Also by Maureen Howard

Natural History

Natural History

a novel

Maureen Howard

Carroll & Graf Publishers, Inc.
New York

First Carroll & Graf edition 1999

Carroll & Graf Publishers, Inc.
19 West 21st Street
New York, NY 10010-6805

Library of Congress Cataloging-in-Publication Data is available.
ISBN: 0-7867-0632-5

Manufactured in the United States of America

To my brother, George Kearns—other stories.

It seems to me not at all unnatural to precede *Natural History* with a list of acknowledgments. So many with seasoned and detailed knowledge have helped me to transform my curiosity and faded memories into the entries in this novel. I hope the Bridgeport friends will forgive their facts turned to my fiction: David W. Palmquist and Mary Witkowski of the Historical Collections, Bridgeport Public Library; Robert Pelton of The Barnum Museum; Charles Brilvitch, architectural historian; James Callahan who knows his McLevy and Lennie Grimaldi for his extensive research, a continuing act of loyalty to our city. I want to thank Charles Silver of the film department, Museum of Modern Art, and Paula Frosch, the Thomas J. Watson Library, Metropolitan Museum of Art. The books will never balance, for I'm heavily in debt to Walter Bernstein, Lee Deigaard, Nancy Edwards, Jack Ennis, Betty Fussell, both Hatchers, Gerry Howard, Loretta Howard, Cleo McNelly Kearns, Emma Lewis, Gloria Loomis, Andy Marasia, Janet Marks, Michelle Novak, Sonia and George Tscherny, and YOU BET—to Mark Probst.

Contents:

Natural History: I

From above, start with the privileged view. Lay on the page a neat grid of neighborhoods, the quirky crosscuts of routes that followed secondary streams or an Indian footpath, what was decreed by nature or habit and is long forgotten, long a dead end or confusing turn in the city—the lost logic of a marsh or a stubborn farmer's lawsuit that will not let you pass. Though you are above, remember? Bird's-eye view. See-it-all as though know-it-all, as though you can with practiced calligraphy, with India ink on the nub of your art-shop pen, label the streets—North, Parrott, Main, Iranistan, Golden Hill—and in labeling possess them. As though you are a recording angel on the ceiling of a glorious cathedral—not here, not by a long shot, but pictured up high, say in the abandoned RR depot or above the stage in Klein Memorial—depicted with your compass, plumb rule, and telescope, all your outmoded apparatus, to measure the depth of Ash Creek, the elevations of Tunxis and Chopsey Hills, the wide mouth of the Pequonnock, the acreage of Brooklawn Country Club larger than any public park, the cramped property lines of poor folk, broad boulevards of the rich. But already you have left off the scientific, are coloring in. Conventional road-map blue for Long Island Sound, watercolor waves feathering against the lighthouse at Fayerweather Point, desert tan for beaches, peaceful green for the parks of Park City and for its cemeteries—St. Michael's, Lakeview, Mountain Grove. In these you draw miniature crosses to mark the dead and move on to sketch in steeples, the white hospital on a hill, two eccentric onion domes, all landmarks for the living, as though the living can see what you see from above—where they are heading or that the amusement park across the bay is shaped like the extended siphon of a clam or that the city seen upside down is an ear, the whole harbor scooped like an auricle with deep inlets, canals trapping words, for you have left off mapping and are well into a storied topography with whaling ships, trading ships, tankers set afloat. You line up factories as toy battlements along the river.

As though you have given up the ancient art, which, after all, is best accomplished by accurate messages from the stratosphere, you doodle a decorative border on parchment paper—livestock, cornhusks, teepees, silvery-blue mussels, and squirming lobsters of burnt sienna flashing bright gills. Cartoon city: poor battered ear with rust strip of the last century's railroad bed across it like a bloody Band-Aid, the recent sinuous thruway draining its life like a rubbery tube. As though to draw the eye from such injury, you settle to the flat panoramic view, mark in the toot of ferryboat and factory, the oiled hum of sewing machines, whirr of Frisbie pie tins and jazz notes above a spinning Columbia record—Louis Armstrong or Benny Goodman, who recorded in the city—as though . . . well, as though demoted to your draftsman's table you must put down as legend on the faked shading of your parchment the sounds natural to this place and can't remember sparrow tweet or gull's caw or rustle of Norway maple, but only bus fart and father's whistle, which seems unworthy, and so you print in the rat-tat-tat of test shots from Remington Arms and the Nubian tiger's growl with many r-r-r-rs, the trained elephant's muted honk which makes it as legend in this imaginary landscape. Now you are driven to vignettes, capturing in cloud shaped frames a circus tent with clapping seals, hobo clowns, the hard heeled march of the Socialist mayor, all that is marvelous in your view of the city, cleverly incorporating an ink blot as witch marks on the breast of Goody Knapp, hanged for harmless hysteria in 1643. Driven to words now, literal legends, you write out "There's a sucker born every minute," attributed to P. T. Barnum, late, late of this city, and resort to the old vaudeville line "When you're not on Broadway, everything is Bridgeport." And topple off your stool as though North Wind with puffed cheeks on a very old map blows you down, as though the horned sea dragon of a vast uncharted sea buffets you with its paw. Down to earth, in a windowless place you set the uncertain boundaries of recall, with stub of an Eberhard No. 2 draw in small figures below the simple, wavering horizon.

Easy does it. Boy and bike. His Columbia come to life, out from under the claws of bamboo rakes and strangling coil of hose, wheeled past spare tires worn treadless gray but saved along with empty 3-in-One oil cans, jars of rusted brads, ruptured sled, the license plates off a prehistoric Model A. James' bike is out of its winter grave. He swipes the deep red of its fender with a cheesecloth rag, rings the bell once, twice, in a ratchety grind, then, full and satisfying, rings it out across the double drive. Ping. Ping to the street, which is quiet, carless at this hour. He's off—going where he's sent each Saturday. This Saturday the sense of live earth in garage dust; the very grit under his foot has a manly rasp. He's off—destination only Mr. De Martino. So what! The fact of his music lesson slips quickly out of sight behind a clear view of himself straining uphill, a champion effort, then, at breakneck speed, coasting down Anson Street through every stop sign into the day's adventure.

A twenty-eight-inch bike, last year almost beyond him: he sets the seat up a notch, throws his clarinet and music book into the wicker basket, where dead spiders lie in the gay shroud of a candy wrapper. A queer Saturday in March, false spring, and off he goes, easy down the long asphalt drive unaware of any danger into the city street. What is there to fear? Unless, like his mother, a figure clotted milky white, spying behind her curtains, you thought of him in grim detail—crushed skull, mangled limbs. Oh, he's had it with her caution, pedaling easy on the crest of the road when a manhole cover assaults him. Clarinet case jumps. Hard leather saddle rams his behind. The tires of his bike are flat. Suffused with innocence, freewheeling joy, he's been riding on the rim.

Watching her son's come-uppance, Nell breaths easy. Boy and bike safe on the sidewalk by Coyne's, wheeling round their ash cans with the lids half off. Ashes, for they still get the load of cheap coke, their furnace unconverted, poor untidy Coynes, their ashes blowing at her boy. Safe now, no more danger than a cinder in his eye and he's sensible at last, at least in from the street where he might be killed.

Her pleasure would be to drive James to Mr. De Martino, but for the hint of spring that brought his bike to mind, and this Saturday the jamboree. Catherine to chauffeur across town. Cath impatient at the kitchen door in her skimpy Girl Scout uniform, sleeves and waist riding high, the hem let down. Cath, far from bacon grease and butter smear, the blast of the hot-air register cruelly fluttering the precious scraps glued so precisely to her poster-board display: COTTON, QUEEN OF THE SOUTH.

"King," James had said. "When cotton was king." And threatened the whole beautiful project with a blob of jam until tears gathered in his sister's eyes. "Bro-ther," James said and off he went to dig out his bike, but not before his mother, pretending to be cross, said: "Ride against the traffic, James. Watch at the four-way light!" The soft grate of her warning she could not help.

She could not help herself with him, could not stop the

fears—scenes, really, in which she saw his body limp, dangling from treetops or bloated on the sandy rim of Seeley's Pond. James splayed on the railway tracks. Quick glimpses of her boy horribly dead, and that is why she stands behind the curtain in the dining room, not to be seen, not to be mildly despised by James. Yes, she is searching out her car keys and the purse, but must watch his foolhardy start, then watch as he walks the invalid bike ceremoniously past Coyne's, Grillo's, Shea's, past the jack pine that towers over the little gray box of Louie's grocery store, until James, safe and sane, is out of her sight.

At the kitchen door, guarding COTTON, QUEEN OF THE SOUTH, Cath has seen him, seen him unearthing his bike, could have rapped on the kitchen window, called out, "Flat tires, bozo," but why should she when Queen was what she meant, Queen of the Old South. She had leapt ahead from Scarlett, smudge on her regal brow, sweating in the burnt fields of Tara, to Victoria, slip of a royal girl, blessing the Industrial Revolution. Both queens beholden to cotton, for her project swept through history, the straight line of it—small brown seed to the patent number of the great Lowell loom. Painting the gold title on red posterboard, she had trembled for fear of splotches, the cotton lint, sprung from its pod, wobbling dangerously as she tacked a nice thick tail on her Q. With her beautiful display, all wired and pasted, she'd earned her badge, but this was the day long awaited, this Saturday of the jamboree. The competition, for that was what Miss Sullivan called it in the chill cement basement of St. Patrick's School. "I say we enter Catherine in the competition."

Enter QUEEN OF THE SOUTH, not Cath, but the girls knew Sullivan's talk, no pussyfooting around. Miss Sullivan was tough, her trim green uniform and overseas cap ready for the salute, the command; her hair shaved in the back like a man's. The seven mile hike, campfire in Beardsley Park, knots and signals her natural way and all Girl Scout baking, sewing a terrible chore. Catherine had come to the meeting with her unheard-of project for the badge. Odd and independent, never asking could she, Miss Sullivan, do history? She'd already put them through folk dancing, made them jig to her Virginia reel, twisted them up in a morris dance, Sullivan sticking to the cement floor in her gum soles. Not asking, just coming one Wednesday night with the big red posterboard. Mr. Bray holding the basement doors open for his daughter, coming into their meeting where no man entered, flicking his ash.

QUEEN OF THE SOUTH: alone, up in her room, she'd cut out the picture of an antebellum portico, its massive white pillars dwarfing slaves bent in the fields. She'd drawn the boll weevil's pincers and the equally nasty fingers of the cotton gin. All labeled and dated, her display bore true legends of fine Egyptian thread and the trials of Eli Whitney. At the end she had cut the many types of manufactured cotton into petals and pinned them to her posterboard in an artificial rose. Catherine Bray was entered in the competition described on official stationery from headquarters which Sullivan passed (now-you-see-it, now-you-don't) quickly before her eyes.

Car keys found, her mother said: "Your coat." Mrs. Bray was in her old sealskin, her everyday hat, the lovely Christmas purse from New York on her arm. "Your *coat,* Catherine." She held the posterboard while Cath stuffed herself into the navy blue melton, a childish Sunday coat with velvet collar.

"Back out the car," said Cath. She could not bear to see the cotton boll teeter, the casual way her mother sauntered right into the windy warm day with a smile. "Back out!" said Cath.

"Heavens!" her mother said. You could not laugh at Catherine, not in this mood. A terrible sight, that child's round face clamped tight with her purpose. In the garage, Nell Bray—Mrs. Bray always to the neighbors, for she was naturally grand though unaffected—Nell saw the mess her son had made—the hose, worn tires, all thrown against her old Packard. James in a hurry. James with his clarinet now safely on his way to Mr. De Martino. Her gloves streaked red with the dry rubber hose; the new purse, black lizard, scraped along the back fender as she fought her way to the car door. James was careless, she must say; in another world with his music, a musical child.

Saved—so much saved. The faded bladder of a beach ball, sled hung from a rafter, her very own with wooden runners and a faint stencil design. Saved, all of it, the Currier & Ives ice skates along with the studded collar and heavy chain—*requiescat* Bootsie, Boston bull, of distemper, 1939. That insignificant death: the children had not fed or watered their sluggish pet, but saved—Bootsie's license, and somewhere his chewed rawhide bone. The family riches, all saved, necessary as attic must, cellar dank, useful in some way . . . faceless gold pocket watches, linen dusters, ivory nail buffers, harness and riding crop, mason jars, buttonhooks, back issues of *The Delineator* and *Life* magazine.

Catherine would not come down the back steps until her mother drove right to her with the car. A tipping and bending of posterboard: its pictures and scraps fluttered, the cottonseed oil sloshed in its little vial.

"There now," her mother said, "easy does it."

"We're late," said Catherine, who was seldom easy.

"I don't imagine," said Nell, who did not believe jamborees began on time, "with girls from all over . . ."

"You've never been," said Catherine, and when they got there, way out at Fairfield and Park, the big drive of St. John's was full up, parked tight. QUEEN OF THE SOUTH would have to be carried half a block, its smudges and nicks exposed in full sun before it was properly displayed. Here, in alien territory, three Scouts popped out of a station wagon, a big red dog barking out the rear window. Girls in penny loafers and polo coats, knee socks without the trefoil, no kerchiefs or Scout berets, barked back at the dog, teasing as they ran away, chasing up onto the big lawns. Here, the houses sat far back; the bushes not barberry and privet stuck beside front stoops, but varied and clustered shrubs, the rhododendrons basking this fine day; trees set out for the look of them as well as shade. Cath found St. John's Episcopal Church a confusing sprawl—fortress, meeting-house, thank God for the plain brick of the hall, no steeple. Still, she must say it once more, she'd not enter the church, never would pray there, never.

"It won't be required," her mother said, "that you lose your immortal soul." IIow many times they'd been over the mumbo-jumbo brought home from St. Pat's as to the dangers of the unconsecrated—the very wood and stone of a Protestant place occasions for sin. There was no dealing with Cath's peasant faith or the obstinate set of her mouth as they balanced the red posterboard between them. A wind swept across State Street, which widened here where it left off being downtown and became the residential avenue for businessmen who ran the city, a boulevard for bankers, doctors, and lawyers. The cotton scraps and carefully inked legends of QUEEN OF THE SOUTH flapped wildly as it proceeded up the unholy Episcopal steps. No fear, Cath's project was maneuvered into a big still room, secular as a parlor cleared for a dance. Little girls everywhere setting up the jamboree in a hush.

Nell Bray was not wanted. She stood in the door, a slack civilian, enormous and gaudy in her sealskin and guinea feather hat. Catherine, who wanted her gone, did not turn to disapprove of her mother's laugh, Nell laughing now at the spectacle, a sputtery unshared laughter that came upon her most anyplace—at the beach, after Mass, at the stocking counter in D. M. Read's. Then she was at a remove as though standing by herself on a small stage—on the pavilion while the half-naked bathers disported themselves in Long Island Sound, or on the porch of St. Patrick's, loitering dreamily, looking down on the parishoners as they bought the Sunday *Post.* "There they all are," said Nell Bray's laugh: her daughter hated it, for she was out there bobbing in the high tide, working at the breast stroke; it was Cath saying good morning to the neighbor ladies and Skinny Finn, who passed the collection basket. And Catherine choosing her mud-colored stockings for school suddenly might be—well, anyone, lost in the department-store crowd to her mother, as she was now, one more Girl Scout, and what was so funny about the competition citywide, about the cold Protestant hall with lamps and tables like a living room, no statues of the saints.

Finally Nell said: "Where are your friends?"

"Not friends."

"The girls from your troop then?"

"Obie and June," said Catherine. "Not friends."

Then Nell tilted her child's beret, an improvement against regulations, and said, "It's a winner, Cath," meaning QUEEN OF THE SOUTH, which looked to her flashy in St. John's hall, defiantly red in this Protestant place with delicate Windsor chairs pushed against muted cream walls. She was gone, leaving Catherine to Obie and June, to the jamboree or whatever—a solemn business it seemed, the competition. Down the drive, there was Frieda Kurtz in a trench coat, fat epaulets mocking the military, and under it the green shirtdress of a Scout leader. Frieda, who Nell taught with before she married, demon in the classroom, good fun out with the girls. They'd been the long and the short of it: Nell lofty, lightly freckled, with her crowning glory, that pile of red-gold hair; Frieda scrappy, dark and small.

"Nell," she cried, running, running late.

"They're in there," said Nell. "Mine's among them."

"Not Catherine!" said Frieda.

"Eleven," said Nell with a mother's pride, as though it were her great accomplishment, a daughter who survived eleven years, a son thirteen—what she had to show—and the door of St. John's closed on Frieda Kurtz, who had come with a smocked baby dress to see Catherine in her crib, with a book of mythology for James, years beyond him. Now Frieda looked smart in her uniform, worldly—a little silly in her leader's hat. Unmarried, unlovely, reputed to be a clown, yet a force for all that was new, untried—a power at the Board of Ed. Billy said, "Your friend Frieda," when he saw her downtown. Your friend Frieda taking lunch at the Stratfield, with some hack from the mayor's office. "What a mutt," Billy said. Still, she was down at the Stratfield, wasn't she? It was Frieda in there with the Girl Scouts citywide, her trench coat this season's style. Nell, what did she care, really, in her sealskin worn at each button to the hide. Why should Nell care, rubbing spittle on the wound till the shine of her new purse was restored. Black lizard, far too expensive, Bill's present from New York. She would like to forget the picture of her husband on the front page of the *Post*: the detective, back from an extradition, bearing his gift to her in one arm, the other handcuffed to a gangster.

She cut across St. John's lawn, her heels sinking in the thaw of this fine day. The brown grass had looked firm: Catherine was right, the Protestant church an occasion for sin, for ruining good shoes, not our world. A sign advertised the hours of communion or vespers. You could pick and choose, show up at will for the sermon: *He trains my hands for war, so that my arms can bend a bow of bronze*. Psalms 18:34. Here the Rev. Mr. would spell out his homily, schooled to address the war as a problem, as though it might be disputed that God was on our side. Sunday deliberations for his flock: the bow of bronze was not for Nell. Bill Bray had done his bit the first time round. James was a boy. Tires inflated by now to be sure, but safe on his bike. Her men safe—a crime to think it. She did not need sermons with the world's misery, with the headlines, though she seldom looked at the evening paper. Picking up the living room litter the next day, the news seemed less tragic, though in these last months no less urgent. Nell did not need to speculate on the right of it. If that was their Yankee way, no harm. Enough to remember our men and women overseas with the dear departed, sweep them into "Let Us Pray." Enough, the gold star in Coyne's window. She never passed the sharp glitter of it on a field of white satin hanging above an angel-wing begonia that she did not think of Duddy gone. There was the wrong of it.

Duddy Coyne, transformed from a thick lout, come to life in his sailor's uniform, his whites gleaming as he cut around the corner and headed home. Crisp in the heat of August, a canvas zip bag with his gear. "Mrs. Bray!" Hand to his cap, he gave her a smile;

the flesh worked off him, stringy now. "Oh, Duddy!" she'd said. The only words they'd ever spoken. She had noticed, how could she help it, his neat little bum in the sailor pants. She was clipping the hedge, James' chore. That was wrong. A scorching day, the shorn privet curled limp at her feet, clipping fast so Bill would not scold James. Or punish—so they could all drive down to Seaside after supper, get the breeze off the Sound. James had been playing his scales, then a popular tune that drifted out over the parched backyards. Nell had come to the front hedge with the clippers. Her boy so taken with his music. Imagine—in that upstairs heat practicing for Mr. De Martino, though it was wrong of her clipping past his last jazzy trills, long after she'd heard him slam the screen door and knew he was off with no excuse to Seeley's Pond, or more truthfully, the Rialto. She was wrong trimming the hedge, blisters forming in the crook of her hand. "Oh, Duddy!" she'd said and blushed like a girl, dress stuck to her breasts, the smell of her sweat mingling with privet. She had turned to admire his spit and polish, the flapping bell bottoms, the dazzling backside of him, white and trim. Dud Coyne, torpedoed in the North Atlantic, had not been issued his bow of bronze. It was wrong to let James off the hook. She was sweeping the clippings when Billy came home.

"Jesus, what kind of a nigger job is that?"

"Only the cleanup," she said.

"Your mother," Bill began at the table. That was what she could not bear: her good dinner before them each night—each night a delicate matter, though it was just the four of them at the round table. Her calling them, holding them there. "Your mother wasn't off for a lovely swim," Bill said, "or run to a lousy movie," building his case, and James, who hardly acknowledged—clipped, unclipped—a front hedge, was made to look upon her swollen weeping palms. That is what she could not bear.

In her car, Nell turns to take in the long shot of St. John's Episcopal Church, assess the opposition—smug in its genteel mix of colonial styles, fine corner to sit on, enviable with its big parlor to accommodate Girl Scouts citywide. The high tone of a Sunday, Rev. Mr. from the pulpit, taking his ease to contemplate the war. Trespassing, she swings the Packard up a circular drive under the porte cochere of a shingle house the size of a library, the size of a school. It is the Pisky minister's manse. To hell with them. She laughs at herself, no better than her child cramped with primitive fears. It is Lent, and Cath, who denies herself all sweets, all movies, has predicted that the jamboree will be an orgy of Protestant cookies. There's no dealing with Catherine: Nell can see her at attention, reciting the pledge, the worn sleeve of her uniform weighted with badges—History now mastered along with Sewing, Dancing, Boating, Baking. What next? She sees Catherine with hash marks and medals, very solemn, tricked out in the uniform of a WAVE or WAC, like Frieda Kurtz, absurd in one of those rigid military hats.

Hardly out of the way, by the slightest deviation from her morning errands Nell can snatch James from the treacherous ride home, all downhill. With a twist of its wheels she can stash that fool bike in the trunk of her car. Traffic heads to Main Street despite the rationing, a slow procession of cars with windows rolled down. The good day has them out. Nell, who knows her city, cuts through back streets to the North End, heads uphill to Mr. De Martino. Saturday—children everywhere, chalking sidewalks, whacking balls in the center of the road, showing off on roller skates and bikes. She envisions James, his fair head come to rest on a granite curb, his leg stone-white through the gash in his corduroy knickers, no breath from his pale lips, but to the side the blood red of his bike unharmed, its wheels still spinning.

James looks hard at the notes under the hooded light on the music stand. Darkness at Mr. De Martino's: heavy lid of front porch, clump of cedar grown over side windows; half-drawn shades, split, ragged at the edges. Dark dust velvet curtains hang over the door to where she is, the mother, Signora De Martino. Once—it was Christmas—

James breathed near the curtain and the stink of the dust went down his throat. Waxy and old, with black black hair, the Signora handed him a thimble of sweet wine. He thought he would choke it up. At the end of each lesson he stood away from the dust velvet as though he was that shy, that polite, so Mr. De Martino must take the half glass from his mother—warm milk in winter, sip of sour lemonade when it was hot—and pass her offering to James. "Thank you," the boy said.

Smiling their yellow smiles at each other, the De Martinos would then teach him Italian for thank you. *Gra-zee-ah. Gra-zee-ah.* He never said it. And it was cold always, supposedly for the oboes and piano, for the flutes and clarinets. "Pre-cious wood," said Mr. De Martino, "cannot live in the American home. If I want the Sahara Desert," said Mr. De Martino, his worst joke, "I visit Haile Selassie, leave Lucia home." Lucia was the Steinway, not his mother. Wagging his slick pomaded head, he would demonstrate her upper register. A big black baby grand. The studio dark and cold this fine Saturday in March. Blowing on his fingers, James thought Lucia must freeze her lid. Supposedly because it was unhealthy, Mr. De Martino did not eat red meat, corn on the cob, soft American bread, and what he called—in his precise, hastily got-up English— "your sweets." James knew his diet to be half glass, penny-pinching as the De Martinos' chill cast-iron radiators. They ate macaroni: that was cheap.

"To work!" Mr. De Martino scampers like a cold-blooded gopher in the dark. "Ess-ercise?" Mr. De Martino closes his bright eyes as though guessing, his sallow face happy with this weekly sport. He keeps no record James has ever seen: all in his sleek head that this week in March, James Bray is on Fifteen. F-major scales and arpeggios. "Ess-ercise Fiff-teen!" It is the Method. James has advanced to the second book. The Method is all, all as to breath, fingering, and the embouchure. The Method is "purr-fection," said Mr. De Martino. But then Giardi was perfection. Once, with his mother, he had met the great man in New York, gone backstage after an exquisite concert. Giardi had spoken pure Italian to the Signora—*puro, purrro,* said Mr. De Martino, like a tabby cat. Often they had walked by the magnificent apartment house in which Giardi lived. James is learning the Giardi Method.

Slowly, James licks his reed, screws it to the mouthpiece. Fifteen is old stuff, busy as hell with the left hand. But James has no form with his pinkie today. Buzzes and snorts, stumbling over the slight progressions; he fakes it, never having set eyes on Fifteen. "My reed!" James gutters out.

"Your reed?" Legs crossed, Mr. De Martino lazes back on the piano bench. Over the music stand James catches the tut-tut tap of his toe, a glint of suspicion in the narrow smile. No structure to De Martino's lower face—rubbery, boneless: donated his chin to Mussolini. Not the first time James' fury and a touch of shame invites Il Duce as a cartoon fatty to goose-step the bare studio floor. Benito of the massive jaw *sieg heils* the Method, slams the lid on Lucia, screams in *puro pur-r-r-*o until the Maestro and Momma are brought to their knees.

"Back to kindergarten," cries Mr. De Martino. "Cross the break."

Slurring gracefully from lower to higher register, the simple exercise takes over in James' mouth, easy breath, lips working. Under the one spot of light he squints to see only notes, to cut out the disapproving teacher, and makes a clean sweep of Fifteen, right through to a melody, a reward duly noted in his book, for the good student. "A Scottish Air."

"Quack," Mr. De Martino, pretending James has played badly, well, not so badly. "Da-*deee*-da. A long E," says Mr. De Martino, "not quack-quack."

Now comes the good part. *He* will play "A Scottish Air" on Lucia perfectly, never looking at the score. So lively it seems from this stick of a man, and then at James' request he'll go to the tottery table with a sagging lace cloth on which his woodwinds are displayed—flute, recorder, oboe. Gently, fondly, Mr. De Martino will pick up his own clarinet. It's the way he holds it, easy and light, the way he first puts his lips to the mouthpiece, a quick kiss before some small adjustment. Bold and forthright, he'll play the next lesson—Sixteen, Eighteen, whatever—show the boy how it's done. The instrument hides his chinless state; eyes downcast, not mocking James or the tawdry world of the downstairs rent, a so-called studio on Thorn Street, he's alive and yet at rest as he plays on in the Giardi Method. Easy does it, the music teacher content in this dark cold temple to his talent, heeding what might have been, James thinks, his calling. For this moment he comes to Mr. De Martino, and because next, with a flick of his finger, he'll signal to James. Together they'll try whatever exercise comes next, and when he falters, rasps, sputters, Mr. De Martino will say plainly, "Think. Count. An *open* G," or, what James values most of all, "Fine. A fine legato."

Today when the student finishes "A Scottish Air," Mr. De Martino sits on the piano bench looking floppy, small, folds the wooden cover on Lucia's keys. "And what is next?"

James turns the page where the chromatic scales of Sixteen dance crazily before him, and though the teacher purses his lips, pecks out his tongue demonstrating Giardi's this and that according to the Method, he does not take up his instrument. The lesson over.

Today, like any other, the dusty curtain is drawn back and there's Momma De Martino with the half glass of warm milk rattling on a saucer, but she's in her nightgown, that's what James takes her costume to be—thin white stuff, stained ruffles at her ancient breast, trailing a big flowered shawl. Dry black hair hangs down beyond her shoulders like a little girl's, like Cath's unbraided. "Geraldo," she says. Then Mr. De Martino, mortified, passes the milk to James. Tepid, James knows this half glass, gags it down.

"Geraldo." The old woman reaches for her son, takes his arm through hers as though they are about to go backstage, behind the dusty curtain to their drama. Her cheeks bright, unrouged; her smell sickly sweet as she insists upon her weekly role. A blue medallion, the Immaculate Conception, is pinned in her ruffles like the coy brooch of another time, drawing the boy's eyes and her son's eyes to the décolletage of withered powdery flesh.

"Thank you," James says, wishing now that he could say it in Italian, then runs or wants to, for first he has to dismember his clarinet, slam it in the case, roll up his music, pay. Pay two dollars, usually slipped as though it were a secret message into Mr. De Martino's palm. Today he flings it at the baby grand and he's coasting downhill, hellbent through all stop signs and lights, past the emergency entrance to St. Vincent's, where among the doctors' cars, the white ambulance gleams—silent, at rest.

So that when Nell Bray stole up on the dim porch to peek under the shade, see James at his lesson, there was a small child with blond ringlets, cherubic girl or boy in overalls, perched on a straight chair, spitting into a flute. Sad fact, as Nell drives home, she looks at each corner thinking to find her son along the way, stops only to beg the Sunday roast from Mr. Murtagh, knows her since she was a bride. Mrs. Bray holds herself primly over the stewing chickens while he tucks in the bacon he does not reckon with her ration stamps. In a hurry today, the speckled feathers on her hat ruffled in the wind, and she's half into the stately gun metal Packard, a curiosity in the neighborhood, when Murtagh sees the glove, gray pigskin curled to the shape of her hand, worn through, he notes, and puts it aside. She heads downhill, down home, still hoping to see the flash of her boy's red head and a bike. Sad fact, the garbage men are at her drive, and James, whose job it is, has not put the trash cans to the curb. She hefts them against her, twice stumbling down the back path, thank God in time. Wiping her hands on the soft sides of her coat, Nell skips up the back steps, where she's thrown down her lizard purse and Mr. Murtagh's bag; precious bundles now cradled in her arms as she pushes in the door. Always, Nell's glad to be safe home, safe here at last—inside.

And where is her Bill on a Saturday? Billy Bray, who in his investigations drives the back roads of the county, the revealing circuitous routes. He, with the gift of gab, known at drugstores, lunch counters, bars where he drinks an occasional root beer; Billy known for the gag, the tease, the inside story, but known to elicit, draw forth, amazing tales from the butcher, the baker, and there is actually a candlestick maker in Westport, in a swampy hollow where the less successful artists live, a man who turns out counterfeit brass candlesticks, sells them as antique—a man so crafty he now works in pewter, not to be ruined entirely by the war. Billy knows, for instance, that Murtagh has long used a touch of horsemeat in the chopped steak, that he sells the uninspected veal, half-born, in a caul. Geraldo De Martino—there's a case: poor bastard snitching trinkets for Momma, a scarf or toilet water off the counter at Read's, wanting to be caught and spanked. "It is a dream," he tells Billy. "I am asleep walking," says Mr. De Martino. Billy Bray listening to Momma's boy, drinking weak punch after James' recital—Jesus, what a blowout, all those kids tooting and puffing—and what's he to say—"I charge you, Geraldo De Martino, in the name of the law." Pathetic larceny. Not worth a fart in the wind. Ask Billy, or ask him—Frieda Kurtz? Into her third martini at the Pink Elephant— owning that all these years she's off to hotels (the Waldorf, the Willard, the Copley) with which exemplary Judge of Probate who'll never divorce his wife? "A collection of matchbooks," she says to Billy, smoking her heart out, her cough choked off in a desperate laugh. "What is it now? Tell me," he says, and they do. Billy Bray thumbs back his hat, loosens a button on his vest, pulls the knot of his bow tie, some small move that seems an opening, the gift of his revelation. "Tell me," and in exchange they do.

"Jesus Christ," he says to Nell when he gets an earful, "I should have been a priest." True, and as though he has taken a religious vow his lips are sealed, almost, for there is that secular confessional she's privy to, behind the bedroom door. Nell listens to him, losing a hairpin, chasing a wisp of dust, not wanting to hear that Ed Shea may have his hand in the till at City Trust or the postman's led Billy to believe he can deliver a quick one to the grocer's wife. "God forgive them," Nell says, if she says anything at all.

Or, she smiles from her distance upon his tales of sin and degradation, as if to make them disappear, easy as blowing a spill of talcum off her dresser scarf, which is neatly mended, mellow white. Then she can face her Bill, round and balding, his tilted smile fresh as a wondering boy's, the little strawberry mark like a dollop of jam in the cleft of his chin, big open eyes, for sure the windows of his soul.

Tell Billy Bray. He is a short man, grounded—no shift or shuffle about him, carrying a little breadbasket at his middle these days, courtesy of Nell's blackberry roly-poly, her buns glazed with egg yolk and sugar, her good old apple pie. As though with her sweets she'll take the bitter edge off, for he's no priest. Detective in the State's Attorney's office. The one and only. Detective—as far as Nell's concerned, a job sharply dry like alum, like iodine with a sting to it. She nurses the daily wound that this decent man who stands before her in his BVDs, taking his pajamas from under the pillow, should spend his waking hours often far into the night, with felons and thieves, murderers, that she must listen in her distracted way, though they are not his indictable courthouse cases Nell gives half an ear to, they are sad stories of Frieda, Mr. De Martino, and the like. The nurses at St. Vincent's running for fortunes to the blaspheming gypsies. Murtagh's thumb on the scale. Plain people in search of magic absolution. They must figure the detective beyond outrage and offense, the likely repository of all their misdemeanors. As he taps her flannel gown, "Sleep tight," turns comfortably from her, Nell knows why they tell her husband. It's not his priestly but his worldly wisdom that she fears as well as her own pigheaded innocence. Tell me? Tell me? Why must he ask?

This Saturday, at the courthouse early, he's parked his state car in the empty lot, proceeds to the vast lobby with its Romanesque vaults and High Victorian staircase. The great wrought-iron chandeliers not lit: this fine day only sunlight streaks through the leaded windows in heavenly rays as in cathedrals he'd seen as a soldier in Normandy. The courthouse is more beautiful to Billy than any church: the heavy office doors—Clerk of the Court, Common Pleas, Judge's Chambers—more to his liking than a jumble of dark side altars, more reasonable, even more sacred. Billy's footsteps resound. His smoker's hack comes back to him in a pleasing authoritative echo.

Blind Tupper at his newsstand folds the canvas wraps off his cigarettes and magazines. On a Saturday, on a Sunday, where else would Tupper go . . . and hearing Billy Bray, he has the Luckies on the counter, has already made the change.

"Some day they're giving us," the blind man says, his slack bruised eyelids fluttering as though he has enormously enjoyed the sunshine for the minutes it takes him to tap across from his rooming house to the big tiled hall where he spends all his days.

"Some fine day," Billy says and heads back behind the staircase where an office bears his name—William Aloysius Bray, County Detective. There on a stool is a gnome, a crookback mite of a fellow smiling up through rimless glasses.

"Got anything?"

Elliot from the *Post:* "Got anything, Billy?"

"Christ, Elliot. Eight-thirty in the morning. I got sleep in my eyes."

"You going for manslaughter? Second degree?"

"I'm goin' for coffee," Billy says. He has opened the door to his office with a big brass skeleton key. Any fool could break and enter.

Elliot trails him in, craning his neck up. "You gonna bring her in?" He knows he won't get an answer and watches as Billy fiddles with the trick compartment in his heavy oak desk, finds a small unloaded revolver that he slips into the pocket of his topcoat, a prop.

"See ya," Tupper says as they head out, their footsteps loud on the marble pavement. The two regulars—Elliot and William Aloysius Bray—and in a sense the blind newsagent's right, he'll see them. The courthouse, their second home: it's rare for either the skittery reporter or the swaggering detective to miss a day. There's this about Billy, he does swagger. His heels come down hard in a dress-parade march, shoulders back, chin out. Winter or summer his coats flap back from his solid body, devil-may-care. Up at the lunch counter on Golden Hill Street they drink creamy coffee with crullers, before Billy takes off in the state car to drive down the line.

"Where you gonna bring her in?" Elliot calls to his pal, the detective, as though he'll hop right along to the Stamford pokey or out to the county jail. Elliot's not going far, hard enough with wry neck and birdy bent frame, filing his courthouse stories, catching the last bus home to the excessively clean flat in the two-family house he's bought for his mother. But there are few tricks Elliot misses, never a twist or turn of justice meted out in the county courthouse, nothing gets by him—small matters of juvenile detention, contested wills, pleas and payola, a quick "social call" on the State's Attorney by the local FBI. This is his beat; though he can't run down the line to cover last night's murder, he'll be waiting under the stairs when the detective comes back and there'll be a treat, some choice item he's saved for Elliot. Trust Billy Bray.

Since midnight, Billy's known, one of those calls, there are not that many, that drive Nell crazy in the night. This night the heavy silence of his long listening, his growled response. She will not ask, what is it? Terrifying at this hour—arson, rape. "Homicide," Billy said, settling back into bed, soothing her shoulder.

She breathed so fearfully beside him. "Who? Who?"

"Girl shot a soldier."

"Where?" she finally asked.

"Down the line. Stamford."

"Oh, Lord!" Her voice was easy. After all, he was not getting dressed in the dark, rooting around in the bottom drawer for handcuffs or the blackjack. Bill was safe beside her, half asleep. A girl shot a soldier: they were living through a war. No urgency, no further story. She waited for his hoarse cough, then the rumble in his chest that came before the steady snore.

The handlebars rest so lightly against the plate-glass window of the Sweet Shoppe it looks as though James' bike is suspended miraculously. He's headed right past the comics and candy to the back of the store. There, in an alcove lit with an eerie orange bulb, he buys his cups and ball, flap cards, die box—all kinds of magic tricks. Many he cannot afford—bottomless jugs, the pop-up feather bouquet—but James has saved his church money and a half dollar from De Martino three weeks running. Easy money. Just tell his mother that Geraldo has raised his fee. So here's James in the den of iniquity, the back of Pappas' Sweet Shoppe, playing with the devil's wares. Today he knows exactly what he wants, a day already wonderful, free of his mother's ride up the hill. All winter it has been a long hike down to Pappas' in the Hollow, cutting loose from his friends after school, stealing into Nick's back room to study—*Magic of the Masters, Sealed Vision, It's Easier Than You Think.*

He's never called a grown-up by first name but easily says Nick. And Nick is old—fifty, sixty—the Dean of Delphi. Sometimes Nick will take the coins and do a French drop, a back palm for James, but his hands are swollen at the joints, he's not that quick. Dark, as though the sun shone on him every day, large—he looks to James bloated in his sharpie suit, his white hair sticky. His smell is thickly perfumed when he comes near to pull a Walnetto or a Necco wafer, a licorice cigar out of James' ear or inner pocket.

"You don't tell your daddy," Nick Pappas says. "You don't go to Nick's." And James understands what he is not to say at home.

"You tell him Nick's a clean place." He's never to get to the point where he would say it, though there are wads of gum under the soda counter, dust rats, congealed, cling to the baseboards, and the ice cream dipper lingers in a slop of gray water. James is to say whatever he must for his friend.

Today Nick does not attend to the boy. He's on the phone. There are men in the shop, not buying magazines or candy. One of them spits out the open door. So be it. James will not hear the stories of Cagliostro or Ali Bongo, be shown the Houdini handbill—"If You Fail You Will Die." What matter? Today he has come for the silks, the brightly colored handkerchiefs he will whip into the air to the amazement of his audience, an audience in James' head that's half the usual assembly in the junior high auditorium and half the fans Nick Pappas tells him of who flock in evening dress to some wondrous place, Egyptian Hall. Red, orange, green, the silks will stream forth from a little matchbox in which he has folded one measly square of paper to fool the public, to show how cramped, how small; then—blue, yellow, flaming pink—the vast display, the silken flourish. He will laugh with them, the crowd he's duped, astounded utterly, and take his bow.

"Ah, the silks," Nick whispers to the boy, their secret, but when James puts down his fistful of coins, the Dean of Delphi doesn't stop to count, walks him fast into the sun. "We do the silks," Nick says, hardly a promise as he turns back to the men, the ringing phone, and closes, locks the sweetshop door.

James' bike has flopped cockeyed across the pavement. Its front wheel spins slowly in the breeze, clarinet case sprung open, but all's well. Only the Method has suffered dog's paw in the gutter.

Obie and June stand at attention (sort of) on either side of Catherine. Slouching on one hip, Obie throws out her chest and smiles. June, taller than the tallest boy in school, stoops, pulls at her Scout tie as though it might, please God, open a trapdoor beneath her and she'll be swallowed or cut off at the knees. Shoulders back, tummy in, Catherine Bray looks into the regulation void as the judges approach. They carry long thin pads like one her parents brought home from a bridge party and they are scoring COTTON, QUEEN OF THE SOUTH, fingering the field hands, the calico petals. Frieda Kurtz, her mother's friend, stabs with her sharpened pencil the lint and carded floss. "What a lively interest," she says to Obie.

"Not me!" says Obie, shifting to the other hip, and June laughs or gulps, some noise to back up Obie.

"Such industry!" The three green women poke at Catherine's project. Eli Whitney falls facedown, leaving a crust of dry paste, a white scab on the bright red cardboard.

"A local boy," says one of the judges sweetly, and sweetly she tries to set Eli Whitney back in place.

"Not true," says Catherine. "Born in Westboro, Massachusetts." Her voice is clear, too strong, as though she is reading out to the jamboree, but there are only three green ladies, Obie half dead of boredom, June fiddling with her tie, the great parlor itself a swarming mass of girls at their various projects, at the cocoa urn, at the cookies or setting up banners and flags. "After the invention of the gin," says Catherine, "he lost his patent and came to live in New Haven. At the age of fifty-two he married Henrietta Frances Edward of Bridgeport."

"A local *girl*," says one of the ladies, and they all laugh at that one, even Obie and June.

"Yes," and in dead earnest Cath reports that Mrs. Whitney bore him three girls and a boy, but they are moving on, down the row of tables with Indian baskets, Connecticut broadleaf tobacco, looms and samplers. All the exhibits are colonial, but no one said. No one told Catherine there would be a sign over the refreshments: "Our Founding Fathers. Girl Scouts of Greater Bridgeport." Back in the cement basement of St. Pat's, why had Miss Sullivan not read it out? Oh no—it was send her to the competition, send old Cath into the arena that she might be tortured, torn limb by limb for the general enjoyment, send her under the protection of Obie and June, who don't know history from hokum, from horse manure.

It all blurs—the oversize rugs, oil paintings of Episcopal bishops, American flag, pale garlands climbing the chintz curtains, so secular and weak—all trembles in one watery blink of Catherine's eyes. The tears held back: she will not, will not, standing at attention, and slowly it comes clear. She is looking at a cross. There on the cream colored wall, a wooden cross without Christ, just a pretty polished thing, and Obie off, chewing away at a fresh stick of gum. June galumphing kindly to her with a cup of cocoa. Yes, so fitting—she will drink it, sweetly sinful, scummed and cold.

Billy thought to head up to the parkway. The woman lived in North Stamford. Anyway, the good day, no stoplights on the Merritt. It would mean he'd miss a couple of calls along the way. The Swede had news in Southport for the federal man, but he'd only tell Billy. The Swede saw U-boats skimming Long Island Sound like bathtub toys, had his eye on the local Italian newspaper with the weddings and obituaries. Spaghetti recipes as fascist propaganda. Educated man with a screw loose, once a diplomat, sportsman, art dealer. It was out of courtesy he paid his calls on Selvig, refused the schnapps. You wouldn't want to get drawn into that, lazing in the bay window that overlooked a private patch of Sound and gentle tides, in lounge chairs the Swede's wife had set there so he could defend her safe and serene lookout. The Swede, who even Billy might allow was some Adonis—silver hair, ex-athlete's build, the teeth—the teeth alone would win a contest—Selvig had married a rich woman. You had to stop at the gatehouse. Fair enough, the man lived behind elegant bars. Today the conspiracy would have to wait—a girdle of land mines set in the rocks of Compo Beach, espionage at the hat factory.

A killing last night. Billy bides his time. A slow drive down the Merritt, with hardly a car. Saturday they were down at the shops, careful with their gas. Sunday they squandered for the family drive, the visit. A couple of state troopers putt-putting on their motorcycles in the sun—might be a funeral motorcade at that pace.

When they see it's Billy meandering down the Merritt they salute and speed up. He doesn't want their escort.

He prefers to come upon the house with nothing more than the friendly crunch of gravel in the driveway. He does not know the woman's house exactly, but knows the road, the area— still farmed. Some good old houses with the dates pinned on. Commuters have taken over, rich people, not as rich as the crazy Swede. And the woman's road he knows, where half a dozen houses went up in the twenties, fancy houses with turrets, balconies, gables, and casement windows—all sorts of do-dabs prove you have the dough. Billy knows his territory, the whole of Fairfield County up to the federal prison in Danbury, east to the novelty of security leaks at Sikorsky Aircraft, down to the state line—the tax evaders and embezzlers of Greenwich. The richest town in America, said the *Post:* they got that out of *Fortune* magazine. The lay of the land— soft hills up north, an easy drive; the flatlands pressed to the Sound with all the towns and their factories known to him like people.

And this house, stockbroker Tudor, if he had not seen it, he knew its kind. People who said "We live in Connecticut" built these swank places out of picture books. They had grounds. The woman's house sported a baronial arch above the entry. A wrought-iron lantern hung from a chain, its bulb faint in the sunlight, still burning from when the police came here in the night.

He thought it was the maid, the dark dress, low shoes, chin tucked demurely down. It was the woman, the girl in her shadowy front hall, wearing lace collars and cuffs, a little hankie like Nell took to church in her hand. Someone had got to her. Sweet thing. But the face when she raised her head was painted, the lips dark red, puffed in an everlasting kiss or pout. It was the pout now and she was a girl, not a woman. A little kid with eyebrows drawn on, big lashes gummed at the end to look like a movie star. And she did. He supposed she was aiming at glamour, like all those girls he never remembered as he looked through magazines. Ann Sheridan from Lana Turner—he couldn't tell you, Billy Bray. That was this kid's style, the sassy blonde. Someone had got to her, but the bold pompadour, the breasts poking at him in the novice's costume—she wasn't quick to learn.

It was as though she expected his shield in the leather case, seen that one before, expected Billy or whoever. They sat in the living room. It was like a hotel lobby with new carpet, a few bridge lamps, end tables. The couch. The chairs. No one lived here, and beyond lay a sun parlor—bright this fine day—vast and completely empty. She sat on the edge of her couch, visiting.

"Tell me," says Billy Bray.

Her name was Isabelle Poole. He knew that, and she was married to a major. "Mah husbun," she says it as a grievance, "is 'n It-ahly." Troublesome place, a nuisance now that she had killed a boy. She, Isabelle, was twenty-three: the major had come across her in Texas. And was smart enough not to leave her on an army base. Six months married, she sat in North Stamford along with the new furniture, the cellophane still on the lampshades, department-store gloss on the broadloom rug. Something to come home to.

"It's so co-old," she says to Billy Bray. "Mah husbun's from these pahts." Not really; according to the cops the major was from Brunswick, Maine. She ought to get a taste of Maine.

"We take what we get." Billy smiles at all that sunshine splashing the sun parlor floor. Still, she was right, this room had the everlasting chill. They talk about the radiators. Her husband has wronged her with an oil burner, a thermostat.

"All tha-at," she says, "all that fuss and cla-ank." It's clear to Billy she has never lived beyond the stinking lowly comfort of a kerosene stove. He lets her talk on—how in Texas, how this 'n' that down Galveston, down Port Arthur—all very sociable. And clever, setting herself up as the exotic dame—Mata Hari of the Panhandle come to North Stamford. *This* time we all eatin' peas and collahds. *This* time, aftah suppah," and there follows Isabelle Poole's description of spring—honey and locust, mimosa and lemonade, the Lone

Star veranda so pressed with family, family trying for a breeze, you can't find "a inch to set."

But when she fumbles with a matchbook and Billy takes it from her steady little hand, she loses her routine, stroking the hair on his wrist as he lights her cigarette, a split second, nevertheless. It wasn't a belle puffing smoke at him from the pouty lips, the restless desire in her eyes practiced on a hundred bar stools, or, what the hell give her the benefit of the doubt, verandas. Eyes shallow as mibs, the pale brown shooting marble James lost down the backseat of the car. Eyes not pretty but useful, and she gives that tough mib look to Billy Bray, the luster worn off it years ago, passing it around just as natural as trying for a breeze, the eyes and mouth searching him as she has searched the soldier boy last night, wanting something for herself.

"Thanks," she says to Billy.

"Last night?"

"Ah expect you know 'bout last night," says Mrs. Poole. But he listens again, the girl's soft twang reeling her story off against the middle-of-the-night rundown from the Stamford police. How she went "down street" to meet up with friends and they'd had a beer (you wouldn't know where she'd put it, little thing, ten drafts and no supper), and when she come home this fellah (Private First Class Litwak in full uniform) was crawlin' and prowlin' her place and over by the neighbors and in her bushes whatever you call them. The gun was in the drawer upstairs. She had time. She found time to run up those big stairs led to a balcony, like a hunting lodge you'd imagine with the iron chandelier, the bulbs like steady flame, and into the bedroom with the new bedroom suite.

The bed made up neat when Billy gets there, looking around, hat shoved back, hands in his pockets. You could bounce a quarter on that bed, tight as a barracks, a prison cot, but a spill of thick orange nail polish on the night table (her side) and stockings on a velvet stool with the shape of her thin legs. Tightly muscled legs, like she walked far once, worked hard once. The stockings, the garter belt, the underwear and slippery peach of a nightgown, wave set and mess of metal curlers, instruments of torture to make her Mrs. Poole or the barroom girl. Whoever she is, she doesn't mind Billy in her bedroom.

Photo of a child, white-blond hair frizzed up, pink party dress, no party in the sullen eyes. The mother's full lips early dissatisfied, the mother's worn agate eyes already come-hither. Come hither if you dare.

"Lou Ann," she says, chin up. There was no picture of the Major. "Lou Ann—with her daddy in Texas."

Better off, Billy guessed. How would he know, to be fair. To be fair to this woman who shot a soldier. She stands at the window in a pose, impatient, tapping her fingers on a cigarette case like some society gal in the movies. Billy Bray moves in with the match. She lights her own. This time he sees the splotches on her skin, one side of her neck speckled, pale brown discolorations against the nunlike collar. The afterprint of fungus. He had seen it on boys in the army, a mark of the very poor.

The soldier boy had come in the front door last night. "Not here," she says, meaning the inviolable bed. She'd run up here for the gun.

"Did he touch you?" Billy asks.

"Not here," meaning Litwak had waited politely, hat in hand, for her to fetch the pistol. "Down in the kitchen."

"Did he touch you?" Billy asks.

"Well, whadda ya think?" says Isabelle Poole.

Down in the kitchen a row of empty Coca-Cola bottles and a pack of Camels revealed the room's use. The bride's pots and pans still sported their labels. An organdy apron and cap for a maid lay folded in an open department-store box. The scene of the crime was duly noted as tidy down at the station. Private Litwak, shot four times at close range, had fallen on the new checkerboard linoleum, not a scratch or scuff in sight.

"Where'd he touch you?" Billy asks.

She's ready for that. "In front of the *refrig*-ah-rador." She's ready for anything. The long sleeves of the dress buttoned over her unbruised arms. Not a mark on her—so they said.

The neighbors to the right slowly drag rakes over the winter lawn in a show of spring cleanup. This is at a distance beyond the stretch of yard, big beautiful yards up this way, and they have to lean forward, crane around their bushes, to see Billy Bray and Mrs. Isabelle Poole. She stands shivering in the sun by Litwak's car, his father's car, rusted out, dented, that he'd borrowed for the night. Her own runabout locked in the Tudor garage. Great metal hasps secured the barnlike doors. It is odd she has come outside into this world she hates even with this day's blessing of the sun. Inside, she's won most every round, dry-eyed but taking out the little hankie for Litwak's "ah-*bus*ive" language (where'd she get that one?) and the nasty blood soppin' into the army overcoat as he lay upon her floor. Never cracked; now she wobbles on the gravel in her sensible shoes, embracing herself for warmth, the gracious lady seeing the gentleman off after lunch.

And then he runs to her, the neighbor drops his rake and runs for her, like a schoolboy leaping hedges, clearing a low fence. This tweedy fellow, red in the face, stands by her. Makes a fool of himself over this woman. Billy laughs aloud when he is made to prove himself, take out his shield, laughs at the man's breathless mix of arrogance and fright. You could call the neighbor handsome, the pretty face still holding at fifty, though there was something going, gone under the good luck of his good looks. Ruptured duck in his buttonhole, but he was back to the real world of advertising or Wall Street—in any case, a commuter. The big city. Well, Billy wouldn't know about that, listening to the neighbor's story, the terrible accident, he calls it. The police would have all this, but there was some reason to jump the hurdles, some show of form or strength here that isn't worth it, to campaign against "this Litwak, this intruder," to go on about the dead boy, a Bohunk kid from East Norwalk, to go on about abusive. "Isabelle," the handsome neighbor says, excluding Billy, "Isabelle," panting like a puppy, "they are able to do it. They are bringing the major home."

She trembles, her whole useful little body shivers with the cold, and she puts out her hand toward the dented black fender of the Litwak car, but then rights herself and looks at them both with such contempt, these men. "From It-haly?" she says.

The neighbor's wife, a plump plaid figure, resumes her raking. Billy, driving off, catches sight of this pretense, the woman's scraping at the muddy ground. Some truth in her false gesture, staking out her handsome husband at the side of Isabelle Poole.

Nell's lookout, her vantage point: the dining room full of windows, full of light. Speak no ill of the dead, but her mother kept the green linen shades at half-mast. That had something to do with money or dignity, the Devlins' position in the world. It is Nell's house now, her parents' house with thick stucco walls. The home a castle her father built of his cement, memorial to his trade. She lives on here with husband and children, though the Devlin house is called by her father's name. Old world, the matter of her inheritance—this temple of the middle class passed to her like a poor Irish cottage with a mite of land, or like an Italian villa, the humble village street beneath its garden wall. Nell is both princess of the villa and daughter in the cottage left to look after—to bake, stir, mend.

Soon after her mother died, the sickroom not yet dismantled, her children happily absorbed with cutouts and crayons under the dining room table, she'd snapped up the shades. Light in this house. Now the sheer curtains, pushed back, are rotting on their brass rods never to survive another wash, and Nell, the girl of the house, has become an oddity to the neighbors, dreamy and distant as they imagine ladies, though she knows exactly who they are, remembers their children's ages, each kiddy's name. Strange that she lives among them, driving out in her ancient car to the Ladies'

Natural History

Art League and for every small errand. The mother of a peculiar girl and, of course, the remarkable James. Married to Bill Bray, their Billy. He's easy—catch him in Louie's or the drugstore or backing out of Matthew Devlin's double drive—kid problem, mortgage problem—you can talk to Billy, but she's Mrs. with faded red hair; shabby schoolteacher look to her is go-to-hell grand. The girl of that house and always will be.

The sun is hot on Nell's freckled hand as she picks dead leaves off the Boston fern, if leaves they are, fluttering like moth millers to the carpet, dusty pale brown. On the lookout for James, his lunch long on the kitchen table, a sandwich and the custard he favors. Her head is crowned with rose and amber jewels, reflections from the stained-glass panels above the dining room windows. The colors dance on her hair and white forehead in jerky animation as though she's in one of the Looney Tunes down at Poli's. No boy on his bike—her fault. If she'd not stopped at Murtagh's, come direct from De Martino's, if Bill was not off on a Saturday and the further distraction of Catherine's jamboree, but she is solely to blame and is well into James' disaster—death mask of his face, knickers torn from the crushed cartilage of his knee—when she spots the red fender of his bike thrown at the side steps all the while. "James," she calls, "James," from her post in the dining room, knowing there'll be no answer, no reason to hunt for a note—"Dear Mom . . ." Off to the movies with Pastore or Gildea, and what, after all, is wrong, so wrong with the double feature, and they are lovely boys, Pastore or Gildea, bright boys for this neighborhood. "James," she calls, wasting her breath. Nell's looked right past clarinet case and bright yellow practice book dumped out of the bike basket, her fault, and she feels in her apron pocket for her glasses as the anger rises. She whacks at a cobweb, sweeps the corpse of a winter fly off the windowsill, sucks her scraped knuckles like a child. Nell sees and doesn't see.

Doesn't see how on this beautiful day, James can sit in the stale air of Poli's or the Rialto, rancid oleo on popcorn, candy bar for lunch. Sinful. The day's a gift. Truly sinful, and the sun will be gone when James comes home through the dark streets. A fury comes over her at the lovely boys on a lovely day, at her son's utter disregard of what, of whom, she can't say. Blinded, she has not seen beyond the red fender of his bike, the bakery truck delivering to fat Minnie Brosler; Mary Keating, sinless, on her way to church to pray and pray and pray. March, the Lenten season, but James will eat candy bars, take pleasure in his double feature. It terrifies Nell, what her son cannot give up, while Catherine, you may be sure, will not partake of sweet Protestant cocoa.

The dining room is a box shut upon Nell, a wooden box paneled in chestnut—her father's extravagant choice. Up near the ceiling there's a plate shelf: the papered wall above had always stood empty. Here Nell has set pottery and penny banks. Life in this house. The majolica plates burst with leaves and berries, fish and fowl. Mr. Micawber is ready to spill his beer, the cow her cream. The pickaninny in his cast-iron cap strikes the penny pitch. Clown's dog jumps through the hoop for a dime. Toby jugs and beer steins, all her toys pretend to something they are not. Here she has set her tole trays, fruits and flowers she has painted meticulously from the life, muscat grapes you might reach for, lilacs—you'd swear to their scent. Shut in with her as though by ancient custom they'll sustain her in the grave, as well as the buffet with silver and linen, her initials on the double damask shroud with stubborn gravy stains. As well as the round mahogany table clawing the worn Sarouk with its friendly paws, the nightly table where they sit, for Nell will not have them eating in the kitchen like . . . she'll not say families down the block or the Brays on Division Street in an upstairs flat, just that it suits her—half queen-was-in-the-parlor, half serving girl—to run in and out of the kitchen serving hearty fare. The good food her children must never forget in days to come, the everlasting smells of stews and fresh buttered vegetables, layer cake, berry pie. Forming their cross in the circle: Bill and Nell and James and Catherine. Catherine—dark and stolid, her father exactly, his dent in her chin, his big brown eyes asking of the world. James—long jawed like herself, with her fragile skin and brittle hair of the sandy Irish, the high white Devlin bone poking the bridge of his nose. A genetic joke, the four of them sorted out this way, eating supper under the dining room lamp. As for store cake, packets of macaroni and cheese, the margarine brought on by the war, she'd have none of it. You can have Mr. Birdseye's frozen peas, a feast of them, she'd say, you can have your baloney and Bond Bread when I'm gone.

When I'm gone, an idle taunt. A time unforeseeable when they'd disport themselves at her table, for there she is spooning it out—a touch more, a smidgeon—in their circle of light. When I'm gone—a safe proposal, safe as James is now at the Rialto. Nell could say the row he sits in, way down front with his head bent back from giant faces on the screen. Short-sighted, the Devlin myopia; she can't drag him to the eye chart at Harvey & Lewis, and fears for James looking helplessly for stop signs, the blinker. She fears the softball pitched at him, her boy felled, unconscious in the school-yard. James—not much for sports, his fair head wrenched back for hours in the flickering shadows to see, with no perspective, gangsters, cowboys on the screen. Pleading to her boy in the front row, "You'll go blind as a bat."

Now Nell looks out beyond her own reflection and the red fender, beyond the near sidewalk, across North Avenue to make it out: Sourian has set up his stand, a few green bins have been dragged from his shack, taking advantage, wouldn't you know, of the one good day. He's slit open a sack of potatoes, bunches of beets, and what is it yellow? Carrots half dead in his cellar brought over in the trunk of his car. That empty lot of Joe Morrisey's, which once had an elm and briar bushes, well-known stumbling pits of her childhood, a magic hillock where she might hide, gold to dig for and not be scolded. Queen Anne's lace and wild daisies. Her children had played King of the Mountain in Morrisey's lot when they were old enough to cross.

Now it's Sourian's with a pasteboard shack, all summer his

rotting fruits and vegetables, piles of hard melons stacked like cannonballs. All summer cars driving up, the lights strung like a carnival until the war. A crime for Nell to thank God for the blackout. A commercial property faced Matthew Devlin's house, well, it was a neighborhood that welcomed useful trade. Sourian's fruit stand was beyond her father's, her own, imagining. Bill, even her Bill, can do no more than call the Board of Health. Sourian buys them off—she sees the rats, the filth behind the shack that brings them. Morrisey's lot leveled, scraped raw. There is no elm.

Nell has eaten James' dry sandwich; dampened, rolled, and ironed Billy's shirts. It's two-thirty, three. Catherine has not called, so she'll dash outside in her apron to put James' bike away—when Sourian is seen with the oranges. He appears, a great bearded man with a gleaming smile, like the genie out of the oil jar in her children's books. Not near his car or the shack or the shaky green vegetable bins, Sourian stands clear to the side of his lot facing the Devlin house with a crate of bright oranges as though he has dug them up like treasure or they have fallen from the sky.

"How you do," he calls to Mrs. Bray. It has been a long winter, though that's not why Nell smiles back. There is no forgiveness, no reprieve from their small enmity—never. It's the sight of the big man in his shirt sleeves holding that crate of oranges as though it were light as a loaf of bread.

"You come here," Sourian says. And Nell, for no reason she'll ever know, hops across the street at his command. "You come," he says to her yet again when she stands close by. "Take," Sourian says, and his smile gobbles her up. "Take," he says, but she will not. He lays the crate down and reaches for Nell's hand to show her, to teach her. "Take."

They squat by the oranges. "How much?" she asks. Oh, she'd never buy from Sourian. Her voice is unfamiliar to her, low and halting. Nell pulls her glasses off, feels in her apron pocket for a coin or bill. There is only a recipe clipped from the *Post* for crumble cake.

"Florida," Sourian says. He is wearing queer cloth shoes. His bare ankles are brown. He has been in Florida, and his forehead, big nose, naked arms are darker than she's ever seen from her dining room window. "Florida," he says, "like home." And turns the orange crate so Mrs. Bray can see the label with a bluebird and a happy child pictured in a gloss-green grove. Like Lebanon? Armenia? He holds her by the wrist to make her touch the tight pebbled skin of an orange. Her finger runs over the navel, up to the stem. What of their hatred, real to Nell, which she now believes may be to Sourian some oriental game. There are leaves in the crate, fresh and shiny. She has never seen oranges with leaves, and her hand selects a plump orange, almost perfect store fruit with neither leaf nor stem.

Sourian says: "I pick." His broad hand wanders the crate, choosing divinely. One, two, three, and Nell's orange makes four. Now he pulls her to her feet and spills the oranges in her apron, tucks the ends up at her narrow waist. Sourian counts—four oranges, two sloped breasts above, her long pale throat, trembling chin held high. Sourian smiles with big white teeth, heavy-lidded eyes glistening—and unbelievably he strokes Mrs. Bray on the cheek as though she were a pretty child.

Last ring of the phone missed as she runs in the door. Catherine, poor Cath calling, but when Nell drives to the other side of the city, St. John's is locked against her—vestry, parish house, rectory if that is what they call it. No Scouts. No cars. She drives home slowly through back streets known like the lines on the palm of her hand, laid out with small mysteries, turns you never chance. No feathered hat, her apron under the sealskin, which she clutches around her as she pushes by garage junk, scoops the evening paper from the porch, and runs up into her father's house, safe from Sourian's gaze.

How did Obie get stuck with Catherine and June? She swings into Howland's through the revolving door, scoots by the usual mess of ladies at hosiery and notions to the stairs. No one takes the elevator to Howland's basement. This is not known to Catherine or June. By the time Obie hits the bottom step she has taken off her Girl Scout kerchief, rolled her socks, hiked the uniform well above her dimpled knees. Her hair, with some swift stroke, now falls over one eye, ripples right down to a slouch shoulder. Some hot number.

A descent to hell, as far as Cath's concerned. Not all that innocent, she's heard of Howland's basement, what goes on. What goes on in this unlikely hangout after school she could not actually say. Something dangerous if not diabolical. And not first class: Howland's cafeteria can not compare to the Silhouette Room of D. M. Read's. Obie places her coat in some ritual to reserve the extra chair. The tables are black marble, lights dim: Cath's notion of nite club. She is ready to be burned and scourged.

Obie flashes a silver compact, dabs orange powder on her nose: "No one here Saturday."

Ever so pleasantly, June remarks on women sipping tea, children with ice cream sundaes.

"None of the kids," Catherine explains and could cut her tongue out. She's come to Howland's for punishment, hellfire. No one knows who June is, where she lives. A tall drink of water who showed up in their troop one day, arms dangling out of a green cardigan, stooping to make her height go way. From Pennsylvania, June said, might as well be Paris or Mars. As though promoting her strangeness, her last name is jammed with y's and z's.

Obie, nursing a small lemon Coke, sits at an angle, legs crossed. She's not with these girls, with Catherine and June. She hums, flips her hair, combs it over the table. June is scraping the bottom of a hot fudge sundae, speaking all the while of their wonderful time at the jamboree, of the cocoa and songs, of the nifty exhibits.

Cath can't bear June's sweet words, her voice gone sticky with chocolate and cream, and feels in her coat pocket for a coin. The cotton boll is there. She's ripped it from QUEEN OF THE SOUTH; that pod so tough, so strong, it pulled clean away. This has been the worst day, not merely of her life, end of the world, dark falling upon the earth, wherever that was. Well, she'll kiss it goodbye here in Howland's gloomy basement. Beyond the black glass partitions of the cafeteria—housewares, brightly lit. Out there live people, still breathing, choose whisk brooms, pots, and dishtowels. Once she'd come here, once when her mother's favorite saucepan sprang a leak. No more tinkers, her mother said, and said there'd been such a man who came through the streets like the Italian knife sharpener. The tinker mended your pails and kettles and pans. That was history, Cath supposed. Who cared? Not the Girl Scouts of Greater Bridgeport, believe you me.

"That kitty was the cutest thing," says June. A red cat, doggy shape with doggy muzzle and clouded blue eye, crazed by a ball of string. Hooked into a rug by the troop from Trumbull, the kitty had won second prize. All those Scouts squeezing berries and weeds for the dyes. Cath had worked alone, clipping and pasting her scraps; run by herself to the reference room. They knew her in the reference room—the colored man in distinguished wire-rim glasses who slept by the *Britannica;* a creepy neighbor lady, Sister Brown, deep in genealogies; half blind Mrs. Muller, the reference librarian who smelled of rotten apples. It was Mrs. Muller who gave Cath the picture of Eli Whitney from the official file, a torn gray envelope wound with rubber bands. She'd entered Catherine's silly dream, for that's all it was—pie-in-the-sky for an old librarian with watery eyes and dirt ground into the wrinkles of her neck, for a proud child who always thought . . . what was it Catherine thought? . . . that she'd know more than the rest of them. Special child, running to the reference room, pestering the Department of Agriculture, Washington, D.C., for a real cotton boll.

"Hold the bombardiers. Call Franklin," James had said.

If he was so smart, why did the parcel finally come? Handle with Care. *Enclosed is the cotton boll requested. We wish you all the luck in your agricultural endeavor.*

"Call Eleanor. The Girl Scouts have arrived."

"That will do, James," their father said.

She'd carried the official box and that letter signed by no one down to dinner, lifting the brown pod high above her head, sacramental, as though its white fluff of lint with flecks of seed . . .

"Thy gifts and presents, a pure victim . . ."

"You may leave the table, James," their father said.

What had she wanted from her hours alone, pasting, arranging her pictures and facts, whittling a cork to fit the little vial of cottonseed oil? Cath had not known what she wanted until she waltzed into the basement of St. Pat's, her father bearing QUEEN OF THE SOUTH like a lackey. Sullivan and those chattering girls held their breath. Catherine Bray was a wonder. Was that it? Was that all? The history badge sewn onto her sleeve. Plastered with honors, more than the rest.

Today it was simple: she wanted first prize, saw herself walking up on a stage, flags rippling behind a committee of judges; crisp women from headquarters salute her, gold trefoil pinned on their caps of green gabardine. Faceless Girl Scouts look up to her out of the dark. It's one of the downtown theaters, Poli's Palace or Majestic with chandeliers and red velvet curtains. In a Senior Scout uniform, the dark forest green, she does not falter over well chosen words of acceptance. It was terrible, her sin of pride that brought her to defeat in the Protestant hall. Numb with shame, she glommed on to Obie, trailed after her to Howland's basement, but not before she turned QUEEN OF THE SOUTH to the wall, kicked the posterboard and heard the pictures skittle to the floor, not caring—slaves or the great inventor—but she reached round. Her fingers knew which corner exactly: she would not sacrifice her cotton boll.

No better than June, she tagged after Obie, as though she yearned to know what Obie knew. Obie was thirteen. Her parents owned a hardware store on Main Street. The O'Briens often ate their dinner at Pjura's Restaurant or the Stratfield Hotel. The children, five big brothers and Obie, knowingly wandered the shops and streets downtown. Now Obie whisks her coat off the extra chair for a loose, gangly boy with a B on his varsity sweater. Some dope from Bassick doesn't know Saturday is wrong for Howland's basement. The boy lights a crumpled cigarette. Obie gives him a look, flips her hair in exasperation. It occurs to Cath that she is the embarrassment, not June. June finds lipstick in her shoulder strap purse. She's pulled her beret to one side like Joan Bennett, belted her raincoat tight. Oh boy, *Foreign Affairs*, starring June the Unpronounceable, but it's Catherine who is Obie's trial. To further humiliate herself, she borrows a half dollar from June, looks upon meat loaf in gravy, breaded brown fish and baked beans. When Catherine comes back with a glass of milk and a small dish of spinach in its inky green pool, June has disappeared.

"Caught her bus to Chopsey Hill." Obie drags on her friend's cigarette. They erase Cath from the table. She is no more, in her pigtails and uniform with many badges. Chopsey Hill so far from school, from their weekly meeting at St. Pat's. A lopsided waitress swipes at the black marble table with a sour rag, avoiding the spinach and milk. Cath plays with her pennies, June's three pennies. Under the table the Bassick boy and Obie do something with their legs. The milk and spinach form a chalky coating on Cath's teeth. This is hell and she deserves it.

"So, okay," Obie says. She's been laughing like crazy for the Bassick boy. Now she calms down, stubs out their cigarette, scrapes back her chair. Fooling and fighting, the boy and Obie abandon this hangout, unfashionable today. Catherine scrubs at her front teeth with a paper napkin. She cannot call her mother with three cents. Up at the counter men wash out big aluminum pots and basins. The woman at the cash register is gone; dim lights dimmer. Catherine buttons her navy coat with the velvet collar, tight in the arms, Sunday coat for a child. The pennies slip into her pocket beside the cotton boll and her yellow ribbon. Awarded honorable mention, the most disgraceful moment of her life. Dark is upon the earth, upon the underworld of Howland's basement as she moves through the gleaming housewares. A yellow ribbon, one of many: First Prize to the girls from Stratfield, for their ridiculous village of Popsicle sticks. Toothpick fences. Chipped mirror for their pond. Huge celluloid geese and ducks stalked teeny lead settlers in cowboy hats and prairie bonnets—colonial, my eye. Second Prize to hooked-rug Rover, the terrier cat with clouded eye. The yellow honorables: worthless compensation for every colonial sampler, colonial jar of ye olde jamboree. Some competition. It was all over when Frieda, a woman from her mother's past, came to make it nice. Came to *them*, that was a hoot. The last yellow mention for St. Pat's, Miss Kurtz with a wink for the good old days when she and Nell Devlin taught school. Cath would rather die than touch the thing. June took it. June from Nowhere, Pennsylvania. Obie, the nerve of her, said, "Thanks." Thanks for the booby prize.

Here you have a map, at last, manufactured to instruct. One of those big schoolroom maps printed on glazed cloth, the kind that rolls down from a cylinder to cover the blackboard with the world or North America. This map is both more and less than first intended; more calm, less fraught than you intended, as though it is a ditty written plain, wars and storms, time and place. The large dotted lines define more than your city, which was in fact too dense, an eyesore of names and locations; or too yeasty, rising toward the next dimension while this plan, printed by the hundreds up in Hartford, the state capital, this layout is flat, broad—more than you imagined. The county entire, Fairfield County is shown as fabulously simple, the shallow blue waters of Long Island Sound, the pale green of its slight elevations in Redding and Trumbull, the heavy pink populace of the industrial centers—your city and others, Danbury, Stamford, Norwalk. Less than you imagined; unstoried, general issue, yet you dare not snap it back into oblivion as though . . . as though it is not your jurisdiction.

Billy Bray has left the home of Mrs. Isabelle Poole, due north of the tavern where she ran across the Litwak boy, and made his way to the red brick box of the Stamford police station, where the local cops are dumbfounded by the murder, by the reporters from New York and New Haven, by a feisty woman with a camera from *Life* magazine. Billy does not say that if there was significant evidence up at that fancy house, someone has destroyed it, that the boy's uniform shows no twig or tear of neighbor brambles. He sets up the arrest. It will do to bring the woman here for the arraignment, not to the county courthouse like a common criminal. The Major is on a transport plane flying toward home, and it is highly unlikely that Mrs. Poole will be held without bail, transferred to the county jail in Bridgeport, a few blocks from Billy Bray's home—his wife's house, actually, where the King's Highway becomes simply North Avenue.

The detective goes about his business with more than his usual control, drives by the half-house in East Norwalk, an old company house near the Dobbs hat factory, where Litwak's family lives. A florist truck at the curb, neighbors with nose trouble staring. He thinks to wait, not to disturb. Stretching Saturday into a work day, he travels Route 1, the old Post Road, stops at the Swede's in Southport and comes back into Bridgeport through Hunk Town to pick up the line on Litwak in the bars. He stops at the coroner's office to look at four battered slugs and at the slack baby face of the dead soldier under the bristle of GI haircut.

Billy's wife has driven crosstown, up and downhill in a zigzag of missed connections. Nell, home at last, absentmindedly wanders to the kitchen in her shabby fur coat, unfolds the evening *Post*. There is Isabelle Poole; brassy hair rolled high off her forehead glistens in the flashbulb's light. She faces the camera defiantly in slacks and a snug angora sweater. Nell takes off her distance glasses to better see the common flower face that will fade fast, figures Mrs. Poole bought that sweater a size small, from the look of her a pin-up girl of no account. She doesn't read the story. When she lies in bed beside her husband she will hear and dread it—unavoidable as the header SOCIALITE KILLS. Bill will tell her four shots to the stomach at close range. It is a comfort to throw off her coat, settle, and turn the page to the daily drawings of Pacific islands and the Italian boot with the Allied victories marked on the Adriatic and in North Africa. Jabbing arrows depict the continuing struggle at Monte Cassino, the gains and losses at wherever. Over there—Europe. The Other Side, her family had always called it. The Other Side, too distant for names. Simple, successful people putting Ireland well behind them, they traced a limited geography of work, church, home. X marked the Devlin house in their detailed inset, the stucco house at Parrott and North Avenue where Nell will lie down next to Billy.

On Main Street, North Main Street, there is the Rialto, its modest light-bulb marquee turned on these past few weeks. James watches a tribe of Indian braves make their way, single file, across a high ridge in stately silhouette, a slow thrilling procession. They ride in silence to certain death. James and his friend, the Gildea boy, await the massacre. Will there be the cavalry call or drum beats? Will the soldiers move forward in glorious but foolhardy formation? No, they have learned from the old scout to crouch down in ambush, wiggle on their bellies from rock to rock. The ping, ping of bullets is more deadly than the soft thwump, thwump of arrows into flesh. James has barely left the neighborhood; uphill to Mr. De Martino, down to Pappas' in the Hollow. Endearingly irresponsible, yet we see he has taken the easy way, bound on a Saturday to end up in the front row of the Rialto. Even as the second feature ends James calculates the delights of this day, which are not over, but he could never rank them—the music, the magic, the movies.

It's Billy who's looped far up to the Merritt in pursuit of the homicide, then made the day business-as-usual, put off his return to the courthouse, where only now, at dusk, he writes on a legal pad, then speaks into the round cup of a Dictaphone. So speaking and writing in turn, he builds a case for what is now the State v. Isabelle Poole. Stringer, the State's Attorney, is country club—an elegant man out of Yale Law who gardens, breeds collies. But tough, an unsmiling smart fellow who hates to lose. Henry Stringer is law library, courtroom. The burden falls upon Billy, no direct testimony, so he assembles his circumstantial evidence before he calls Stringer, who's got to know this is a flashy case. The wire men, the *Times* and *Tribune* have descended on Stamford, a woman in army fatigues from *Life* magazine. Stringer, whose wife does not like Billy Bray to disturb him at home, not even for murder, has been waiting for his call and listens when the detective says a cryin' shame that Bohunk soldier was nineteen, but given the Major flying home with his medals, he'd hold it at Murder, Second Degree. William Aloysius Bray turns the big brass key in the door with his name lettered on, strides across the courthouse lobby, and has to laugh at himself—the sweet revolver still in his topcoat pocket. What had he hoped or imagined the danger to be? From that loose little trick, the slippery stuff of her step-ins, the flesh color of her nylons thrown down for him to see. The stain on her neck seeped down under the postulant's collar. She'd give you a dose. No birthmark, original sin, that was the print of her past—you'd know what a woman like that had lived through, guess it from the swell of the lips, pull on the cigarette, strain of her bust against the cheap glass buttons of an artless dress. She'd cut off his balls with one look. Then the switch—her invitation to him in a petulant smile, automatic but more than friendly. Cute trash from Texas.

Tupper is closing his stand. He holds out the Luckies to Billy. Three packs a day. Billy catches the picture of Isabelle Poole in the fuzzy sweater, taken last night, the triumph of killing still in her flecked stone eyes. He's got something for Elliot. Sure enough, Elliot hangs lopsided over Tupper's counter, then scuttles alongside as Billy Bray heads to the state car. Lou Ann. He gives Elliot the towhead daughter, dressed for a party, left behind in Texas. The socialite, the Major's wife, no more than a child herself when she brought that hapless kid into the world. A bit of human interest Elliot can knock together before he makes his way home to Mother.

Catherine has traveled far beyond her prescribed course: home, church, school, library. ". . . no frigate like a book," she's committed that to memory, but today sailed forth unmetaphorically to the heathen shore of St. John's Episcopal hall and the eerie isle of the damned in Howland's basement. Gone long and far—still her adventures do not end at what is now the end of an ordinary winter day, early dusk, clammy wind blowing up from the Sound as Billy heads into traffic. Saturday, the stores are closing, and Catherine, the willful dreamer, runs down Main Street, hell-bent for the court-house, praying God or at least luck must be with her this once and she'll hitch a ride home with her father. Catherine is squat, stocky to be nice about it, and runs clumsily, thinking she'll see him, call to him. And it happens: there at the stop light on Golden Hill, in his unmarked state car, is Billy Bray. She sees the angle of his soft felt hat, his round face, her face with the fleshy dented chin. As the light changes, she runs to him, runs after him as he drives off, tears fogging her eyes. She'll catch up, can almost feel how it will be sitting safely beside him, and Catherine runs out into the street, where she is hit—gently, unimportantly—by an oncoming car.

Blood, policemen. The driver, a foreman at Burroughs on downtown business after the day shift, a kind terrified man, insists on driving her to St. Vincent's. Her mother in Emergency, hatless, clutching her coat over an apron, gone white as the white room. Yards of white gauze, thick strips of adhesive as though she's a major calamity. One green sock lightly spattered with her blood. Her father enters, stunned in the brightness, awkwardly kissing her at last. Now the nurses joking with her father, Billy Bray. Her mother tall, dignified in that dirty apron. There is an ugly gash across the new purse from New York. Now her father joking with the nuns. Her mother looks on: it is one of those awful moments when she is not of them, framed in the glass door with EMERGENCY etched above her long delicate head. There they all are, Nell Devlin looking on at nurses, nuns, the injured child, then looking down to see she wears only one glove when the Mother Superior, who would not for a routine accident come to Emergency, appears. Here is the daughter of William Aloysius Bray brought in with a scrape and contusions. A sister of St. Vincent de Paul, ever serene; the white wings of her bonnet sail across the bright room to Catherine. From the bosom of her habit she takes a religious card with a medal of Jude, patron saint of miracles. Listening to this heavenly woman, the voice of an angel—that is how she speaks—say he is the saint of healing as well, but Cath knows it is a miracle that she's alive.

At the dinner table they eat Mr. Murtagh's franks, Nell's beans with a touch of black molasses. Saturday night fare, but there is an aura of specialness, a solemnity as they pass the ketchup, pour their milk. Playing a legitimate invalid, Cath wears her pink quilted bathrobe, her injured leg propped on a footstool under the round table.

"Contusion?" James asks, pushing to the very edge with mock alarm.

"A bruise," says his father, pulling a stern face that doubles the double chin. "And when you choose to . . . when it is your pleasure to run off to the movies . . ."

It has started now. Nell passes the cole slaw, no one's favorite, but it goes with franks and beans.

". . . you'll have a bruise," Billy says to his son.

The overhead light, its glass shade a rural landscape of misty trees by wandering stream, shines upon them. Now it has started: their four faces too familiar, each dealt a small portion of wrong and pain. Poor Cath has pinned St. Jude to the bathrobe: Nell can see it coming. "Patron saint of desperate cases." This from James. The swift slap of Bill's hand.

"Well, he is," says James, the red mark spreading on his cheek.

"Lovely oranges!" says Nell. She fairly sings out, "Winter oranges." A second miracle: James has not been sent from the table. He sits in a black mood across from Cath, the happy martyr beatified. She has undone her pigtails before supper and dark hair surrounds her plump face in unnatural twists and bends. She looks older, perhaps thirteen. They all stare at the unlikely oranges, as though they are a Lenten punishment. Billy says, "What the hell!" He likes his dessert, a piece of his wife's pie, her bread pudding. "Say, isn't this dainty," he says, tossing up an orange, and the kids laugh.

Nell makes a show of being hurt as the sharp smell of orange peel springs at her, but she's pleased. It has not been that easy to bring them here, to hold them tonight under the dining room lamp. The windows rattle in their frames. She looks up, for a moment remembering, but the stained-glass windows are opaque at night, flat pink, tan, green; the weightless old curtains are drawn and the shades pulled out of habit for the blackout, so she cannot see beyond. Across the street, the disgrace of Joe Morrisey's lot—she will always call it that—shack and cheap crates, entirely gone.

James toodling away on his clarinet. Thank heavens the walls are thick, built to last, the house large so that his parents can barely hear, only take pleasure—James is practicing. Catherine's room is next to her brother's, and even on this night, the night of her accident, she has no say in the matter. Her brother is musical and she bears it, as she bears his pokes and prods, his teasing and correction, which are precious to her—James' notice. She has come to cherish this suffering hour in which, by a supreme act of will, she gives up her studies, her projects, gives herself to "Mood Indigo," "Begin the Beguine." As though, as though she could be James, profligate and easy, endowed as her brother is endowed.

He sways in front of a crazed looking-glass, hips thrust forward in striped pajamas. "When the deep purple falls over sleepy garden walls . . ." James slurs, hurdling octaves. He's got it by heart and glances down at the clutter of sheet music on his dresser for inspiration only: bluish photographs of Woody Herman, Benny Goodman, Artie Shaw. Deadbeat De Martino, maestro of the Method, is abandoned with his fussy promises held out to James of someday the Mozart concerto, someday Till Eulenspiegel's Merry Pranks. Geraldo with his threadbare memories of a rapturous obbligato, both he and Momma heard it, the ravishing sound out of an old instrument fashioned from the rare mgambo tree. But it's good old Geraldo, James knows that, passing the half glass to his one talented and lazy pupil.

Tonight he rushes the repertoire. The silks await, still hidden in their matchbox from Pappas' candy store. Saving the best for last; so unlike him to delay the fun, but James is ever so slow and serious as he puts on his grandfather's top hat, which rests on the tip of his ears. He is Jimmy De Vino, alias King Klang, alias Professor Mulrooney. The trick is not the trick, but always to capture your audience, and to this end he smiles. Hey—are you with me? See there is nothing, my friends, but this simple ping-pong ball. It bounces and now there are two, now three, you bet. One red. One green. Now none at all. Slow, not fast—a little patter for misdirection. No hocus-pocus, ali bim bah. "Beautiful day," says James. "It makes a fella want to get out there and play ball." Twenty, maybe thirty times, his head turning deceptively this way, that way, he does the ping-pong balls. "Beautiful day, folks. Hey, it makes a fella want to get out there and play ball."

Next he back palms a quarter and drops it. "Laugh, go on," he says, mightily offended. "I'm a rank amateur." He picks up the coin, flips it. This is his sucker gag: Okay, you chumps, where is it? Whadda ya know, this clumsy kid in floppy pajamas has made the quarter vanish. James is devoted to his magic. It is all so logical, explainable. Nothing to believe in but illusion. Harry Houdini, he thinks of this often, walked through a brick wall. The coin. The drop. He alters his line slightly, "Laugh. Go on, Ladies and Gents . . ."

Finally he allows himself the silks folded tight in their tiny Ohio matchbox. He thinks to produce them with a flourish, but that is not his style. He holds with a kind of bumbling charm as though—as though it's not so easy—only then is it really amazing.

Ah! red, blue, yellow, green swirling in the air. He tries the dissolving knot. A knot. In green silk. He displays it. (Even the boy in the top hat is credulous.) A knot truly, but when James blows on it— ha!—the knot disappears.

Finished with the evening paper, Bill Bray leaves it strewn upon the couch. Isabelle Poole shares the front page with the President, who is withered, gray in the gray photo. In the midst of Matt Devlin's heavy furniture, of Nell's ornaments placed about, Billy recalls the rooms with no life in North Stamford, other than the life of that woman's hand on his, a split second, then the sway of her hips as she led him to the unused kitchen. How did the soldier come to be in that kitchen? Nell has fallen asleep over her book. She is a great reader. He wakes her, adjusts the thermostat before they climb the stairs. She sits on her side of the bed as she does always to pick the pins from her hair. They are a rusty color meant to match her auburn, but the crowning glory is streaked, quite recently, with a faded yellow-white.

"Socialite, I'll tell you," Billy says. "If that's society, I'm Winston Churchill. I'm Lord Haw-Haw." Though it is her wifely duty, she does not want to hear about the woman who committed murder.

"Jesus, she's some debutante."

"The poor boy's dead."

He tells her a number of things: that the State's Attorney is a busy fellow, a vestryman on Sunday, so Mrs. Poole may have till Monday. She had better go to church before she's charged. The Swede has not sighted a U-boat; this week it's espionage at the corset factory, the enemy within. And the Mother Superior after him . . . her nurses are running for luck to the gypsies. They want to hear the long voyage, the dark stranger. What's the harm? He can't close the gypsies.

"No harm," Nell says. The air in the bedroom is thick with his last smoke of the day. She does not want to hear about the nurses' venial dreams or the Litwak family's request for a military funeral, though they do not yet have the body of their boy. Unfair to Bill, but she does not want to hear about that woman in the angora sweater, her assortment of men and crimes. Her wish is granted, for there's a clang, a rolling clatter of metal. It is the empty trash cans James never brought in. She's halfway out of bed when Bill grabs her.

"God damn him!"

What a tragic figure he looks to Nell in his rage, in his wing-tipped oxfords and pajama bottoms, his little breadbasket heaving. "Leave it. Leave it," she cries.

What a fool he is out in the cold with the gun in his topcoat pocket, the lid of the trash can held up like a shield against the first flakes of a blustery snow that will turn to rain.

Catherine has half listened to a mystery show, full of squealing hinges, creaking stairs. Her mother had brought the portable radio in, read to her from *East o' the Sun and West o' the Moon* as if she was a kid, years ago. Then it was time for the mystery. No one even asked about her project. She had lost her yellow ribbon in the kind man's car or in Emergency. It is as though there never was a competition, yet Cath's sins will not be forgotten. Pride, then desire: she had seen her father's soft hat and red bow tie and all she wanted, running blindly, was to have him safe with her. She is convinced her leg is in great pain. This is the day she nearly got killed. God's hand held back that car. Such marvels happen in her world, the good as well as the bad. Eli Whitney assembled ten thousand muskets for the army before he ever saw a field of cotton. Juliet Gordon Lowe, struck deaf on her wedding day—one more example—rice thrown in her ear, then she founded the Girl Scouts. That is history. You are marked. You know, as Catherine Bray now knows, that she is called. She will give her life to some great cause, to some invention. James has fallen asleep with his light blazing to the world. Her father passes her door, funny in his coat and pajama bottoms. She hears him in James' room swearing at the magic apparatus. She shifts her leg: it is precious. This is the day she got hit by a car.

Pretending sleep, James hears his father whack the ping-pong balls, scatter his coins, mutter the name of his friend the Dean of Delphi. His father, the detective, turns out the light. Billy Bray stands in the dark hall between the one child who will always know what he wants and the one who will never get what she wants. He feels his way back to the bedroom. "Jesus, that's a good one," he says and slips the revolver into the drawer of the night table, his side of the bed.

"What?" his wife asks. She can hear he's easy now.

"It's snowing," says Billy. And he thinks he must not tell her the Greek runs a front for Ernie Cozza: he must make a move on the candy store. And thinks he must not tell, what with the trash cans and Emergency, that Private Litwak was invited, not a doubt in his mind—an assignation with that girl. And says, as though this is most remarkable: "They fly the Major home from Italy and we haven't won the war."

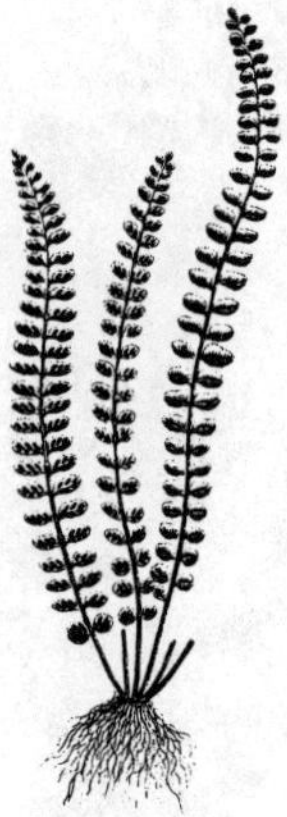

Museum Pieces:

The Witness
Sister Brown
Closet Drama
The Lives of the Saints
Double Entry
The Music Man
Screenplays
The Spinster's Tale

The Witness

If I bear witness of myself, my witness is not true.
—John, 5: 31

And then. And then. All forward march, in careless phalanx the family coming at us; Dad straining comfortably at the leash, sniffing out hometown corruption and crime. Like father, like daughter; the girl marches in precise imitation, chin up, eyes forever wandering to check the overconfident hup-two, hup-two of Daddy's gait. Mother in step vaguely, drawn off by the daily mysteries of unmated sock, scorched collar, pan sizzle, glisten of fresh egg. Her hand reaches back automatically for the boy, always an insolent step behind. The father so red-faced, puffed like a cock rooster from their two-block excursion to St. Patrick's, we do not even have to ask, and then? Who will be the first? Who, coming at us over the years, will first break ranks? Peel off—toward life, toward death.

Lala Litwak sees them. Sitting outside their church on a Sunday in the very car, his father's pocked and battered Chevy, his brother drove to that woman's, drove to the scene of his death. Parked behind a van that sells the Sunday papers, Lala watches the good parishioners who have attended late Mass, singles out the Brays, observes their descent down the steep granite steps, a light breeze blowing the mother's dress against her narrow thighs, ruffling the father's bow tie so Lala could grab it, swing him like a dead cat against the carved stone saint, Patrick with his staff and bishop's hat. But never. Lala only watches, shifts to neutral, whams the choke. Sputtering, the Chevy scoots a half block ahead of the Brays. On the short blocks to their stucco house they now trail him in the rearview mirror, holy after their holy mass, pursue him under the first leafed-out elms and maples. And weeks later, remarking upon the heavy-headed dahlias and the last of the rambler rose, they follow Lala, unaware of his notorious car, recently dusted for prints, photos of this sorry vehicle admitted into evidence. Then Billy Bray might be stalking Litwak of murderous plots who would leap to the sidewalk, twist a shiv in his ribs, or, taking aim from the Chevy, would shatter his florid go-to-mass face. But never. Billy is laying out the order of the day as Lala draws up to Sourian's curb, abreast of melons, oranges, early peas. The Brays cut this blight upon the neighborhood out of their view as they come dangerously close to the old Chevy. Once Lala rolls down his window so it would seem that Billy Bray cannot help but see him. But never. Billy, full of his *paterfamilias* role, is boisterously ordering the day—what ride to be taken, Sunday roast to be eaten. And once, the boy is fooling with a half dollar which rolls off the curb right in front of the Chevy and quickly scrambles after, so that Lala in the idling car could crush Billy Bray's son, make his bright blood run into his bright hair. The kid sees the man with a porkpie hat, a skewed mustache, sees Lala hunched over the wheel, smiling at him through the murky windshield.

Not smiling. It is the way Lala's upper lip pulls over a slightly cleft palate so that he is always smiling even when, as he tails Billy Bray, his heart is pounding with hurt and hate of the man who did not send Isabelle Poole to burn in hell for the death of his brother. Did not even send her to prison. She's free somewhere in her snug sweater, tits pushing out like hard fuzz balls, sour balls left in a pocket. She is breathing on a bar stool. Lala sees her as Eddie must have, swiveling round, offering it. Some hell of a prize. She is lighting up now, boozing somewhere while he sits in his old man's Chevy watching the Brays cross at Parrott Avenue on a summer Sunday. Half in the bag and in eternal night where Lala's cast her, Isabelle Poole displays her barroom charms. Her red mouth breathes death, but she is breathing somewhere, gone from the big house where Eddie died. Taken off, moved on. Billy Bray, who could use a shiv in the ribs, a blast in the happy red face, has let her live. Lala Litwak is not smiling.

It is his misfortune that he looks lighthearted, his upper palate patched in a screwy smile: and that his name is Lala. Could never spit the d in Ladislaw, so Lala he became, pet name and taunt: sweet in his mother's voice with the liquid slavic L, silly to kids— tra-la-la or Fala as though he were the end of a song or, *arf-arf,* the President's Scotty dog. Barked at, sung at, Lala has no defense against his indelible smile. No fool, but made to look the fool, that's his further complaint against the detective. Not against Henry Stringer, the State's Attorney, stuffed-shirt, courtroom rhetorician, as unfathomable to the immigrant population of the county as a nineteenth-century New England preacher. Stringer's patrician voice might be the humdrum prosecution in a radio drama as far as Lala is concerned: "Then, Mrs. Poole, is it correct that you . . . ?" So low and controlled you'd think she'd parked by a fireplug, run a red light, not drilled a soldier boy at close range. That is correct. Eddie Litwak's dress uniform with four neat holes like big cigarette burns is numbered and displayed. What does the remaining Litwak boy care for Stringer's stone face, the judicious clearing of his throat as he launches dispassionate arguments in a court of law? A big shot, not fully human, how would Stringer identify Mrs. Poole's "in-truder" as his perfect baby brother who, until he went off to the army, slept in the same bed, whose breath Lala still feels and some-times thinks he hears, a troubled sigh, so he'll have to cover Eddie or, like long ago, lift him downstairs to the toilet in the night? Why would Lala imagine his knife in the State's Attorney's trim ribs or his buckshot blowing off that remote Emersonian jaw?

It's Billy he guns for. "Tell me," Billy Bray had said. That was the Sunday; two nights and one day had passed since the murder. "Tell me." Lala, dead-eyed, sat upright on the couch. The room—stuffy and low: flowers splayed wide and high in baskets all around. Cleared place for a casket: Eddie's body, not released to the family, holds its secrets in the morgue. Finally, it is quiet here as though the insistent reporters, curious neighbors, consoling Father Nolan, even the Litwaks, mother and father, know enough's enough and stare at the unanswering ceiling over their bed. The quiet is heavy, no better than weeping and words to Lala. He doesn't like talk, doesn't talk well. To Eddie he spoke with a shrug, twitch, blink of an eye.

It is Sunday and Lala, who works in a foundry, should be on his shift to end all wars. He sits in the powerful silence, his hands, competent and large, rub-dubbing his knees. He hears the kitchen faucet drip, a settling of the stairs as though Eddie were about to come down in his uniform, blond bristle head damp with brilliantine. He hears the cars pass slowly by, Sunday drivers gaping at the Litwaks' half-house as though the flaking gray clapboards will reveal the grief shut up inside. Lala wishes he caught the bus to work, to the screech and clang of metal turning. There he loves the noise, the thunder of sheet metal and sharp whine of the lathe spewing brass filings. He is the prized worker, a foreman now. Lala of the golden hands. Genius in his touch, any problem, any fine points, ask Litwak. He loves the loud high shop where the workers do not speak in the din, hours without a word, and the joke's if enemy ears are listening they'll have squat to tell. It's whispered that the shafts and findings turned out at Lala's plant are shipped across town to Chance Vought for the Corsair. His nuts and bolts fly four hundred miles an hour, the only glory this Litwak boy rescues from the war are his Corsairs zooming off carriers, strafing the last of the German resistance at Monte Cassino. Rub-dubbing his knees, today he misses the earsplitting noise of the foundry.

"So, tell me," Billy Bray says. He does not flash the shield. Seated low on a collapsed punching bag of an ottoman, he dangles his hat between his knees. The detective might be praying this Sunday at the bereaved brother's feet, his voice a murmur of consideration. "Tell me, son." And Lala, with so little use for talk, tells all he knows, how Eddie took the old man's car and they'd go down the Log Cabin together, only that night Eddie gave the high sign. Lala knew it was some girl. "A libe un," Lala says. Eddie stinking of after-shave and brilliantine, in his dress uniform, sharpshooter ladder pinned on his breast.

The story tumbles out of Litwak, so many words, telling of his fears that night. Down here, here where he punches his big fist into his stomach. Telling all, his eyes fill with tears above the inappropriate smile, the whole sorrowful story from when Eddie was his baby brother. "He tawk fo me," Lala says, and Billy understands Eddie spoke for his brother; Eddie who was handsome, unimpaired, who left home Friday night turned out for dress parade. Eddie on leave from gunnery school, someplace down South that the Litwaks, Jadwiga and Witold, never bothered to locate on the ragged map of America pinned up in their boys' attic room.

And Lala takes the letter from his pocket, defense-plant ID pinned to its flap. He is dressed in his clean workclothes, this day like any other. *Are you getting any from all the hungry women?* Eddie had written in his last letter from Fort Benning, Georgia. Billy Bray takes note of the soldier's rank and outfit. Lala, smiling, watches the detective read: *We'll hit the town. We sure will pick up their morale, those lonely dames.* The pretty blond soldier including his silent split-lipped brother in the fun: Eddie who had the girls and the gift of gab for both of them. The detective hands the precious letter back. Nothing to go on, the soldier boy's hormones pushing their case. Alone, Eddie could operate.

"A libe un," Lala says. Sad, given the tragedy, to see the gleam in the big brother's eye, the vicarious pleasure in what might be an empty legend, Eddie's making out. Gave him the high sign

and Lala sat with his parents, here where he pats the couch. There was music on the radio but he could hear the Chevy's battery grind, pick up in a sickly cough. If only the car had conked out in the cinder lot behind the Log Cabin. Here, Lala punches his gut; he knew it here. Billy Bray remembers the Litwak car, dull with age, dented, an eyesore on the clean raked pebbles of Mrs. Isabelle Poole. She was a live one: the sharpshooter was dead.

Lala talking, never said so much in his life. He speaks an easy pidgin, now Billy understands, that works its way around the labials and dentals. How Lala waited up, liked to wait up, more like Eddie's father. Like a mother to the boy. And worried. A late child, Eddie, the Litwaks' American soldier. Papa and Mama had no idea what went on out there, what kind of women, even what kind of war. Through their barely functional English, the radio news came in as so much static between polkas. Down at the Dobbs factory, Wiltold stitched the leather sweatbands into civilian felt hats. The Litwaks live with their small American family on an immigrant isle. On their trips to the mainland—Bridgeport—they would sometimes buy the Polish paper as well as piroshki, kielbasa. They would pray for the armed forces, that coda to the Mass, at St. Michael Archangel, protector of Poles. Polish pastry, Polish saint: the sweet and sacred erased the pain and hunger left behind in a Livonian village that was not on the map. One colonel, another commissar marching an army through the single muddy street. Safe in their company half-house, the Litwaks had not tracked this war with no occupying forces, an American war for their American sons.

All this useless to Billy Bray, for who in the dead boy's defense would want to play down the great moral conflict, liken it to any cossacks' skirmish? The movement of the Allied forces in the European Theater as mystifying to Mama and Papa Litwak as a cruel form of baseball, and Eddie—the only action he ever saw an ambush by Isabelle Poole. No hero, the little ladder of awards pinned to his uniform passed out to the boys like C rations. Still, the detective is touched by the running babble of Ladislaw Litwak, his love for the glib, girl-chasing brother, the sad end of their lifelong collusion. Stringer can use Lala against a society whore. Even Stringer, making the people's case reasonable to a fault, can get hold of the drama in this one. Put Lala on the stand, bereaved flummox who cried through his harelip to state troopers and then to the local cops to give him the body, to give his kid brother a military funeral. Billy's noting this in a bent-eared pocket calendar, courtesy of Bridgeport Savings and Loan, when Jadwiga and Witold appear, ashen, dulled, no more surprised to find the detective than some stray Russian foot soldier stealing the last chicken in their yard.

And then: "Ladislaw Litwak to the stand." At first he did not hear the tall gray prosecutor call him. Then he could not speak, forgot all the detective taught him to say, sober, affecting answers as to names and places, time. Mr. Bray had coached him to a point, as though coaching was needed on the nature of Eddie. Blank, smiling at the Bible, the hush was not to Lala's liking: a stirring and shifting of jurors on their benches, whispers in the crowded room until the judge called for silence. Silence in the courthouse, the monkey's gonna speak. Like the game they'd played with him till Eddie called them off. Lala's uncontrollable smile meets the chaste courtroom gaze of Mrs. Isabelle Poole. Speak monkey, speak. "A libe un," Lala says, as yet unsworn to tell the truth. "I fell id ere," punching his gut, gut fears that night. The court reporter stopped dead. And it seemed to Lala, above the gavel's call to order, that he must speak now to save Eddie, and if he says it right he'll call his brother back. So help him God, is Lala laughing at the Bible? Court called to order. Swearing anyway, only to himself: Eddie, he says clear as he can, comes down the stairs, gives the high sign. Seven o'clock. Lala smells the brilliantine. The Chevy stalls and Eddie is trapped listening to the radio. *Come on the Manhattan Merry Go Round/We're touring alluring old New York town.* The kid is safe in his dress uniform, not chasing cooze. Called to order. No, he has never seen the woman in the navy blue suit, except in the newspaper after she shot his brother. Called to order.

It was Mr. Bray who led him to a point. "Tell me," the detective had said, and Lala told his story. He had practiced—seven o'clock, Log Cabin, a libe un—then Mr. Bray had abandoned him to the law. Not abandoned. Billy has made a judgment, his experienced call. Lala might be the strong figure to arouse the emotions of the jury—defense worker, big bereft guy. Or might fail. The broad blubbering face could seem at times wild as the story unfolded . . . unraveled. And the indelible smile, which played well in close quarters, might appear, under cross examination, as a crude counterstatement, defiance of the court. Not abandoned him to the cold eye of Henry Stringer, who cannot direct to proper answers the passionate testimony. Billy had given up coaching—Log Cabin and libe un, the Litwaks' radio show of that Saturday night—knowing his witness could fall apart, but had never calculated Lala's sputtering outrage at what is now a sly smile on the face of Mrs. Isabelle Poole.

Stepping down from the witness box, Lala knows he has been made a fool of for one side or the other. The war in Europe over by the time of the trial, he wanted to say how Eddie counted on finishing off the Japs. The defense does not wish to cross-examine.

Isabelle Poole cries on the stand. Her hair is drawn back in a sleek knot which fails to make her prim.

Defense counsel, arguing a total absence of direct evidence and a ridiculous weakness in the circumstantial case, moves to dismiss. Henry Stringer does not oppose.

Billy Bray, man of the people, turns from the outcry, leaves the courtroom abruptly.

The Major in crisp suntans, field ribbons, cleaves to his wife on the courthouse steps.

The mother and father of Eddie Litwak make no sense of the headlines. It has always been thus; still, Jadwiga Litwak did not expect that woman on the front page facing down her sin, nor the picture of her boy, Ladislaw (story continued on Pg. 3), his hulking form centered under the portal of the courthouse with a smile she knows is not a smile on his flat blond face. Jadwiga folds a form letter from Eddie's company commander, a letter in which "execution of duty" is deleted, "uphold the cause of freedom" and such phrases are left intact, inside this historic *Bridgeport Post* and locks it away in a tin box with immigration papers, baptismal certificates, and her Livonian velvet vest many sizes too small. Eddie, in uniform, remains on the radio cabinet and then takes his place on the first console TV, the photo dusted, set on an embroidered scarf. It is his mother's daily wish that like his brother he'd been maimed at birth.

State v. Isabelle Poole is not closed. Lala tails the man who betrayed him. With all his heart he wants to do in the detective and buys a knife in a stiff leather sheath, a hunting knife for skinning rabbits and squirrels. And then he tracks the Brays to Sunday mass and once to St. Michael's Cemetery, where they pay their respects at the grand Devlin obelisk, the Mrs. deadheading geraniums while the girl wanders off to pray before a marble Virgin. From his hiding place, a gnarled cedar hedge, Lala looks straight into the pious brown eyes. The girl crosses herself, smiles at the harmless smiling man. He disappears down the slope to the new graveyard, where insubstantial immigrant markers poke up through the weeds. The war effort winding down, Litwak is free to stalk the Brays at Fairfield Beach on a Saturday—their striped umbrella, sandy towels, Thermos of lemonade. He steals up beside the Mrs., who sits apart in a pavilion, comes so close he could touch the sleeve of her voile dress or turn the page of her magazine as she looks out in a weary reverie over the smooth waters of Long Island Sound.

Each of the Brays is confronted on occasions of great daring in Lala's mourning muddled head. It's only Billy he's after. Billy whistling in the cemetery. Billy in his wool bathing suit, sizzling in the sun. Once, the detective spots Lala: it is at Candlelight Stadium, a small-time baseball field. News of illegal betting has reached Stringer's office. Billy passes himself in. It's back to minor league ball, the war in Europe being done with, and the floodlights play up into the sky of the North End, casting a theatrical glow from the railroad crossing at North and Lindley to the gravel pits, all that remains of Matthew Devlin's empire of asphalt and cement.

After the blackout, the lights of the stadium are inviting to the workers at Bridgeport Brass and the smaller factories along the river, still running a late shift. No more driving home in darkness. The whole neighborhood has a holiday air. The summer sun never fades on the home team, a raggle-taggle bunch, the Bridgeport Bees—old-timers and 4-Fs, but the news is Hispanic boys, the darlings of the first wave of Puerto Ricans up from the island for war work. When talk of making book on Baby Gonzalez surfaces in Stringer's office, Billy Bray, delighted with this assignment, heads out his front door, crosses the railroad tracks, cuts through the empty lots that abut the Pequonnock where billboards and bleachers define the Candlelight field. Into this blazing arena he saunters in summer dress, his white linen suit, his panama hat. Cops give the salute. What crimes are afoot at the ballpark? He wanders through the clubhouse, a hencoop affair. Sinking into the long sloppy innings with a bottle of pop, Billy watches the Bridgeport Bees beat Waterbury, Reading, and Pittsfield. No one catches Ladislaw Litwak at his game, waiting for the perfect moment. It will be one night during "The Star-Spangled Banner" or the hullabaloo when Baby slams a ball clear into the river. An almost perfect setup: the dim wooden bleachers, the diversion of hecklers and fans. Night after night, Lala watches for the detective, then moves down from his cheap seat, stakes out Billy in a box.

Billy loves baseball; in his misspent youth had tried out for a sandlot team, better than these fakers, a shortstop when he was thin and fast. On a hot July night, his shirt and jacket limp, he's up on his feet cheering with the crowd. The panama waves above his sweaty bald head. Litwak moves on him, unsnaps the stiff sheath.

"Come on, you bums," Billy yells. The bases are loaded. Lala's knife slips down into the dust, into the never-never land of soda bottles and half-eaten hot dogs, peanut shells, the litter of pink tissue carnations from ladies' night. The detective sees his would-be assailant, guesses at his weak intention, but has missed a stupendous double play. "Clear out," he says crossly to Eddie Litwak's brother. "Clear the hell out, Lalapalooza."

Obediently, Lala climbs back to his seat, not sure of what he's done. Eyeballed the enemy? The crowd still cheering as Baby Gonzalez scores. He has hardly heard Mr. Bray's mild, belittling reproach. Now the would-be assailant is assaulted on all sides, turned round and round, as though he's playing blind man's bluff and will be headed off in fate's direction. They are Spanish girls clawing at Lala, all in thin white blouses, the straps of their slips and bras visible on dark shoulders. Red mouths, red nails, bangle bracelets. "Baby! Baby!" Laughing, wild with the scoreboard's good news, they make free with their captive, a large timid man. A kiss. Lala gets a kiss from the most raucous, least pretty of the girls.

"Anna!" they scream.

"Ai!" she says, wiping the bright imprint of her lips off the man's cheek, a bold stroke. "Anna Banana," they call her in their chatter. Not an exotic Latina flower, Anna's plain and hardy as the wild yellow asters that grow beside the dugouts. Her eyes are bright-black, clever. Making up for lack of beauty, Anna plays the clown. The big pale man settles close by. She takes his constant smile as a come-on. A come-on to come on. The game fades in the light of their flirtation. This night little Anna is less the fool for her friends. "Baby! Baby!" she cries when her hero leaps for a spectacular fly, but her head swivels from the scoreboard to the blond man. She is suddenly shy.

For the fans of the Bridgeport Bees, the summer moves toward a triumphant season. VJ Day wraps up the war. Now Lala makes his way to every home game, down Route 1, stoplight to stoplight on the King's Highway, passing the Brays' stucco house on his way to Candlelight Stadium. In late July, the night of a double-header, the Chevy breaks down in Black Rock. It's the car Eddie drove up to Isabelle Poole's, a car Lala revered as though it held the answer. Sitting on the curbstone while a mechanic attempts a miracle, he yearns for his Anna. Now the rusted fenders of the Chevy look hopeless, the torn upholstery only fit for Jadwiga and Witold to make their runs for sausage and sweet Polish bread.

The following day, Ladislaw Litwak takes his savings (it is his only crime) from Mechanics & Farmers and bribes the used-car salesman, the great sleaze of Norwalk, procuring—ahead of doctors, lawyers, wealthy merchants in the area—a 1941 two-door 88. "Anna," he calls, loud and clear. She's a lively dark bird hopping to him up the bleachers. Her head, with thatch of black hair cut close as a boy's, comes just to his shoulder. Smoothing her skirt, she brushes his thigh. When, at last, he drives her home to Boston Avenue where Anna lives with her aunt in the shadow of General Electric, they come to each other in Spanish and babbling English with perfect understanding, the almost new Oldsmobile wrapped around them with its promise of what everyone is promised that summer, plenty and peace. And then, "Anna Banana," he says, botching the B. They were born to speak a happy patois and will speak it for years to come, their language a lovely invention. Often Anna is quiet, no longer in need of the adulation of her pretty friends. Lala talks freely; like having Eddie back, yet it's Anna with her nice ways, fixing his collar as she listens, turning his big hand over, a marvel with its downy growth of yellow hair.

Their children are big and fair, small and dark: one for him, one for her in the tidy script of Lala and Anna's blessed union. And then the two Litwak children with Spanish first names are sorted into separate bedrooms as they move from an apartment above Anna's aunt to a double-decker on Noble Avenue to their own home in Fairfield with fledgling shade trees and two-car garage. Eddie's picture in his dress uniform follows their fortunes.

Somewhere out West, Mrs. Isabelle Poole divorces the

Major, or the Major divorces Isabelle Poole; a small item in the paper in which the Major is identified as an insurance agent in the state of Maine. Lala reads this while Nilda, dark and small, hangs on the arm of her father's wing chair. In the same way, Lawrence Litwak (that name's easier all around) learns that James Bray has become an actor in New York. Feet up on his desk in the pine-paneled office of his tool and die company—he's a gifted man, knows well what he knows. Not an inventor, he designs clever bolts, tricky valves; design is too fancy a word for the magic which resides almost solely in his hands. It is Anna who negotiates the world, a worldly wife who instinctively knows an American story—it is one step from foreman's bench to managerial office. And then a small shop: the bidding, the contracts, the pine paneling tacked up on weekends, but the door to the works always open to the pleasant whine and clang of metal parts in the turning. It is here that Lawrence Litwak reads a notice sent by a press agent to the *Post*. Off-Broadway Chekhov, only a local paper would bother with the head shot of James, the narrow nose and long chin sculpted by studio light, "son of the former Nell Devlin and the late William Bray." He remembers that grand lady who looked through him, her tired eyes on the distant shore, and the sweaty detective he meant to kill at the ball game, the first night Anna kissed him. And reads in the *Post* that a spur to the Interstate will erase the big stucco house, but skirt the old Candlelight Stadium where no one plays ball.

It's high summer once more when Anna Litwak, still in her hospital coat, hears the boys come in—Angel, tall and fair, with his friends. She's been to St. Vincent's, where she interprets for Hispanic mothers who bring in sick kids. Tuesdays and Thursdays: professional, no volunteer, Anna works toward her degree in social service. The babies have not been given their shots, are sunburned, blossomed with bites—that's the least of it. These girls will not believe in the white patches of strep throat or that the sun is real on the Connecticut shore. She knows these island people, their herbal remedies. She has known their angry pride, their reasonable fears.

The Mother Superior is fond of Anna Litwak, who is compassionate with all her clients, yet she can break it up, make the exhausted interns laugh, lighten the sorry work of the clinic. Still in her starched white coat, Anna in her kitchen is unpacking groceries when she hears them— the boys. And then: Larry slinging down his golf clubs against the front banister.

She will ask Angel to count how many for supper. The boys' voices, husky adolescent voices, trail away to the sunroom, where she has sensibly installed the television. When she goes after them, there's a stray boy in the living room, a lanky kid she's never seen, trained to be polite to parents in an unfamiliar house. Anna listens to her husband speak. She is proud of his sharp consonants and dentals brought out by the therapist, though she will never give up their private language.

The boy is admiring the family photographs: "Is that you, Mr. Litwak?"

"Hell, no," Larry says, always smiling, "that's my baby brother. He died in the war."

Never that easy to withdraw into magic or music. As you know, a strict world of practice. Hours lost in it—ball under cup, coin in the cuff, two-faced card. Four of hearts either way, so you can't go wrong once you've slipped it in the deck. Cut the pack . . . but why would I give my trick away even now, useless as it may be to amuse you. I'd try anything from the old routine to have you back at the dining room table after they had gone to bed, the light inscribing its small arena. Too small in that you might detect my cunning moves, but never did. Ball under cup, Catherine. "Which cup, Catherine?"

And you'd never guess. I practiced so that you could never guess and waited for your little gasp of awe that came with "Oh, James!" And you'd have those clownish daubs of white stuff on your face over the blotches that surfaced and disappeared and, like one of my more sinister illusions, appeared again—those years. Sometimes your head in a towel wound high like a sultan, Ali Baba, Pooh-Bah or what I supposed a comic version of such a personage to be. The scrubbing and washing of those years as if you could make it all go away, what was happening to your body. The smell from your side of the table was always soapy, carbolic, superclean. I stank. Of myself and the stolen cigarettes I smoked in my closet. It's a wonder I didn't burn that house to the ground. I stank of my bodily emissions and even on insufferable nights when the curtains hung still at the windows, I wore my brown suit jacket full of the smell of me, but with all the secret places where feathers and flowers, dollar bills and the real four of hearts could hide. Black rims under my bitten nails as though by design; in that light my filth alone might distract you. "Which ball, Catherine?"

"Red," you'd say in full certainty and out of the cup you had chosen the little rubber ball would roll to you—inevitably the green.

And the cups again, dancing under my dirty fingers before you had finished "Oh, James! Oh, James!" making a soft sandy shuffle on the mahogany table after they had gone to bed. Those years when we would wander down for food or a schoolbook and find the house was ours. Her table clawing the rug, her lamp chained to the ceiling; his butts and ashes, evening paper thrown wide, making sure we knew it was a temporary setup, on loan. We—their children who never got along, or made up squabbles in conformity with funny-paper families and B movies, but in truth those nights were fine. The best we ever had. Practiced, you bet, but fine. We got down our lines, and you'd sit on a dining room chair, the stiff black leather seat built for an eternity of meals. You sat unwillingly at my command, pretending my tricks were a bore, when really you'd come down to find me, heard my feeble tooting stop, my footsteps on the stairs, the icebox door. Once, you claimed that you heard through the suck of bathwater draining, saw in the fogged mirror as you swaddled yourself like a clairvoyant, that I was down there with a turkey leg and the last of the pumpkin pie.

"Okay, Cath. Take a card. Any card." A long reach across that table, test of my skill holding the fan steady, waiting through your serious deliberation. Each time real thought, the true selection,

when it didn't matter at all which card, Cath. Not how it works—
the joke, the trick, ball under cup. My God, what an audience you
were, perhaps the best I'll ever have. First row center in the stolid
chair with your Latin or French grammar set aside and the girl
magazines you read in secret, profane texts. Girl magazines to teach
you to be beautiful. Those years, it seemed such a significant reversal, when they went up to bed and left the dining room to us like
some after-hours club. We said nothing I can recall—turkey leg,
icebox, Latin verbs, *parley voo, mon frère,* and the patter of my
routine. *Comme ça,* nothing said, and it was not often. High esti-
mate: a dozen times. Ten years past and for at least half that time I
have carried it in my head that we talked across the reach of the
table, because I have talked across the mahogany reach through the
smudged yellow light to you a hundred times. You sit there and
listen; fingers puckered white, thick hair drying to a snarled mat,
tidy bale of your body inhumanly clean. The small gold medal stuck
in the damp of your throat, Our Lady, miraculous in her cloudscape.
I smell you, Catherine, sharp as the lye in a cake of Octagon soap,
and we talk. We talk—you say, then I say:

"It was always easy for you, James."

"Balls, Catherine."

"Effortless, the music. For pity's sake, I wasn't deaf. The
magic. I wasn't blind."

"Just . . . I didn't know you had a sister." This from the girl in James'
bed, the bed a depleted mattress on the floor. One room with hot
plate, poor excuse for kitchen table. White paint in excess, as though
to make clean what cannot be cured; surface disease of the walls has
spread to the split bathroom door. One alley window. A first hazy
light which reveals nothing beyond a brick wall of Hell's Kitchen,
close to the Great White Way where James Bray intends one day
soon to perform. Black top hat, black cane on a hook, classic black
phone, a few books. All else a dead white, whiter than the soiled

sheets and ivory shoulders of the girl. As the sheet drops, her perfect porcelain breasts are tight and round as oriental teacups. Her Edwardian pouf of black curls has slipped to one side in a floppy tam-o'-shanter. So pretty, James would say, so notably beautiful nothing renders her foolish, bare-breasted and disheveled in his dingy sheets. Though at a disadvantage; she did not know James has a sister.

"She is younger," he says, which says nothing.

"The phone rang?" The girl, puzzling things out.

"Some time ago." James stands above her fully dressed; his brittle bright hair, striped tie, the muddy green of his summer suit are gaudy in this room—a young banker or lawyer out of his element. Down in the Village, in her cozy apartment with the velvet settee, majolica plates, the carpets from home, his sister has swallowed a bottle of pills, then walked to the emergency room of St. Vincent's to forestall a bitter end. Out of danger, they said; "She's in a peaceful sleep." No point his running down, but James dressed and sat out the night watching by the bed of the wrong girl, as it were. The beautiful girl slept in languorous containment, stretching, smiling in her dream, while Catherine haunted him, daubed in unmiraculous ointment, lumpy and moist in a terry cloth shroud.

"Is it anything awful?" the girl asks.

"She gets herself in these pickles," James says, not about to tell a pitiable story.

"Like what?"

"Oh, you know." In a light stroke, he speaks a line from the play he's rehearsing with this girl: *A man happens to come by, sees her, and having nothing else to do. . . .* James Bray is best in mannered roles—Restoration fops, pettish Noel Coward boys, Brecht's movieland gangsters. He is rotten so far, plain rotten, in Chekhov. Playing the tortured young writer in *The Sea Gull*, he delivers Konstantin's speeches in a thin complaint, sentimental to cynical. Who'd give a damn about his fate? She, on the other hand, the girl in his bed, is an ideal Nina—open, unfinished, malleable—with a coarse grain of ambition at her center; the notable beauty from the Midwest perfectly cast as provincial. Shameless, she rises now and walks slowly to James' bathroom. He hears the water in the tub and watches her march businesslike to fetch her canvas bag, the kit she carries to rehearsals with herbal tea, pure glycerine cream, dried berries, cereal stuff growing in a jar, and her precious class notes on affective memory, organic forms of feeling. "What do you think?" she asks James. "In the first act my hair loose, ribbon in the back? Mary Pickford style."

"Good enough!" he says. She got on to Mary Pickford last night. Looking over James' room, performing the necessary dalliance with his cane and movie books before they ended up in bed, a picture of the silent film star as Rebecca of Sunnybrook Farm had caught her attention—the coy smile with a suggestion of milk teeth, those adorable curls. No use his explaining that Miss Pickford in gingham, swinging her sweet basket down a country road in the exaggerated innocence of 1912, should in no way serve as the model for Chekhov's ingenue . . . Nina Mikhailovna in the white lawn dress all stitched by peasant hands, sacrificed to the last gasp of Romantic idealism. Not to mention timing: the girl was already naked as she closed the book on America's Sweetheart and began rotating her head in a private exercise of relaxation. When that ritual ended, he'd brought down the lights, taken her in his arms. What followed was better than their rehearsed scenes, well done, if not inspired. Limber and ardent, they played together for the first time. He could have chosen to say: *My enchanting darling, dream of my life*, with some conviction, slipping inside her tight-tuned body. Her legs high, extended like a dancer's, made his greed artful. Her moans were surprisingly guttural, unlovely. James held back, chose the moment to come, to call out her real name. She slept almost at once, the way she cries on cue. In the first act, childishly afraid to go home late, Nina's tears pour down this girl's cool cheeks while James with Konstantin's real wounds, unloved, a pathetic figure at his mother's feet, cannot weep. He is twice directed in the script to weep.

"In the last scene," the girl asks, "my hair up? I'm older, you know, worn."

"Never!" says James.

"Like Duse," she insists, twisting her hair in a crown. Duse is referred to in *The Sea Gull*. Ivan, their director, has carefully explained Eleonora Duse to his discovery, the notable beauty from the Midwest.

"Like Ellen Terry!" James says. "Or the divine Sarah!" What's the point of jibes or recriminations? She's off with some unguent to his tub.

The point is Catherine's enforced peace. No point, they said; she'll be hours sleeping it off. "My sister," James calls. There is a gurgle, a splash of surprise. He has the decency to go to the split bathroom door, loose on its hinges. "My *sister* is all . . ." James will not go into that story. He sees his Nina Mikhailovna Zarechnaya, *a young girl, daughter of a rich landowner,* soaping her lean thighs. She is ecru in the chipped white tub, the color of lace. Lace afloat in tea. He remembers his mother at the kitchen sink, a tangle of lace emerging from a basin of cool tea, scraps of pink stuff, the sewing machine. "To soften the color," his mother said, "you dip the lace in tea."

"One lump or two," James had said. Nell Bray laughed, but the sad outcome was Catherine in pink taffeta and Lipton lace, waiting for her beau, her solid body unyielding in the boudoir froth of the gown. Gilbert and Sullivan, her matronly flutter when the boy arrived, trill of surprise at the ungainly orchid she pinned far above her breast. "One lump or two," James said as his sister minced out the formal front door.

"She looks *very* nice," his mother said.

His mother said many things to correct his ways. She said to comb his hair, clean his nails, thank the Lord. To thank his father, always that. Thank the maiden aunt for Christmas underwear and gloves. She said it all without force, her words dipped in indulgence, yet it was hard to forget her lessons. So in the middle of the night he had dressed up in his one suit as though going to church or to play the clarinet at assembly. He was going to Catherine, who had neatly saved herself, not the first time. What would his mother say to that? "Be kind, James" . . . something mild, uncomprehending, wrong script entirely. Courtly, well groomed, he had waited until his leading lady rose from the mattress.

"Ivan will have a fit." The girl's voice suddenly shrill with self-concern. Yes, Ivan will have a fit at James, whom he's miscast. James suspects he's within days, if not hours, of being replaced. Ivan has accused him of conventional continuity, of wearing a verbal mask. Ivan wants what he calls moment-to-moment Chekhov.

"The call is for ten o'clock!" The notable beauty is having her fit: just dawning in her sudsy head that she'll be dealt another young man, a more passionate Konstantin she might not outplay, even in bed. He hears the furious splash of her rising as he steals out his door, down to the empty street. It's not quite true what Ivan says, that he has no emotional recall, cannot enter the actor's trance of *as if*, for it's as if he hears the cultivated voice, the scourge of his mother's extravagant tolerance: "James, when you take a girl home you do not care for, be courteous in the morning. Be kind."

Which is to say, Catherine, life in Nell's house was hard, not in any way apparent, soft as a feather bed I couldn't sleep in, sweet as penny candy to rot my teeth. Devout peasant girl, Maid of Bridgeport, the ribbons and citations pinned over your desk, still there at the shrine to your terrible hard work. *Ad majorem*, Catherine. Curled, fading—do you review your honors when you visit? When you walk into the stale room spooked with your girlhood, rosary thrown on the tarnished tray with junk jewelry, doesn't it kill you to think of it all preserved? The twin beds so you could have a girl chum stay and never did. Nell's crocheted spreads and the dressing table, that secular altar she never prayed at. Doesn't it grab you, Catherine, to stand at the door to my room? You dare not enter to look upon my mess; the tricks and jokes abandoned, the sacred clarinet case, the reverential pile she has created of my worthless college skits and plays. Rings on every surface left from soda bottles, years older than the beer can stains. As though we are still there and will wake in the morning, hear them downstairs in the kitchen, their mumbled conspiracy mapping out the day, and wait under the blanket—I speak only for myself—I wait under the red plaid blanket singed with careless smoking, listening for his motor to turn over, for our father to be gone in the state car. God, how I wanted him gone.

You were known to run down the back stairs in bare feet to get a look at him, a hug, one of the Billy Bray roughhouse specials before he tooled off to the courthouse, where he led his real life. "Jesus, you'll catch your death . . ." That was his line. I may never have heard it, huddled in my covers . . . "in bare feet, your death of cold." Doesn't it seem the damnedest thing, Catherine? Even then your risks greater than mine. One of those nights, our good times, the shadowy white O on her table. I was up to some fool thing, pouring water in a top hat, and the contraption left its mark, there under the circle of light a milky ring, and you did your magic with a drop of oil and the heat from the palm of your hand—rubbing, rubbing. I will never forget our fear: her table stained and all the things in that room, the blessed objects, frowned upon us.

"Fooling around," you said, eyes cast down, rubbing, rubbing, and Presto!—it was gone. "Never again," you said as though it was through—youth, laughter. Always something grand to relinquish. Joy—no more of that. And you showed me the blisters raised on the fleshy pads of your hand. Draped in your towels like a teenage sibyl: "No more, James."

And I took the grim ace of spades out of your pocket, a feather from your ear, a dollar from the Biblical folds of your robe. "Stop. Stop it," you cried, crying, really crying in that helpless laughter I reduced you to. "Stop it!" I can't stop, Catherine. I can't stop fooling around.

Good times, that room to ourselves. In the misty-eyed script you make of the past, you won't remember how we hated the spell to be broken, the grimace on your mottled face, your grunt of annoyance if they so much as called downstairs . . . *Lock up, children. Children, put out the lights.* By what right could they ruin our fun? By every right. It pissed me off, Cath. And it pissed me off in the morning when she said it: "The lights blazing, James. The back door left open to the world."

Our petty crimes. He was already down at his courthouse with the riches of fraud, arson, rape, homicide, grand larceny to set up Billy Bray. He put her up to it. Nell's tepid delivery of his melodramatic lines: "We might all be slaughtered in our beds, James. Door open to the world, an invitation to whatever murderer or fool." You writhed for the both of us, clutched your schoolbooks to your chest, the day in ruins before you, while she scrambled my eggs soft as I liked them.

Where were the killers in that neighborhood, Cath? The Siegal boy, trained to sell potatoes and onions from a wheelie cart? Boy of forty who could not count his change. Rita Murphy, laughing her way to Newtown, to what we called, so ignorantly, the loony bin? Where were the thieves? With keys under every doormat and the upstairs porches any kid could climb like a second-story man. What, for Jesus Christ's sake, Catherine, was worth stealing in those houses? Open to the world. The kitchen light left on and you running for the North End bus to school as if from hellfire. There were ploys, rules to the game. The way I see it, you never will catch on.

There came a night worse than water rings, more dreadful than the kitchen light inviting the parish cuckoo to stab us in our beds. A stifling heat always in effect, that night Billy came upon us to check the thermostat, so he said, his gumshoe surveillance, obvious. You were scrubbed, waiting for me, deep in your book, your hair rolled in untidy nests to make you curly. I was setting up—the climbing billiard balls or miser's dream to amaze you, my multitude of one.

"Go on. Go on," he said, an awkward moment. I stood in his place. Though the table was round, by some decree against geometry, our father sat at the head. Queer to see him sink into a child's chair, so small. Though let me tell you, Cath, I give Billy Bray no more than five-six in his stocking feet. Hear this: pure bounce, his stature; the little man's strut, Cath, bantam in the ring.

"Go on with your show," he said, and I was obliged to make the ping-pong balls rise, spring from my hand as though balanced in thin air; the coins multiply, unholy loaves and fishes. How perfectly I wanted to perform and did, as if my life depended on it. All careful calculations, the balls, the coins delivered that night as if by magic. The practice worth it to audition for God Almighty. Well, it was only Billy Bray.

"You're good," he said. "Pretty good." Wilted in his shirt sleeves and suspenders. "It's nice to be good at something." There it was, the self-pity before us, shocking as one of Nell's new recipes instead of the same old apple pie.

You said: "Do the cards, James."

"The cards," he said. "Well, that's some kind of talent, son. Maybe you'll have better luck than me." And he got up and came back with the evening paper and a glass of whiskey, Billy Bray, who never took a drop, humped over his booze . . . maybe it was stage whiskey, tea. My entertainment ruined by his tragic smoker's hack.

"That's a lovely thing," he said, "to be able to fool the public."

"The fine art of deception. It's only fun," you said and looked as though your Topsy wads of hair and raw scrubbed face would melt in grief.

"Fun," he said. "Fun. I guess that's what it's all about." You had not noted the evening paper, which he now unfolded.

Exhibit A: front page of the *Post*: our detective, mighty unhappy on the courthouse steps. "All's fair in love and war," he said. "Go on, James, with the tricks." If there was ever a dismissal . . . I've been to open calls where I wasn't asked to read. While you took in the headline, NOT GUILTY. You took it hard, though it wasn't the first time, Catherine, that your daddy flubbed a celebrated case. This girl had killed her dying father, not a lover. Shot him in the head.

That house was too grand. All the big ones—anger, sorrow, pride—ricocheted off the walls. Girl shot her father, I'm sure it was that one, Cath, not the bimbo with the soldier boy. A big beefy girl shot her dying father. No one cared for our detective's indisputable evidence—the girl declared merciful and mad. He came to where we enjoyed ourselves and I thought, I'll remember the hunch of his defeated shoulders, the loser's uncertain eye. I'll remember the tremble of the Jap-yellow fingers, the Jap-yellow nail tapping the picture of himself humiliated. Noting my first knowledge of finely burst veins, the strain against his collar of too much flesh, as if I were studying a part to play it—a man finished, self-abasing, lured by death. In a matter of seconds, he managed it—weakness, age. I guess I should have noted that the tears ran too freely from your wounded eyes.

"Put me out of my misery," he said. "The gun is in the bureau drawer. Load it. You're smart kids."

"Daddy! Daddy!"

"It's legal. We got that squared away."

Daddies to the nth degree.

Then: "Shoot me, Catherine."

Admit into evidence: People's 1—my cards on the table, proof that I was frivolous, dissembling; People's 2—your homework and holy medal establish you as good; People's 3—ACQUITTAL IN MERCY KILLING. Under oath the big girl could not recall the gun or hour of the night. *They say I killed my father.* Who was on trial that night? I should have noted how quickly you rose to the bait, too quickly, eyes feverish, and mounted the defense to save your father's life.

"Tell me," he said, "tell me, Catherine."

You launched an argument passionate as that girl's crime, the corkscrew jobbies on your head bobbing in all directions. With Billy Bray in his terminal slump, you'd not play God, by God, could not construct the mitigating circumstances. For five minutes you had his full attention.

"That's my girl!" The value of life settled under the dining room lamp. Why retract your argument with a bottle of pills? Nell came at the end of your rousing summation. In her bathrobe, the brown plaid rag she wore in the night when we were sick. She stood in the shadows, held herself tight as though it was cold in her big hot house.

"Come to bed, Bill."

"That's my girl," he said, coughing through his cover of smoke, somewhat embarrassed in front of his wife that he'd brought his front-page disappointment to the kids. Billy at the thermostat now, bonny and courthouse-bright. "Jesus, what did you think, Nell? I was out on the town." Arm round her waist that night. I knew I would remember the clog of phlegm set loose by his laughter, his quick shift to jovial, more amazing than the Spooky Dollar or the Devil's Touch. When desperation appears only briefly in the plot, I should call it up, his quick turn from your splendid validation to Nell, who had his number.

"Come to bed, Bill."

Their mounting the stairs together, their stop on the landing and her hopeful words: "Children . . ." that reached to her husband's discredit, your crazy litany of daddies, the untouched glass of amber whiskey, whatever must be put to rest that night: "Children, when you come up, turn out the light."

Nurse Know-It-All reads from the chart, grams of Miltown taken by, pumped out of Catherine. She does not accept James, with reddish hair, arched nose, business suit, as brother to the dirty dark girl strapped in the hospital bed.

"Saturday night." She offers her diagnosis: "Saturday night." Taking her patient's sluggish pulse: "Occupation?"

"Actor," says James and soon as the word is out of his mouth knows it is Catherine's job she must fill in. What to say? Cath tidies the work of others, checking tenses, caps, and semicolons, at best dates, place names in remote parts of the world. "Editor," he calls her, though he knows his sister's job at the Luce emporium is menial. The nurse sniffs, she moves about Catherine's bed with a demeaning efficiency. The snap of her uniform is a reproach as she draws the white curtain that closes James in with his sister, who, the bitch is right, along with many of her charges could not withstand the terrors of Saturday night.

Here it is like a tent made of bedspreads and sheets when they were very small, a makeshift place. Thinking they were unseen . . . only Cath is not with him plotting and hiding. She is laid out in a dead sleep James presumes has no dreams. Even, soft breaths. Her hair is unnaturally black and crimped: the remedial process continues. God, she does look like their father with his head thrown back to play down the double chin. The bedsides are up like a crib. James lets them down. He loosens the straps on her arms and the one that cuts across her belly. Why should she not escape if that is what she wants? Why wake to restraints? To Sunday? They could play in the white tent if she'd come around. Too serious she'd be with little cups and saucers; the spill on the oriental carpet full-scale disaster. He'd laugh at their game being ruined, run from his mother's scolding, "Honestly, James!"

"Why did you ever think it easy?" James says aloud. His sister's involuntary snort is the answer.

At this moment he should be looking over yesterday's notes on his script. James is a quick study: it's the jealousy, rage, hopelessness of the sensitive Russian boy he fails to get. The call is for ten. Ivan will stage his predictable fit. "Dye your hair," his Nina had murmured, as he rolled off her, in the half minute before her untroubled sleep. "You're not dark. Dye it." She was right, only the look of Konstantin might pull him through.

Now he should be marching crosstown in the Village, keyed up, a young actor on his way to a Sunday rehearsal, for the artist the work week never done. He should stop to observe the daily displeasure of the newsman on Eighth Street, the way he flips the change at his customers in disgust, the sexless gaze of a hooker, peddling ass early across from Grace Church . . . all useful, useful. And now carry his threadbare pride into the dark cellar called a theater toward the unmerciful light on stage, toward his fellow actors, who do not believe in him. Ivan has begun to suck his teeth loudly when Konstantin Gavrilovich enters the scene. James should, at this moment, recite portentously, *"Oh, you venerable shades, you who drift over this lake in dark of night, rock us to sleep and let us dream . . ."* or rail at his actressy mother, or tear up his clumsy manuscripts before his exit stage left in search of the gun. Now his Nina of last night will be well into her cruel flirtation with the handsome old queen who plays Trigorin. Time seeps by in the white tent, dreamy, slow as the sugar water dripping into Catherine's vein until her eyes open in slow motion. A weak smile forms on her lips.

"Heaven," James says. "This must be heaven."

"James?" The tears well up, naturally.

"What you see is what you get." And he takes his sister's hand. Ball under cup, Catherine. He has not held Catherine's hand, not since they were kids crossing the street. It is a stubby, ink-stained hand, the cuticles ragged. Now he is clean: she is grubby, her hair gummy, pitch-black against the pillow.

"Up to my old tricks," she says. Not so old. It is the second bottle of pills. The rest has been wild talk, calls in the night, Billy Bray bluster. They are perfectly quiet behind the white curtain, not saying:

Don't tell Nell.

Would I tell Nell?

This never would have happened if he hadn't deserted.

Resting, cozy in the grave. William Aloysius, d. 1955—all that chunked into the Devlin granite.

I am missing Mass. Unholy.

I am missing rehearsal. Unprofessional. God damn you, Catherine.

"I was thinking," she says, whispering in the tent, "last night thinking of Sister Brown. Big Saturday night in New York and I'm in there seeing her broken straw hat, her silk gloves, lace-up shoes." A tick of laughter propels her words, Cath's launched: "Sister Brown, at her white old throat, cameo pin with Greek maidens dancing. All night seeing the sparse bun of white hair, spectacles pulled down on her nose. Sister Brown, imagine! I couldn't get her must smell off me." James watches his sister laugh. There is no quiet in her, no stopping as the story spills from her. "She was a witch."

"We made that up."

"You believed it. You wouldn't touch her fence. Sister Brown. Whose sister?" Cath, laughing a trembly laugh. "Older than anyone. You wouldn't grab a kite out of her tree. Her barn—no one had a barn, a well, a rusted gate. The shingles on her house queer and round. Fish scales. Her house the prow of a ship. Poor woman, she rose from the dead." James can't figure his sister's lengthy recitation—manic, sure, but poised; can't fit the assault of her laugh— brassy, insistent—into her ghost story. Giddy, tossing her head on the pillow: "She wasn't one of us, James. Her genealogies—shaking the dead tree. She had no kin, no husband, no child. I knew her in the end. She called me by name down in the library where no one laughed at her, where Mrs. Muller brought her dusty accounts, flaking tomes, she was *Mrs.* Brown. Whose Mrs., James?—full of pesky questions. In winter—*'Do you suppose you are an Indian, Catherine?'* My ankle socks, bare legs—she found them foolish in the cold. Winter—not the witch's hat, black felt like a fry pan. Every day at the big oak table copying from the Bibley books, spotty records with gilt edges. Fine inky script. *'Catherine? Was it a port before the bridge, Catherine?'* I smelled her ink last night, yet something sweet, heavy."

James can't make it out—why his sister's words quiver with hilarity. It's as if she's sailed away in her story and he's stuck on shore, as if she's off on the *Richard Peck*, day-tripping to Rye Beach, set upon the fun she must have on the roller coaster, the Dodg'em cars, and he's abandoned on the sturdy pier with the workaday factories of Water Street churning behind him. "Last night," Cath says, "thinking of Sister Brown, how she'd come to stand by U.S. History where I sat, look down at me. *'Consider that you live on the King's Highway, Catherine.'* And she was right. North Avenue was property of the crown. Sister rose from the dead last night; in my nostrils, not any human smell." A jolt of laughter. "Here, in New York."

"What's funny?" James, his own voice hushed: "What's funny about the bottle of pills, Cath?"

"Ladies in the library, the two of us. Sister Brown. Whose sister, James? With her drawstring bag of precious notes. Spectacles on her skinflint Yankee nose. Pointing to her powdery throat with the oval brooch, *'The Fates or Muses, Catherine?'* I figured Muses, wispy, draped, and dancing, but I'd never know if I was right. She only wanted me to be there till the lights went on all down the reading room, poor Sister Brown, and we would pack up separately and separately take the North End bus. Separately walk home. She was never one of us."

"Sister—some Protestant sect," James says. He has lost patience with Catherine's shrill aria. "Old Protestants in some cemetery the other side of town."

"That's not it. Anyway," Catherine says, seeing for the first time that she has been strapped down, "anyway," she says clearly, soberly, "she rose from the dead."

James can only believe he's been replaced. Ivan's had a dark Konstantin or two waiting in the wings. At best they are rehearsing around his scenes. Today the aging actress who plays his mother (an aging actress) can rage against him with good reason . . . *"a capricious, touchy boy."* Her haughty repertory voice appropriately corny . . . *"It is a pity that a young man should waste his time."* But now he must go and find the authority, whoever that may be—nurse, nun, doctor—who can tell him what is to be done with his sister, here at St. Vincent's on a Sunday. They have fallen into silence in the white tent. "St. Vincent's," he whispers at his sister. Nothing more need be said: it is the very name of the hospital at home where they stood together not that long ago and watched their father gasp beyond endurance for his final breath.

Black pit of a theater, unsprung seats scavenged from a movie palace. James sits in the last row with a tough little overnight case in his lap. Cath's Amelia Earhart luggage, how she cried at this gift from the parents when she went away to the Mesdames de Sacre Coeur at Marymount. Aristocratic nuns fine-tuned his sister. A splendid motor when they finished her, programmed to run on holy oil. *Caterina Maria,* her name called in Latin at graduation. Watching her sedate passage toward her honors, James thought his sister in the black robe had the class of a solid prewar car—Nell's Packard. The yearbook foretold a scholar who would make her mark: she plugged away at names and dates. At the courthouse there was no end to Billy's pride, each week you'd think she wrote the magazine alone. Nell, that was peculiar, thought it only natural that Catherine take on New York, affairs of state, the culture. But his sister, they could never see the danger, was overwhelmed by *Time* as she had been by the matched set of luggage: not more than she could handle, more than she deserved.

The Amelia Earhart overnight case, made to fall from great heights, slips and slides on James' lap. He'd like to hurl it across the blackness to see if it will spring open with his offering of stockings and underwear, blouse and skirt he must bring to Catherine. He is so damn sorry, still, she's too much, all that talk of a neighborhood eccentric, old stuff—haunted house, weeds choking walk and gate, cats wild in the barn, old stuff in an unfunny recitation, and then when he went to Cath's apartment—for she had either walked naked down Jane Street, crossed Greenwich, headed for St. Vincent's, or something unmentionable had happened to her clothes—when he went up the narrow stairs to her cluttered rooms and stood in the doorway there was the evidence: a pair of large brown trousers hanging from her dresser drawer, a dish of broken crayons, one Mickey Mouse slipper, incredibly small. Sister Brown, indeed! Who has Cath harbored? Who mothered? It would take Billy's investigation of the premises to say if his daughter slept with brown pants in the narrow bed or lay on the couch with the Mickey Mouse child. Catherine's brush (James cleans it) is clotted with white-blond tangles of baby hair. How long had they played house with his sister? When did the phantom husband and child pack up, leave their touching domestic traces? Leave her to the careful overdose on a Saturday night, to the apparition, or simply the lie—Sister Brown? Who—James is sorry as he thinks it—who's play-acting now? Scratching the indestructible surface of the overnight case, he'd like to face down the bounder who has ruined his sister. He is sorry for the story Catherine cannot tell.

Jane Street: the scale crazy, as if the big house they grew up in had shrunk, or its castoffs—bits of china and silver, tattered carpets—had swollen to giant size. James knows a majolica jug, tole tray, letter opener, celluloid hair receiver on the dresser as he knows the freckles on the back of his hands, the light growth on his chin that casts him in unheroic roles. Other objects he sees as eerie doubles: Cath's rummaging the Village shops to make what's past live on in an inkwell, a fern stand, a blue and white bowl; the dark print of Dutch landscape, reproduction of a reproduction. Stale, no place for the young, he has never liked coming here for meals, though his sister, no surprise, is a studiously good cook. Only the papers and books are professional—Catherine, a long proof sheet with her caret marks and deletions, semicolons and typeface confirmed. Page-perfect as hard work can render it perfect. Atlas, encyclopedia, Audubon guides, registry of House and Senate, red pencils, three-by-five cards with all queries answered—Tigris and Euphrates, intermediate range, Fidel, Enovid, Baghdad Pact.

Correct, unlike the file cards in high school with contradictory facts and arguments which James and his sister assembled for the debating society. Both sides of a question. Resolved: that the Electoral College be replaced by Popular Vote. Resolved: death penalty or atomic weapons be abolished. Catherine, missing the game of it, cried out "I don't *believe*" before arguing feebly against labor unions, socialized medicine, as if in the school auditorium she exploited the poor, let the unfortunate die, though her words rang with a zealot's conviction in defense of the United Nations, the minimum wage. In the rebuttal she was Antigone, Mrs. Roosevelt, Saint Joan. Billy despaired of his daughter, the fervent debater; approved of James, seeing in his son's tricky arguments, his ruses and recoveries, the making of a brilliant trial lawyer, not the actor he became.

He turns the cards on Jane Street—Farouk, Faubus, Fermi, Flesch, Floyd, Franco—his sister's verified data for *Time* magazine. No doubts, no gray areas in Catherine's file. That's the other side of the room where Mickey Mouse and baggy trousers muddy the clear appeal, where nothing is proven as James sees it: neither goodness nor sin in the fallout of an affair. Easier for her in high school, to take on matters of life and death, the great issues of the day. James shuffles the three-by-five cards for the one-finger break. Soft, uncoated, they don't respond, or he's lost his touch. *"God give them wisdom that have it; and those that are fools let them use their talents."* The first time his father saw him on the stage in New Haven, not the platform of debate where he thrilled Billy with forensic hoopla, but the stage with footlights, scenery, greasepaint, velvet jerkin, bells on his toes when he played the fool in *Twelfth*

Night. The old man, hacking his disapproval, was smart enough to know a rotten performance. Only Catherine thought him a minor miracle, enchanted as if she'd come for his magic at the dining room table. Ball under cup, Cath? Didn't she love it then, along with Nell—*"Virtue that transgresses is but patched with sin, and sin that amends is but patched with virtue."* "Wonderful, James!" At the time he believed it.

      With Catherine's file cards fanned idly in his hands, he believes he has destroyed some order—Fromm, Frost, Fuchs, Fulbright—a setup more than alphabetical . . . side steal, the gambler's shift. Order in his sister's mind: the desk with its clean blotter, sharpened pencils, roll of stamps, is bruised with their father's cigarette burns. It was Billy who might have burnt Nell's house to the ground. So Catherine, favoring scars, a little mad, James grants that, would work at the desk where Billy paid the bills. Catherine under observation, scruffy and sly in St. Vincent's, will be released once more into his care. Her laughter off-center, disturbed and disturbing, had something to do with confession, acquittal. He had not picked up on the cover, the dodge—"Sister Brown" was like . . . only like in the telling—the set pieces Cath brought home from college of Augustine and Aquinas, discoveries told with unhinged, greedy elation. Catherine *con brio*, enlightening them all at Christmas dinner. Abelard with the mince pie: she quoted the unhappy lover's skepticism, pretending to a play of mind, informing Nell and Billy it was Abelard who proved there are questions that can't be decided.

      "Not proved?" their father put it to her for the State.

      "Sort of—" she had said in her uncertain debater's voice.

      "As in 'sort of true,' is that it, Catherine? Sort of false." She laughed to please him; Billy's girl put nicely in her place, laughed strangely, lost the case she never believed in. In the white tent James had not recognized her misdirection, making merry of Sister Brown. Cup under ball. Drawing his eye off. Which ball, James? What's she after? Walking near naked to St. Vincent's, sending him to her mockup on Jane Street, her unconsoling view of home? What's it about—her calculated miss? His art, her pills? James fumbles the cards. Resolved: practice does not make perfect.

Now they appear in a boisterous row. Ivan in coolie jacket, shaved head, Chekhovian pince-nez riding his fat nose. The ripe old girl cast as Irina Nikolayevna, the glamorous mother, swirls a silk cape back from her ample bosom. His Nina is pearly, more notably beautiful than James recalls with the dark pouf of hair she imagines to be Russian sloping over one cold determined eye. The troupe complete in a theatrical procession except for James crouched in the back row. Lights up as the players take their places. The awkward setting about of folding chairs and weak-kneed table into the dining room of a country estate (once grand), barrels and wooden crates for sideboard, hatboxes, valises. James watches the scraping and clearing, hears the actors' banter turn to the strict silence that precedes the moment in which they enter the play.

Act II: with scripts still in hand they work toward a comic agitation, the bittersweet Chekhovian tension of imminent departure. There are those who leave. There are those who stay behind. James watches his Nina betray him. Ivan with his heavy mid-Europa accent (it is ludicrous) reads Konstantin's line: *"Chenge the bondage for me, Mama."* Words of the wounded boy, would-be artist who has, in the first act, put a gun to his head. James walks, a silent specter, down the aisle. In his nice business suit, he mounts the few steps, is under the lights. He sets down his sister's tough little suitcase. *Change the bandage for me, Mama. You do it very well.* With his sandy hair, his lean Irish mug, James is Konstantin Gavrilovich Treplyov—angry, shamed, injured, sorry. Without script, without manner, he plays as he never hoped to. Ivan, Nina, Trigorin (faded star of stage and screen) draw to each other like children or workers in the field, witness to an apparition. *"You've hands of gold. I remember, it was so long ago when you were still acting on the imperial stage—I was a little boy at the time—a washerwoman got terribly beaten. You bought medicine and washed her children in a tub. Don't you remember?"* Irina does not remember. *"Lately I've loved you as I did when I was a child,"* James says to the aging actress who is his mother, and when the time comes his bandaged head falls in her lap. James weeps.

A second nurse has come. This one ruddy and fat. Kind in the way she settles the patient back in the restraints. "We'll see," she says, running a wet flannel cloth over Catherine's face. "We'll see all about it, Catherine." Soft meaningless words so much like Nell's, and then she swoops round the bed, curtain in hand. The white tent is gone. "There," she says. "We'll have company."

A young black woman with a glistening scar on her temple, foot in a cast, smiles at Catherine and draws back at once into her own pain. A window on water tanks, tarred rooftops. This is New York. This is Sunday. James in his olive-drab suit going to mass—not likely. Crucifix over the door. No Christ. Catherine can wriggle her arms free. She is perfectly happy to be in the big baby crib, sides up. Quiet, she's quiet now, and breathes with satisfaction as though she has accomplished—what? Eisenhower is President. It is September 1957. She had answered all that. She had told the doctors it was Saturday and in something like a flare-up: *God's in his heaven. John Foster Dulles is Secretary of State.* Sunday. The rungs of her bed are cool and smooth. She will not escape. The smell is gone of stale toilet water—the heavy scent that caught in her throat of lavender and dust, old ladies' lavender.

When she had perceived that she was to be abandoned last night, to be left to the timeless editing, she thought quite naturally of Sister Brown—conjured her up. So, her words to James were sort of true, all true her rehearsal of fish-scale house, lace-up boots, *Mrs.* Brown—the dread honorific. The black felt hat, heavy as a fry pan, fit her own head with terrible ease. Ladies in the library hung up on the past. A reticule weighted with facts cut at Cath's wrist, but she had opted for pills, then run in some queer costume—unwashed, uncombed—out onto Jane Street. Here in New York. It was not the first time Catherine had seen the old neighbor woman emerge out of a white mist. Once, come home from college—it was a holiday or holy day—she had seen the black silk bag, the hatband assume their reality. Maundy Thursday, perhaps. Cold but not winter. At breakfast her mother had said, "Sister Brown passed away," just like that, bringing her up on newsy events.

"No. Oh, no!" Catherine said, thinking at nineteen or twenty the world as she left it must be intact.

"The other day. Your father saw them wheel her out. It was the mailman or paper boy found her nearly dead. The cats were so hungry they came begging down the street."

"No," Catherine said. It was just the two of them in the kitchen, her father down at the courthouse. James had already quit Yale, was acting in New York.

"I'm afraid so," Nell said. "Poor Mrs. Brown. She had a little girl, you know. We played together. She was sickly. We played inside—cutouts, checkers. She was a clever child."

Catherine, flustered, had run through the swinging door to the dining room. "You never told me," she shouted back at her mother. "A child? You never told me that." She had dashed out then in a raincoat and kerchief as though headed for church—it was most probably Easter vacation—but had turned in the opposite direction, charged blindly into the morning mist. First the silk bag, next hatband, then tip of old boot—black bits assembled. Next, the flesh pink of cameo; Fates dancing at the throat, and then Sister Brown, the ash-white face with its quizzical tilt. She stood holding her broken gate where the dew beaded like tears and she poked a silver drop. *What is the density of water, Catherine?* Catherine had known the answer, but could not speak, and the old woman drifted back as though swept by the fog to the fish-scale house no one entered, her black reticule with what researches dangling from her hand.

And there was no mystery. Mrs. Brown had simply come around when they got her to the hospital and demanded that she be dismissed. The next week she died. Catherine was still at home and read it in the *Post:* "Bella V. Brown, wife of the late Harold."

"Late!" her father said. "It was fifty years ago."

Now she would like the tent pulled round her. Now she would like to sleep. It was sort of false, the dry old maid resurrected for James, but there was no mystery. Last night she had smelled the cloying lavender; heard the simple, unrelenting question—*Catherine?* And how could James forget? They'd all had a high old time, had so enjoyed it—the story of Cath running home in terror when Sister Brown returned from the dead.

Closet Drama

Obviously, when mastery exists, then the question
of the heart comes up. Without mastery the heart
isn't worth a damn.   —Jerzy Grotowski

I

In the dark.
    Ba-ba black sheep. *Microphone static.* Its fleece was white
as snow. *Spotlight tracks the mike boom, which dips down, hovers.*
Fleas. Fleece. Blah. Humbug. *The mike withdraws.* Under spreading
chestnut tree, village smithy stands. *The mike descends. Spot grows
to include James Bray lounging in a square black leather chair. Bray
in sneakers, jeans, work shirt: unshaven, boyish, aging. Cool, slow
smile, he leans into the mike:* You don't know enough about me to
stuff an olive.
    You—you face the screen. The dark theater. More likely,
more's the pity, you sit on a couch or propped in bed like big dopey
stuffed animals and can't know that happy end on Victorian FRONT
PORCH, that kiss was shot before the principals met, before they had
to deal with the dead middle, its dead confusion, dead hair-raising
suspense. Making the moving pictures—space-time travel, practical,
you bet. I'm talking insurance, who can afford sequence? Ship that
equipment, crew, moody actors, many of them mood-elevated, imperial director halfway across the country again, plop the whole

operation down on FRONT PORCH? Insure that scene. Art director's affixed gingerbread, weathered FP to romantic perfection. Plotline having gone to the wars or action in the big city, the filmfolk can't be sure that on their return the rocker will be at the correct angle, not to mention degree of honeysuckle bloom, even with the stills and cover shots, elaborate notations—smudge on her apron, sweat on his brow—even with the cobwebs reattached in upper left corner, the porch will be detectably wrong, can't be left to memory or imagination. FRONT PORCH: seal it. In the can.

      I'm watchin' movin' pictures here. *James leans back in his chair as though rapt before the big screen.* Only the good flicks, good ol' pictures. *James for some time playing audience—passive/enchanted.* Knowing that somewhere there's a contingency, somewhere FRONT PORCH *in toto* with rocker, cobweb, gnats stuck in the screen. Call it magic. Hey! I'm watchin'—darkroom, screening room—beautiful room, one of many. This is one beautiful chair. One of many. *Lights up a notch to reveal square black leather chairs on an otherwise empty stage. Dipping along, the mike counts the chairs—three. James in the middle chair.* Bewildered by turn of events, you find me sitting pretty in a Grand Confort, black calfskin model, with the luck run out. Hey, I'm aware of the vagaries of the market. It's more than okay watchin' the ol' movies. *His trained voice husky; delivery high, bright. Light flickers on James.* That is one effect: fibrillations from the old black and white projectors. Why they called them flicks—and then lost it, threw the whole pulse beat out with dull wash of color. Start with the classics—Chaplin, Keaton. I watch Charlie with the cane, the billy club in *Easy Street,* watch the pants in *Gold Rush,* the graceful skirty things he does with the extra flaps of material, dainty movements, coy tug at a place below the rope belt, just to the side of the button fly, his dance-hall humiliations undercut by the masterful way he uses those pants. One secret: you know there's an ACTOR in that getup, every improv under control, every object a possibility—plates, chairs, beans on the knife, spaghetti, OF COURSE the spaghetti.

James spent, slouches back in the chair. The revolving door, you bet, the wide world a shaky set invented for the Little Tramp. It's where I start, that's all—watchin' Charlie, watchin' Buster, their light flickerin' over my face, my body. CLACK. Lost my nerve. Clack. *James' voice unmiked, stretched thin.* Clack, when the take ends, making the motion pictures. Like you see it in the movies. "Cut," the director's line, then the hinged black board with the zebra stripes down the middle. CLACK.

Whatzis? *James up from the chair.* Hey, two years I've had a couple of walkbys, one feedbag commercial. I'm workin' up here in the dark. *The mike returns slowly.* Ba-Ba Black Sheep testing everywhere that Mary went. *The mike screeches.* Forest primeval. Murmuring pine, hemlock. *The mike adjusts. James settles, edgy, tapping the arms of his chair.* Or a close-up of Keaton illuminates the room—still white light. Buster's hooded eyes, head lidded with famous hat that casts no shadow. Still shot, he knew everything about moving in the moving pictures, when to be still and let the screen throw off the white face, white so melancholy his skin acts. I've been watching Keaton's skin, the living mask. It would be instructive at this point to have projections: Charlie plucking at his pantaloons and the long flat powdered face of Keaton. Dead flesh surrounds survivor's eyes.

Hey! I can't run a lot of expensive equipment, show film-school clips off the back wall, stoop to video where you can't see Charlie's pants are striped, striped morning pants cast off by some bloated banker or butler, pants that speak of station, class, decorum. I choose not to see Keaton's hat reduced to a plugged nickel, lose the wild undefeated dream in those eyes. It's not share and share alike here. I see what I want to see.

Another effect: the room is not, in fact, not that dark. You pick out the chrome that cradles the chairs, contour of black and white vase, a statue, books on a shelf, zigzags on Navajo rug. No window. No door. As in the movies when people make love in the dark—you have to see them, don't you? Blue-black look of night not totally concealing, lens choosing its drama, sequence of alarm clock, phone, white sheets, bare breast. Or the warehouse—dark, movie dark—illegal crates, hovering steel beams, glint of gun barrel. Guys chasing up open stairwell. Hey! You want to see the action? I am here. Out of work, unshaven, in the dark.

Lights up. James in a spare, stylish room. Black and white Indian pot and terra cotta statue on a thick glass table. Hung on the back wall, a Navajo rug. Cabinets, shelves with books and baskets artfully arranged. No door, no window. Three Cube chairs, Le Corbusier's classic Grand Confort, face out as in proscenium theater. James moves to the end chair, stage left.

A couple of paydays. One feedbag commercial.

"It keeps you out there, hon."

That's Glenda. Glenda's the agent.

"This is all good news, babe. You were overexposed."

Glenda's like having Marjorie Main for a mother. I go back that far. Like having Margaret Hamilton with the blacked-out tooth and the poison apple on your side. Glenda is tough love. I've been with Glenda longer than the sum of both my marriages, twenty years. Currently, hoping Glenda will not call.

"We got a lot of interest."

Perhaps the worst line in the daily jingle. I have zip, no interest at all.

"What you want up there? Food stamps?"

Glenda says the field must lie fallow, full of such wisdom. I say let it lie fallow, don't spread it with shit.

"Love ya, babe."

Love ya, Glenda. I do love Glenda, a procuress, neither bad nor good. Every day she wakes to the bloodsucking demands of filmland and goes into the field, a hardened missionary among the savages. She has learned their language, adapted to their ways. Glenda listens like a foreign operative to what's going down, conspires for her people. It's godawful to think that every day Glenda thinks of me—whether to keep me on the back burner, whether to polish me up or try me on some casting agent, tarnished. My wife and child go about their business, forget me sulking in my room, but I'm Glenda's daily business.

"This is the best news we've had," Glenda says. "There's a kid actor. They're calling him a sensitive James Bray."

"Like I'm dead."

"Like you're famous, the galaxy." (Glenda knows my hide-and-seek game.) "I thought you didn't want to work?"

Sooner leave my wife than leave Glenda. *James moves to get up.* I left my first wife, my first child, as though walking off a set, as though they were actors too difficult to work with. Glenda's for the long haul, knows me. *Sunk back in his Cube.* While I . . . know nothing . . . about Glenda. Whether she has boyfriends or girl-friends. Whether she's from Tulsa or Bayonne, or Bucharest for that matter. Whether she lives with her old mother or cats. Once I detected a clot of white fur on Glenda's black pants. "Angora," she said and went on to elucidate the favorable terms of a contract. I will never know if Glenda had been with a sweater or a goat. Love ya, babe. Love ya, Glenda. *James, eyes closed, speaks so low the mike swings down nearly touching his lips.* In her pigsty of an office, Glenda. The dead plants and moldy yogurt cartons, a sea of press releases, scripts, mountain of trades—like a 1942 studio set, AGENT on the glass door, all within the computerized glitz of Agency Numero Uno. The legend she has become, my Glenda, bird-boned, sexless—Elsa Lanchester, Bride of Frankenstein, pop eyes, pucker mouth—daffy but harsh, harsh among all the softly lit head shots of her people. Up on the wall, beautiful people. Talented, successful people. Okay—the nightmare is: I come into Glenda's mess. My picture is gone. Ingenues and vamps, men's men and women's men, American boys and girls, fun fatties, old timers who have signed on for the big production number in the sky. No blank square on the wall. No empty frame. *James whispers.* Hey! It's not that I'm gone, no, no, no. I was never . . . never up there at all.

Blackout. The phone rings and rings.

II

Black and white pot, terra cotta statue, phone on glass table down front. Chairs pushed back to form a small overlit arena, in which—James Bray. Noise. Shattering noise. Shouting. Ziff come . . . Ziff come . . . *Noise dies to a gentle whirr.* Shouting to prove we could withstand the racket. It was Ziff come in a helicopter, better effect than the modest Porsche. The stunt horses reared. The junkyard dog howled at his trainer. In the desert—we were in various degrees of agony, skittery and hot though the sun was hardly up over a big red rock formation, the only point of interest in a desolate expanse. Except for GAS STATION. We were here for GAS STATION, an abandoned one-pump rig. *James places the terra cotta statue to be GAS STATION.* GS from the days of the flying red horse. They touched the wings up, put a couple of dented old Nehi signs on the rotted white clapboard.

An ugly script, the director aiming at pretty shots, getting his forty, fifty takes, already over budget. We put up at a creepy motel featuring lizards with blister-red eyes and huge scorpions from outer space. Our trailers drawn round like covered wagons, the generator pulsing, but across the yard, field—whatever you call tumbleweed on scrubland—no more than fifty feet away, there was a camp. Pup tents and propane stoves. Students digging for shards, skulls of Indians with the old professor, a gentle, weathered man in a floppy straw hat, perfectly cast. We were legal. They were legal.

Some royal screwup. Or a wee bit of corruption. It was their holy and official site, their designated site. Site A. *James places the black and white Indian pot at Site A.* Our location man had paid off the county for GAS STATION. We were to have the usual coverage, cops stopping traffic on a two-lane road through the desert, hadn't been used since they made *High Sierra* or W. C. Fields tooted out there to sell choice real estate in a Model T. Nary a state trooper on the horizon, they were someplace cool, counting their cash. So the diggers were there—these earnest kids in bandannas and sandals with sieves in their hands and little picks and shovels, ready to work in the big sandbox. And we were there, the filmfolk, ready to play.

Good scene, better than our script. The director, no longer in the business, pops a fistful of Valium as the whirlybird comes toward us, dark angel across the desert. Students flank the old man—defiant, silent, ready for the plucky last stand. Actors and crew shouting through the noise, making our own racket. *The mike hovers over James' head.* The helicopter, awkward in the air, delicate as a moth landing. We wait for the apparition: Morty Ziff.

James collapses in the nearest chair, his back to the audience. He reaches for the mike, drawing down lengths of cable. Even, plainspoken: Haven't trod the boards . . . in many years. Broadway had not beckoned. When I first came out here, my résumé read out failure. Angular, Eastern-effete, nobody's true love, nobody's hero, I watered their dry lawns, vacuumed the scum off their pools, chopped their mesquite, diced their shallots, read unproduceable scripts with the lowest of the filmfolk. Born lucky, I never despaired. Some funny gigs: pouring the sip of wine, I stood back while the fella tasted. You bet I waited, this was only the time of trials. L.A. was one of 'em, driving the spread of it in jalopies, sleeping in squalid bungalows with a changing cast of anxious characters many of them too old to be hopeful, many of them too self-deceived to accept the peripheral life.

James gets up, pushes the chair around to face the audience, balances on the arm in profile, offering the good side of his face. When asked about the early days, I say born lucky. It had not really been that hard. Hey, an exclusive. I choose to confess homesick. You bet, homesick—I longed for the filthy sidewalks of New York with many breathing bodies, live faces. This pathetic longing for my flophouse room in Hell's Kitchen, a matter of blocks from the big time shows. Now, I can say how one day, walking out into the mean dirt yard of one of those crumbling L.A. bungalows, I saw the dusty spikes of a hideous growth, this plant with freaky head, orange and purple beak, and knew my luck had run out. Longing for the green parks of my childhood, made peaceful with deliberate shady paths, with vistas of Long Island Sound, with playful streams feeding the Pequonnock, I killed the thing. The Park City, a pathetic slogan for a factory town, became my Eden, and the one red maple, the privet clipped like heavy gumdrops binding the rough stucco of our house to its narrow city lot, was a garden of lost delight as I decapitated the bird of paradise in West Los Angeles. Okay, it lasted half a minute. I thought the luck ran out.

James faces the audience, the audience which he turns on and off with his engaging smile, flip of the cable. And then, mid to late sixties, that war, I was suddenly right, being nobody's true love, nobody's hero. Morty Ziff found me you might say, or you might say he took the pulse of the nation—jumpy, embarrassed, first perception of maybe second-rate. Or pulse of the business, Ziff already in the muck of it, cutting deals. My wife got me in the door for a reading. She'd come to hate the movies. She was a painter and for a living painted mattes for Universal, those strangely old fashioned backdrops for the action. Super-real, the moist roots and undergrowth of the jungle, the rooftops of hazed Montmartre, crisp Regent's Park, the sexy silver dials of cockpits. A troll in the workshop, she executed on demand each lifelike frond and billowing puff of smoke. Artists leading our undiscovered lives; we made this central mistake about the nature of my calling. Making the moving pictures why I came out here, not the rent due, baby on my back—lines I actually delivered. Other cheap thrusts at her naive political positions. Let's say a decent woman mistook a crate of college books, my disdain for the jolly volleyball Cal. culture, for *serioso.* In any case history, my son swung from the ceiling like an angel in his baby bounce chair, above the fray. No real fray, my ambition crude and easy as the woozy seductions of a psychedelic poster; only the sprout salad wilted and the space in the pasteboard apartment grew heavy, heavy with her honesty. I walked out on the mother and my boy as if for a breath of air. Let's say one of life's ironies, my wife, the artist, got me the reading. Ziff and this casting director turned on to my uptight Eastern voice; checking the long chin, sharp nose, baby blues you might remember—offbeat face, perhaps a useful actor. In a sendup of the Western, I rode with the bad guys.

You bet, I loved the few scenes over and over as though always rehearsing. One angle, then another, same moves, same lines. From the first day hooked on the apparatus—chalk lines and cables, the brute lights lighting the night and day, mikes flying after my every grunt and dying word, loved the small professional audience so taken with their machinery. Nuts and bolts laid out, no make-believe, just magic.

James, center stage, twirling the mike over his head. Noise. Shattering noise in the desert. We wait for the apparition of Morty Ziff, no one uses the Morty. The door of the helicopter springs open. Ziff, unbuckling the safety belt—slow, slow climb down the shaky rope ladder, calculating each step as though landing on the moon, his investment in GAS STATION the giant step for mankind. Solemnity. He is capable of solemnity, what he presumes is a gentleman's reserve, rather than loudmouth histrionics to get his way. From above, the big guy got the picture, a two-ring circus: our mishegas, the diggers' containment.

Ziff strides across the nasty side yard to the sand pit, faces off with the old professor. Pith helmet to broken straw hat. Colonial guvnah come upon the natives. You know who'll win. You know this slick piece of Hollywood shit will come on like visiting bishop with shabby parish priest, like the man from headquarters with expendable manager of works. It's quick. The kids are laying nets over Site A, placing their shards on cotton, packing their gear into a disreputable Volkswagen bus. And naturally they come to watch us. Irresistible—watching the filmfolk, pure process of doing our stuff. Even the bewildered old guy comes to stand with his students, blessing our childish enterprise.

And we start to roll, placing the cameras, rehearsing the

scene. I drive up to this halfhearted gas pump. Dog barks. Get out to stretch my legs. Yaller dog crouches, snarls, lunges at me. A young woman runs at the cur to save me. The dog, a pro, stops dead in midair, looks up at the pretty lady, then to his trainer, who is mildly miffed. We laugh, the assembled crew, the wimpy director and his camera man. The actors laugh, naturally for once. Ziff, too, though time is money and we've already lost the fuckin' sunrise. Then she gets it: the pretty lady understands she's the innocent intruder and there's hilarity all round. A veil of honey-blond hair falls over her face. She stoops to pet the dog.

"Thanks," I say. "That was nice."

She looks at me as if I'm real in my powdered-down makeup and quasi-Western outfit. The first words Lilah says to me—steady, unembarrassed: "I'm good with animals." *James has been walking this scene through, now he pushes a chair downstage, settles in, releases the mike, watches it suck up to an approved station.* What it's like—those times when Chaplin meets the girl. In the midst of his shrewd tricks, outrageous tactics, her face is incredibly sweet, so pure—it's the other side of grubby and clever, the other side of the world. A shame I couldn't go on with this guileless scene in which I meet Lilah at GAS STATION instead of the programmed blood and guts that followed, such a shame that in six months Lilah Lee Hulburt is my wife. My second wife.

Meanwhile Ziff has noticed she's a knockout, what he calls "new talent." "Stick around," he says. "We could use a little help with the animals."

She got him in one take. You can't be that beautiful, even in California, and not learn to dish it out to the posse of hopeful horny men. The mongrel was licking her dirty hand, "Poor fella, poor fella," she said, aiming that at Ziff. She does not think much of our production. Directing her crew to get cracking, she does not think of us at all. Then I realize she's not a kid, has an edge on them, an assistant to the brittle old man. Her body strong for the desert digging, and womanly—full breasts flopping in faded plaid shirt, real hips in the jeans. Her face too fine for that hard light, yet in the clean structure of the cheekbones, classic modeling of the head, something austere. Rose in the desert, wasted on the desert air. My second wife.

Dog barks. I get out of the car, stretching. Dog growls, lunges at me as directed, stopping with teeth bared at the command of his trainer. A scrawny gray man in overalls comes out of the gas station. His wife in worn washdress hushes the dog. She's scared. We go through our lines. I spot the gray man as a small time punk, the ex-con who knows the dirty secret I'm after. Wife framed in the doorway, quivering hand to mouth. We had lost the sunrise. Someone said it was 110°. I remember watching Lilah Lee Hulburt fasten the back door of the bus and go around, climb up in the driver's seat. It must have been an inferno in that can. I wanted to go with her.

James slides down comfortably in his chair for the end of this story. The director having his terminal fit, we shot the scene. I drive up. Stretch. Dog. Gray man with pasty look of prison still upon him. Faded wife in doorway. The wind machine blows sand against the tin Nehi signs, against the actors. We are chalky, shouting our lines through a dust storm. I remember the food was rotten on that picture and that I asked Ziff at lunch—we were in the air-conditioned Winnebago for the talent—how he got rid of the professor.

"I schmeered him," Ziff said, making that movement with his hand, thick thumb across the fingers.

"Cash!"

"Don't be dumb, Jimbo. Pay the damages. They want to dig bones and beads off the reservation? They come back and sift that crap in style." And then—he could not resist it: "I got a little something extra here for the lady scholar." Hands on his package: "I got a treat for Greta Garbo."

James makes his way to the cabinet, fiddles with a dial. Voice on, his own voice in polished delivery. Born Morgan Pfitzer to Lutherans in Plainfield, New Jersey, his parents tithed to a strict branch of that church, Dutch Reform. *He begins to speak with the tape, turns back, switches off the machine, in a fast rusty voice goes it alone.* Dutch Reform, decent people, neighborhood of solid houses built for commuters before the First World War. Every day Morgan's father rose early; ferryboat across the Hudson, train to Penn Station, subway downtown to the paper-box factory where he designed packages for soap and toothpaste, for cereal and Mazda lamps. "My father was an artist," his son would say in later years with a shrill hyena laugh, "an artist of tabs and slots." At five o'clock, Fred Pfitzer reversed direction, ate his dinner, dozed over the *Courier-News,* allowed himself milk and his wife's thin icebox cookies, so to bed. Blanche Pfitzer's cupboards and cabinets in order. Her curtains emitted a strong smell of bleach. Floors and furniture shone. In the living room where brocade lounge chairs faced the silent radio, the Bible lived in a Dutch Bible box of oak so old its carved fishes and crosses were all charred black.

On Sunday—church in the A.M. then religious instruction for Morgan and little Pearl, then roast chicken, then a ride up into the Watchung Mountains, then cold chicken and the Bible lifted from its box. Frederik Pfitzer read in a dour voice favoring the bloody books—Judges, Jeremiah, Leviticus—while Blanche and Morgan and little Pearl sat with heads bowed, hands folded in their laps. Pearl pale as her name, but limp; Morgan florid, barrel-boy fat. Pearl fond of paper dolls and playing house, was crocheting a long lumpy brown tube that looked like a string of hot dogs with the idea of making a rug, but alas in her eighth year was taken with the dread summer disease, a decade before the Salk vaccine. For a while the house was lively with doctors and nurses. Morgan's job was to boil big pots of water, though he was only ten. Then little Pearl died: that is what happened to the Pfitzers. It would have been most of their story were it not for Morgan, who tore the heads off every paper doll and cut his doomed sister's raggedy rug chain in a hundred pieces. Why? Many years, many thousands of dollars later he revealed to a doctor that he had neither loved nor hated his uninteresting sister. He was not happy when she departed, nor did he suffer the guilt of the survivor. Why then had he gone to that doctor in bad faith? Why had he told Fred and Blanche that God was in the funny papers? God was Dopey Dwarf, green cheese. Blanche choked into her hanky.

"You are the very devil," Fred Pfitzer said to his son.

Morgan was a hellion from then on, scourge of the neighborhood, where he was known as Morty, then Morty the Grifter, for he was full of schemes to anger and annoy, schemes that involved tipped garbage cans, slashed tires, jimmied windows. Other kids would do things for him. He was like one of those tough urchins in the old movies who seem to be blessed with no parents, only their gang. Except Morty was a loner. Often at the movies by himself, sneaking in the side door of the Strand or working a scam with a roll of red tickets he'd swiped from the church hall at Dutch Reform. On Sundays the Pfitzers no longer bothered to look for the boy when it was time to drive across Route 22, up into the Watchungs. He was at the movies. In his wisdom, God had taken little Pearl and dealt them a wicked boy.

But smart, their Morgan was smart—cut the kid stuff— smashing milk bottles, robbing junk and petty cash out of neighbor houses. He ran the numbers in junior high, set up pools on varsity games, faked the size of the pot. It was about money, and his teachers could see where he was heading, this thickset boy in flashy plaid jackets they were sure his parents did not buy. Brash, persistent, he got the Elks, Kiwanis . . . Johns Manville, the butcher, the baker took page ads in the yearbook, underwrote the senior operetta, glee club tour. Those teachers hadn't a clue where Ziff was heading or how he spit out his lawful name. A boy without friends, with admirers and flunkies, good girls warned off. He was like a grown man with his desires, arrangements in Newark, whores in Jersey City. It was a joke that he was a high school boy at all.

It was a joke he still sat, a star boarder, with the Pfitzers in their neat living room with the Bible and a Magnavox TV. He watched sports with the weary box designer and dashed up to his room to make book on the trotters, up to his room where he'd put in his own phone. When Blanche and Fred went up to bed, he watched late into the night, and for a while they thought they had their Morgan home. He sat on watching, watching all those other lives, not stories so much as the stars. Gary Cooper. Linda Darnell. Lucky people who had changed their names and changed their fortune. Cary Grant. Dorothy Lamour. He was short, burly, with the build of a middle-aged man never cast as the lover—Edward Arnold, Broderick Crawford—the heavy, the extra cop. Big lumps of knowledge on Ziff's forehead, and his beard came in dark below cheeks so inflamed he looked perpetually bullish, charged up. A pity, for it was the lithe smoothies—Claude Rains, Dan Duryea, Richard Widmark—stirred him. Bogart, of course, Bogart. Watching Cagney play a psychotic little tout—*White Heat,* a favorite—his face was radiant as the twelve-inch screen. He was no actor. The voice from Ziff's block body was pitched high—scratchy, demanding. Wisely, he chose one role to last forever, unlike the rest of us, projecting ourselves again and again in the dark.

James stands. A stint of deep breathing, knee bends, then ambles to the back wall, rips off the Navajo rug. Backlit, he is a shade blown up on the white wall behind him. James shadowboxes, pivots round. Unlike the rest of us, children again in the dark, easy dreamers, happy to see ourselves in whatever the story, Ziff wanted one transformation. He gave up his petty crimes and the women he paid for in Newark; a rehabilitated adolescent, seemingly with no more ambition than to transfer his residence to a fraternity house at Rutgers, which in prehistory was founded as Dutch Reform. Though hardly his intention, pleasing Blanche and Fred his last summer home; glued to the late shows, harmless, or idling down at the Paramount or Strand. Unlike the rest of us, talkin', foolin' around after the lights went down beginning of the movie. Unlike the rest of us, drifting up the aisle when the show was not truly over. At the Pfitzers', alone in the middle of the night. . . . *James steps to the side* and a big silhouette of bulbous armchair sprouting round, heavy head appears on the back wall. The real show was not over. Alone, face aglow in the semidark, Ziff sat at attention, eager for names— gaffer, best boy, assistant assistants. The lone realist, reading the credits. Hey! Even Ziff had a soft spot—waiting in the shadow of Fred's black Bible box, in the wax smell of Blanche's gummy polish, their devil of a boy breathless, waiting for the magic moment. *On the back wall in stately succession—Columbia the Gem of the Ocean holds her torch high; the noble head of the MGM lion slowly swivels before his mighty roar.* You bet, icing on the party cake, meat next to the bone. *Warner Brothers' heraldic crest; the great searchlights of Twentieth Century-Fox sweep the sky.* Ziff watching the sweetest show of all. *The small world spins within the universe of Universal.*

Lights up: James, to his audience, nervy, pacing the apron of the stage: EXERCISE! Close eyes, flex fingers, toes, elbows, knees. Drop jaw. In preparation for what, pray tell? The show, game, act? Choose one from list of three. Sway like breeze in the willow's hair, like doggie's tail, pendulum, sotted sailor, like the old tire swing under resplendent apple tree, and, yes, like the empty sleeve of World War amputee. EXERCISE! Close jaw, open eyes: the terrier's tail is cropped as is the boxer's, the Boston bull's. Digital works, amazing lifelike prosthesis. Grant the sailor his sea legs, the willow shallow roots, short life. Stand on your head. Flex pinkies, piggies. Stick carrots in your ears, beans up your nose. An extra, you do not go on just yet. Thank the powers that be.

III

Music: Benny Goodman—"Body and Soul." Gradual warm light, dawn stopping short of day. James in a floppy double-breasted suit jacket over work shirt and jeans, penny loafers, slouched in one of the chairs, downstage. Navajo rug laid out, center of the dim room. James

speaking over the clarinet riff as the music fades: Thusly attired . . .
Jesus, I must have been a treat. The jacket still smells of boy-sweat,
of cigarette and leaky unconsummated sex in the front seat of Nell's
Packard. My trick jacket with the secret pockets, double lining up
the sleeves. Summer before Yale, I donned the magic jacket, heavy
petting, born lucky, as I say. Lucky enough to own three punishing
calfskin chairs. Okay if lost in a movie, otherwise slippery like dancing with a dog you don't want to dip with, some girl of good family
your mother has her eye on. Not memorably painful. Beware the
classics, leather-bound.

  Meanwhile, Morgan Pfitzer and I are of an age. While
he's ordering his priorities *re* the big career, I'm wearing this stinking jacket every night in my mother's car, trusting one of my dates
would fly me to the moon—a term I actually used. When I didn't
have a gig—a term I actually used—in a kiddy swing band. Unem-
ployable—we rehearsed nightly in a damp rec room. The drummer's house, his family leading their stunned half-lives above the
din. Every night, high hopes, real dreams of the Ritz Ballroom, even
a gig at Pleasure Beach as we launched into the first set. Then,
clarinet thrown in the backseat of Nell's car, I would drive to one or
another house where a girl waited on the front porch, ran down the
steps in a fresh ironed dress, fresh washed hair. They all had these
baskets that summer, comb and lipstick tucked under the lid, undo
the damage as we drove home from Seaside Park.

  James strolls to the Navajo rug, assumes lotus position.
Mike dips for the story. Predictions as to my future in filmland: front
seat of Nell's car, I delivered an unconvincing performance. Foreshortened bedlike expanse of prickly gray plush, feet play clutch
against brake as I reach for those nice Bridgeport girls. Soft breasts,
nipples at the ready, but they would not. "You don't know what this
does to a guy." A line I actually used. Smooth thighs up to the warm
strawlike wetness there. My prick did its one trick. Gearshift in the
ribs, I'd implore. They would not, nice girls. Until one came along
who advised I get my butt out from under the steering wheel and

come down to the beach, where we spread my mother's lap robe on seaweed and mussel shells and the nice girl directed the rest of the scene.

The true drama of those hot nights reserved for the kitchen. William Aloysius and me. *James plays as though to Billy Bray across the jagged black and white pattern of the rug.* Ghost of himself early on, thinner, at last, pale—his black hair, what was left of it, had begun its transformation to tufts of dingy snow, and I believe it had started, the suck of blue-gray lips for air. Come from his Dodgers that he watched however long the innings, my father appeared in full armor, emerging slowly in his cigarette haze, a stagy effect. The undershirt of his summer BVDs revealed the fallen-away muscles, chest with the shrunken flesh old men display as a shield. Who'd harm them? If I'd not been a boy running on lust, I'd have seen the ghost of my father in the nightly apparition of Billy Bray, his suspenders looped over the pants he wore to the courthouse. No matter the season, his heavy oxblood shoes. He never changed to lighter clothes, that was faggedy Ann, la-di-da, so that as he shuffled toward me he could almost pass for a stout fellow, a boxer with fancy footwork, those lithographs of Irish immigrants putting up their dukes. In my boy's books there were such pictures of noble lads. Thrusting out his dimpled chin: "Been out with the girls?"

I tapped my clarinet case.

"You must be worn out with the music."

So he carried on through the sweltering nights of August with the interrogation. "Taking the sea air?" he asked and answered: "We needn't send you to New Haven. You'll have a fine education before you pack your bags."

Thinking how soon I'd abandon the life in that house, I did not counter, which left the kitchen to the empty creak and rattle of his anger. My silence to his demeaning banter. There's more to male violence than fisticuffs and pummeling. He wheeled around in a stooped maneuver I was to learn when stabbed or shot upon the stage, staggered back to his ball game. I know and don't know why we disowned each other. Hell, William Aloysius Bray. . . . *James leaves the tight arena of Navajo rug, reaches for his mike, plays to it.* I took delight in Billy Bray as though he was Victor McLaglen in one of his puckish roles, or a "character" like Harry Truman. Turning from me, clutching his upper arm. . . . A hundred years later in a screening room—Hey! it's Billy grazed by a mobster bullet, Little Caesar with the tough line to deliver: "You can dish it out, but you can't take it anymore."

I've been watching, crippling my coccyx. Moved on to glistening nights, mean streets, as they say, of killers. The flip side, my father was Little Rico—that scene in which the focus goes blurry, Edward G. Robinson loses his nerve, can't shoot the kid he loves, Douglas Fairbanks, Jr. Billy couldn't finish me off, just see me skimming by, as though I was one of those water skiers who appeared on our beach that summer, nonsensical to a man who had experience of real danger. He seemed, in that dim night kitchen, to be fearful as well as feisty. Let's keep it simple, maybe just pissed at a boy who would not watch a doubleheader with his father and by a trick of fate he'd been blessed with a daughter who was in at the television, waiting on the big brown couch to replay every pitch he missed in loving recitation. I scored with the nice girl in Seaside Park if not with the swing band. Later, with the acting . . . I believe he was waiting for my fall. Now I could tell him it will never quite happen: a special effect, I walk on water, resemble the agile adventurers I play. Beautiful room this, one of many, still the hand of fear upon me as it was upon that smart-ass kid, his father lurching out of the hot kitchen, fear that Billy was the gifted actor, that I'm standing in the wings with sand in my scrotum, seaweed in my hair, an impostor trying to fill those real oxblood shoes.

Lights down. James lays the mike on the glass table, draws from the pockets of his slouch high school jacket—the enchanted handkerchief, the flying goblet, multiplying cigars, the devil's key ring, disobedient match, and a deck of cards, which he shuffles then flings high and wide in his beautiful room. Fifty-two pickup! *Then the whisper:* Hey, I'm fifty-two years old. Mother of mercy, I could use a little backup. *Music: bright clarinet of Woody Herman—"Cherokee."*

IV

In the dark. The telephone rings and rings. Mike static. Fumbled phone.

"Thinkin' about your instrument," Glenda says.

Silence.

"You there? I been thinkin' about the lower registers come into your voice."

"Glenda, this is painful. In the dark here! Severed an artery with the Native Amurcan vase."

"So, I was thinkin'," Glenda says, "about the husky quality, like trust. This is a voice to believe in."

"Mother of mercy."

"Total new infrastructure," Glenda says. "Classy—the Brooklyn Bridge."

Silence.

Glenda, on futuristic Hollywood set, determined as an old music hall hoofer to finish a folding show: "For me," Glenda says, "this is once in a lifetime."

"Whole-grain commercial?"

"Grow up," Glenda says. "Major network, prime time. I sold a switch: you play it as a grown-up. A series, Jim. You are the mature man at the precinct."

"An old cop? You want me to play an old policeman on the television set? Babe, I got a hernia shovin' these friggin' leather chairs in the dark."

"Talk to the people. A series, Jimmy. Don't say no."

"No."

Lights up. James tidying the room. He finds the mike dis-

carded in his chair, yanks it like a vacuum cord: it recoils overhead. He picks up the Navajo rug, wears it as a prayer shawl, totters to the cabinets with their display of books and baskets, audiovisual equipment. Packing. Lilah Lee Hulburt packing up . . . make it bearable for me when she's gone. Curtains back from the cleaners. We got the view. My wife not a curtain woman. *James stumbles toward one small window now in the set, peeks through the curtains at a narrow slit of light.* We got the views—the Channel Islands lying out in the Pacific, San Ynez Mountains rising up from our pasture with the BIG CLEAN adobe barn, eat off the stall mats. Patio: dwarf lemon trees either side of plish-plash fountain, path of gray-green eucalyptus. We got—mother of trees, Moreton Bay fig, pulpy purple fruit, vulva pink inside. You want to see all that. Below, city at night, handful of jewels thrown down the hill. Only our little girl, a gloomy sixteen, has funereal drapings at her windows. Black gauze above Jen's windows, as though the fireman who might have saved her died. Here, curtains 'cause I'm watchin' the movies, curtains to invoke the dark. It was hell the day she sent them to the cleaners, Lilah making it bearable for when she's gone. Her anthro books gathered on one shelf, texts she hasn't cracked in years, lemon trees, mammoth cactus all repotted. She's placed the vase—*scusi, scusi*—POT, and priceless statue here. Beautiful objects to be left behind.

But she was the beautiful object, Lilah Lee. Sun's flaked the glossy California tan, hair darkened. She has taken off the silver bracelets.

James sluffs off the Navajo rug. It slaps the pre-Columbian figure, a smiling, crouching fellow with deep slashed eyes, a conical hat, who teeters, but rights himself. Babaloo! Close call. *The microphone whines.* "Well, you're not a boy. You're just mature." *The microphone sputters.* She was a child / I was a child / moon never beams bringing me dreams / Beautiful Annabel Lee." *The microphone descends, offers itself.* Call Ziff, no pride in this line of work. I could work tomorrow. Pick up the phone, take Glenda's series seriously. You go down there, talk with people think they want you.

Schemes and projects. You fly to New York, to Aspen. It's like the plans we had, boys in the North End, to build our own boxcars, put on a show. Let's get the Big Band out of the cellar. Only there is money. Talk and money.

With the mike downstage, working the audience—intimate, husky. I watched my wife take off the Indian bracelets, silver bracelets, old pawn, beautifully worked, some set with turquoise. My gifts to her. We go out, she displays them on her brown arms, her only vanity. We come home from our neighbors a while back, greedy art collectors, but blessedly Eastern neighbors, blessedly liberal neighbors among the tasteful fascists who live on our hill. We're in our white livin' room with all the Injun stuff. "What it's *worth,*" says Lilah, exasperated at our blessed neighbors, how they groove on their pictures. The Hockney, bargain basement. Pollock, a steal. Budget Bacon. "And *good* people." Lilah won't figure that one out. A while back, Christmas ago, the gaudy Mexican candlesticks set out in her white living room and my wife knelt by one of our baskets, the Chumash presentation basket with a lid. One by one, she took off the silver bracelets and dropped them inside as though they were so much cornmeal. Hey! Packing away the beautiful things. She was the beautiful thing.

At the bookcase, James dials. Voice, his voice in recitation— seductive, stagy. Rose in the desert, Lilah Lee, a day's drive away when I found her. . . . *He rips out the speaker wires. His voice— sputtery, weak—from across the room.* Those tales, the arid material of Hollywood and Vine. *James rips out the second speaker. Silence as he searches, finds the mike stuck in the Mayan statue's arms. Low, untheatrical:* Ba-ba. Testing. *The mike spits.* O Captain! Captain! Fearful trip she's done./ Ship's weathered rackareno. *James releases the mike, which floats up to a respectful distance.*

Lilah Lee Hulburt. A graduate student digging in the desert when I found her. It was like being discovered, she supposed, those tales of adorable girls at drugstore counters who ended up in Goldwyn's Follies, but that was the arid material of once upon

Hollywood and Vine. Her mother knew all those stories and believed them. How Lucille Ball and Paulette Goddard. How Lana Turner. Such fame was just a drive through the desert away, that's what Hetsie Hulburt would have her daughter know as she snapped beans or shucked the corn for supper. About the only good thing Hetsie could say for Riverside, California, was they had enough backyard to keep them eating. The house a four room shack they did not own.

Seven Hulburt kids running around the vegetable patch, skinny and dirty. When Hetsie tried to count the towheads, it seemed like seventeen. And . . . there was Lilah. She came in the middle. She came when Boon Hulburt had a county job with the dog catcher and stayed awhile at home. That's why she was different, Boon being settled. That had to be the reason for this girl who never ran wild, who sat on the front stoop reading any paper or magazine. She was apart from all the ruckus, not even looking on, so sometimes Boon would say, "What's a matter? You don't live here?"

She looked straight at her father, "Oh, I live here." Her considered words might have come from the far side of the moon. She was beautiful. That happens in a family—dishwater eyes, all the slope chins, low foreheads, and flap ears get handed out and there is a perfect spill-off from the gene pool, produces a Lilah Lee. If Boon wasn't home that year, you'd think Hetsie got her from a movie magazine. And she was so treated by her brothers and sisters, by teachers and neighbors, a visitor among them. Tranquil and good, a champ at schoolwork, unlike any Hulburt. Those kids always in trouble—truants, bullies, cheats. The older girls bred soon as they were able. Too dumb to jump-wire, the boys swiped aerials and hubcaps.

James satisfied in his Grand Confort, gentleman at his club with the fireside story. From her earliest years, Lilah tended to the chickens, bantam roosters, geese and ducks, later a pair of pheasants that were useless, Hetsie said. All cooped in the side yard, cleaner than the Hulburt kitchen. As Lilah fed and watered her fowls, you could see how easy she went about it, more at home than she was with people. Once, well it was when the girl was thirteen, Boon, after some months on the road, turned up with a cocker bitch swelled with a litter. Hetsie gave it to him about the mess, not to speak of money.

"Didn't bring the bitch to you," Boon said. Lilah bedded the dog near where she slept, spent her egg money taking her to the vet. When the puppies came, tumbly small things, curly wet, Boon said: "If she could of, Lilah woulda had them pups herself." It was that summer he took his daughter to the horses. He couldn't teach her; only a hand, a fellow who worked rodeo, driving the trailers, at best a groom, at worst just shoveling shit. To the other kids, no surprise Boon took their beautiful sister to the horses.

"To the Wild West Show," their mother said. Hetsie from San Diego, growing up had never seen a horse except on screen. As though Boon was servin' time, she didn't allow talk of rodeo. That suited Boon, one of those men don't want family cluttering the professional life. That was his profession, working rodeo. He loved the wild ponies and the broncos, the bars and gambling, roughhouse women. Listen to Boon, it was a long shot in a John Ford movie— noble beasts and brave men riding in dignified procession against the sunset, against God's own cathedral, Monument Valley, riding out to claim the West.

"The Lone Ranger," Hetsie said. He came off a destroyer from War in the Pacific, a sailor from the Texas gulf. Electrician first class, would not even fix the toaster. Hetsie was sore, mean when Boon was away, owing the milkman, the grocer. She'd strut out of the shack on Lemon Street to catch the bus on Lime, proud like she was shoppin' down to Reynolds', make her way to the Air Force base, clean house for the officers' wives; or the children would find her gone in the morning and know she was off to what was left of the almond groves, picker for the day. "Like a wetback," Hetsie said. When Boon turned up, her sharp tongue softened. So, it seemed a good thing when he took Lilah for the riding, that sweet child among them cowboys, but he'd have to bring her home in time for school.

James, the mellow raconteur, moves from his chair to accomplish stage business—pour a whiskey, fill a pipe—but the lights come down, darkness in his screening room, only the back wall with a bright projection—a fresh American girl, one touch too hearty for a picture book princess. She sits a sturdy white horse, reins looped loosely in her hands, smiling for the world to see how proud and happy. Yellow braids, new red boots, blue plaid shirt—this shot is color, so clear it could win an Eastman Kodak prize—and the sun so bright in the girl's gray eyes that she squints slightly, another clue she's human. In the background, far away as shepherds on the Tuscan hills behind a Virgin, the row upon row of dwarfed, cheering, madly cheering fans. In the movie dark, James turns his chair so that he, too, can look upon the child, Lilah Lee.

From another time. . . . *His words unsteady, then carefully paced:* Those cowboys did not bother Lilah. From another time or world, she spoke to them directly, as she spoke to everyone, from her deliberate distance. The worst of the carnies felt bad if he forgot himself with Lilah. An angel come among them, yet she earned her keep. Craziest pony, wild cow—she had the magic touch. In weeks, an old cowpoke had her ropin', ridin' the barrels, not like she was at a dude ranch with her daddy. T-Bar Rodeo, small outfit but the real show. Rolled in a blanket, Boon slept with the men on the floor of a van. Sometimes she'd see women in there, too. They put Lilah in cheap motels, travelin' from town to town on the second rate circuit. It was her first time without the sleeping bodies of her brothers and sisters all around and she took her joy in silence, embraced the stained carpet and peeling paint, before falling into a bed that was all her own.

Each night, eyes wide open, she dreamed of the horses. Lead and gait, flank and withers came like her native tongue. Now she knew why Boon left them in Riverside: partly for drink and women, mostly for hard work and horses. Knew why he took her with him. The American West—her day's ride across the desert. In a scenario much like her mother's, Boon saw her turned out in silver spurs and buckskin fringes, Annie Oakley without the gun. He saw his beautiful daughter as Queen of the Rodeo, and they did dress her up in a swell outfit, let her ride one show and then another. Funny thing is, learned lady I picked up in the desert, turned out to be a star. Weaving a big white quarter horse through oil drums, that little girl came in for the money. Over the loudspeaker: Out of Riverside, California, Lilah Lee, girl wonder, rare as the desert rose. When Boon packed her up and took her home to school, she knew what he wanted was what she wanted. She knew that back on Lemon Street, where Hetsie had let the cocker pups go all to hell.

The back wall blank, no more prairie princess on white steed in what must be a shabby fairground mostly hired out for stock car races, flimsy Ferris wheels and loop-the-loops of traveling fun fairs. In the dark, James stumbling among the chairs. The big time, Tulsa, Santa Fe. . . . *The mike without juice.* Hey! Tulsa, Wichita, BIG DEAL Santa Fee. . . . *A spot sweeps through the room, catching James at the dead dials; scruffy half-grown beard, cool blue eyes blank with fright.*

In the dark: a woman speaks—second-generation, assimilated California voice—pleasant though now and again arriving at a slow burn that flares to anger: A German story . . . we read a German story in anthro, UC Riverside, variation of a legend in which a mother and father sell their beautiful girl. In other versions, Scandinavian and French, it hadn't struck me I was that child traded so the family might prosper. Summers I worked the circuit and for four years after high school it was the big time—Tulsa, Phoenix, the Calgary Stampede. And Madison Square Garden, the ignorant audience expecting Minnehaha, Bronco Bill. *In the dark, a childish harrumph and hum, a competitive clearing of James' throat.* My father managed me; Boon Hulburt steppin' out in silver buckle, lizard boots. He promoted other acts as the years went by—rodeo clowns, then a couple of country and western singers who worked the shows.

They called me Lilah Lee, riding the women's events for big purses, but I could jump Razz-Ma-Tazz through fiery stockades, fleeing the rustlers, dance to the tom-tom beat on Eldorado. A black Indian wig—yes, the trick riding was much like a circus, and I gave my life to it, training and grooming, working dull office jobs in the winter season to buy extravagant saddles and a fancy quarter horse, my sweet one, Baby Doll. A life of total dedication, obsessive hours added up to years, and it never occurred . . . *A distracting clink of glass, a scramble among cables or wires.*

Lilah, steady-on, continues: It never occurred that I'd been sold like the beautiful child of poor family in our classroom story. Boon had his RV. Hetsie her tract house where she turned on the sprinkler to water a few flowers, telling the neighbors she'd been saved by Jesus. They had all of them been saved by Lilah Lee. The kids, unbelievably okay, settling to undemanding jobs, to marriages with many babies. The whole crew came up to Pasadena, catch me, Lilah Lee, at the head of a posse. I exhibited a rich man's palomino, wearing chaps with silver conchas, cream leather boots to match the horse's mane. That riding club—doctors, lawyers, financiers—wrote it in my contract—professional makeup, red roses to be woven in my hair.

What the woman teaching me her folklore could not fathom was tough trade: I sold myself. *On the back wall a mounted showgirl waving to the crowd, Tournament of Roses, full-blown red roses in her long blond hair. The saddle extravagantly tooled, etched silver horn pure flash; bridle and browband inlaid with turquoise. Who would notice the rich men and women riding behind her, playing Western, their club shirts of red satin, white Stetson hats? She rides alone, knowing she's the draw, passing her clean white smile to the crowd, who look up dumb, adoring. Then there is music, "She Wore a Yellow Ribbon," by a dandy marching band. And the announcer's voice pitched toward glory: "Girl o' the Golden West! Lord, ain't she special! Lilah Lee!" She rears the palomino up. Dancing in the air— unearthly creatures, they cannot be merely in California, merely in the Tournament of Roses to please the crowd before a football game.*

In the dark, the woman's voice, sharp, instructive: My story not fit for that woman's class. Hell, give Boon and Hetsie their fancy meal ticket, I wanted that life with the horses more than I ever wanted people. Wanted to be Lilah Lee. Our teacher, a stuffed wise owl, decidedly angry, said it was always a girl, always a beauty traded away for good fortune. I spoke up: "The girl in the legend is not unhappy."

"As long as she sleeps, in the Celtic version, as long as she keeps her eyes shut in the Brothers Grimm," said wise owl, blinking at me through her glasses. "She is a commodity traded from her father's house."

Older than my classmates who could not see it: the girl in all these stories is forbidden to look upon her lover, often forbidden to ask his name, but it's not so simple. "Beauty as a commodity," our teacher said.

"That girl," I said, "that girl is not unhappy until she breaks the rules." There was no point in arguing with the plain professor, no point in getting personal. I was that beauty: sold, just as surely sold myself to the horses, to the elation of being up there in the saddle, warm horseflesh between my thighs. From the first day, riding high. My mastery of those big animals was some kind of transgression fit into the story. Better than sex, it kept sex at bay.

James in a dim ray of light at the window, clutching the mike: EXERCISE! Humility—try that. Naked in a room, no props— try that. Sounds: cow, dog, cat. You are nowhere near ready for gorilla snort, elephant aria. Small, domestic: me-oooww. Bark in your birthday suit, no way ready for words—for you say, then I say. Stale tradition of the theater. Devices—open larynx, upper thoracic respiration. Stock moves from your repertoire—flailing arms, sunken chest, hand to heart. Banal gestures of caricature, selling yourself, shoddy goods.

Bumbling in the dark, James works with the mike down-stage: Whinny, neigh, stomp in your stall. Bloated with green apples, the flies gather on your eyes, squat on the wet rim of your nostrils, stir your mucus with tiny legs. Fool, you have gobbled those apples. Powerless against the heavy green horseflies. Flick, flick your tail.

Discomfort or pain, which is worse? The self-inflicted tummyache of childhood or the niggling *Musca domestica* buzzing your moist eye on its way to your rich manure. Discomfort, you say—the informed choice.

From the dark, the woman's sharp laughter: Charlie Chaplin meets the girl! It never occurred to you? Never occurred, I was bare-assed in bare room?

James, steady almost inaudible: EX-ERCISE. You are permitted one direction, bare-assed in bare room. Let it be this: "Actors should be like martyrs but alive, still signaling to us from the stake." Anto-neen Artaud.

The woman's laugh again, then an intimate whisper: Later . . . yes, later, I gave my self to one cowboy, then another, beer breath, Westerns on TV . . .

Blazing light. Infamous chairs in their lineup. No James. The phone rings and rings. From the bottom shelf of the cabinet, a muffled shift and fumble, door flaps open. There, in cozy cradle position—James, who speaks to thin air. What you may do is tie my wrists and ankles, secure the door with sealing wax, bind it with stout cord. Sailor's knots. The Houdinis did it, Harry and Bess. The Metamorphosis. Exchanging places in three seconds. *James rolls from the cabinet.* We could learn that one. In three seconds Lilah Lee is bound by my restraints *and,* LADIES AND GENTS, I stand free. *James takes a bow, looks suspiciously about the room, up at the blinding lights.* Control effects. Cover set. Contingency location. Check it out, that's a live phone. No shame in this business. Call Morty Ziff.

"Why didn't you telephone?" Ziff says.

"Didn't have a nickel."

Lady in the Lake, Ziff says. 1947. Trick camera. Robert Montgomery, arty-farty Marlowe.

The woman's voice, Lilah's—weary: Ziff again. Ziff on the line. Check it out, the artful dodge, contingency story. One cowboy or another . . .

James collapses, sits Houdini-style, lashed and gagged in the Grand Confort. His wife's words are faint, hesitant, then lulled into a reverie as the light mercifully fades: One cowboy . . . or another. Beer breath, the smell of liniment and pot to ease their pain . . . back to business in the morning like it was a dream. All that, much later. Time of the story, it was godawful hot. I come off the road behind Boon, who drove the big air-conditioned horse van into Cody. I remember being in that can, no real air, no daylight, covering Baby Doll with her blanket. Godawful hot in the paddock. Fourth of July, big weekend, big money, the cowboy's Christmas.

First day, pretty much as always, I done real well. Boon delivered me to the press back at the motel. I spoke my piece about what I loved was hardship and the freedom—same as the cowboy, that was romance enough, 'cause no, I had no boyfriend, gray home in the West way down the road. Chill cocktail lounge, cold vinyl and a tank full of tropical fish, speckled and striped, and this one shiny guy fluorescent blue. Lit from inside, he's swimmin' furious around coral castles, under a plastic bridge, through green, orange vegetation, and I thought, he is the only living creature in this room. Leave. I wanted to leave that interview so bad, I almost forgot to smile, forgot to thank them for the taco chips and 7-Up.

I was eighteen years old. In the elevator there's this boy and girl with bare feet and a guitar, touchy-feely kids, but with time enough to laugh at my rodeo shirt like I didn't know Trek talk, like I didn't know Lyndon B. Johnson was diggin' his grave, like I didn't know nothin' but ponies. Well, it was not the first time I wanted to say, I work for a living, I work hard. And then hate myself for it and I didn't know nothin' but ponies and watched how the boy leaned into the girl and laughed like it wasn't an accident when he got so hot kissin' his toes twanged that guitar. Kissin' to show me.

I had nothing but my boots off when the knock came at my door, thought it was those kids come to laugh at my leather vest, my white shirt with red rose. It was cowboys, three men from next to the fish tank lookin' for Lilah Lee and lookin' funny.

"You boys doped up or somethin'?" One was at my prize buckle. His clean manicured nails. "You boys with the rodeo?" Another stood close behind me. The smell off him, perfume. It was something how these dudes were dressed, like it was Christmas, all right, or maybe Halloween. The third was screwing the top off a silver flask. "You need that stuff to come on to a girl?" I wasn't scared. That's the truth. These fellas, looked like the Junior Chamber of Commerce got up some wild idea 'bout Lilah Lee. The rest is half dream pictures, half forgotten, but I recall three white bodies without a bruise or scar and I recall I wanted to be hurt, that I was ready, really ready for the men's events I could not enter, there being rules and regulations. Bronco bustin', you stay on eight seconds, that's the law. Well, I rode these men hard and long. Nothing scared me—not their tight hard buttocks or their soft ripe balls. Three and Two watched while One had me. One rolling off, Two slipping up inside. Three to go. Three or Two making me come again with his hand. And I kissed them all as my lovers. When their time was over, they put on their outfits and went off politely, leaving the silver flask. It was my first drink of whiskey that night against the chill. The next day I rode Baby Doll, I mean I rode her. We stole Cody.

Lilah's voice, sharp, fast: Later, one cowboy or another. I gave myself to their admiration, as I gave myself to the whoopin' and yellin' of the crowd. I could have told the Anthro class, so taken with their signs—drop of blood, porcupine quills, pecker, foreskin of a clam—why I wore, quite innocently at first, the famous white satin shirt, its yoke embroidered with a single rose. I could have told our teacher there was no enchantment, I wanted my hurt. There was once a girl who let in three dudes and later, much later, turned a mongrel to prince in the desert. That, too, was of my doing. How could that teacher like me? I sat speechless in the back row, burdened with my textbook beauty, obscene as a centerfold. I was the distorted image. We went on to giants, ogres, a greedy crone with three wishes who must live forever with a pudding on her nose— our professor comfortable with grotesque notions. Glass-eyed, stuffed, she looked pleased as she sought me out, a marked-down item.

In his chair, James tears at the restraints. Lilah's even, placid recitation: My scars not visible when I was thrown. I invited the magic moment, let my attention wander to a billboard with an enormous glass of beer. Beads of sweat big as my hand. The immense golden pool beckoned. For some time I wanted the hurt, an instant in which I lost concentration, riding careless and fast. Baby Doll panicked at my betrayal—faltered, threw me, stomped me in the dirt with bewildered fury. I did finally want to get hurt. Silence: the alarming silence; sun hazy and one last clear look at the receding stands, the mass of expectant faces. This is what they'd come for.

On the back wall, close-up of a woman's face, streaked hair pulled back, symmetry of sharp, perfect features; weathered skin. In this blown up photo of a handsome woman, the color is washed out— all but the eyes, zinc gray, wide open. James wriggles free at last, turns to see his wife's image, then quickly looks away. Lilah on the screen listens to the voice, her own, anticipates with a sad, knowing smile each turn of the story: The time had been coming: it wasn't the dust or muck, the traveling, cowboys with no future. I don't believe it was the ugly ropin' wild horses, stupid steers, the bets or payoffs. Contests against time, against nature. There was no rustlin' anymore, shootouts, chuck wagons fryin' up slab bacon. I could have told my lady professor how I wanted to get hurt, told that lady who never heard the like, the lively terms bronco stompers—a subculture— used for women as part of their mythology. No dance halls with good whores hoping to go straight, just big self-conscious country and western bars, guys and gals with tough rules for the game. Frontier—developers out of Phoenix and Houston, leasing the arid overgrazed land. A carnival girl, I played my role in a slick reenactment of roundup, the occasion for simple competitive sport made up a hundred years ago by bored and lonely men.

Laid Lilah Lee to rest in the white satin shirt with its suggestive rosebud. Something happened in my fall, a magic bump on the head. I woke up real sore, Lilah Hulburt, in the uncostumed present. One thing: I handed in my neatly typed paper for Anthro, a correct account of Yurok boy/bird transformations, knowing my story was extreme as any tale we'd read, knowing I couldn't tell it. Where to begin? With that class of sweet California kids and half-blind teacher who had never seen, for starters, the magnificent rosy . . . the large erect penis of a stallion or the temperamental dignity of a mare in heat.

Sold myself to the horses, but inevitable as my tumble in the dust, I fell for one of those cowboys . . . another and another, bare-assed in bare rooms. Fairly innocent men, not always nice, mostly timid fellas who switched channels to find Westerns on TV. Crossing fully into their world, because the motel rooms were too empty or when the satin shirt and boots were off for the night, riding for the crowd was being no one. Lilah Lee.

V

In the dark. James, false and bright:
"Hi!"
"Howard Hughes there?" Glenda says.
"Speaking."
"Still pacing the cage? You want the network people fly up? Mountain to Mahomet."
Silence.

"Pre-production," Glenda says. "Development, these people are committed."

Silence.

"You're the crazy," Glenda says. "Get your ass down here. Prime time. They're talking Thursday."

"My bowling night. Better you sell me the Brooklyn Bridge. Besides, I haven't said . . . I'm . . . Glenda, I'm a forty-eight short . . . growin' a beard . . . comin' in Santa white."

"You needed to broaden your base, sweetheart."

The screening room remains dim, big shadows play on the walls. Shadows of banisters, of window and door frames, alluring ominous shadows, blown up, tilted. James pacing through them, jittery. Sound track of muted Nite Club music interspersed with muffled shots. He moves from chair to chair, reaches for the phone. His voice crackling, barely controlled: First time west of the Mississippi. Extraordinary and Almost Incredible. Agent hangs up on Star. Oh, Glenda, my Glenda, fearful trip is done. When too smart for my own good, Nell. . . . Hey, very like my mother, helpless with her flip boy. She'll not make me clean out the garage, kowtow to network mafiosa. With filmfolk—always the improbable move, even when trapped, fingers clutch cliff or ledge of skyscraper high above city street. Always the rescue, not to mention stuntman, composite—stomach-wrenching long shot, close-up of fingers slipping.

James in a hot spot—black silk pajamas, gold crest on the pocket. His beard has come in black with random tufts of white, thinning red hair in disarray. He pit-pats around with a fifth of Jameson's, Waterford tumbler. Look, I'm cool. Anytime now, I go to the phone, call Ziff. Hey, babe, long time. . . . or watch my movies, watching all the darlin' gangsters. I mean back, back before I did my shit. *Kiss Tomorrow Goodbye. Ace in the Hole.* I'm sitting here watching *Double Indemnity.*

Back in his Cube, middle of the row: the beautiful room, one of many, set out as in opening scene. Introduction of closed door, slit of light at narrow window. Movie-dark. City at night. Headlights, streetlights—bar, café, beanery signs. No people. Mean streets as they say, say, say. Danger, this shiny black danger like a grown-up toy you shouldn't touch, forbidden and sooo . . . so wonderful. American Hell. *Streaks of light play over James.* Familiar, seductive as the dim neighborhood alleys back home, mysterious pool parlor, other side of town where things happen. Things you can't know. Hey! I am like any other poor bugger sitting in the dark watching the show. You think I'm watching Fred MacMurray different? I'm watching how he is all washed up—dazed eyes, deflated, start of the picture? You think I'm listening to his voice fuzzed with guilt and pain? But diction, the guy's got great diction? No, I'm gone in the dark, these crazy patterns play all over the walls. *James turns to see the menacing scrolls projected behind him, runs toward them as though to embrace the snare.* You bet, listenin' to Fred MacMurray. He's spilling the beans into this old Dictaphone machine with the cylinder, telling all the lousy things he did into this tube before he dies, like the machine in my father's office. Billy Bray would get these poor crooks and frauds, speak into the tube. It was before Miranda and they would tell him, like Fred MacMurray is telling how he killed for the love of this bitch. I'm sitting here and it's sunshiny Cal. day and Barbara Stanwyck is coming downstairs with this ankle bracelet, reads out whore. Glint of it under silk stocking. Fred and Barbara, tough snappy lines, dirty little lust notes. I'm any dope in the dark, except I am thinking Billy Bray as I take in Stanwyck's tough mouth, square fuck-me shoulders.

Turn that woman off, Lilah says.

Close the door. For Chrissake, close the door.

Not till you turn that woman off, Lilah says. The second time this week I've come in to find her devouring that flabby man.

Lights up. The shadow of a woman cast against the back wall. James moves toward it: in silhouette their bodies face off.

I'm leaving now, Lilah says.

Silence.

I'm going into town.

Silence.

Pick up Jen from her tests. Not medical, if you're interested. School tests, Lilah says.

I'm interested.

If you're interested, she'll die if she doesn't ace them.

It's winter, then?

We've had Christmas, Lilah says. We've had New Year's.

I can't see you. I can't see your hair or eyes. Let your boots appear, your arm with the silver bracelets.

I'm gone like Fred and Barbara. Like the detective in the oxblood shoes, Nell and Baby Doll. I'm gone like Bess Houdini, but your daughter, sweetheart, you lost track—she's long gone. *The silhouettes disappear. James watches, befuddled as the silver bracelets, an armful without the arm, move about the room. The Mimbres pot travels from the glass table to a shelf. The pre-Columbian statue levitates, dancing through the air, clutched by the hands? the arms? that display the old pawn bracelets.* Watch your cops and robbers, Lilah says. *The Navajo rug comes off the wall, skittles across the floor.* Project me, James. Worth a thousand words, Big Sky Country, Amurcan West, slide show of Lilah Lee. *The back wall remains blank. James flails about after the silver bracelets. An Indian basket comes off a shelf. The bracelets disappear with a noisy clank, so there's no telling where she is—Lilah Bray.*

Sight gags. Cheap sight gags.

Cheap? I can't compete with the tramps in your movies. *The pre-Columbian figure floats back to the glass table. The imprint of a body is seen on one of the chairs. James downs his glass of whiskey in one gulp. Hands over his face as he draws near the disembodied spirit, reaches out blindly.* Lilah? Lilah?

Lilah Lee Hulburt Bray appears, shadowy, transparent—then in the flesh, black riding boots to blond hair—stark beauty, her good looks buried under the history of a false extravagant flowering, a lonely marriage—transactions that never quite worked out. From a distance you can see it still—Queen of the Rodeo. Close up, the first fine netting of age over her face and throat is cruel. Braid down her back like an Indian woman's, bleached by the sun as though she has not kept up the cosmetic treatments: it's natural, the hair, scooped body, attenuation . . . what she has done to herself determined to be natural, to remove herself from human accommodations. A distant woman but alive in some system she has staked out for herself, a protective code. She caresses the surface of the terra cotta statue, a touch to the conical hat and stiff loincloth before she turns to this man in floppy silk pajamas, the man with his head in his hands who begged her to appear.

VI

James in sweats, towel around his neck, energy up: Here the business with Ziff.

    Lilah beating a riding crop against her thigh: You say, then I say? Then the business with your daughter, Lilah says, with Jen while you're in the mood.

    What mood?

    They sit side by side, mike dangling between them; the room aglow as though lit by parlor lamps.

    What mood? Business with Ziff? Fucker don't return my calls.

    Heard you, Lilah says.

    You bet, average once a month, like he's calling Blanche Pfitzer in Plainfield, can't crawl to the Bible Box. Once a month, cash-and-carry view of humankind. Multidirectional deals, video rights sewed up in Tanganyika, studio eating kibbles out of his hand. "How's it goin' in solitary, Jimbo?" Jimbo written off, fuckin' mother, fuckin' maiden aunt.

    Better you do Jen, Lilah says, it's your goddam hideout, your show.

    Be my guest.

After, I'll do Ziff. I'll do that bastard. *Lawn.* You take it from lawn.

James snaps his fingers for the mike, which jerks toward him reluctantly. Gesture of obeisance, he salaams the mike. My bunker. No lawn. *He moves toward the one slit of artificial daylight.* In our humongous hacienda, no lawn. My bunker faces the patio, as do all the swell rooms . . . face each other in a squared-off smile. Imagine, if you will, my wife, her shadow across Mex tile, no lawn to blur the edges: Lilah leaves the house, her shadow absorbed by Spanish Revival fountain, fragmented by potted plants on her way to the stable. Imagine the bunker in darkness behind you, audio-visual off—out there a scrawny goblin, our girl's shadow come home late, and wonder as I do if her mother sees it, too. More often, in a long triangle of light cast across the tiles, see the puffball of our child's Orphan Annie hair wobble as she leans over her book.

Amber gel, suffused light, comfy here, you have to see it, don't you, the two of them goin' at each other. You say, then I say. His way out—the skinny window, more likely that door: were he to slam it, the whole set would tremble. Proscenium arch slip your mind? *Playbill* rolled in your lap, satisfaction of a tasty supper before the show, body to the right of you, body to the left. In the dark watching he says, then she says. You Jane. Me Tarzan. Spells relief. *Lingua franca* of love story. Pretty confident I'm not gonna get into some downtown frame, twenty years ago, have the audience up here with the priceless pots, nifty chairs. Honest, not gonna wander the aisles soliciting. Hey, my room, my show I'm working on Jen up here, orphan, born of actor and horsewoman. The way she wondered about that, it seemed to Jen—half name half claims her—she was left on our doorstep. She had a right to wonder where she came from: her mother taking the hurdles, hunter class; her father making love in movie dark to a chit might be his child. *James standing behind Lilah, who sits tall in her chair.* Silent, no longer wonders, our girl's fallen silent.

Mute, Lilah says.

Time was our girl wondered, couldn't get enough Riverside, enough Bridgeport, wondering down at Hetsie's house that's paid for, where the Jesus station plays morning to night. We listen through Tabernacle Choir to tales of the Dust Bowl, Jen pryin' out the lost family's flight to California, short takes of grindin' hunger and patched dresses, stories Hetsie don't like to tell or, as she says, can't half remember. Trials sent by the Lord, she says, except meeting Boon when he was a sailor out of Texas. "Texas!" Our Jen, wild to fit that in. "Never been there," Hetsie says. "Funny thing is, no cowboys down near Galveston. They got oil rigs, bayous . . . lot of French people down there, no cowboys." And Boon, silver tips on the boots, silver tips on the lariat tie, sits on the couch that's paid for, won't talk about that old stuff, but will recall for Jen the glory days Lilah Lee flipped somersaults off Baby Doll.

James fiddles with switches, dials. Lights down. On the back wall a shadow swings, steady as a pendulum across the face of a young woman in hip huggers, dashiki. The colors are off, bleeding orange and ghostly violet-blues of faulty film stock. The woman's hair, uncertain grape brown, hangs lank to the waist. James, frantic at the controls, unable to blank this sequence while the woman on screen shoves backpacks, duffels, a milk crate of 78s across worn shag carpet. The woman—sweet flower-child face, hoop earrings—sways toward the swinging shadow, reaches up, grabs it like a sack. It is a baby she takes from its bouncer. James, powerless before his dials and buttons; then montage of palms and refracted glitter of crystal chandelier across the fragile mother, no more than a girl. Her grave dissolving face. The baby's cry overwhelmed by Tchaikovsky: "Serenade for Strings." Clear view of potted palms, tea tables. James cannot speak.

Lilah turns to the scene: Palm Court of the Plaza!

Silence, then James, barely audible: On my side . . . my side . . . Catherine to offer. Catherine of holiday phone calls and the reassembled life. My sister exposed to a kid's curiosity at the Plaza. On location in New York . . . caper movie, shooting in deco restaurants, a teched-out loft. Lilah flew in with Jen, our California foundling taking notes on the unrecoverable past. Palm Court of the Plaza. *Silence.*

We said, your aunt is delicate.

James continues, subdued: Lilah's word I picked up on, delicate—meaning to say troubled, attempting to cover the times Cath's been out to lunch, or, put it nicely, not of this world, so you might proceed with delicacy and just as the twelve-year-old historian gets this . . . *Literally rising to the occasion, James puttin' out:* Enter Cath, big and hearty, delivers a rundown at times bawdy, on the flora and fauna of Bridgeport . . . Easter bonnets with phallic feathers at high mass, fleshy orchids for the prom from Tom Thumb Florist, the unrestrained sex lives of neighborhood dogs and cats, our own confused Bootsie humping Nell's leg.

Music at the Palm Court, appropriate schmaltz for Catherine's lewd tintypes, sepia tinted views of Nell and Billy, grandparents of one Jenny Bray. They come on as dear, infuriating Irish Ma and Pa routine, Maggie and Jiggs—that reference lost on Jen and Lilah. The Flintstones, that may do it—our mother all sensibility, keeper of hearth and home, purveyor of middle-class manners; our father all bravado, fumbling player in the public arena. Cath reeling off true detective, clues and deductions, Grandpa in pursuit of the Cozza mob, Billy crouched in a shootout, corner of Main and State. My sister had nifty plots, telling them to her niece with the violin playing, as though she held her finger in the mystery to keep the page where the detective wings a gangster in mini zoo of Beardsley Park, runs through the spooky arcade to D. M. Read's. Plots, Cath gave them to the gullible child from plotless California. And a hero. I did not recognize the storybook detective, but sure knew Cath as she gobbled little sandwiches, the hungry look in her eye for Bill's approval. And Nell's. May they rest in peace, she said, folding her cartoon panels, Sunday funnies passed on to a child along with a muddy blue shawl.

"Handwoven," said Catherine proudly. "I spin and weave. That's what I do."

Lilah laid the shawl on Jen's shoulders, where it looked, in the Palm Court, a drab artifact from Ellis Island. We said come to California, recommending our climate, our pool, the waltz muting our frivolous words. "Our ranch," said Lilah distinctly, which made Catherine, the big bundle of her, choke on a scone. She didn't invite us to her loony loom—"Whatzis? Spin and weave?"

"That's what I *do*," said Cath with a slam of her teacup, and Jen can see she's kind of delicate. So, spin and weave, okay—at an address within easy reach of our childhood. Jabbing at sugar lumps, Catherine obliged to say how she did love my movies.

"Which pictures, Cath?"

Her untrue stories, deflections, and what's more when I laughed, called for the check, my sister knew I hardly require she take herself to a vast mall and watch my shenanigans . . . ball under cup, which picture, Cath?

"Oh, James," she said, caught out, twisting for any route of escape, perhaps a leap to the Plaza chandelier. I saw how tremendous her effort: she's studying the timetable, fingering for dear life our mother's pearls, bending to Jen with a stage whisper: "They did their best. Our parents did the best they knew how." We brushed the crumbs from our laps and rose, popping the thin skin of family bubble. Someone said, "James Bray." And then another, gaping at me. Path cleared by waiters. Why did I do that to my sister? Bring her to the Plaza so we could hide from each other behind the potted palms. *The back wall blank, light narrows to a spot on James— exhausted, eyes closed.*

"Her hair?" Jen so desperate to know.

My sister, black Irish as Billy, had rolled her hair in a net. It looked fake, smooth as links of blood sausage. On each temple, Cath had clamped a dime-store barrette. Her terrible hair, her limp hopsack dress against the starched linen of the tea table, the strange matter of spinning and weaving—we were known, unknown to each other. Her goofy smile of relief as she ran for the Fifth Avenue bus. She would not take my hired car to Grand Central. Free of my favors. Free of us.

"Her hair?"

"My sister never had a way with her hair." I stood on the front steps of the Plaza with my beautiful wife, my curious daughter: the jaded doorman, porters staring up at me—someone to notice, but no big deal—world at my feet and I envied my little sister pulling her bulk up into the bus, not knowing she was mighty queer to look at, yet invisible. Now you see her, now you don't. Cath's was a better trick than mine.

Slowly the lights come up to reveal Lilah enthralled with James, with James doing Jen, and Jenny Bray in her chair reading. The girl in black, cultivating adolescent misery: wire-rim spectacles, wild corkscrew hair an unfortunate blend of her mother's true gold, her father's burnished penny red. From time to time, she looks up— then back to her book, underlines, checks the index. Silent.

Post Palm Court, Lilah says.

Their child is another sight gag: split screen—she plays, they play.

Immediately, post–Palm Court, Jen gave up on where she'd come from—Rancho Grande by way of almond groves and Seaside Park. Our foundling moved on to computer chess and ancient Rome. Born lucky, the next job I was able to show my daughter aqueducts, Colosseum, Arch of Constantine. Hey, my last feature film, costar . . . in which a predatory widow. We're not sure where she comes from, but Jen grooved on the Campidoglio, stood beside Marcus Aurelius surveying the Forum laid out like De Mille's great studio set before her, peopled it with emperors, slaves and soldiers, the early Christian martyrs in her books. Thrilled—we had not at that time lost track: from the rented villa on the Aventine, we watched her, a deep child, steal out in the morning to touch the rose-red tufa of the garden wall, old as the looted columns and capitals which flanked our security gate. Thrilled. You bet!—our little historian thrilled to death. *Toweling his face and beard, James collapses in his painful chair.*

Jen throws down her book. It slides across the glass table to within an inch of the pre-Columbian statue. Her insolent shrug. She shuffles to the cabinet, where, among the row of ragged texts, she finds one to her fancy, returns to her chair, which has grown small as Baby Bear's. Darkness with harsh flashes of light, phrases of jazz, breathy woman's voice: "I lived by the railroad tracks. It's a blue sick world." Donald Duck squeal of fast forward, glass breaking, dog growl, movie music rising to crescendo, man's voice: "Her whole body had gone soft as custard when I slugged her with it."*

Lilah paces, beats her riding crop against her palm, whisks it into the air, shooing the mike away—a horsefly in the barn. Now I say cows. I say Morty Ziff, tax-scam cows. Holsteins he'd never seen, though photos of big black and white cows hung in his black and white tile bathroom, which was rather like a butcher shop with its marble counters and slab table for the masseuse to pound him. Drain in the floor like a slaughterhouse. The cows he called them affectionately, as if they were pets left behind in Plainfield, as if the pictures sent to him by the General Partnership of Breeders were of the very beasts he owned. "The cows, you want to write off maybe two, three hundred K, Jimbo?" James flashed the indulgent smile.

James now gives that smile, speaks in an insistent nasal whine. "You got an attitude, Jimbo. You know you got a fuckin' attitude don't make you popular."

True, Lilah says, half of what Ziff says is true. James Bray, a bread-and-butter actor, easy to work with despite the attitude—removal. *Natural, not studied. Lilah sits next to her husband. They seem to look for a moment at Jen reading, her mouth pecked tight in disapproval.* Natural, James' way, and why women gave themselves to his adventures, adored his . . . inattention, each one hoping it'll be me, just me he'll search out with the baby blues; why men could savor his triumphs with no envy. An attitude, Ziff was on the mark.

"You don't respect your material, Jimbo."

Wrong: day I met my husband in the desert, I understood he set no value on the entertainments which came his way, but that he loved his work, the dailiness of making moving pictures. By the time we married, I understood his dedication to the lens and, as a movie actor, how quickly he cared about the lines, letting now . . . this take, this minute's emotion enclose him. The necessary gift of dropping in on anger, tenderness. If there was condescension in the performance, it never showed. Toward Ziff's cows, his attitude: "You call Bossie in at night? As a limited partner, you get the front half or the back?"

Breed cows, profit potential, not to mention depreciation and something down the line called phantom income. Grazing in upper New York state like queens on this gorgeous farm, Ziff had pictures, papers. His cows pedigree.

"You don't mess with the bull," Ziff said. "You get the cow hot with chemicals. She goes into super ovulation. You vacuum the uterus. You got maybe twenty eggs, freeze them. It's beautiful. You got a cow maybe pop fifty calves a year."

"Chicken in every pot," my husband said and we laughed at the dairy farmer of Malibu. James did Ziff—vile jokes as to the frozen embryos, wild calculations as to value of the herd. Poor cows, I'd say, a relief to laugh. From the moment Ziff came clattering down in the helicopter, making the desert over, our site into his location, I hated that promoter. *A spot on Lilah, sound of the crop beating.*

James from the dark: Deal out fear, that's power, Jimbo. First-class shit travels first class.

I hate my husband's connection to the guy—it's like that first day trying to make sense through the backwash of the rotor. The whole apparatus—Glenda, PR, the easy-come girls he works with on a picture . . . Boon off to the T-Bone, but I reserve my contempt for Morty Ziff, his locker room intimacy with my husband—all one dirty male joke. Cruel jokes on pretty talentless girls, Ziff setting them up with studio big shots turn out security guards.

Rotten jokes . . . surprise birthday for withered art director, old lovers in attendance tattling to new little boys. Ziff, whose only political allegiance is to Bebe Rebozo for planting a life-size blowup of a naked girl in Nixon's bed.

Out of the dark, James: I wouldn't give you diddley-squat for mick salmon. The Excelsior, wop flophouse.

A spoiler, James made him out to be a fool—his best performance takes on Ziff—the creepy falsetto, face thickened with vulgarity. As for the rest, when I married James Bray, my mother said I'd died and gone to heaven. Word of the Lord, Hetsie's little girl had crossed the desert. But there was Ziff, another gift from Jesus. *The spot on Lilah grows. The room seen whole, James' screening room now with the door ajar. Lilah draws back the thick curtain and a pink light—dawn? sunset?—pushes an artful pattern of green-gray leaves against a graceful Spanish scroll at the window. Jen, out of her chair, slings the old textbook back on the shelf. The Mimbres pot, the Indian storage baskets teeter; she's out the door.*

Sorry, Lilah says, I've invaded.

You bet! Catchin' the old movies.

Silence.

Go ahead. I say. You say. Death and taxes.

Never rid of him, Lilah says.

Past tense, bastard won't return my calls. *Lilah looks away from the pink light, moves fast for the door. He blocks her.* Do Ziff, goddam livestock. Take the jump, darlin'.

She pivots, hooks the mike down with her crop, testing. Bare-assed in bare room. *The mike blasts.* Golden beans in a basket. *The mike calms to her gentler testing.* The Ziff factor. James Bray, the actor, shipped down to Riverside to hand over the check, not much publicity in that—college deans at a small dinner. Not much money, barely enough to get Site A working again . . . for, as I understand it, James' filmfolk had trashed our dig for the shot of bloody sun melting behind the outcrop of soft red mesa. "Why so angry?" he asked me. Gruff movie voice tamed to intimate, he'd addressed us during dinner, speaking of our California heritage, beloved coastal Indians, getting the tribes all wrong. The gratitude over, I was nobody, teaching assistant, Miss Hulburt. He saw me look long at the Minute Rice and chicken provençal, so that I would not laugh out loud. That is how I fell in love, mocking, fighting. "Because you ruined something," I said. "You people get away with murder."

"Look, did we move them to the reservation?"

"Don't talk stupid. You're not a stupid man." James Bray looked at that moment anything but clever. Not an actor, just boyish . . . a wounded handsome man. I thought, there's something to sift through and recover. Then we never fought when we were married, other than the Ziff factor, blight on my good fortune. We moved up the coast from L.A. scramble, removal from Morty Ziff. I hardly notice how I co-opt myself into the spectacle of laughing at that man. Brothers: good brother and bad, only the fable gone wrong. Ziff knew exactly what he wanted and James . . . to James it all came easy, there was never any quest. I came easy . . . so I collected my Indian pots—pots not vases, pots. Baskets. An actor's wife down at the small museum of natural history, I classified arrowheads and shards. A docent, honest work become hobby until we had Jen, who was happy and fat. She talks, they say she talks in school. *Lilah sits in the Baby Bear chair.* Cherub fat, rubbery wrists and ankles, and such a noisy girl. Words when they came were fresh milled in her mouth, spilled from her, golden beans from a basket. *Again James tries for the mike. Lilah ducks out of the little chair.* In school, they can't shut our Jen up in school. And, lovers at the end of a story, we were content, if not always happy. Until the cows.

Screw the cows, darlin'.

Cows, horses, big difference. *Lilah persists, attempting Ziff.* Big difference, Jimbo. Gimme shelter. So *horses,* talk to the man, you gonna be fartin' through silk.

She comes to rest by the window with its theatrical light, a cosmetic glow that softens her face, restores her hair to gold. Low, very fast: Tax return discloses first purchase of a brood mare, house declared a ranch. I went up to Palo Alto, bought the Arabian. Baby Doll, the hot blood who threw me, half Arabian. Alive, out of the dream my mother called heaven, ordering the stables refurbished, old horse fence repaired, feed pellets and vitamins. Pleased as the girl with her menagerie by the side of a rented shack in Riverside, and then the next mare and a pricey stallion put to stud. Purebred Arabians purely for breeding—chestnut and bay, pranced in our pasture, tails carried flag high in action. In a matter of weeks, broke my solemn vow and was riding English saddle, training to train my horses. A matter of months, I wore the black coat and velvet hard hat—awkward in the fine art of dressage.

By choice I rode a mare, Falada, clear chestnut, as though desert bred, perfect balance of a great Arabian, her temperament so loving all stories confirmed of mares sleeping next to the masters in their tents, feeding on dates, white rice, camel's milk. *Lilah rests her hand lightly on her husband's shoulder, then settles at his feet. They look a comfortable pair.* I didn't bring Falada into our Spanish Revival bedroom, but favored her over my husband and child. Never bred my mare, kept her only for show. Oh . . . my concern all for James and his career, for Jen and the beginning of her silence, but I lived with my horses . . . with Falada, morning to night. Smelling like a rose with trace of manure, I served what the Mexican cook prepared. Seldom a family at table, horsey people, filmfolk. I would try to attend . . . not look toward the eucalyptus path leading up to the pasture or turn to the kitchen where the intercom connected my life to the stables. *Lilah, head bowed:* Consumed by stud books, thoroughbred registers. I wanted to know Falada's strain, every sire and dam that made her, champion bred of champions, my sweet Arabian mare.

James raises her up. Enough, darlin'.

I'm doing Ziff, Lilah says.

Come on, now. My room, my show.

She tears the Navajo rug off the wall. Lights dim. Home

movies of grazing horses. Dull, poorly lit close-ups of trailers, dark stalls; unsteady shot of California foothills. According to plan, Lilah says, the calculated loss, nonrecoverable loans. Insurance: figure the coverage on Al-Mashaar, for stud at three thousand. "Jesus," Ziff said, "that horse delivers a load." Vet's fees, manager, ads in Arabian horse journals. Each spring the mares foaled and foaled. Falada, I kept her out of the action. We were the team to watch, Scottsdale, Louisville—class shows. My husband, not a stupid man, envied the passion of my performance. By the time the scheme folded, he could catch me in English tailoring, sitting Falada hung with blue ribbons . . . understand I was driven beyond sport or dedication, no better than Lilah Lee flashing her white satin with the sleazy embroidered rose.

James, foolishly blocks the back wall with aerobic leaps: Lineage, darlin'. Do the lineage. Sultan's pack, copper jugs.

I say, Lilah says, poking James with her crop. Out of the mare Nejdme. Out of the stallion Manakey. Before it all came down, I knew Falada's lineage, out of the mare Nejdme, out of the legendary stud brought here by an outfit that performed at the Chicago World's Fair. Along with belly dancers, fakirs . . . out of glorious horseflesh exhibited with worry beads, copper jugs, tourist trash in the bazaar. Step right up, folks . . . last of the Ottoman Empire, trying to hold its own with an offering of Arabian horseflesh against the Ferris wheel and Cracker Jack, against Veriscope and enough white marble stuck on landfill in Lake Michigan to rebuild our Jenny's Rome.

On the back wall, a slide show of brownish photos, perhaps postcards: men in elaborate desert costume—turbaned, fezzed, skirted and pantalooned, some with scimitars, lances—mounted on magnificent steeds. It was in Falada's bloodlines, Lilah says, the show ring, the ribbons . . . You bet, Jimbo, like Buffalo Bill with whooping show-biz Indians, worse as I see it, the Wild East Show, those beautiful Arabians in a hyped-up simulation with camels, gazelles. Three times a day, Bedouins attack a caravan, rob and kill. Three times a day they abduct women for their purposes and the women are rescued by Syrians the program calls "their dusky friends." One trick I envied: A veiled woman stands with an orange in the palm of her hand. Mohammed Delbani charges, divides the orange with his sword. The severed slices fall and she dances, uninjured, her bracelets and bells tingling in the hush. They went broke. . . . *Lilah cracks her riding crop to clear the screen.* And we lost a shitload. Fuckin' livestock, Ziff said. The Hamidie Hippodrome, too much competition at the Midway Plaisance, bare-breasted women, Little Egypt's *danse du ventre,* Irish castle, French can-can. The devoted masters sold off every horse for the passage home—thus the lineage of my Falada. "Fuckin' cows," Ziff said.

Would that they were, James says.

This is serious, Jimbo, dump those nags. No more buybacks, Lilah says in Ziff's hysterical whine, foolin' around, it's history—tax reform cows, horses herded out of their shelters. Always Ziff, you said, as though that bastard had called off the deal. My Arabians, a drug on the market. It had been, hadn't it—a market?

James moves on her.

I'm doing Ziff, Lilah says. I'm taking the hurdle, darlin'. "Stay with the horses," says you, gentleman farmer.

"What you got there is dog food," Ziff says.

Arabians died mysteriously for the insurance. Mafia, in it all along. Japanese had syndicated money on the hoof.

James moves on her.

I'm doin' Morty Ziff. I'm doin' Ziff, darlin', and I'm no better on the books than greed breeders who played fast and loose with lineage. Arabians hip with hip investors, movie stars didn't know croup from crap, sheep dip from Shinola.

Baa-baa, James says.

I say, Lilah says. Sold: stallions, colts, fillies not green broken, gelding—reserve champion, hunter class. Trailers and tack, props hired off to another set. Only my brood mare left, I'll never show her.

James throws the Navajo rug over his head.

Leave it to the rodeo clown, Lilah says. I say. I say—that's the deal. And by the time I took off the English gear, Jen was well into her silence.

You bet! Hadn't worked in a couple a years.

She whips the rug out of his hands. First-phase Navajo, 1840, Lilah says. They were good to their livestock. *She follows James in something like a tango until he backs into the baby chair.*

Ba-Ba Black Sheep.

No mike, Lilah says. No more projections. Unless you want your goddam girls, Stanwyck and Crawford. Mean-mouth Ida Lupino, all those bad girls. This is Rancho Real, James, nondeductible. When I came down from the stable, you'd had a couple of paydays with the stars, youngsters in need of professional adhesive. And the commercial. I know, darlin', that indignity, cast against type . . . because who'd suspect James Bray? You bet, love 'em and leave 'em, who'd suspect that guy with the recognition factor, oh, *that* guy! Who'd suspect he loved slurpin' down cereal. Underneath the cool, one more American boy.

You pistol whip? That something you learned in motels from the cowboys?

Lilah holds the blanket breast-high like a shield, its black and white ziggurat pattern small defense for her sorrowful face.

At the cabinet, James dims the light, works his dials. His bunker again, his show, he turns to watch city streets slicked with rain, pattern of headlights, streetlights; unnerving flicker of badly spliced footage in which the girl with waist-long hair, hip huggers, baby in her arms appears again. The film catches: once more the girl continues to shove her belongings across the stubble of shag carpet toward a door. And James—it is James shockingly young, surfer's shorts, long- ish Beach Boy hair, the blue eyes washed out in this murky color film. He unhooks the baby bounce chair.

Lilah watches with her husband, who makes no move for his dials. It's now plain that the young woman on screen with the grave flower face is leaving this place. She flings the door open. Cal. fine day on street of shabby low houses, half-houses. Yucca, cactus, rampant bougainvillea, wild geranium. Cab at the curb. Cabbie, a square-set Chicano—bell bottoms, mustache and sideburns of an era—helps the girl. Her few belongings fit easily into the trunk of his car. In the doorway, James jigging to entertain the baby, just old enough to wave bye-bye: spitting image of his father, penny-red hair, slope baby jaw. James jigging in boyish hightops as the girl and child disappear. Insufferable bright sun down to a distant red stoplight. Close-up, the garish palm trees on James' shorts weep into the mother of all Waikiki waves in this lousy print. The film slips during his wild waving, bye-bye. Flaps at the next splice—tap, tapping his toes—flaps and cuts to . . . phew! professional movie dark, chrome glint, background chatter, piano bar blues.

At least, Lilah says, I held the reins when I dumped Baby Doll. *Silence. She clutches the Navajo rug to her like a child.* It's all out of the past, darlin', you say, then I say, actors doin' their best stuff in B movies. Trapped in the dark, Jimbo. Do Harry and Bess.

Truman?

Houdini—come on now, slip the knots, darlin'. It's your father, Billy Bray, you're watching.

A House Divided, James says. Universal, 1931. Walter Huston. Billy Wilder.

Billy Bray, I never knew. Do the Metamorphosis, sweetheart. Didn't he wear those sloppy topcoats, dented hats, pack a gun to shoot the gangsters? Didn't he have a clever boy who wouldn't believe his stories? Murder, bad girls, duped men.

House of Strangers, 1949. Mankiewicz. Fox. Richard Conte.

Corruption in the neat old-fashioned city, all-night diners and bumper cars. What you got there, Jimbo? A feature film. Slip the knot, sweetheart. I scratched rodeo, at least it was my show.

James grabs for the Navajo rug.

Ziff again, Lilah says, huffing and puffing, ugly body ruling the ugly mind, loves you the way the fat boy loves the graceful kid with all the luck; playing yourself, real easy, everyone's movie star, product of his imagination. I think of it that way, James, now that I'm out of the stable. I think how Ziff made you and how you loved your work, like having a barnful of beautiful horses. Now, it's one boy in one chair with the reruns. And you loved Ziff, the way the bright boy of good family can't get enough of the slick article from the wrong side of the tracks. Loved to talk filthy, Nell's boy. I know so little about her, about them. Summary, like one of your treatments—but I think Billy Bray would make some swell movie. Billy Bray would have the guts to throw Ziff behind bars. *Lilah flings down the Navajo rug, taps him with her crop before she heads out the door.* I meant to say, Lilah whispers, it's terrific, darlin', the white that's come into your beard.

VII

In the dark.
    Glenda?
    Silence.
    We got a bad connection?
    Least of it, Glenda says.
    I'm comin' down.
    Thought you retired, Glenda says.
    No foolin', I got a project.
    Silence.
    Glenda—you still my girl? Get Ziff on the line.
    I thought you were married to the guy, Glenda says.
    Lovers' spat.
    May I ask the nature of this project?
    Good as ol' gold, Glenda. We need Ziff.
    We? Glenda says. Don't sell yourself short.
    Not selling myself at all.

You selling the Brooklyn Bridge? Glenda says. Roebling cables? You sound funny.

How funny?

"Well, you're no boy," Glenda says, "you're just mature."

Joan Bennett. *Scarlet Street*. Hey, I'm not watching the old movies. I sprint, maybe five miles up and down hill.

They'll want you to put on weight, Glenda says. The series. But this is good. This is good you got a project, make the prima donnas at the network feel insecure.

No network. The fat old cop's a dead issue.

Love ya, Jimmy.

Spot on the mike, stage left. Spot on James in his sweats, stage right. Yes sir, yes sir, three bags full. *The mike squeals.* Just stopped in here. Look at the old homestead if I may? *Sputtering, the mike follows James.* One for my master. One for the dame. One for the little girl lives down the lane. Hey, I just stopped by, old buddy, drawn to the scene of the crime. *Bright yellow Cal. sun streaming in the open window, door to James' room flung wide, distant country-western music. He carries the mike with him as he checks out the equipment, tilts his head at the bookcase to read the titles, selects one, adjusts half glasses, opens to what seems from his astonished smile a familiar page. In full, ripe voice:*

What doctrine call you this, *Che sera, sera:*
"What will be shall be?"—Divinity adieu!

Mike blasts.

These metaphysics of magicians

Mike juiceless.

O, what a world of profit and delight,
Of power, of honor, of omnipotence
Is promised to the studious artisan!

Swollen head, youthful dreams, you bet. *Mike politely on.* Every kid actor in New York believed the day would come he'd sign on for *Faust, Hamlet, Playboy of the Western World* . . . hereditary memory of theater, still with us as we grunted our actor's exercises, back that far—the unmiked stage, trained voice, diction coach. Bless the camera, picks up the narrow range. Give Glenda a heart attack: I wanna do *Lear,* another go at Chekhov. She knows too much, even about the dreams, how conveniently they die. Born lucky. And I know nothing about Glenda, for instance, how the fuck she comes by Roebling cable? Once, after a confab, she drives me by this house, Pacific Palisades, "Thomas Mann," Glenda says, head bowed in respect. "Ah, *Dr. Faustus,*" says I. Immediately, Glenda speaks of a three-picture contract, how we get cash, up front, on the table.

The mike pulls out of James' hand, swings to the bookshelf. Sneaky little taskmaster. *The mike hovers over the old texts.* Jen? You want I should finish Jen? Loaf of bread, jug of wine, thou. *The mike assaults James with its fast-forward babble.* What, my friend? Lost your taste for claptrap? Have it Jen's way, *molto serioso,* only remember I haven't worked in a couple of years. Sprung from the dark room, I am a recovering mushroom. My daughter has caught me reading books that travel with me, short shelf of faded spines: *Federalist Papers, Elizabethan Drama, The Lonely Crowd,* and a crumbling paperback—*Biology I,* man and beast on the cover to be discovered in a puzzle of muscles, nerves, bones. She comes upon me with my reading glasses down on my nose, looks at me as though I'm acting. I'm reading, okay, books I never finish. I leave them splayed under sticky Moreton Bay fig, by dribbling fountain of Rancho Unreal. Jen picks them up, amusing items . . . as if an early Mickey Mouse with the buttons on his pants, a Scarlett doll, tape of Uncle Milty. She comes on smart, not mean, just smart the way she flips the pages, not speaking. Not speaking, the lecture to me. Books is where she's gone, daughter of an actor, gone to the page which at sixteen she trusts. Not beautiful like her mother, she thanks God for that; her contempt, a psalm to her pin-straight body, nest of brass curls. Shut off, she doesn't hear me—Ziff on the line . . . that picture of me I cut to—glasses, scruffy beard attempting *molto serioso,* half reading Marlowe, half listening to bullshit. Doesn't see her mother steal out at night, up the eucalyptus path to her mare, the adored one. Goes without saying, our daughter never gave a damn about horses, but her black curtain flutters at the window and she hears her mother on the tiles, rustle of the eucalyptus branches underfoot, high slide of Falada's whinny. Far up at the stable, she can't see Lilah kissing the jibbah, that extra bone of beauty on Falada's head, far enough so with my child's trick of concentration . . . the page, the words . . . she can't hear the choking cry, her mother mourning lost horses. If ever Jen looked up she'd see a shadow on the tiles tall as a harmless giant. *James comes to stand behind his chair.* The shadow, still as a chair or table, and when the sweet talk, the sobbing, stop, the eucalyptus crackles underfoot—the shadow goes away. Goes back to its old schoolbooks with a flurry of attention as though to complete the thought of thirty years ago and failing that, not quite having slipped the knots, becomes dark figure in dark room. Not quite having bought the cure, flicks the switch to watch, let's say, the heavy eyelids of Robert Mitchum droop to conceal the very worst, not what we see, what we presume he knows.

　　Lights down. James at the window, looking out across the patio. My daughter works till her forehead falls against the halogen lamp. I keep track so she won't boil to a spot. Tonight she's wired. Pages. The words. The words. Score off this map, Jen buying out of here, as her father bought out of Bridgeport with meager talent, her mother bought out of Riverside with beauty. Buying out of Paradise with brains. Her head, alive with need, not a maze of gray matter under dead filigree of nerves on my obsolete *Biology I.* Hey, that's a poor little rich girl not to know her Aunt Catherine with the terrible hair worked this hard at the books. And so did an Irishman work hard, Matt Devlin off the boat, who made his small pot of gold in

Connecticut and so did the dirt farmer work who lost everything in the Dust Bowl and headed to California. How's she to know, our silent girl consumed with words, long lists to memorize tonight, black on white, nearly useless words, using them in two improbable sentences so they will always be her own.

VIII

James reading. Phone balanced on the square arm of his Grand Confort. I invent the seasons here. Summer—more of a good thing, hope of a hot Santa Ana to mix it up. *James centers the phone in front of him on the glass table.* It was on a summer day, the numb tranquillity . . . my wife came to me. I was watching in the dark. She talked of breeding while the self-assured face of Mary Astor loomed like a white enamel lily. Heat seeped into the cool room at the door where Lilah stood.

Lilah, *at the door in her jeans and stable muckers.*

Breeding, Lilah says, the years gone by.

The smell of Irish whiskey and manure. I had a drop taken against the air-conditioned chill and my wife saying the years gone by, Lilah feeling as never before, not even in rodeo—guilty. Mary Astor was opening a letter from Dodsworth, her lover, played by Walter Huston, older than I am now. Her face cool yet radiant. How can that be?

Close the door.

If you'll turn off that woman, Lilah says.

James turns to see his wife standing firm in the doorway. She comes to him, kneels, a supplicant: It's getting late for my brood mare.

Yes?

I want to breed Falada.

Breed her.

It will cost, Lilah says.

I reach out for her, but her look is kiddish excitement. An unworkable combination—my sudden lust, her glee.

BREED HER. My wife runs for the door as though there's a stud waiting in the hall. BREED HER. You need my permission?

I could do a Ziff, Lilah calls. I could work a package deal.

She traveled with Falada to the sire both researched and dreamed of, no sperm bank, thank you, for those beauties, and came back, stars in her eyes. The mare kicks during mating. Her hooves are tied in leather booties, her tail bandaged so its hairs will not cut the male member. Ain't that a day at the races, Ziff said. How much you lose on them nags? Now, I have to believe in the triumph of reinvestment. Recoup. Recoup. Recoup. Recoup the loss. Recoup— the sound of toilet plungers that created horse's hooves, or so we believed, listening to the radio . . . Hi Ho Silver trotting off. Now, I say it's winter with the fog lifting off the Pacific for another perfect day. My wife rides Falada with the bellyband extended. Early, they start up the trail. Arabians have, I am not totally ignorant of my investment, extraordinary endurance, large nostrils, big lungs. Think desert, desert of geography books, big splotch of Sahara tan . . . camels with multiple stomachs, dunes, great distances. The trail behind our backyard leads up . . . steep, dangerous, I suppose . . . to some top of the world clearing, heavenly view I've never seen.

It was summer when she came in here to deal with me about the breeding. Mary Astor opened the letter from Walter Huston and I had thought Lilah was packing up, leaving me, the house so arranged. A museum of pots and baskets, implements. *James comes to the very edge of the stage, presses his hands against the invisible wall.* As in a goddam museum. The servants gone. Down to our half-day Maria, a frightened child without a green card.

Look, I'm easy, the luck's turned. *Bright yellow sun at the window. Soundtrack of chirping birds.* I only stopped in, put *Dr. Faustus* back on the shelf. Hey, that script is unreal. Mad scientist sells immortal soul. *The mike swings at James.* Get this nut: defender of high art. *Ear shattering signal from the mike.* Blah-blah she sells sea shells. *The mike keeps its distance.* When I was young an' twenty,/ heard the wise man say . . . *Coyly, the mike inches toward James.* IF you can keep your head when all about you. *The mike dips flirtatiously in James' direction.* I have been one acquainted with the night./ walked out in rain—back in rain./ outwalked furthest city light. *The mike collapses at James' feet.*

Mute with the heavy burden of her books. I'm doing Jen, the way the days go. All too ready with answers, talks a blue streak in school. No child more articulate. Now, I say it's winter with my daughter off on the bus, down into the morning fog that lies over the privileged kids at the privileged school, Hope Ranch. I'm out of here, you bet. The Project, metaproject, FEATURE FILM order of magnitude . . . resurrection and the life. And Lilah's not leaving, not yet. With Falada, saddlebags packed with horse goodies, she climbs to their view; their waiting, their womanly lying-in. *The mike lets off a musical ping.* Yeah, Jen . . . finish Jen, this bright winter day, another perfect day with the heavy weather of her silence.

IX

Spot on James standing against the back wall stripped of the Navajo rug. His huge shadow mocks him. No mike. Seriously, *molto.* How I was born again, or the luck not run out. Same thing. How my wife came into this room; invasion being some low level of concern . . . mirror to the mouth of the dying. How my daughter discarded our small histories. How the moving pictures are made so we believe— even the flops, sit in the dark alone and believe, if nothing else, the process. Wool pulled over our eyes and we love it. *Big shadow of James, his grandiose gestures.* I been telling true. How it came to pass I went out into the eternal Cal. light, got my ass out of the swell chair—no knockoff—out of the swell room. How Glenda is my loved one. How Ziff . . . I'm saving the best, if not the last.

In the dark: Notorious, *title and opening music on the back wall. Staring Ingrid Bergman. Cary Grant. Claude Rains. The phone rings and rings. Soundtrack muted, James finds his way to the phone.*

If not the last, near last: Ziff saying, shaft the networks. Shaft the networks before they shaft you.

I want, I said, breathing into Ziff's spiel, I want . . . son of a bitch never return a call. *There's a tinkling crash on the terrazzo. In the tattered light, James sees,* I see—my story—that the telephone cord has knocked over the pre-Columbian statue, already deprived of its hands and feet, now decapitated. The Indian head with its peaked hat stares up at me, steady, unforgiving. The big Swedish face of Ingrid Bergman is soft, entirely innocent, yet her mouth, a stroke of perfection, is bitter. How can that be?

What I want? To make a picture.

Something will turn up, Jimbo.

How long you been losing interest? End of love affair with Jimbo.

Keep your socks on.

No socks. Movie, I want to make . . . direct my picture.

Silence. Ingrid tosses her head back; full, thick throat, those white teeth; free, hearty laughter unheard, but when she calms down I swear her eyes are cast lovingly at the juglike Mayan body.

Figure low budget? Ziff's high-pitched titter. "Twenty million do it, sweetheart?"

I say: rotten bastard. Continue in this vein for all the years I've done his bidding, for all the lousy pictures Ziff steered me into. I say: I coulda bin a contendah. I stoop to pick up the Indian head with its wounding, puffed eyes.

Easy come. Easy go, Ziff says.

What's easy? Shitzola? Then list my forgettable work, litany of gunfire, car chase, explosion; thumping and humping of interchangeable actresses, all the while holding the Indian head in my hand.

Don't shit where you eat, Ziff says.

I'm unleashed, damn Morgan Pfitzer, who played me for his boy. Ingrid looks strong at this moment, as though she can take the Cary Grant charm or leave it. Easy come. Easy go, yet cocking her head to the side, you know she's vulnerable, and Ziff saying every out-of-work actor wants to direct a movie, but just a fruggin' minute, something has come over his buddy. Jimbo who's dropped in Ziff's ratings, been eased out of the game, lost his cool when that's all that's left of the reputation.

Ziff switching to another call: record contract, digital sound, happy sci-fi summer movie, every kid in America.

Ingrid's face is smooth, so smooth the gray contours. My voice scrapes with raw need: I want to make a black and white movie.

Black and white movie, Ziff says, wouldn't give you the sweat off my balls.

What's working is Ziff's pleasure, listening to old Jimbo writhe, beg for his life or his movie. Same thing. The movie about his father. Actor with no previous record of angst proposes this murder mystery solved by his father.

NOT SOLVED. Shouting, flipping the phone cord in the dark room. Never solved, that is the POINT, sweetheart. End of the war—soldier, society dame, detective—no ANSWERS. For a moment, I feel I should have gone down to Malibu, confronted Ziff with moral complexities, lives that got lost, manipulated into patriotic lore. SOCKO! At the end of the show you'd be in that position, in Billy Bray's position, faced with no answer. And it comes to me this is what they wanted, my father and mother, their careless boy to be a hero, a fine fellow who tells it true. Claude Rains, he is married to Ingrid—I don't want to believe that—an effete Nazi with uranium stashed in the wine cellar. Ingrid, in grave danger, searches for the key.

Ziff thinking: video rights to summer sci-fi, every kid in America, while Jimbo's on—Jimbo directing (amateur hour) artsy murder, pale shades of *film noir* (kill that the first round), *cahiers de*

Cinecittà, but what's he hearing? Crisp cash. What's the novelty item? Cynical actor plays his father. He can see the angle, publicity, stop-the-clock reviews. Get in a writer. Get in a hot new actress. Big bucks to the soldier boy. The camera loves sweet boys from the sitcoms. Ziff thinking he made Jimbo a star. Lucky is all, class act, no range. That love affair over. Why go out on a limb that's dead-wood? Ziff thinking he's got four maybe five projects under development, slim pickin's. Breakthrough, movie star turns actor, plays his father.

We'll do lunch, Ziff says.

We got a package?

What's she wearing? Bergman? She got the black hat, Ziff says, with the snap brim? Yeah, smooth like they shot her through a gel. You ever notice she has those plug-ugly eyebrows.

Fuck you.

You can get the Pope, Ziff says, the freakin' *New York Times,* actor play his father. You can get kiss-me-ass *Today* show, don't sell tickets to the theater.

Money where your mouth is?

Jimbo, Ziff says, you got a concept.

Lights up. James leans forward in his chair. In the dark room, in the death seat, I'd come across the story probably haunted me all my life. While I exchanged coded messages with Gregor in Vienna, blew the cartel's speedboat in the bayou, wrestled with a dicey blond in the studio sheets, the real murder had been there. No fooling, big as the courthouse on Golden Hill named for the Golden Hill Indians, which can't have been their name. The hometown murder loomed large . . . and real after foolin' around, playing cops and robbers. I felt empowered to deal with Ziff who double-dealt even as he signed me on, to place my bet on Falada—that future, to wonder seriously, quite seriously, why my daughter unpeopled her bookish world.

Glenda said, You call this a contract?

Give the devil his due.

I'm into the fine print, Jimmy. Crooked counsels and dark politics.

We'll sign, I said. It's my movie.

Let's get smart, Glenda said. The series. Don't say no.

No.

So much for Glenda, her sorcery melding the classics with Spiegel and Zanuck, so displeased with me she might be Nell.

Ziff again? Lilah says on her way to Falada waddling proudly in the pasture.

High as a kite, I call Catherine where she's leading the spinster life. A woman says my sister is not home.

"Which murder?" Cath says when I get her. "Leave well enough alone."

Nothing stops me, not even the notion I'm the gravedigger. Billy no longer a ghost. Leading man, wasn't he always? I smell his Lucky Strikes, feel the thin lisle stuff of his BVDs, invoke the night he stopped me on the back stairs, that last summer, scooting out to Nell's car with the clarinet case. Face to face in such close quarters, the hair on his chest sparse, white, girlish paps sunken; the cheeks of the broad face too bright yet (and this is the story) ashgray as a dying face in black and white movies. Suspenders looped, top button of his pants undone for the gas, and he put my hand on his heart to detect the eerie pauses and zany thumps that would do him in. I felt only horror in such close quarters. Tell me, he said, how does it feel to be leaving home? Tell me . . . and I could not, yet I couldn't run from him like a small boy up to my red plaid blanket or out to my play. Kneading the shoulder of my magic jacket, he smiled then, it was charming, and turned himself into Billy Bray. You'll do us proud, he said, the worst thing he could say, putting his hand again on my shoulder, gently arresting me: Well, then, how does it feel to be going off, leaving us? In the close company of our breathing: Sad, I said, it's sad. I don't know, now or then, if I was lying. *James up and out the door, reenters.*

Getting on to summer. Lilah's done whatever to the

lemon trees in their pots by the fountain. Together we glued the head on the pre-Columbian man.

Mayan, she said. A god—they had many. Shamans to keep you company in the tomb. Gods for corn and to toot the evil away. This one probably held a flute in his hands.

I'm sorry.

He was a fake, she said. You don't think I put second century Mayan in your playroom?

Now he reproaches me with his stiff necklace of indestructible epoxy ooze. I never noticed his godly lips pursed to play away the bad season, never noticed his face decorated with delicate tattoos, maybe a beard of two dimensions.

The gods should stay at home, Lilah said. I wouldn't have real Mayan. Not as she instructed me passionately after we bulldozed Site A, but with the wisdom of the mended figure she held in her hands. Her face is beautiful, not as it was when she came from the sand pit with no regard for her beauty . . . worked now with sgraffito of age.

Why the Indians, I'd asked her years ago.

Because of the trick ridin', Boon's ballyhoo. So the Indians by way of reparation. Indians because she had sinned showing off those ponies, parading herself like a trained animal. The Indians, when she found what was left of them on the first field trip, were for real. They'd been here making their ceremonial pots and coiled baskets. The Indians, she said, herded like so much cattle by the Spanish to farm the missions, coerced to Christianity. Lilah Hulburt as I knew her was some swell schoolmarm, digging with the old professor in hopes of a bone, a shell, a coral bead. They were *here*, she'd say, the Hupa, the Karok. Her unaccented California voice could not match the marvel of it. Here, as she said it, was the coast where the freeway runs, where the dolphins clown at Sea World and Disney reigns, and out through the desert where the condos metastasize—what is called the Inland Empires—where the greenest sod is rolled over Sites B and C. Her Indians; how the missions lured them in with chow, worked them to death in the name of spiritual progress. Here, she'd say, meaning the ticky-tack crafts fair, surf 'n turf fern bars of Cabrillo Boulevard, here the Chinigchinix staged their rebellion, fled the priests and the conquistadors, fled to the desert, and it was hard, they'd lived off the sea. So you could find a basket hung with abalone shell out at Site A. You could find worked mussel and cockle shells and the broken pots killed in the mourning ceremony to release the spirit so that a bowl or jar might comfort the dead. You see, it wasn't so much this life, Lilah said. Their finest objects were broken for the grave.

When we were first married, she told me her stories, not real personal, of cowboys and indians. It was then she bought her priceless baskets, her bowls and rugs that she displays here in the Spanish Revival ranch. Booty of the conquerors. It was here she went down to sort the bits and pieces at our little museum of natural history, the movie star's wife, yearning for a skull that might ring true—a tooth, a feather.

James pushing the window, which sticks, pushing until it flies open. A breeze in his face, a few gray-green leaves blow into the room. You bet, Ziff's pot o' gold, the luck restored. Lazin' in the classic *Confort,* playing against the champs, the good ol' movies, I feel as my wife must have, squatting in the pit of Site A sifting, and sifting she'd come across a turquoise, so her Indians had traded with the Crow or with the Zuni, and sifting come across glass beads from Venice—cheap stuff to buy off savages. I'm dusting off . . . hey, my chunk of authentic, the bloody murder that will see me through.

Lights down, then James against the plain back wall. A spot follows as he walks slowly forward: Okay, Okay—center stage. EXERCISE! Loose practice clothes. Naked asks too much, too much, I agree. Floppy, indeterminate costume of prisoner, beggar, postulant, clown. I am not allowed to touch the satchel at my feet, a bag of tricks.

Act—as if I traveled from a place where rambler rose, the heady scent of lilacs, thin skin of winter oranges, apple pie and the like, never were,

as if, having arrived, I smell, touch before tasting the odd prickle spike of agave, before inquiring of lemons, stalking the innocent fig,

as if the mystery didn't exist to be solved, being mystery.

Act as if—Mute Waif, Magic Boy, Rose in the Desert, Maiden Aunt, might chance the one wrenching move beyond caricature,

as if I lived in a city where dust never settles, the air white with fumes visible as limbs under rubble, the catastrophe seen, unseen, as if the night sirens, their wail,

as if the domestic discord, the inadequate plot.

Act as if on the fault line, no bunker, no cover set, you miss a payday.

Beyond all exercise, all preparation,

as if offstage. And far, far from the lens—

X

In the dark. Jen standing, her brass corkscrew curls blocking the klieg lights and tangled network of wires above. Then half-light as she kneels toppling the tiny black chairs. Her large hands set them right. She picks up the wee telephone, listens for the dial tone. It works! It really works. Shifting, she knocks the little cabinet. Cute objects scatter on the shelves—an Indian charm, adorable control panels with mini-dials and switches, tiny books with titles she squints her eyes to read. She lifts the lid of a little basket and golden beans spill out on her big black knee; lifts the lid again, silver bracelets fall into the palm of her hand, her mother's old pawn bracelets which she puts on her fingers. Boxed in, voice muffled, Jen speaks: You are looking for the *best* answer. Even if you feel sure you know the answer. For example:

Clandestine. Omnipresent. Opulent. In a clandestine move, I surreptitiously enter the room where my father is omnipresent. It is not opulent, my mother's penchant being for the stark but never mundane. The tone of such passages is often *ironic*, though whittle is to stick as chisel is to stone. Minuet to dance, sonnet is to poem. Problem: When the girl was little her brother came to visit, not to stay. Strictly speaking, he was not fully her brother, but that fiction was maintained. Those weeks were festive with many candid moments of elation recorded by the boy's Hasselblad 500. Joy is not to sorrow as anguish is to pain. Being older by some ten years, the boy was presented with dirt bike, surf board, tennis racket, catcher's mitt, walkie-talkie, infinite Adidae, tape deck, videocamera, and professional water skis. If a child is so glutted, surfeited, plied with attractive goods, he will soon be either an ingrate or flagrant in his dismissal of such booty, bounty. Improbable as it may seem, the little girl was not envious and toddled after her brother, even wanting to sleep on her baby blanket, a transitional object, outside his bedroom door. His name was Eamonn. Her father, a thespian, who was, not incidentally, also *his*, came from the Irish-American bourgeoisie. Her mother, an equestrian, was of an impecunious family of Okies. A poignant heritage, indeed. Problem: plotline having gone to the wars, if one more of the lit signals was out on the front of the bus above, what percent of all the rear signals would then be lit? If x is a positive integer and $x^2 + x = n$, what's the box office, sweetheart, residuals, possibly, probably, of n? Go. Go to the next page.

Jen flicks her hand across her brow, brushing back a gnat or strand of hair, flicks again. It is the mike, small as a black beetle or large peppercorn when she has it in her hand, then lost again, lost against the black of her black shirt or black pants, only to be traced by its high disconsolate whine. Jen's stifled voice, in stuffed room. Propinquint. *Capturing the mike between her thumb and index finger.* Poetaster. *The mike zings, delivers her words clearly, however big, however small.* Eamonn, how I loved him. How all I ever wanted to know really is where my brother came from, where he went. Up the coast in California where his mother lived on a peninsula that juts into the sea. There she painted wetland grasses and rocks, wildflowers close, so close up, he said, she might have been a hummingbird, a bee—and they lived with a carpenter who studied Mao or Tao. I was small and can't remember. How he was twelve when I was two, fourteen when I was four. That was the hardest problem. Eamonn is twice as old as Jen. Five years ago he was three times as old as she was then. How old? I thought I could catch up with Eamonn. How I wanted to know where he went with all that stuff his mother and the carpenter could not afford. He stopped coming when I was ten, the year our father bought Eamonn his second car. With dark red hair and taller than James Bray, my brother was more conventionally handsome. Lineage. Do lineage—out of blarney, out of Dust Bowl, the imperfect gene spill, whereas Eamonn, it was weird how thoroughbred, endowed. Antonyms for mutt, for striving. Weird the last time Eamonn came, he brought this girl. By weird I mean discomfiting to us all. How she was an airhead who lay like a stunned fish beside the pool, greased for frying. They say you must never skip this passage: It was summer when Eamonn came, the two-week agreement always in summer, and the girl was peeved, petulant, annoyed. Only these dreary reruns on TV. "Oh, I remember that one," she'd say, "Gloria forgot to take the pill." Or, "Gimme a break, Sonny's droppin' acid." And Eamonn, my Eamonn, bringing her gallons of diet soda like he was selling cancer of the bladder. Question: How do you turn two weeks into a hundred years? And all the while this objectionable, opposite of inoffensive person saying *weird.* My mother, my father, the less-is-more decor of Rancho Grande—all weird. Whispering in her strident *sotto voce,* "That kid is weird." By weird she meant foreign. We provoked her naive, childlike, uncomplicated laughter much as aborigines once tittered at the camera. The *ethnic* passage is invariably *positive* or *inspirational.* Well, at least this girl sure liked the camera, liked Eamonn to take inexhaustible footage of her escapades, adventures. In one scene she flops, faceup to backside, like the sharks down on the wharf with one more flip left before they die. In another she spills diet soda down her front and screams like it was flesh-consuming acid. Chary. Castigate. Raconteur. I was foolhardy, not quite the opp. of chary, the times I came into this room to turn on Eamonn's video. Many times while my father was on location, as though to castigate or punish myself, I listened to the girl. Weird, she says, as my mother lathers down her mare, meaning she found the process repellent and my father is like weird without makeup, meaning off-screen he is getting old. And yet I might say that our banal guest was a fabulous raconteur for weird means fate. To make the text suitable we have altered style and content. Weird means destiny. Why I have never seen Eamonn since that summer. He's holding the indulgent camera, so I can't see him in his maladroit movie. How I see my brother only in my head. I run it off, the day he left flat fish shriveling by the pool and took me downhill in his car, along the freeway, off at La Cumbra. We did not speak. Eamonn bought jamocha almond fudge. How I knew the day was weird, enchanted or foretold. According to the passage, the author implies that:

A) The carpenter's pursuit of Eastern philosophy is pretentious.

B) Diet soda instills fear in primitive peoples.

C) Eamonn is dead or has disappeared.

Jen opens the small cabinet. Her large hand scrambles inside, flips out cans of film and cassettes, which she plucks at, unravels. She is up to her waist in a mix of black Mylar ribbon and brittle gray and black celluloid with its old-fashioned ratchet holes. Go. Go to the next page. How Falada is the name of a talking horse in "The Goose Girl," a tale more cryptic than abstruse. How my mother knew that when she bought her mare. Now that is weird. Falada's head is chopped off—some story for little kids—fetid, malodorous, it hangs over the village gate and calls out that the Goose Girl is the real princess. How in the end this wicked serving maid who pretended she was a royal is stuck naked in a barrel fitted out with sharp nails, dragged up and down the streets by two white horses until she is dead, dead, dead. If you finish before time is called, they say you may check your work in this section only. In the above figure, a square piece of paper BCDA is folded along the dotted line QR so that B is on top of S and D is on top of T in the cheap motel, then folded along TS so that A is on top of R in the Paris Ritz. A teeny, tiny semicircle cut out at F and Yo-Ho, you got Swiss cheese, paper doll, imploded star. My brother's contract was up, my father said. Often he says inappropriate things, never intending to sound malign. STOP. How Eamonn became a banker in London. Now isn't that chimerical? They say my brother wears braces, underdrawers, a vest. He sent me this inane, not exactly syn. for vacuous, picture book of these royals, children plunked in pony carts, romping with stubby overbred dogs. How Eamonn has received the golden handshake so I presume, surmise, he will buy British, lots of stuff. When I am eighteen, time to relinquish, disown, stop, stop—it's no longer a problem—when I am eighteen, he'll be near thirty. STOP. Do not work on any other section. They say my brother wears and I say never. I say Eamonn will not grovel, forswear, betray. No word yet invented. I say Eamonn will never, ever wear a bowler hat. STOP. You are looking for the *best* answer. Even if you feel sure you know the answer. For example:

    A   Light reaching earth from the most distant stars.

    B   Stars reaching earth from the most distant light.

    C   Earth   reaching   light   from   the   most   distant

    _____.

STOP. STOP. *Jen stands. The film and tape form a black pool at her feet. The room is big around her, bright. Her mother's silver bracelets shine on her arms. The mike rises from the floor before her. She can't move or speak.*

XI

Another perfect day. James, fit and tan, beard trim, enters his room in best of all conceivable jeans and work shirt, ultissimo in calfskin boots. He carries an aviator's jacket, photographer's satchel, soft felt hat; slings down his gear, looks the place over, sets himself up with the audience, molto sincere: We are lost. We have been left, my sister and I, in the deep woods. The glossy green place of story books, sunlight flickering through high branches, dancing in flecks of gold at our feet. Our shoes are stout oxfords meant to last the school year, to withstand the scuffs of city curb, asphalt pavements, and they sink in the resilient carpet of decayed leaves and pine needles so that we bounce along the path as though——carefree. There is a path and I have dropped the soft white crumbs of Wonder Bread so that we will find out way home in the dark if there is moonlight. Smart move, but when I look behind the birds have gobbled up my crumbs that were to show us the way back. We are truly lost, truly hungry. My sister grabs at my belt when she stumbles. Her bare legs, round and firm, blossom with bites and scratches. Her cheeks are flushed, rouge-red, like one of the Campbell Soup kids caught in their endless, energetic play. Her eyes shine with our adventure in this difficult dappled light, but when she looks up at me her smile is forced and brave, too brave. I do not know if we have escaped or have merely been abandoned. I can only lead on, disguising my own fear with a song:

> K-K-K-Katie, b-b-beautiful K-Katie,
> When the m-m-moon shines over the m-m-mountain,
> I'll be waiting at the k-k-k-kitchen door.

A peculiar choice if you think of it, First World War hit passed down to us by our father in his once sweet, once tenor rendition. Upbeat love song of a returning Yank which fails to cheer us, though I sing out in brash vaudevillian to the approaching night.

K-K-Katie, beautiful K-Katie,
You're the only one that I-I-I adore.

Catherine, my sister, trips on the gnarled root of a tree, the scene having switched to a barely visible etching of angular black limbs and gray undergrowth. No moon. No path. Vines reach for us. She says, "I am starving, James," and brings up the matter of my profligate distribution of the Wonder Bread.

I thought—

You thought wrong, Cath says.

Quarreling, lost, we have only each other, so make it up quickly. She, after all, is not costumed in a cute but threadbare Austrian smock. I wear no feathered Tyrolean hat. We are American children outfitted at D. M. Read's, our city's best department store. Innocent to a fault, yet we are on to the fact that there will be no false rewards of a sweetmeat house with spun-sugar windows, nor punishment by a cackling witch with her ovens hotted up. The time is our childhood, before the tackiest news of this century. The place is probably the untamed grove of beech and pine, a mere rim of wild that surrounds Seeley's Pond, a place we are forbidden, though we have never been told what might happen to us here and now our feet are wet, cold. Wings flap in the darkness. A purple, theatrical glow comes up to violet, then raw pink-and-yellow sunshine in which our parents appear at the edge of this terrifying forest. I remember my father running toward us as though to the scene of a disaster and my mother thanking God. She stands beside the county car, that in itself alarming, the black Ford coupe that was not our property, in which she would never ride. My father cannot arrest me, I am his son, but he cuffs the side of my head. I will not say it was Catherine who begged for a taste of danger, for the trip to Seeley's Pond.

It was me, Catherine cries. I made James come.

But they do not believe my sister: neither my mother, who loves my waywardness to distraction, nor my father, who has successfully interrogated killers and petty thieves. I believe it was that day I became an actor, sitting in the backseat of the off-limits Ford, playing out the wronged hero in silence, a silence that held them in the palm of my hand, a silence I'd keep to the grave, and when the car was full of their discomfort or even shame—it can't have been long, for Seeley's Pond was two blocks from our house—I began, as though it were my utmost private thought, to hum, then very softly sing . . . K-K-K-Katie, K-K-Katie, when the m-moon shines . . . and my mother turned round with a knowing smile to Catherine, whose cheeks were stained with tears, for I sang it so well, an exact, only slightly mocking imitation of my father, the boy tenor, stuttering his doughboy song.

James takes an airline ticket, cash from his pocket. At the cabinet, he thinks to take one of his old books, thinks better of it, puts the ticket and cash into his satchel. He turns off all dials and switches, including the microphone, locks the windows. I bring up a version of that day when some kid asks the inevitable question:

When did you decide to become an actor, Mr. Bray?

Decide?

Christ, the presumed intimacy of the interviewer: At what point, Jim?

At a point forty feet off North Avenue as we turned into the driveway. My sister and I had been lost in the neighborhood woods and my parents found us. I was a mimic, a perfect little monkey, and I realized . . . I realized, I could make them laugh. I could make them cry.

When did you decide?

You don't decide.

Well—

Well, there was Robert Mitchum. I'm not sure I'll get this right. Mitchum is from Bridgeport. I didn't fully understand. I thought he was a guy I'd met who worked in movies, you know, Mount Olympus, big career. I'm talking years ago, over the years, and I got this. . . . *James makes for the door with his traveling gear, turns to hear his voice doing voice-over:* And then I came up against a wall, you bet. Been out there a long time. Hey, it's not like playing wide receiver, outfield . . . the afterlife, you plug beer, coach the youngsters. WHAM! Up against these swell walls, bought and paid for. Fifty years old, struck down in my prime. This is heading in the wrong direction. You come up against a blank wall, at least you watch movies. They are like friendly wall paintings all around you in the tomb. Some not so friendly. *James moves to the glass table, turns on an answering machine now connected to an elaborate phone. The red signal lights run their program. He makes for the door. Voice-over again:* Look, let's pull back to Mitchum. *Night of the Hunter,* arguably his best film. I have nothing against cinema gab. Director: Charles Laughton, 1955. Score: Walter Schumann. Mitchum's GRAND, that's the scale of his performance. The voice swells out of his chest, Oh, LORD—he's a preacher—Lord, with his mad conviction. LORD, he sings, crossing the line to crazy. You ever want to see, to know malevolent, watch Mitchum curl his hand around that picket fence. Maybe twenty times, I watched that movie. The walls crumbled. Maybe thirty, I sat my ass in Corbu's torture barrel until the walls came down. *Out of the Past.* Mitchum runs a gas station. In the sunlight, I'm tracking down a two-lane highway. The sign reads, you bet, Bridgeport, coming into this perfect American town, no bridge, no port. Inland California, on the map—this real, other place. God's country, idyllic lakes, mountains all around. Mitchum runs a gas station, courts a pretty girl, until they come and get him. *James sits in his punishing chair.* He's a guy making an honest dollar. The gas pumps have these milk glass globes on top that just say GAS. Gas is twenty cents a gallon—don't get hooked on that stuff. Mitchum is squeaky clean, his hair dark, face fresh as a Bridgeport schoolboy, which he was, Harding High, other side of town. I cross over. His lines are my lines.

    The phone rings and rings: I'm off. Leave the message.

    Off the map, Ziff says. You goin' to Hicksville? My bankroll, Jimbo. We send a scout to Seattle, maybe Denver. *The red lights dance to their silent tune.*

I cross over, my lines are his lines. They come and get me, a detective in the past. Let's get this straight, a private eye, and I pursue this dame. *If I don't talk I think. It's too late in life for me to start thinking.* A dame with a rod, but ladylike clothes, pale dresses, matching gloves and hats, neat little suits might be your sister's or the college girl's you got down to New Haven on a weekend. Giant steps ahead of Bob Mitchum, this girl laughs at the black piano player: *I thought the guy was going to break out with "Melancholy Baby."* Night now, always night. Repeated shots of french doors and windows. The screen's a game board. *Sometimes the devil wins.* All this confessed so she'll know the worst, the nice Bridgeport girl he's engaged to, all this in Mitchum's velvet low-keyed voice, voice-over like I'm telling you. *James puts on his jacket, the soft slouch hat.*

Voice-over: At that point, his lines were my lines, voice-over you get a sense of destiny. It's in the *noir* kit bag along with the double-cross, the seductions, and this motif: past with its dark secrets, future one punch away—*The Set-Up*, 1949. *Asphalt Jungle*, 1950: *I'll buy back the farm . . . go to another country, to another life.* Let's not take that tack—*Out of the Past*, Bob Mitchum, stunning cinematography, impeccable script. Hey, it just happened I was in the dark, delicate, you bet—watching the old Hollywood movies. Look, at that point I crossed over. My voice, his voice: *I think I'm in a frame. All I can see is the frame. I'm going in there to look at the picture.*

James hoists his bag, puts on a pair of super Ray-Bans. Too cool, he takes the Ray-Bans off, heads for the door. The phone rings and rings. I'm off. Leave the message.

Jimmy, Glenda says. You still my hot property? No wisecracks, babe, it's Glenda. You come on home. *The answering machine blinks with the urgency of its message.*

Mother of Mercy.

XII

James in his sweats. He is electronically retracting a large white movie screen which stands between the audience and three club chairs. Hey! At GAS STATION the plot lurched forward. I remember 'cause I first set eyes on Lilah Lee. When the diggers drove off, the filmfolk got to work. Ziff's chintzy triumph, the schmeer, paled next to our miserable scene. The yellow cur growls, goes for my jugular. Saved by the stale gray man. Wife in the doorway. Old people, frightened. I drink a Nehi and ask questions. The wind machine blasts us with sand. Miller. The guy says his name is Miller. All of this recorded later in a studio. Bugs Mulligan, I say, Bugs who knows the gangland secrets, the whereabouts of cash, who killed cock robin. I believe I was an independent operative, not FBI. Old dame with a shotgun, she must have been some doll. I done my time, Bugs says, just as a car, fast black car, approaches, might be any traveler speeding in the desert, but the script requires I run for the hills. GAS STATION explodes. Yellow dog ripped open at his master's side. The Mulligans dead with their useless secret.

Best angle to shoot me, spread-eagle in the sand, looking back at the inferno, looking forward to GULCH's gory sunset. The best angle was inevitably Site A shoveled over, rigged up with tumbleweed and flowering cactus to relieve the desert gloom. In GULCH, shot before the almost lighthearted CASINO, a stuntman rode his stunt horse pretending to be me. Easy shots they put me in the saddle. I looked half-assed in the rushes, happy they cut GULCH with its soundtrack of gunfire in the canyon and those horses playing dead. It was a movie that the pretty lady, Lilah Hulburt, fierce in those days, never cared to see. *He's out the door.*

Silence in the dark. Glint of mike, chrome harness of nifty chairs, dials of audiovisual. Green minute jumps within the digital hour. Red eyes of the telephone. You have to see that, don't you? Static crackle. Distinctive clicks, whirr of reeling film. On the back wall. Overcast Cal. day. Bleached blue sky, milky caul over yucca, palms, bougainvillea, low pink stucco houses, half-houses. Location rickety, marginal. Angled long shot (student work) down an empty street to red stoplight. The light turns green. Bye-bye welcomes. The taxi reverses, zooms back into the curb. Chubby Chicano—mustache, sideburns of an era—jumps from driver's seat. Mother and baby ejected from the car in the funny fast moves of playback. Sight gag of luggage, LPs unloaded, baby flung from mother's arms out of the frame. Her long mahogany hair swoops down over ethnic smock, over violet skin, big serious eyes, set chinny-chin.

James flapping his baggy shorts furiously in doorway, swift little Chaplinesque dance steps. Bye-bye is come-hither in rewind, in this electronic skit which reduces all emotion to motion. The actors, sucked back into the house, are hilarious in their wind-up-toy gestures, their squealing gibberish.

Hey, the camera swivels in the movie dark, catches the lot of us laughing, tears-come-to-our-eyes laughing. The release long sought. Manikin mom, baby bouncer flying tick-tock, fast as a metronome set for the minute waltz. Their sad (saddest to them) story mechanical. Tick-tock. Take back. Unpack. Where we long to go, to reenter . . . unutter the sharp word, the pitying sigh.

Stop. The playback stops, color not leached, clear now as one fine day on the back wall. His face, long-jawed, young, handsome, you bet, luck o' the Irish. Still: the flour-white actor's face fills the screen, mouth a comic scar. Puddles well on red rims. Still, as though James knows everything about moving in the moving pictures, when to withhold the smile, the trail of salt.

The mike careens overhead, takes slaphappy passes at baskets, pots, books; tests each chair, settles for center stage, twirling, twirling; pings on, guttering, wailing:

Ah! What avails the classic bent
    And what the cultured word,
Against the undoctored incident
    That actually occurred?

And what is Art whereto we press
    Through pain and prose and rhyme—
When Nature in her nakedness
    Defeats us every time?

The Lives of the Saints

Observe the dyer's hand, assimilating itself to
what it works in.   —Dickens, *Our Mutual Friend*

Matins

Catherine dyeing her wool in a rusty brew of onion skins and black
walnut hulls, vinegar to soften the water. Her vats must come slow
to the boil or the yarn hardens. A slight adjustment of the flame
snuffs the burner out. Temperamental, it will not come again without her coaxing.

"Come off it." The burner puffs, pouts, behaves. "That'sa
baby!" The moody, ancient Caloric is the one variable in a process
she's got pat. Blindfolded, she could measure mordant of alum,
cream of tartar into her dyes. To the steady flame as though it were
the willful family cat: "Well, thanks a lot!" So the kitchen is alive
with friendly demons this morning: the stained double sink on its
high legs drips on the half minute into a plastic bucket; the refrigerator moans in the first heat of summer; the chairs—split, ill-men-
ded—have strayed far from the chipped enamel table, essence of
kitchen hygiene fifty years ago. Yesterday's skeins, the yellow of
marigold, hang from ceiling racks. Baskets of pokeberries assign
tomorrow's work.

Today, set out as she must live it. In the room beyond, her

spinning wheel, her loom with shuttles dangling, will bring Catherine through to midafternoon, when she allots an hour to her correspondence with the crafties, the sisterhood of weavers who buy her wool, sticklers for the natural thing. Then the draining, the drying. Then the arrival of her particular friend, Mary Boyle come home from hellfire, slightly singed. Their early supper, then TV news, Catherine's mystery story. Then—prayers of a sort and bed.

Pardon me boy . . . sweeping a mess of hulls and onion skins, she sings. So good in her frayed Keds sliced for the bunions; unlikely Cinderella, there'll be no lost slipper and God willing, no prince. Catherine is fifty; her hair uniformly misted with gray might have been dipped in one of her vats; coarse hair chopped in a child's Dutch bob so she'll never have to think of it again. Her body, thick with the denial of her sex, is a woman's body nevertheless, ample breasts, broad beam but no swing, no give. Her cheeks—beet-juice bright; dress, root brown—a square sack, the wool gone harsh in a fast boil. Good enough for her. Sturdy as a nun, working order: working order, dedicated to the day, not the rewards of the life to come. What life to come? Speculation scaled down: will the flame hold steady? the dye set? the wood of Catherine's loom tighten, swell in the damp?

Not a musical bone in her well padded body, she sings, *When the red, red robin comes bob bob bobbin'*, and then a reprise of "Chattanooga Choo-choo," and then, devil may care, *Gonna take a sen-ti-mental jur-ur-ney*, recalling first lines, fragments, sweeping right out the screen door. Hot. June turned summer in Connecticut. Her herbs and bedding plants flourish in neat-as-a-schoolmarm rows, the big maple at the bottom of the yard exuberant, all freshly greened out. Turning back to the Caloric, "What *was* that fuss?" A white elephant, its admirable low flame, aerodynamic dials, and dead moderno clock now aim to please, come on as user-friendly.

Good Works

Today, Mary Boyle's prim in her seersucker suit, authority reasserted in its regulation stripes, smart lapels, ladylike skirt. After Memorial Day she suits up as the school year winds down, the little kids in the project soon to be consumed by steamy asphalt playgrounds and incalculable hours of daytime TV, a lethal combination that renders some listless, some violent. The dread summer vacation, how these children long for it as though they'll be released to green fields and family excursions; a blessing, surely, that they blank out last summer, all the damaging summers they've survived. The air already taut, edgy in Father Panik Village: Mary Boyle holds to the school year, a flimsy structure at best for her cases, no golden rule days but any small thing, the order of coming and going, something to hold to—assembly, lunch, dismissal. The seersucker suit maintains a standard for Mary Boyle, no one else. The end of school now her mission: each day she knocks on the doors at the project with her folders and, as though there were no aberrant behavior, despair, mass grave of the stunted and fatally wounded, she asks if the children, not the adolescents—she's long given up on that smartass crew—but the little kids, are they nicely in school? Has the head of household received and read nicely the notices sent home? Sweltering in her suit today, her blue-black curls stuck to temples and nape; Mary Boyle, small and spunky, eyes startled by everyday's degradation, yet a pretty thing: and yet a version of Catherine, that's to say maiden lady and once a real nun. Mizz Bee, as she is known, reads out the Xeroxed sheets sent home from school as to when Pilar, Dallas, Mercedes, María, Jamal, La Toy will be tested, inoculated, taken on the class trip to the Beardsley Park zoo; makes a federal case of scattered worksheets of math and spelling and oh my, social studies left undone and scolds the head of household in the way Mizz Bee scolds, flipping from anger to sorrow to her own flustered guilt.

"Why you mad at me, Mizz Bee?"

"I'm not mad," says Mary Boyle, just that cupboard of inflated snack packs and jelly doughnuts—lard, sugar, air—sour milk, good supply of cold beer; just you let that man back in your bed. Big Boy, not dealt his medication, has kicked through the door. Money for shoes, Mizz Bee? Oh, in the armor of her seersucker suit she doesn't contemplate what happened to last week's money for shoes. It's something of an early holiday for the inmates of Father Panik Village when Mary Boyle pursues the end of school—minor matters of truancy, disability, disobedience, gang scuffles—a few weeks' respite before the summer course in the big ones—incest, addiction, grand larceny, upon occasion murder—end of case.

"You mad at me, Mizz Bee?"

Saint Hildegard

Mary Boyle, Little Boyle, Sister Mary Rose, Mizz Bee. As a novice she chose to be Hildegard.

"Hildegard of Bingen?" Amused, her superior did not fault her at once for the sin of pride, not in those days when God's given name, her patronymic, followed a girl into the religious life. Sister Mary Boyle she would be to the world, but the honored ritual remained on the books: pronouncing vows you hooked up with a compatible saint.

"Hildegard of Bingen," she said smartly, Hildegard who taught Latin at the age of eight, who testified that in her ecstasy she was wide awake. Mary Boyle, a self-starter from Pittsburgh, seemed impetuous, perhaps caught up in the passing fashion. Hildegard, Abbess of Diesenberg at an early age, was newly resurrected, one might claim her as a feminist saint. Long on learning, short on humility, she named God as her coauthor. Who's to tell where she got the moxie, Little Boyle from an undistinguished parish in Pittsburgh, placing herself under Hildegard's illustrious protection. Later Abbess of Bingen, designed her own cosmic illuminations to set beside her divinely inspired words; Hildegard's Eve is bodiless, indistinguishable from a lacy flower; her Satan a black hand; her God a coil of fire touching the muck of firmament in a bizarre—heretical?—creation. What woman giving herself to Christ during the spiritual readjustments of the early seventies would not rejoice in the accomplishments of a saint who had made of her calling such an admirable career, turning a deft hand to poetry, music, science, nimble debates with the Church Fathers—as well as the mystical life.

Little Boyle was asked to pray, naturally, and to reflect upon her choice during the long Lenten retreat, to consider Hildegard's *Scivias* (Know the Ways), her *Nine Books on the Subtleties of Different Kinds of Creatures*, the *Book of Simple Meditation, Causes and Cures*, her *Symphony of the Harmony of Celestial Revelations, On the Activity of God*, and the *Book of Life's Nativity*. A good deal to contemplate, when Boyle would teach, for years to come, the fourth or fifth grade. Well, not to read all of Hildegard's elevated self-expression, for so little had been translated from the middle Latin, and was she not overly excited by the Abbess as activist, fund raiser in the midst of her particular unjust war, long forgotten territorial rights within the Benedictine order? Assigned six weeks of silence, Little Boyle, who wanted to be good, to succeed at being good, confessed to herself that she was drawn to Hildegard, who would not allow the body of a revolutionary youth to be exhumed from her convent grounds, who laid her nuns end to end upon the earth when the diggers came. It was that woman who enchanted her, not the Baroness who witnessed Pentecostal fires, soared into distant and holy worlds; proclaimed, perhaps wildly, humanity's divinity. Spectacular soul, no doubt, but Blessed Hildegard of Bingen was never fully canonized, the gentlemen in Rome having the last word. Mary Boyle gave her up, at the time harder than poverty and chastity, that she might be worthy. Weeks of silent meditation proved Hildegard to be a spiritual error, a selfish aspiration. On Easter Monday, Little Boyle submitted the name of Rose to the Reverend Mother, Rose of Viterbo, an obscure saint, third order of Saint Francis, a girl who preached penitence and lived in friendship with the birds. She would take Rose, but append it to her own Mary, that shred of her independence exhibiting a lack of grace.

Of all her names, Mizz Bee was what she liked, a pet name in the Village, humbling yet kinda close. Rapping gently on doors, her fuckin' misericordia folders of their motherfuckin' lives in the crud-brown tote bag says she helped those goodfolk bring you Big Bird TV, that shit. You gotta check out Mizz Bee. What she buzzin' in the pucker suit? Sellin' school is all. That's nice shit. Language as a piece of aggression, you got that down, Mizz Bee? You mad at me? From door to door, Mary Boyle in this truly dangerous place, not imagined by the Rhenish mystic Hildegard (said to be in touch with the most important people of her time), or preachy Rose tweeting in Viterbo (home of desirable pasta plates, top-drawer faience), Little Boyle marches forward with her mission, end of school year, wilting in her uniform until she envisions a field of children affixed to old screwed-down desks, all in tidy rows stretching from Father Panik Village to redemption in this world, where else?

Today there is Peaches (in the file Benner or Benez), last of her childhood in a sweet layer of baby fat, age uncertain in the folder—nine or ten. Mizz Bee leans hard on the bell, finds the lock broken and the girl, color of honey nougat, playing on her pallet bed.

"You sick?"

Peaches cutting a paper bag into bad mouth, evil eye, cauliflower ears—a gay item against grungy flowered sheets.

"Where's Mama?" Mama Michelle's a working girl, seems to Mizz Bee early in the day to be turning tricks. "Where's Michelle?"

"I'm foolin' aroun'," Peaches says.

"I see that." What's the use, Peaches hardly the first child to be abandoned, and they know, they know to cover up.

"She's visitin'," as though Mama's at the neighbors sipping a cup of tea. The look of the kid, closed but not hard, soft full mouth pouting seductively at the social worker, gold-flecked eyes and a tangle of dark curls with red glow. The father Benez or Benner? The face of an imp or cunning angel so bent on her play that this woman with her bag on how folks live, messy and mean, that load's a pain in the butt. Peaches, chin up, says, "Visitin'," not afraid, Mizz Bee notes, and not defiant, busy inscribing with Day-Glo lipstick a jagged slash on the brown bag face. And itching, Mizz Bee picks up on that itching, bends down and oh, oh my, the cooties chase round the ringlets on Peaches' adorable head. The child filthy, deserted, unfed, yet this bad scene, well, look at the file, an improvement on most of Mama's shit.

Catherine works ahead on a busy pattern, large crosses bloom into stars—Gentleman's Fancy. She's for plain coverlets on the overshot loom but weaves on order; the forced ingenuity of Chariot Wheel, Lover's Knot, Gentleman's Fancy, never her choice. One thing set: she works only in blue, her secret indigo, and white. The festoons of colored wool are sold to the crafties, as she calls them, laughs at herself being in their number—the quilters, potters, stencilers, weavers of baskets and herbal wreaths. Up north in Massachusetts and Vermont, in New Hampshire, the crafties might wonder at her in a split ranch hovering over Bridgeport. The city lies to the south. Mind's eye, she can see it splattered, an untidy blot on the Sound, bigger than it should be for a run down blue-collar town, what she calls, with a hollow laugh, Greater Bridgeport.

She believes the desecration of lovely streets and gracious parks, the abandonment of theaters and department stores, believes what Mary Boyle tells—won't see firsthand—lets Mary bring home tales of ignorance and crime, circle within circle of the damned. Her particular friend goes to hell and back each day, to the world for the punishment that nourishes, while it's seldom that Catherine goes beyond the yard; once a week for the groceries, two or three times a year up north for her supplies, trading with crafties for linen warp, scutching tools, for hackles. Whatever would they think of the master weaver, perched in a prefab house above Bridgeport, the city she can't go to, can't leave? With their untainted wisdom, hand-dipped sensitivity, the crafties in their heavy scented shops would label her unnatural, hovering above the rusted railroad yards and blind-eyed factories the turnpike flies over; yes, even the Interstate arches above the city—not to sully its white lines.

"You *will* make it Gomorrah," Mary Boyle says.

"Gin Lane," says Catherine. Their one small argument and a perpetual mystery, why she's returned to this place with her meager trust fund, courtesy of Nell Bray, who lived to guess a nightmare scenario for her daughter who never married. Trust fund and loom, Lord, she is a main-line craftie, shuttle flying today in the four-to-three-to-one, one-to-three repeat of a checkered field in Gentleman's Fancy. Plying her prized indigo, a professional secret unlike the mystery of living in a clogged suburb outside the city limits, her raised ranch on concrete slab, one of several models— splits, capes—that seeped over the Connecticut farmland after World War II, gray box with black aluminum shutters stuck to its sides. Catherine works on today in the rooms commandeered for dyeing, weaving, for Mary Boyle's files of sad family histories that make soap plots into nursery rhymes. The narrow bedrooms intended for postwar children assigned to Mary, bride of Christ with her divorce papers, to Catherine driven mad with the bitter pleasure of taking it on her thick Irish chin from inappropriate men. Breaking the even downstroke, Cath thinks today: Mary Rose sluffed the life of the spirit; I wore out the life of the flesh. That thought like an omen.

Repetitive, demanding—colonial dame's fantasy of crosses abutting stars, the four-to-one-to-three, three-to-one reverse, execution of an elaborate draft. Most days her body a machine without thought, like the big blanks in a tripper's head, brownouts after a bender. Catherine was there and remembers. Remembers not remembering when she broke, went away, broke the frame and stepped right into an unfinished story where she communed with her mother and father, with stern teachers, wacky neighborhood types. Never cruel, their calling her to account washed away the indifferent eyes, the smothering body of one or another truly married man, and she'd be their bright girl again, comforted by back-handed love meted out to her as she crossed at Parrott and North, came down Golden Hill on the way home from school. Away, then back to some upscale center for living where she'd be taught—now, today, this minute, four-to-one, three-to-one—until, as though learning to walk again, she toddled back into the unforgiving present.

Today she can't get Mary Boyle out of mind, in that suit like a WAVE's summer issue for parade, not the combat zone of Father Panik Village, and the street names of Bridgeport play like static—distant Worden and Hurd, buried history of Noble, Lafayette, Iranistan, yes, memory-drenched Parrott and Lindley tick off—a perverse incantation. Catherine at fifty, her hands ghoulish green, nails jaundiced, holds her gray head unable to will her city gone, Gomorrah. To that end she lives at the city's border, so that one day she can swoop down, spread her brown gunnysack wide, silence with dark wings the dreadful place that won't die. Not Gomorrah, but City of Brass, its very existence what she fears, what it might say of her, of them—Nell and Billy Bray in the stucco house that was their castle. What the city might tell if factories woke churning and clanging; if traffic came honking to life at Main and State. Or if, as in a child's ghost story, the pressing voices she has heard might issue from the gutted buildings, scary parks. The long desolate streets.

Company

School, school! School is all Mizz Bee's chatter as she lathers Peaches' head, digging her nails in, scrunchin' them cooties. "Ow-wow!" But the child's laughing, flinging suds at Mizz Bee, seer-sucker skirt all clammy with Michelle's Highbeam Caresse won't kill head lice. Michelle's bathroom a chalky Pepto-Bismol pink: bottles of nail polish (muted melon to orchid outburst) in the medicine cabinet with instruments of beauty—eyelash curler, hair pick, callus scraper—and Mizz Bee knows a roach clip but shies away from a violet zip case. Oh, my, Mama Michelle's dainty apparatus for the douche.

School with its juice-and-cookies goodness, the least of this kid's problems, but Mizz Bee finds in a cardboard dresser respectable underclothes and a mini mechanic's jumpsuit, Indy 500 in sparkling silver script. The taffy-smooth girl kinda good natured, watchin' Mizz Bee mess around with Mama's stuff, rattlin' through cover cream and press-on nails to find an elastic band, snap back the child's clean wet hair.

"Ouch!" says Peaches, but she lets the woman ream out her ears. "Mister Tambourine Man" Mizz Bee is singing, sweet words, sweet birdy warble tunes out Mizz Bee's tight-ass talk. She hugs Peaches—clumsy, like a teacher hugs. Peaches percolatin', bops of laughter as she pulls Mizz Bee down Mama's funky blue-green hall, stops at a scarred knobless door, flings it wide. "Da-da-da-Dum," quite the little impresario, "PRESENTIN' . . .!" Presenting, a living room alive, vivid reenactment—Mizz Bee attempts to name it—diorama, 3-D freeze frame of Peaches' family life.

There's Michelle, purple satin hung with crystal beads, hip-hoppin' with Frank. Scarecrows, half human size, stuffed with pillows, towels, rags. Both of them high, both of them sporting new ninety-dollar sneakers (tin cans the child has padded round with toilet paper). Mama's hair a newspaper nest of inky curls, Frank's grungy beard fashioned out of raveled soda straws. Mizz Bee knows them, knows them all from her files. Peaches does not have to name—Lloyd, Paco, Dewboy, and flyin' Frank—the men who came for a while to hang their pants on Mama's bedpost. The child has called them all up, pasting and coloring, wiring their sick, sad bodies with coat hangers, propping them with mops and brooms. Each effigy a wicked caricature, cross eyes, slobber mouths mocked by every stroke of the child's crayons and cut of the blunt scissors she's stolen from school.

Yes, Mama is dancin' like a fool, fake eyelashes flappin', and Peaches tells Mizz Bee (as though she does not have Michelle's episodes with these men in her folders), tells Mizz Bee she got that shit all wrong. Paco was nice, a candy man, shinehead she's greased with margarine, soft belly hung like a bundle over his belt. She's got Paco bringin' home a sack of chocolate kisses, doofus—smilin' at Frank as if pimp with black leather heart wasn't humpin' Michelle's bones. Dewboy cursed her out. Peaches runs back to her soiled bed to fetch his head, not fully rendered with its lurid lipstick gash, in need of Brillo . . . Mizz Bee, Brillo? Tapping the caseworker's limp hand, the kid's already got it—Mizz Bee, her patron, her procuress. So Brillo, when Mizz Bee buys it, will make Dewboy's harsh, hurtful beard. His head will attach to his thick body already stoned in a corner with oh, oh my, an exaggerated male member poking up in his jeans while Lloyd is readin' *Playboy*, pickin' his teeth with a matchbook, strapped in the fat chair. Lloyd whacked Mama and her for good measure, ate big suppers laughin', at "his sweet slap gals." Skinny and mean, better'n Dewboy, Peaches knows all: "Lloyd wuz Mama's cash machine." She's called them up and it's Christmas with the Nevva Shed tree, lots of presents, and now Peaches swivels Mama so she can smell the musk oil on her cereal bowl breasts, so Mama's lookin' at Peaches, Michelle's flamingo lips smilin' that pretty smile says they are both little girls.

And that's not the end. "Oh my," says Mizz Bee when the

child tugs at her seersucker sleeve, makes her sit—kids together watching TV. Not Frank, but Mama Michelle stopped in her jumpin' jacks, too, all watching the photos of Chi Chi and Ty taped onto the big Sony screen. The little boys who have been taken away, first Chi Chi, then Ty; wards of the state, removed in the wake of Michelle's disasters spelled out in Mizz Bee's files. Oh my's spill past a clot in Mary Boyle's throat as Peaches demonstrates with the remote how Chi Chi and Ty are famous on TV. Their large baby heads are surrounded by colorful flashes of light, by music and voices. Now, like plump amoretti playing their own game in a lighthearted fresco, the little boys smile in the glow of Mexico, Canada, the East and West Coasts of a fair-weather map. Pleased, Peaches nestles up to Mizz Bee, who smells the moist clean of child from a tub, fumbles in her canvas sack for a hankie. Chi Chi and Ty were beautiful boys. She cannot imagine the day when Michelle dressed them so nicely, fussed over their hair, took them to a photographer's studio. "It is . . . just beautiful," says Mary Boyle.

"It's company," says Peaches. The Scotch tape which holds her little brothers to the screen whitens, thickens to bandages during the dull news of the world. She clicks to groovy chase music, the familiar wham-crash and screeching halt, settling Chi Chi and Ty into the nifty apocalyptic flash of a Road Runner cartoon.

Saint Catherine of Alexandria

Doo Wop. Scat. Sarah Vaughan scooba-doo. God, Cath used to love . . . used to attempt "Tisket-a-Tasket," Ella at the Savoy. Singing, nonsense phrases, doo-ba-doo . . . way beyond her. Time was Cath would try most anything. Give her a couple of drinks and she was sassy/classy, your Hepburn, Roz Russell career girl. Really, there was that touch of big city glamour. Crackerjack smart, island hopping in the Luce archipelago. Well, it was swell, Time-Life, the Village apartment, cheap lunches at Chez Napoleon, Brittany du

Soir. Catherine Bray, the world's best rewrite: in the end—before it all came down, not *Life,* just Cath came down or went away. You'd hang around her office for the mockery, the wit; bark braver than her bite. Invited to her flat—flat being an English term tossed off? How would the men who climbed to the clutter of her charming walk-up on Jane Street know flat was working class, two-, three-family houses in the neighborhood back home? So they mistook her in many ways, the flip of her hand at Devlin cut glass, her mother's Limoges stuffed in a cramped front hall closet with galoshes, umbrellas: "The China Lobby. Ha!" That was Cath Bray—martini glass in the freezer if that was the gentleman's fancy. Breezy in the kitchen, bold hand with the garlic, predicted spirit in bed. A pal, that was Cath's appeal to men, all safely wed. Few found her out: she'd wanted long term, like your simple unamusing woman, to sit at the foot of the table, lift the top of the vegetable dish with its faded gold rim, serve yellow squash and turnips, not lovers' lasagna, the sinfully indulgent torte. Her laugh—sexy, offhand—had seemed in place for the affair's duration. It was a hell of a jolt to hear her clever lines crack in the wrong places, reveal ordinary pain.

No more Ella at the Vanguard, Mingus at the Half Note, rooms dark with blue smoke, scit scat, new chords. Her own life was old riffs without resolution. After many ill-thrown pots, half-quilted quilts in tense unhomey retreats, Catherine had settled to the weaving. Almost at once it had taken her beyond the therapeutic to the cloth for its own sake. Careful as editing, but there was no page; and no words with their worrisome halftones and shadings. Now dark blue was her famous indigo. Blue and white her loom colors, the Virgin's colors. Oh, please, Maryology—it had crossed her mind, chattering when Mary Boyle first came to live in this house, her foot locker still stenciled for the convent, Mary Rose.

"Blue and white, all I work in," Catherine said. "I'm into limits." Into self-preservation. How they did run on in parochial school about the Virgin's colors, blue and white general issue out of some religious warehouse. First trip to the Metropolitan Museum—

she was maybe nine or ten—Madonnas in rose velvet, gold Florentine brocade, Zuiderzee merchant-class brown: Catherine was torn between the dumpy parish she believed in and the blandishments of secular marble halls. A like dilemma with her name, Catherine, actually a family name in Ireland. Which Catherine? Nell would have to look up if it was great-aunts in Mayo or cousins in Cork. Which saint? Which Catherine? She had been a wearing child. Her father had turned to the Proper of the Saints, submitting the big Sunday missal in evidence, speaking with rough authority as she believed he did in court. "Here now, we've Catherine of Alexandria, Catherine of Siena. Doubly blest. Make your choice." And he read the thumbnail lives of two exalted virgins favored with visions as though prescribing for his daughter with a solemnity he could pull off, good enough for church.

How Cath told that in New York: it was one of her routines and had its versions, mostly it was that no one cared. Oh, not just her parents, the whole RC Church. The saints were bit players. Star system with Christ and Mary, but wouldn't you know she plunged into kiddie research. Which Catherine? Alexandria, that storied place—then switching allegiance, fairly schizzy, to Siena, *that* Catherine who healed the Great Schism. Schism? History was that shameful. Popes taking off from Rome. Perhaps you'd need a quick take of Bridgeport in the forties—war work of Sincerity City, black lunch pails, this patriotic lore—to get the child's alarm at history books beyond her, exposing fake French Popes with their so-called Papal Palace, its zoo and scented gardens, ornamental swans. Well, she'd prayed in the public library for Saint Catherine of Siena, who trudged over gray hills (blurred photo in *Catholic Encyclopedia*) to hector the Pope back to Rome where he belonged. Poor woman, running into plague, patching family quarrels, dictating God's instructions in a trance. Heavy duty for a solemn little girl.

By the time she hit Marymount, Alexandria was in the ascendant, plucky Siena gone to her eternal rest. This Catherine was beautiful and bright, a noble girl, many suitors turned away. It was how Catherine Bray told it, the terribly American business, ahistorical—any old Catherine, any old county, Mayo or Cork. The limited enterprise of Bpt. Conn., getting on with your life so that there was neither curiosity nor fancy. Shaping the story about her name, editing out Billy's grand palaver and all the times Nell would chose a volume of *My Book House,* sit between her children on the brown couch, launch into *Robin Hood* or *Kidnapped* or *Hans Brinker and the Silver Skates,* to be interrupted by the potatoes boiling over or one of her brother's exasperating tricks. Cath a touch cruel, but funny, "the assimilated Irish," packing the truth away with the cut glass and Limoges.

"Gorgeous, rich, bright—think Radcliffe." *Her* Saint Catherine had learned all there was to know in the libraries of Alexandria by the age of seventeen, an arrogant chit: "I'll have a husband who's smart as I am." An old ploy, isn't it, to ward off the boys? "Clearly my saint," said Catherine Bray, a doggedly bright woman who was never beautiful but had her day. Long story short, Catherine of Alexandria is presented with the infant Jesus in the night. Now He's smart as she is and calls her ugly, speaking of her soul. Next thing you know she's humbled, converted to Christianity, which was, though dates uncertain, all the rage.

Cath's chin up for this one, the telling of *Which Catherine?* to a man who'd want to know more, but not overmuch, about this accommodating dame. Gal, dame—she once kept track of the dated slang men used on her—babe—as though she was second lead, the tough commedienne in a lively Broadway musical. Chin up, infectious laugh, Cath would tell it . . . gold ring from Baby Jesus in what is called the mystical marriage of Saint Catherine. Laughing, she'd run it off, then sober up for the Catherine Wheel, sensational story of miracles and torture, end with her wry, self-deprecating smile as though she'd revealed all there was of herself, pass on to office gossip, the next drink, the withering casserole.

Once, she had told *Which Catherine?* in bed. That did

change the pacing, the pauses, entirely and the man beside her, one she cared for (but then didn't she always?), this one more than any other in that he was the least likely with an invalid child and heroic wife, and she had spun off the cartoons of Nell and Billy, herself the unyielding child . . . now woman on Jane Street, a fan swirling in the open window, redistributing the city heat, mixing a distant aria with faint *Kojak* and the almost pastoral silence of the West Village . . . telling *Which Catherine?* flat on her back and the man gone gray with early worry, propped above her, looking down at her pale, attractive moon face, for in those years a pleasing energy transformed her.

Telling of that Catherine who read all the books in the great libraries of Alexandria. Haughty, privileged, she must have been something in moonlight, her lustrous black hair spread out on a fourth-century pillow. The story came out of Cath slow and deliberate—no laughs, as though someone else was speaking of the mystical marriage and the Infant Christ who said, "Now you are beautiful," meaning subdued, meaning Catherine was mother and wife to the child yet famously virgin, and Maximinus (Maximian?), the Emperor, made lewd advances to her, a cruel man she rejected, lecturing him on his heathen ways. He could not refute her and called in his pagan scholars; the serious voice from Catherine Bray telling these weightier details long edited out. Maximinus' scholars, all learned and eminent men, Saint Catherine persuaded by syllogisms, by quoting the philosophers and poets, convinced them of the error of their thought until all were converted to Christendom. And all buried alive, the soldiers in the Emperor's palace, too, plain men and illustrious, all of them martyred. Flat on her back in the dark *Which Catherine?* became another story, the man withdrawn to his side of the bed on Jane Street, groping for socks and underwear as she told herself; her voice, it was her voice growing in anger, how Catherine had been imprisoned, the old story, how men do fear a girl with a case of the smarts. Shouldn't the Infant Jesus have warned her, like Billy Bray warned his daughter: *You'll catch more flies with honey.* Wanting what? Surely not her sexual achievement.

The sheet wrapped tight around her—dog's bark to man's whistle, tugboat toot, but quiet there as a country lane on Jane Street—then Cath sputtering as though the signal has been lost in this never told *Which Catherine?* Retuned, the words are soft, inward speaking. Is that all then, that men are such babies, as we say, and Jesus, Saint Catherine's husband, looked on like a little boy, a peculiar voyeur, waiting and watching as Maximinus invented the wheel for Catherine, four great wheels with sharp, bright blades and ragged saws to receive her beautiful body, tear and grind her into a mass of bleeding flesh. The bloated, wavering shadow of the man, half dressed, moving politely in the doorway. Crack of yellow half-light. The lamp in Catherine Bray's parlor, left on in romantic urgency, now seems to him oppressive, vigilant as the night-light in his suburban home. The electric fan, its sway and whoosh blanking half her words as she turns to it for small comfort, telling how it was the legend of a woman of Alexandria, perhaps a certain Hypatia, Neoplatonic scholar, woman centuries ago, and until this night she'd always told *Which Catherine?* without much terror on Jane Street, how the wheel looked in paintings no more than the wheel with ratchets spun at a carnival booth or a symbol of torture stuck on Saint Catherine triumphant.

Then she had risen from her bed, flung on her robe, marched to the door of her flat, where the man had let himself out, hooked the fragile brass chain against the night, washed up their wineglasses, their dishes, and never told *Which Catherine?* again, hearing her father's courtroom voice, "Doubly blest," seeing Nell's worry that Cath was so in earnest. "Make your choice," turning to find Billy, bow tie and suspenders, next to the silver creamer brought from home. Well, she had chosen not to tell the alternate ending, for there are two: that one in w. 'ch Saint Catherine, who would not play dumb, was torn to death; the other in which Saint Catherine touches the terrible wheel and it simply vanishes. Patron of scholars, grinders, wheelwrights, turners, spinsters, and intellectuals: that is who she'd chosen and honed the story into shtick. A great sin, like the jazz she loved deprived of its progression. Singing her childish lyrics at the loom, four-to-one, three-to-one, she cannot permit herself to think there was a time when it could break her to recall a night on Jane Street, the one time she might have told it—every word. *Which Catherine? Which Ending?*

Weaving: the drafts of set patterns rule out the original stroke. Catherine might be any woman trained in this household craft from 1700 until the great mills of New England declared her obsolete, or any woman in the hand-hewn sixties gone back to slow and earthy, but she's not really of the latter-day calling, loathing in particular the arty weaving, lumpy and often erotic, displayed by crafties cheek to jowl with crustaceous mugs and plates, tortured silver set with amoebic jewels, all of it hideously personal, yet hopelessly unoriginal. She might be any woman of a self-denying sect, Sister Bray, a celibate Shaker, her signature an indulgence, though they were known to sneak a name, a date, a characteristic thread into the cloth. Thick fingers to solid toes, her body is programmed to turn out her skeins, weave yards of repetition, set herself going in the morning like a great cast-iron loom, heartbeat of New England, long hours, only she's better, thoroughly reliable. Infrequent breakdown: what it's all about, Catherine's manufactured life, no time for the slipped cog, the belt worn thin, power failure in a dry season. Alone all day in her squat development ranch, not a high loft over the Housatonic; an invincible fifty, Cath's not a mill girl—Irish girls, farm girls glad for the twelve-hour day, nourished on boardinghouse bread and potatoes, dreams of a man.

She sings, *A mule is an animal with long funny ears* and *Charlie Brown, he's a clown* from her repertoire, but this day's wound down to the dangerous past. She is tired of Gentleman's Fancy, sits silent, idle at her loom when Joey de Sousa comes to the door. He knocks and she can hear him shuffling, retired postman with sore feet, lonely neighbor man with Doll, the sickly wife. Today she does not want to hear at great length about Doll's seizures and sitz baths, the next switch of prescription. Today, Joey with his harmless need of her seems yet another married man. And she hears him go away with his daily offer to fetch a quart of milk, to tote and carry, stuck back in his pocket. Mean, doesn't she feel mean. Nor will she reply to the inquiries of a dippy herbalist: Will blue salvia shrink hemorrhoids? How may jewelweed be applied to warts and corns? Not in her line, but Catherine will look to her famous indigo. Many trade secrets, this one she'll never divulge, not even to her particular friend, Mary Boyle, how she ferments her urine, scrapes the dry indigo into this chamber lye, simmers it with the doors and windows flung open. The content of the ironstone pot under her bed, sealed in layers of plastic, has arrived at a state of perfect, pre-aniline authenticity. Mean as sulfur and molasses, the lost recipe of Catherine's craft: stirring her brew brings her back to the sustaining tasks of the day, and she does love to think of the lady who'll pay hundreds for Gentleman's Fancy, a woman so pleased with her purchase she draws the sweetly pungent coverlet right up to her postcolonial nose.

Evensong

Thank God, the slam of Mary's brakes, next the soft thud of the unruly screen door. "Finishing off," Catherine calls.

Mary Boyle calls back; "I'm fine," though she's not been asked. "Fine!"

Catherine discovers her—rumpled, standing aimlessly behind big sacks of raw wool. The seersucker suit not charmed today; honeymoon with school days over, no doubt, the hard season of knife fights, filthy hypodermic needles, burned babies set in. Then Mary slaps the newspaper against her narrow hip, flings it on the kitchen table among the fluttering onion skins and tumbling walnut shells. The *Bridgeport Post,* banished from this house, is folded carefully to some feature, not front page news.

"You might as well," says Mary. "You better. . . ." She who tidies her sentences.

"Read that rag?" Catherine says.

"You'd better."

"If you can't tell me what they're up to in that hellhole," says Catherine, "I'll start supper." And so marches in her splayed Keds to the refrigerator where last night's roast chicken awaits them and the half bottle of Blanc de Blanc. Catherine's glass and Mary's glass; she sets them out hoping the domestic ritual will trigger their ordinary evening of comforts and evasions. The *Post* says otherwise, though she does not read a word. Mary, wilted blouse, shapeless suit, confusion gone out of her, stands at the back of a broken kitchen chair as though it's the altar rail, nun in mufti.

"Have they killed each other off down there?" says Cath.

"Best you sit down."

Catherine does as she is told. *James Bray, the actor, will return to the haunts of his childhood. Reached at his California ranch, the rumor . . .* Haunts! Please, Catherine knows this snappy provincial journalism. Rumor! James plans a *major motion picture* in Bridgeport. *Claiming previous commitments, Bray would not confirm, a project under development involving one or another notorious murder . . .* So it's more than an unsettling phone call, more than his passing fancy. The heart's gone out of her. *One or another notorious.* Cath might well be at the round dining room table, James not revealing his hand. She reads on: his admission of *a sister in the area.* There follows the summary of his career, a file called up two or three times a year, and brief misinformation on their father—*on the force from 1933 until his death.*

"He was county," Catherine says to Mary Boyle. "My father was courthouse." But that's not the hurt of it: "*Twenty-nine* until his death, and he was a goddam legend, Billy Bray."

"I don't know," Mary says.

"*Notorious.* Do we need the remake in a punk town with gangsters?"

"I don't know," Mary says.

"Do we need my father dished up in brass buttons and a billy club?"

"I don't know." Pat-patting Catherine's monstrous chartreuse hand, Mary wonders why she brought the paper home, home being what it is. Why is it necessary to instruct her friend? Mizz Bee with a hangover from her days with the doped and self-deluded. Mizz Bee insisting on reality when she's fallen head over sensible heels for Peaches' truant dream, lied to the computer on Golden Hill Street, actually deleted the child's name as though to abduct her from Michelle's dead-end drama in Father Panik Village.

Catherine's bark of laughter. "A sister in the area. Now isn't that the limit?"

"I don't know," Mary Boyle says blankly. She feels blank, not the sharp woman who stripped mod theology of its glamour as she opted out of the convent, not the wily social worker who can milk the dry teat of the city budget. Cut-and-dried dumb, like Catherine's weeds and pods; Catherine who sweeps, cooks, weaves while she meets the world totin' her bag—"What ya got there, Mizz Bee? Pro-files, histries—all that shit, the dem-o-graphics?" Yet on Catherine she has the thinnest of files, bare bones of a story, that the family came from these parts, that the father cut a figure, that James Bray is the face seen in the dark intimacy of a movie house. Along with millions, she's taken the screen's enlargement of near-sighted blue eyes, cracked bone in the nose, sharp cut of the jaw for offbeat handsome. It was a treat to drive to the mall in the convent station wagon, one of those transactions with the culture: reject Disney, steal, naughty girls, into the forbidden movie, watch James Bray mount . . . motorcycle or naked woman. No hurry—he was famous for it—confident, the kind of guy they would have wanted, confessing to it as they thrilled to the further treat of hot fudge sundaes. She had lived in this house with Catherine for months before she knew James of the discarded childhood, James of two wives and panoramic views of the Pacific, was that James who looked down from the Big Screen with his sly smile and, mightily amused, pegged Sister Mary Rose as an uncertain virgin.

"Yes, *that* James," Catherine had said. "I haven't laid eyes on him in years." Closing the books as she liked to do, as Mary Boyle favored it, so they lived by the day's cases, the day's dyes and hank of wool. Wasn't that terror enough? Mary had been stabbed in her small breast with a nail file, spit upon, tires slashed, mugged by a pack of children. Catherine could weep over a flaw in her patterns as though she still believed in mortal sin.

"Would you think it was James?" Catherine flaps the picture of her brother with a trim salt-and-pepper beard, shrugs off Mary's touch.

"How the hell would I know?" Wounded, though she'd known Bray at once, but how the hell would Mary Boyle know why men grow beards in middle age to look like Freud or Willie Nelson, some important dude, Fu Manchu, General Grant. Any more than she'd know why a woman opens the door to the man who beat her, or know an addict's fingers digging into flesh, or know the childish inattention of girls like Michelle who walk out on their babies. And thinks she knows just how much she doesn't know, moving quick down the hall to her narrow room, where she shucks the seersucker suit, stretches out on her neat bed made up with a coverlet Catherine has woven. Spare here, spare as her own file: a good girl not fulfilled by goodness, one way she sees her departure from the convent. It was safe, far too safe: one answer to justify her embrace of evil, she uses that word now for misery in the Village.

Once, teaching grade school, Sister Mary Rose had been at a loss for the holiday pageant and resorted to a Samuel French script of *A Christmas Carol.* The Ghosts of Christmas Past and Christmas Yet To Come had little appeal to children of good family glutted with reruns of interstellar adventure. That poor folk, all those Cratchits, should be grateful for a roast goose was inconceivable. Then she had found a picture of Charles Dickens, quill pen in hand over blank pages, dreaming his characters, wicked and good: Marley, his old face ravaged with loneliness and greed; Tiny Tim an angel at death's door. She had needed this illustration as much as the children to get the pathos of this nearly tragic story. Now it seems as if Michelle with her hard brown boobs, her satin flash, surrounded by pimps and dopesters, floats out of the ludicrous tote bag, the very papers of Mizz Bee's folders in angry disarray, spewing out the characters of Father Panik Village . . . the downy altar boy, lean athlete, girls fresh from the islands, their heads gasping above water in a sea of emaciated addicts; the amputated diabetic, gross, helpless among known killers and petty thieves; good men beached in their lives; good women dependent on luck or Hallelujah . . . all toppled on one another—a crowd scene of hell, shoving, pushing to dissolution, a solid mass of limbs, bodily parts . . . from her neat updated file, there rises a disembodied baby's head, a glistening shaved skull, here an eyelid peeled, there engorged lips of vagina, moist heart throbbing—bones, bones, rattling string of dry vertebrae, broken dish of pelvis. The computer printouts shredded so that there are no stories. No hecklers . . . what she totin'? Mizz Bee's files snowing, snowing on the crabgrass and chickweed in asphalt cracks and on Mizz Bee unable to teach her class, unable to direct the skits of Father Panik Village. Yet she is determined, her sweet unaging face—like any number of Dickens' child-women at bedsides, gravesides—quivers with the effort to know.

Mizz Bee out looking for trouble. Today she has found it in the inventions of a plump picture-book waif and the photo of a movie star. What can she know of Peaches, alone now in 4C, behind an unlocked door, with Kentucky Fried and the grape soda she begged for? Mizz Bee wondering if the child has finished the dreadlocks on Lloyd, on Dewboy the Brillo beard, if Chi Chi and Ty, still taped to the Sony screen, are enshrined in the evening game show. She won't tell Catherine, her particular friend, that she's deleted Peaches, cut her out of the ugly system. What can she know of

James Bray? Publicity notices: profile of some Hollywood liberal, but that might be some other guy, Redford or Sam Shepard, with horses and a nifty wife.

Riverside Drive

In the sprawling apartment on Riverside Drive where Catherine Bray met up with Mary Rose Boyle, someone had hung a Tiepolo print of Mary Magdalene being assumed into heaven, or so it said: "The Assumption of the Magdalene, Giambattista Tiepolo, 18th C." Brought here by an exile out of a rectory or convent as artifact from home, tacked up on the kitchen wall, the drawing's faint inky strokes and pale gouache browns were lost in the muddle of pots and pans, unmatched dishes of former lives, bright steel sieves, fancy double boilers for ambitious beginners. In this halfway house it was mostly instant coffee, jug wine, order-in Chinese or pizza. Catherine had looked long at the print that no one owned. Magdalene is collapsed into the arms of ministering friends, winged angels and a putto. They swirl around her body in rhythmic exultation. She is central. She is earthbound, still young, beautiful and presumably dead, eyes shut by death, but the luxuriant hair spilling on creamy paper is seductively alive. Her plain garment, disrupted by much reverential care, reveals bare breasts, naked leg, a shapely thigh. A show of flesh, Flora Dora girl. They can't lift her, not to a Tiepolo ceiling, never mind the heavenly realm, she is so weighted with her story and her name.

On Riverside Drive, Catherine Bray came to live among the floating population of men and women, mostly Catholics—the divorced stripped of their church, ex-Jesuits and nuns, their commitment fading like the final guitar strums of a folk mass. Devotion and debauchery: she'd said that about their curriculum of self-discovery. Endless late-night confessions, yet histories foreshortened into nicely edited CVs for the life to come. In this crowd, she was the dresser, knew the Upper West Side bars, the "family" restaurants of Little Italy, what remained of her jazz clubs in the city. That apartment a maze of passageways, deadending in bedrooms and toilets. The many doors of French farce, but with such earnest sexual endeavors. Cath played the permissive housemother. She wanted none of their games.

And there was Mary Boyle, who as a child of the sixties had imagined the convent as an exciting place to be, all systems breaking down, she'd be on the ramparts, though of course protected, so. . . . So, she hadn't fully understood her motives and the system had been in place for two thousand years. It allowed for the foot-stamping petulance of your Little Boyles over matters of colonial wars and racial violence, just as it had once allowed, with what largesse, homage to Catherine of Alexandria until that legend became somewhat overwrought.

That Catherine was depicted too ardently as the patron of the University of Paris; the *prefecteurs*, not a woman among them, made use of her anti-authoritarian stand. Students pinned the red ribbon of Catherine to their shirts and she was found to be a certain Hypatia or no one. Just as the other Catherine, the dyer's daughter of Siena, shuttle diplomat to rival Maeterlinck, Talleyrand, our own Henry Kissinger, got knocked out of the ring. They matched her against Francis of Assisi, a mystic heavyweight. The Dominicans in Catherine's corner, while the Franciscans . . . it was a matter of building funds, the chapels to Catherine having sprung up like strip malls, cutting into Franciscan turf. So it was ended by decree, that cult of that Saint Catherine. Francis, a blue chip in the long run, Christlike with his rough habit, feeding Umbrian wolves from his hand, saluting Lady Poverty, lying comfortably with Sister Death. Tricky investments in which a saintly stock rose with the value of women's submission, declined with a soft market in visions.

So who'd blame Little Boyle, not holding to her spiritual course, when, past the middle of the twentieth century, large heart in small body, surfeit of *humanitas,* all she had was zeal—not listed as a virtue? Who'd fault her for the next healthy step in the direction of Father Panik Village? A backstairs route to martyrdom? Could be, though no saint she——on Riverside Drive. Catherine Bray watched the girl's inept flirtations, sidling up to Moore and Doyle, all three delighting in their gaudy unisex sweatsuits after the clerical garb. Mary Rose going after her man as though completing another assignment from the Columbia School of Social Work and she landed Tim Doyle for a week or two while their exploratory passion ran its course. Confused, wings clipped, Little Boyle played Judy Collins ("Hard Lovin' Loser"), James Taylor ("Lonesome Road") fifty times each, then the heartbreak was over. Call it a miracle, Catherine thought, the girl's a virgin.

On Riverside Drive, Mary Boyle turned to Catherine as though to learn, what better model, from the life of an experienced woman. To this warm night, pedaling with a vengeance at her wheel, Cath can't say what cautionary tale she told the girl, or why Mary Rose wound round her spent heart, strong as three-ply thread.

Craft

In Tiepolo's *Assumption of the Magdalene*, white bone protrudes from under the dead saint's garment. Upon closer inspection, it's not bone but a twisted foot. Whose foot Catherine could not say, for Magdalene is seen laid out complete in her swoon and all her angelic followers or early Christian friends can be accounted for limb by limb within the crests and ripples of their sumptuous garments. Her dress is scant and plain. Though they hoist her upper body, Magdalene's hips lie flat, grown into the ground, no room for another's leg beneath her, unless . . . unless it is the foot of Christ this harlot washed with tears, dried with her hair, anointed with perfume.

Surely it's His foot, toes pointing toward the pearly gates.

His foot turned toward us with an earthy sole, worn by dry hard paths, jutting rocks and roots, a place Tiepolo rendered with a dusty roadside bush, a scrub olive that offers no shade. Not scenery, a landscape of grubby pilgrims' journeys—on foot. That foot, if it's Christ's with the toes articulated as swollen and crabbed, is attached to Magdalene, so she's a freak like the Polynesian princess with three breasts, Scots piper with cyclops eye, Chang and Eng, the dog-faced boy—though a freak of art, not nature.

On Riverside Drive, that murky print on the wall—reduced, ill reproduced, lost in the culinary litter, whoever hung it long gone from the training camp. Catherine Bray was on her way out, but didn't know where. No more Jane Street. No more stand-up comic in the sprawling Luce empire. Away to a place this time of her own choosing. She had been missing her first attempts at the weaving, the satisfaction of making the day's work grow, work of her making. Living among men and women who courted extravagant transformations, Catherine imagined the small balanced step to the present. One day she comes out of her room where she line edits Americana—summary texts on the Gold Rush, robber barons, Copperheads, Reconstruction—working free-lance, how her fellow boarders admired that term, one picture book after another: Catherine fears these facile histories will soon catch up with her. And someone has hung a plastic bamboo scroll: SZECHUAN PANDA COCK-TAILS FREE DELIVERY, a garish thing with stupefied red and gray horses by an electric-blue stream, hocks and heads of these creatures jammed together in misunderstanding of Western perspective. Poor Magdalene can't compete under her film of kitchen grease.

Washing the kinky Assumption, ammonia wakes Catherine like smelling salts from a faint. There, in the lower right-hand corner, fallen away from the central drama, is a skull. For months she's taken it to be an extra stone. A white skull, exquisitely drawn and pleasant enough, that says, after all, we're only human. What Catherine has been missing is the feel of rough wool, the lively beat of the treadle without personal demands, yet in marriage of heart to hand, the daily challenge. That night Catherine packs one bag with her few belongings.

Close to her old hometown, she sets up as a spinner and weaver, trades she has learned when last away in a house not of her choosing, the most peaceful time of her life watching the patterns emerge. A novice, but not for long; it's in the nature of craft to be mastered, and this Catherine does, working early and late, until in a few short years she is celebrated among the crafties, and somewhat mysterious. There's nothing mysterious about her craft, the warp and web of it, trusted tools and re-creation of design. Buonaparte's March, Freemason's Folly, Cloudless Beauty are dazzling to us in their intricacy, but then Catherine is a master; her stained fingers fly as she threads the loom. Her bale of a body sways with the grace of a dancer. Near magic, her down-home proficiency, bringing life to repetitive abstractions of pine trees, blossoms and stars. *B-I-N-G-O and Bingo was his name*, singing her nonsense as she comes to the end of yet another coverlet. Her blue strands, her white strands, securely tied off.

Art

Peaches thinking music, how there should be music. Can't find the boom box, knowin' it's been traded like the mess of gold chains Mama buys and sells and buys again. Shit, there's this honky radio, pink plastic—all over beach umbrellas like she's supposed to lie on the sand, salsa pulsin', while Michelle car-hops down at Seaside. Batteries low, but she can kinda get it goin'. Should be Latino dance hall, even rock 'n' roll. These songs are slurpin'—(Sinatra, Mel Torme, crooners Peaches doesn't know), but music. She plays a flashlight over Frank and Mama slow-dancin', not clubhouse jive. And high-beams Dewboy who cursed her, in the corner good an' dead.

Peaches would know why the skull has tumbled off center

in Tiepolo's drawing; because it is perfect there, like the lime-green Nerf ball she now places at the very edge of the speckled carpet so it looks like Chi Chi and Ty were foolin' and dropped it. She would never question Christ's disembodied foot with its knobby ankle bone and puffy toes. That's how you make it, like the raggedy tree she's making, ripping up ol' clothes—Mama's, her baby brothers' left behind, and her very own white lace First Communion—tying strips on the Nevva Shed Christmas tree till it's hung full, blooming with . . . she could never say prayers, wishes, any more than Peaches Benner or Benez could describe the skull as standard iconography for Magdalene, a woman who thought hard about her sins. Who cares? Peaches knows what Tiepolo knew: draw it in, lift the crayon, stand back when a raggedy tree is finished. Maybe finished, for her own work contains an ongoing narrative which she manipulates with a play of light or song, a rearrangement of figures. No one has taken Peaches to a museum where pictures and tableaux are set, once and for all, behind glass.

No one has taken Peaches to the Akeley Hall of African Mammals in the Museum of Natural History. She has never seen a diorama other than her own, and Akeley's *Gorilla, Gorilla* is the world's most famous, a happy domestic scene. The dominant male beats his chest; female collapsed in the wings, chomping, ever chomping leaves which hang untidily out of her damp mouth. From Mom's withered leather breasts, we assume that adorable baby gorilla is weaned. So real—the dirt, dry twigs, and moss imported from the Belgian Congo. Vines hung with bedstraw skillfully drape the scene, the habitat as it is properly called—sealed with smudged glass, framed all around with black marble. The gorillas are not stuffed; their hides are stretched over clay subsculptures of gorilla, each nostril bulge, furrow of slant brow, ripple of Dad's musculature absolutely real, in a process conceived by Carl Akeley, who died in West Africa, where his gorillas are posed in his instructive story. So real, two extras of the extended gorilla family climb onto the brightly lit set, into an always nice day.

It is all wonderfully correct, worth Akeley's life, hacking through the jungle in 1926, no antibiotics and a fever. He'd moved up from useful taxidermist to romantic explorer wanting the *Africa, Africa* of his dioramas superreal: black and white photos to work from, casts of leaves and tree bark. The rhinos *en famille*, the giraffe's watering hole, Lybian desert, confrontation of ostrich and warthog already accomplished, there remained his most arduous dream—gorillas.

The accuracy of the trampled foreground in *Gorilla, Gorilla* is played off against the false shimmer of leaves (silk or fine rag paper) of the overhanging trees, here on the middle cliff where the raspberries (wax or painted clay) will never ripen. The background painting of Mount Mikino and its valley, curved though it is toward 3-D, is calendar art, no brushstroke evident, impossible attempt at wide-lens photographic. The two volcanoes of Kivi are represented: benign lavender clouds float from their gentle mouths, real as nature improved on.

It rained every day of the gorilla group expedition. The volcanoes spewed angry fire, molten lava. The bearers took ill and sensibly ran away. Carl Akeley should lie in his diorama, displayed on a litter, wasted by his Africa. The heavens should open behind the glass which encloses his moldering fantasy, for it's not Africa the visitors to the museum look upon, but an American landscape of bright mornings, of time stopped at the innocent moment of discovery before guiltless acquisition, before the gorillas looked back at us in furious recognition.

Peaches stops the music, places the half-eaten bucket of Kentucky Fried before the flickering rim of late movie. There are night noises in the hall, scuffling, intermittent cries. In this first summer heat, more than the usual sirens convene on the project. The whirling red spot of a squad car against the broken windows of 4C make her figures shift and sway in a light show. She gives Lloyd in the fat chair a torn book instead of his limp magazine; deals Paco, that doofus, a crusted chicken wing; turns pimpin' Frank away from Mama; kisses the slick photos of her brothers. Peaches steps back from her effort: her rag tree needs maybe a few dark tatters of T-shirt or jeans. And she wonders at its beauty, worries that it will not be finished ... for who? What occasion? ... follows the flashlight down the eerie blue-green stream of Mama's hall. And so to bed in Father Panik Village.

Once Lilah Bray could tell about the rag tree, that it is found in cultures as disparate as fourth-century Celtic and contemporary Haitian, that the human scent on cloth carried messages to druids and shamans, could tell a class of Anthro 1 that food left for the dead may comfort the living. Yes, the grateful dead, and further bring home her lesson of offerings and rewards to California kids—milk and cookies for Santa, carrot for the Easter Bunny. The magic of keeping in touch.

Now she lies in a stall with her mare, Falada, a stall she will enlarge for the birthing. It is actually only for a moment, after oiling the protruded nipples, that she stretches against the mare's swollen belly to listen. She hears the foal's heartbeat, then hears it fumbling in its sea of dark. Falada's soulful eye looks up at her with resignation, her nose hot to her mistress' touch. Lilah speaks to Falada, tells her of the few weeks left when she'll walk by her side in the pasture, whispers to her of sire and dam in a soothing mantra. Aga out of Sultan Bey, Sultan Bey by Futurama out of Bey State out of Champion Bel Shamir. Back to Nejdme, Manakey out of the desert to the Great White City on the shores of Lake Michigan, whispering the splendor of her bloodline into to mare's noble ear. Falada nibbles at Lilah's hand. They are together in this perfect genetic plot, reeling it forward—Manakey out of the desert, sire Shalimar out of Harady son of Sula and sire Temptashun, reeling it back to this night when they lie together for a moment in Southern California.

A disembodied breath of hot Santa Ana sweeps across the

pasture and follows Lilah down the eucalyptus path to the patio, where she is caught by the halogen glow of Jen's Tizio lamp. Jen does not lift her tousled head to see her mother standing there full of horse smell and teat grease. Now that the term has ended at her private school, she sleeps the days away and wakes to nocturnal endeavors, reading and reading, writing in speckled notebooks through the night. Free to do as she pleases, her father off at last to make his movie so she doesn't feel that she's lamentable, insufficient, or more accurately, perverse. Lilah passes into the house, a woman who is never lonely, yet in her way she misses James this time, listens for the soft thump-thump of his running shoes. This time he's gone off by his own design . . . wanting something she can't provide. Lilah chides herself for that cheap shot, goes to the door of his screening room, flicks on the light. The place is flat without James' boyish agony. The wind blowing down San Ysidro Pass rattles loose tiles on the roof, whines through the Spanish grillwork at the windows. She longs for the distant soundtrack of old movies that accompanied her husband's growing pains.

What he has in mind . . . James would never use the word . . . what he has in mind, let's not get heavy, may be art. Used straight, the word would shatter the entire construct of the Ziff and Glenda setup into crossed telephonic signals, arteries clipped, dangling wires bleeding brass. Art suggests the limits of James' craft. With a small *a* is all. Hey! An honest movie. He's rusty on stuff like origins, the source, where you *go* as in some long-forgotten acting lesson, to come up with . . . Small *a*, not as Ziff must have it, BLOCKBUSTER. It's occurred to James, going to stake out his property, that there's justice in the industry's term of approval, blockbuster being an instrument of massive destruction. So who's the enemy? Who?

James is feeling love, well, like a lover on the trail of a reluctant girl, which must be half the turn-on. In his mind he goes over the story: lost story of a soldier and a wicked woman, dark story as he sees it. Let his father be the hero who can't win. Let the city be prosperous and innocent, seemingly innocent. Let the script be as he writes it in his head, scene after scene unfolding as he flies across the continent toward Bridgeport, making it up, a tale of his desire . . . small *a*, please, so James can name it art.

While his sister is torn this night between wheel and loom. Catherine never works after supper, but can't settle. The meal ruined, Mary sulking. Cath's chosen escape, the nightly mystery, fails her—eccentric village lady plies the curate with cream tea, sniffs clues at the fishmonger's, eavesdrops in the hedgerows . . . but damn, goddam, she remembers this one: Lord Ainslee did it with a poison dart, long secreted in Mombasa chest. Rubbish. She slams the beater on the loom as though she can barricade herself with a few sticks and length of cloth. "Damn, damn James," she cries while the clacking undertow of her treadle calls to him, "Come back. Come back."

Saint Patrick

Never a tick of interest in his saint, whether James the Greater or James the Less. Named after his Devlin grandfather, Matthew James, who made whatever money built the stucco house with stained glass windows. As a boy it was stained glass windows he first considered art, not the upscale fenestrations of dining room or landing on the front-hall stairs with landlocked water lilies, pearly-violet-green that shone upon him. It was church, St. Patrick's, where naturally enough, the windows told the story of that saint. James, squirming in his pew, constructed a little drama, shepherd boy to bishop, but there were many windows where he drew a blank as though pages were missing in his *Tales of King Arthur* or he'd skipped installments of *Jack Armstrong*, for it was a boy's adventure. On Sunday he followed the windows front to back to middle, depending where his father chose to sit.

Asking, he got no answer from the frightened women who taught him. The same old stuff—Patrick bringing the pagan chieftains to their knees, charming the snakes out of Ireland, which explained two-tenths of the windows. That left Patrick with eight miracles, better than the illusions in his first magic set. His grandfather's name was under a window: Gift of Matthew J. Devlin. Celtic letters, his mother said, and seemed annoyed. "The cost of it! They were always after him." That was another story. In the Great Depression his grandfather had lost a lot of money. James gave up on Saint Patrick, just took the stained glass windows to be artistic, blue sea and mossy shore, white lambs and golden boat—storybook artistic. He did not want them to be real, they were art, even his grandfather's window in which Patrick kneels for some reason by gloomy purple rocks. Soon he stopped seeing the windows, which were in fact splendid, Arts and Crafts Movement; shades of William Morris in sinuous etched robes of saints and sinners, of La Farge in opalescent clouds and fluid landscape. James looked at people during mass and aped them—transfixed to dutiful to bored.

In Ireland he'd been taken to Croagh Patrick by a darling girl. That day they were shooting scenes without him. British soldiers in a roadblock, which, naturally, the filmfolk had set up in the untroubled South of Ireland. British soldiers stop the death van chock full of explosives driven by two dewy lads. The blast that followed, an expensive setup. An Irish girl, who sang for a bit in one of his scenes, had driven James out at dawn. He had felt Irish, not really, but got into it quick enough. The countryside was as green as he could wish driving through Mayo with a silver mist on the hood of the car, soft hills with sheep and little whitewashed cottages, at times a flicker of sun and weathered old men in caps and Wellingtons walking the side of the road.

She took him to a great mountain where the grass ended in a bleak stone path. That was Croagh Patrick, with fog at its peak. As they climbed up and up, the sky turned moody gray as though the lighting cue had changed. "The pilgrims," the girl said, "do this in bare feet." And up into the thick damp she led him until they came to a tiny ice cold chapel, a ruin with a cairn of stones beside it.

They were the rocks in his grandfather's window. "Where Patrick did his penance, instead of the real purgatory the rest of us are bound for," the girl said, half laughing at James, the film star. "Lord, do you really want to hear this?"

He did. She had a darling voice, the darling girl. Strumming some ancient instrument, she'd sung "The Rising of the Moon" in a scene where he comes into a pub looking for whoever in the conspiracy. She told him what a fella Patrick was, a foreigner who converted the King of Tara's daughters, caused a darkness to come over the sun and the snow to vanish (that was Joe Scully's window). Patrick struck a wizard dead, drove a cart over his own sinful sister. "We were ever a violent people." She was putting James on. "Sure and he cast the blackbirds out of Ireland." So it was birds, not snakes.

"It's all stories," she said. "They'd just as soon you didn't hear it, how he bargained with God Almighty like a horse trader and, don't you know, was favored for his hardness. Ah, all we do is talk." They were in the dank unspectacular chapel not fit for this scene, the petitions to Patrick on scraps of paper, on holy cards, a clutter of lurid votive lights around them asking Patrick to heal, to forgive. "If you credit them," the girl said. She had a long Irish face like James and was sandy with pale eyebrows and lashes; his freshly dyed for the movie.

"I credit them," he said and knew she'd come back with him to the seedy Georgian hotel in Westport, knowing that she sinned with him already, her breath warm against his cheek. There was something of the actress about her, for after all she sang. It might be the end of a ballad: they came out into the light and the fog lifted somewhat so that the Bay of Clew could be seen below them, magnificent and lonely from Patrick's Penance, and she came to the last verse, how the saint, forty days and forty nights, had made the sign of the cross on himself from one canonical hour to the next and prayed here by the rocks, driving his hard bargain with God so that when the houses of Heaven and Hell and Earth shall come together on the final day, it's Patrick will judge the men and women of Ireland.

So James had been taken round the stained glass windows of his parish at long last. He scooted to the car with the darling girl just as the first tourist bus of the day spilled out Boston Irish, some of them barefoot, Americans like himself in search of legends. He was fairly reviewed, fair enough, though that movie, strangled in its plotlines, flopped. He remembered the Irish girl, dropped in the final cut, but understood no more than a boy why a man suffered himself to crouch by wet rocks atop Croagh Patrick forty nights and forty days.

Particular Friends

Joey de Sousa mowing his lawn: coming round his row of baby pines, he swings so near Mary Boyle's window she wonders if he sees her stretched out on the bed in her white slip. Free of his slow postman's route, he rides that mower like a hot rod, swooping down the front bank into the rock-garden curve. Part of their lives, Joey plowing them out, charging their battery, mowing his lawn—then theirs. He calls them the girls. On holidays they go to neighborhood parties bringing Catherine's sour cream cake.

In the convent it was not allowed, particular friends, not as might be coarsely imagined: affairs of the heart were with the Lord. Mary's family had come once to this house, made their way up to the Easter show at Radio City, tacking Mary Rose casually to the end of their tour, not to reveal unspoken fears. A carload of Boyles from Pittsburgh shuffled about awkwardly in the kitchen, still visiting in the convent. They had exclaimed over Catherine and her loom with desperate smiles, figuring the older woman as Mary's lover. Easter Monday—Mrs. Boyle brought chocolate eggs and a tin of feather-light lemon bunnies, believing Mary and her sturdy friend were not allowed treats. Pop Boyle took a broken chair and sat apart. A union man who had survived the goons of Republic Steel, he looked to Catherine like one of the lean socialists—soiled tie, frayed cuffs—who had worked the old Bridgeport city hall and looked as though he'd prefer a union bust to these visitation rights with his daughter. Unsure of the new regulations, the Boyles—Mom, Pop, Sis with bickering boys—left at twilight as though Vespers had rung. Lord, how Mary and Catherine hooted as the Boyles drove away. Like children, really, and then withdrew to their separate shame, barely spoke for a week as if they were, in fact, practicing the profound silence of the cloister in which it was revealed to both of them: the absence of physical desire, two half lives patched to one.

Mary had packed her bags and gone to Pittsburgh after that, a twice-yearly trip to the family who were bereaved when she entered the convent, embarrassed when she left. Now they give her a whirl: turkey and mashed potatoes, cookouts and scenic drives along the Susquehanna. Pop manages a quick fix of Pirates and Steelers. Once his daughter thought it was her father's dedication to real steelers led her to the convent. Now he's Pop, the fan. In Pittsburgh, Mary feels she visits a theme park called Home. Only Deirdre Boyle, that sister with the scrappy boys, dull dutiful husband, and some further disappointment she must tolerate, gets on Mary's case. Dee Dee, who has taken up aromatic synergy, presses healing ointments and balancing Boji stones upon her, hoping transcendental essence will break the spell of the sorceress' workshop, the charm of a cranky woman, Mary's particular friend.

Sharp rap at the window: there's Joey de Sousa with a sappy smile. Odd, Joey is Catherine's pal. With an apologetic tug at the bill of his cap, Joey is yelling, "Out of gas." A relief, even if old Joey's been giving her the once-over, and she calls to Catherine that de Sousa will not mow their lawn tonight. She calls out over the slam of the loom, but when she runs out to the living room—the workshop—Catherine has switched to the wheel, is spinning off her indigo. Her chopped hair pinned back, she wears pearls that Mary

Boyle has never seen, lustrous against hopsack.

"My mother's," Catherine says, for she knows what Mary's thinking, that the very nature of their enchanted house has changed. The carded wool spins, even and strong, onto her spindle, the wheel's revolutions perfectly timed. "The worst chore," Catherine says. "I do love it. So tiresome they told stories . . . the lazy girl who wouldn't spin, the poor girl who spun her thread out the door to catch a lover. Briar Rose pricked her finger, she had to meddle, didn't she?"

"Sorry. I-am-so-damn-sorry I brought that lousy paper home."

"One or another murder." Catherine's eye on the wheel's whirr: "His own advance man. Leak it out, no one will guess which grave to be opened, which body exhumed."

Spiteful as a neglected child, Mary Boyle grabs at the blue yarn. Catherine slaps her hand away and makes repairs. "One murder or another, don't you believe it. Tempt the audience. He'll be here tonight . . . tomorrow."

"Not here!" Their house is a poor thing now, hunkered on its concrete slab, kitchen with pretension to artisan's shop, a mess of weeds; narrow bedrooms and a bath that's popped its pearlite tiles. Both women smell the oppressive woolly odor of the room. Cath wets her fingers in a little bowl that swings off her spinning wheel. They have never noticed—below, the oak floor is sodden, gray with water stain.

Compline

Mary in her bed: no longer sorry. The first summer night at the window, her body in boyish pajamas stretched out between the sheets. Her window open now so that de Sousa can scratch at the screen, she wouldn't mind, have a look at her. Not much to see, unless without the glass between them he'd get the scent that she's alive tonight reviewing the sins of the day, that habit never shucked from the religious life. She's not sorry: deleting Peaches from the system, toting James home to Catherine. Worldly gold eyes of the child assessing her power over Mizz Bee. Page folded to the publicity shot of the actor, aware that she was teasing, testing. The worst, tangling Catherine's yarn. Bad Little Boyle. She's not sorry, not for any of it. Ministering angel or meddler, she's had her day. Her hands move up under the pajama top over the sharp pokes of her rib cage and cup her breasts. So little flesh: her body fed on meager experience, nothing to show for it. She tweaks at her nipples until they are hard, the ordinary thrill self-induced, and gives it up tonight, no fantasy of defrocked butt or blasphemous balls to sustain her.

She will bring it about: the rescue of Peaches. The child's hot hand in hers drawing her to that room, godforsaken and inspired, the kid's vision of family. Half the day was gone when she drove Peaches to school, knowing her cherub would lie to the teacher, invent a crisis. In the Indy 500 pitsuit; enormous orange lozenges dangled from Peaches' ears.

"Take them off," she'd said.

"They Michelle's."

"They attract attention." The kid got it. Mizz Bee was going to let her stay in 4C, not evict her from her life.

Reviewing the day of marvels: she'd winked, unused to complicity, then let the child out a block short of school.

"Lyin' low," Peaches laughed. At the crossing, she held her chubby hand up to wave. Oh, my—a clattering armful of Mama's bracelets.

School, school. Mizz Bee gave up on that one, rushed back to the office, whizzed through her daily proposal from the flabby custodian. "When you gonna marry me?"

"June. I want to be a June bride."

"Can't wait allaway to June."

With her sack of files, that shit, Mizz Bee sneaking past

Vic Benino, lazy head of human services. Vic playing with stats—birthrates, deathrates—in violent pink and green pillars on his computer screen; prepped out this hot day in cords, crew, mock turtle getup. Vic, son of Bridgeport, desperate to drop the connection. On tiptoe she'd made it to the communal terminal and zapped Peaches. No child, abandoned with head lice, ever existed in entry 4 of Father Panik Village. Benner or Benez, Peaches was no more.

Mary triumphant in her bed. As a child, she feared the recording angel who wrote down each of her sins on a scroll to last forever. Future husbands, employers, teachers, friends had access to the record. The angel knew, like the FBI, and would constantly betray you. Well, she'd zapped Peaches and told no one, a dangerous game. And what does she want with a fabulous child? Leaping ahead: repair the lock on 4C, take in whatever mail marginal people like Michelle . . . As she has always plotted, each step of the way—her devotion and lack thereof; now I will relinquish the nunnery, now I will lie with Tim Doyle; now go among the needy; now it is appropriate to live with Catherine. Now redeem Peaches. Now bring about the reunion of James Bray and his sister. And never asks why this day. Grace or luck? Havin' a nize day, Mizz Bee? Luck. Pure luck, she's not sorry.

Mary turns in her bed: a miniature barroom mirror stuck on the wall, Jack Daniel's giveaway. She'd won it at a country fair, trip to buy linen warp and pattern drafts with Catherine. Crap for a kid's room, the mirror blinks at her as a car drives by. Air at the window—still, waiting. The dim blue TV shines out of de Sousa's, meets moonlight on his newmown grass, on the lilacs in such heavy-headed bloom they might be carved in stone. Outlines of trees, bushes, flower patch tremble, push toward a third dimension. The de Sousas are news hounds, Joey and his Doll, as avid for any one-alarm fire and skirmish in city hall as they are for hijackings and unprecedented famine. Morning, noon, late into night, now that Joey's no longer on the beat, they gobble the world, tell the girls which channels, which hours they prefer, which anchorman they favor. Unlike their house and yard, the world's an untidy place: vigilant, they take it in, but take no stand. Mary, the union official's daughter, is shocked to think it: the de Sousas have never registered to vote.

Breaking the order of things—her costume of seersucker suit thrown on the floor with Catherine's coverlet, she's not sorry, turns in her bed to the wall. Summer, after all the fruitless years, the excitement within her as she putt-putts out of safe waters. What seems a dream: having salvaged Peaches. Why? Well why, in God's name, should the Village claim her?—Mary Boyle had coolly filled out reports to the parole board, requests for family mediation, routed the ambulette to the lame and halt of the Village, endured Benino's review of cases, Vic's only input to his city's miseries administered with gay kindergarten graphics at the end of each day. What's real: the gifted child, plump elf in cottontail pajamas, stardust in her hair. Mizz Bee will keep her in . . . a tower as yet unformulated, with fresh milk and warm oatmeal, clean sheets and infinite, yes infinite care.

Mary Boyle's never sinned: nunniness, priest in her bed all sensible progressions, if somewhat theoretical. In truth, for a shade over forty years, her angel's scroll has been empty. While she sleeps it can be writ: her self-induced demands of now or never, godlike disposal of grace and her favor, shocking absence of contrition, obsessive first love. Out of your depth, Little Boyle. Pitiful load, Mizz Bee, pull you way outta line.

Catherine in her bed: defying the season she wears a voluminous flannel nightgown as though to invite the frost. A big jolly-faced moon shines down white as snow on her neat rows of herbs and flowers, stuff she grows for witch's brew—feverfew, tough marigolds and yarrow, lavender she's nursed into a mangy hedge. She'll whack it all down in a bitter harvest; so unnecessary, not one color in the dull colonial spectrum she couldn't order from a catalogue, any number of born-again crafties churning out ocher, brick, acrid sage green. Cottage industry, Carolina to Maine. For that matter she could order her indigo wool, hand spun, predyed, unsmelly. No concern of hers once the piece left her loom, blue and white of her patterns easy to match with lampshade and curtains. Let them display Cloudless Beauty, Tennessee Trouble over their ruffles, tuck them under pillows. Her work should lie flat, simple fare for simple people . . . white walls, bare floors. It's been an elaborate ruse, her craft, her busy work.

She lies atop her bed sealed in her hot flannel sack. The big moon mocks her solemnity, a moon in a child's book or on old sheet music that lived in the piano bench, bright and comically oversized, turning lovers and back-fence cats into silly silhouettes. Not the end of the world, Catherine, that's what this moon says.

Rising to pace her cubicle, she sees the great ghostly shape of herself projected on the wall. Look at the size of you! The goblins will get you. Not goblins—James, he always could. *Previous commitments,* draw her eye to the left-hand flourish. She had dismissed his call to her . . . *Which murder?* Never a word to Mary Rose, kept it not to but *from* herself, an unspeakable secret; and now James is here, not in the quarter acre of woods left behind de Sousa's, not prowling this homely development looking for Bray on a mailbox, but in the vicinity as they say on the police blotter. He'll be approaching the domicile. And she stops to pity Mary Boyle, who surely must be suffering. For the first time she's seen their house as sad without men and children, something Cath could have told her particular friend. But the real story once again consists of what she didn't tell, never told Mary Rose of the time she went to meet her brother for tea at the Plaza, wouldn't Nell have loved it. Made a fool of herself to James' wife and gullible girl. Beautiful woman—though she liked the first wife better, quick tongue in her head . . . and Eamonn, the name all she recalls of that lost baby boy. She'd told ribald tales in the Palm Court, brought a shawl woven for the pale daughter, a pathetic sight between her handsome parents. To Mary Boyle, she'd made it seem a hundred years since she'd seen

James, as though no more than the holiday calls . . . as though she'd broken with, even feared her brother. Pacing in her bare feet the bare floor. In her mother's pearls—she'd slung them on tonight as though she was off to the Plaza, a dress rehearsal.

Catherine sits on the edge of her bed. Under the flannel the pearls are warm against her breast. She could kneel and tell them one by one instead of Aves, how she had put them on after she looked at his picture in the *Post*, how he'd know them at once, remember the Christmas their father, sick-gray, came swaggering as of old down the back stairs with the red velvet jeweler's box, how Nell had hightailed it to the pantry so they would not see her cry. She could tell each bead through the decades to the clasp. The clasp had tiny diamonds. She'd slung them on, combed her hair: visiting day. Not the Plaza, James would see she was in Danbury.

Their father's confusion when he spoke of the federal prison in Danbury. His contempt for the better class of criminal—businessmen and politicians in for tax evasion, perjury, fraud—but his awe when he spoke of their power, their grand position. "That fella," he'd say after some routine transaction with the mighty who'd fallen, "yacht, putting green, seat on the stock exchange. That fella could make or break you with a call. Millions!" The glisten of that word on his tongue. "Well, he's in Danbury now, country-club prison." James would see she had signed herself into Danbury, in for life. Minimum security, recreational activities. Her murder mysteries a nightly addiction, puzzles with neat solutions, the recycling of these stories. For the privilege of drawing a pleasurable blank, she could always forget who done it—until tonight when she remembered: the handle of the poison dagger secreted in carved Mombasa chest, Lord Ainslee having begot dusky son by African princess when the Empire. . . . Bloodless prose, mannered crime.

Laughs at herself. Pacing her bare room, Catherine picks up the thread of it: she, the happily deluded audience to her formulaic mysteries; James come home to make an entertainment of real murder. There was only one. Society woman kills soldier.

Solved. Unsolved, but only Cath knows that, and knows why she was drawn back to the scene of the crime, stands guard over a few scraps of evidence which lie somewhere in the occluded heart of a failed city. It's only on this night, the excitement and terror of James' coming, that she understands her fruitless task of fruitless years. So it begins: what Catherine Bray once thought would be her trial may be her deliverance. The notorious murder, unsolved. For years she has known the answer. Come to rest on the edge of her single bed, she hopes James has not written the script, for there's only one story, one ending.

Again pacing, each touch of anonymity revealed to her in moonlight. Bare walls, plain weave of her coverlet contains no romantic fable. She'll keep watch over this house in which she's constructed the numb comforts of the present, the nightly thriller and prayer, what she calls prayer, computation of the next day's work to the half spoon of brew's measure, pokeberry, pot stir, strokes to the inch—one-to-four-to-three, three-to-two—of pine tree or star, the terrors of bedtime stories thus held at bay.

And again lies on her bed. "What's the story?" he'll say, her big brother, fifty-two. The years flip back to any number of times when she'd put out for the inappropriate man. "What's the story?" James would say kindly, knowing the repetitive and ugly plot. Plot with so much gloss, psychiatric and therapeutic: with comforting catch words—denial, negative image, delusion, and the soothing, guilt-free inappropriate. "What's the story?" So kindly she could not bear it, for he was careless with their mother's love, with his wives and children. But he had cared for her: literally, made the arrangements for his sister to go away until Cath could no longer bear the burden of his kindness, for her brother had not grown into that sort of man. She had managed to evade him these decent if constricted years, years without a crisis, years in the slammer. James would see she was in Danbury, laugh at Mary Boyle, her convent ways, Mary Rose, who, until she looked at her brother's picture tonight, was the living soul she cared for.

"What's the story?"

"I'm under house arrest."

She watches the moon, which will not leave her alone in darkness, through the insubstantial wall hears Mary turning, turning in her bed, and at the mended screen the rustle of the past. On and off, Cath dozes. Wakes to laugh at herself, sweltering in her flannel gown: she will wear her hairshirt. Wakes to cry! James with that speckled beard, her own gray head to be expected. He had looked actorish, naturally, in the *Post,* and she remembered back to the start of his career, he'd bleached his hair for an ingenuous role. Their father had nearly died of it. Wakes, believes she wakes, to sigh. When they chalked off the driveway for a game there was a safe place to run to if you could. There, no capture counted. For years she has lived home-free, now she's frantic, dodging the chalk lines. "Millions," she calls out. "Millions. I'm in Danbury."

"No, Cath," James says kindly, as he tags her enormous flannel nightie.

"Yeah—" She's out of breath with running. "Oh, yeah. You . . . you underestimate my crime."

Antiphon

Mary Magdalene spent the last years, thirty years of her life, in the desert to expiate her sins. At each of the seven canonical hours she was lifted to heaven for nourishment, for in the desert there was neither food nor drink. Each day the angels came (so it is told in the *Golden Legend*), came with the rustle of garments, the beat of their wings, to cover her body, to heave her, to feed her. It is the start of that arduous round trip which Catherine studied on Riverside Drive, which Tiepolo drew but could not render unto the many thousands, those journeys—the repeat, the repeat.

1				
2				
3				
4				
5				
6				
7				
8				
9				
10				
11				
12				
13				
14				

In the beautiful concept of double entry bookkeeping, the debit and credit must always agree;
no inaccuracies or altered circumstances are
admitted, no rambling daybook or mere journal
will stand the check of the other side of the
ledger. Dip in, flip back or simply read on. Read
on—you are free to follow the story.

Double Entry

Silence. Aerial view: Float above smokestacks, wooden water tanks of factories, church domes and steeples, above housetops in tight identical rows; zoom in on billboards—Lucky Strike Green Has Gone to War, Cream o' Wheat (Uncle Tom servin' up his darky smile), Victory Bonds (V. in white toga, debutante pageboy). Silently skim the tops of leafed-out trees, peek through fluttering branches. Follow the white balloon swooping up through Technicolor blue until a mere pinpoint of child loss. Dip to the sun flashing off trumpets and tubas.

BLAST of marching band. Down Park Avenue they come—Girl Scouts, Elks, Sons of Italy, Odd Fellows, Ancient Order of Hibernians, Raybestos Brakettes. Flags and banners flying. Starched white skirts on Greek Orthodox schoolchildren. On Masons, the red fez embroidered with gold T-square and compass of that mystical fraternity. Cream Cadillac convertible with this war's hero, Colonel Mucci, handsome as star of stage and screen. Open touring car (old Auburn or La Salle), with two shrunken Spanish American War vets, one bright-eyed, one blind but alive, alive! Pan the crowd; then, one by one by one, the faces—broad Muscovite cheeks of drum majorette,

Statues

Balancing her scales
blind Justice awaits the arguments;
so they are empty on the courthouse steps,
saucers of air. Who will produce the tilt?
Cartoon strokes—Daumier, Nast—of the glutted
sunk to porkbelly reward while the gaunt poor
rise heavenward in their rags,
                of course.
Some balancing act, but once she learned to do justice,
to await—unbiased, stone cold—coin of the realm,
mealy grain, butcher's thumb, his head on her platter—
A skill they say you never forget,
                like riding a two-wheeler.
Never forget the blindfold. Standing or seated,
what matter. She is porched.
Who will weigh elegy above the ode?
It is some other goddess hefts the torch
            of Art and Song.

James' patriotic entertainment scheduled before the curtain, to speak in the old way, rises on the tragic story. Horse(shit) before cart you say, not buying into the romance of the city. Here, on the other side where in truth—flags hang limp, banners fade, unflapping. Cheering over the Bethel Fife and Drum in their tricorns of colonial militia, I work the crowd like a shill, drag 'em in. Who can resist the undrilled businessmen sporting ribbon sashes, boutonnieres, calling to friends and relatives along the way. Men's clubs formed in the last century by a rising middle class for comfort in a city with foreign ways. The Slovak and Hungarian orders come into their own. Not in evidence 1940–45, the Schwaben und Schuetzen Vereine.

Odd that in recalling the Odd Fellows etc. our director forgets the Knights of Columbus, who held white-tie banquets and balls well into this century, grand affairs altogether, in imitation of the Protestant gentry. James' first production tricks set up in his grandfather's K of C opera hat. Not a contraption, the hat was unfortunately real.

Darkness and light divide the course of time, and oblivion shares with memory a great part even of our living beings.
          —Sir Thomas Browne, Urn Burial

map of Ireland on freckled Eagle Scout, big Polish mama in peasant dress, stolid Jewish merchant, poppy in lapel, overseas cap (Argonne or Belleau Wood). Memorial Day—think Life photo essay, that fleeting, self-conscious art form.

Against marching legs, the wheels of a bike spinning, spokes twined with crepe paper—you got it, red, white & blue. The camera traveling with a boy, one of many wavering slowly on decorated two-wheelers alongside the parade. Bridgeport: Honor Guard enters Seaside Park, marching through triumphal arch. A boy—sandy hair, long wiseacre face with its own purpose, cuts out of the line of march and races, no hands, toward Long Island Sound. The kid now circles the colossal statue of P. T. Barnum, throws down his bike. Turning his back on the parade, he looks up to the kindly giant settled comfortably in his bronze chair.

Close-up: desire in clear blue boy-eyes. Fantasy music: jazzy pipe organ of movie house cutting out faint glockenspiel of Central High Band as James Bray scales up the pedestal, pries open the book in Barnum's gigantic hand, sticks his grubby boy paw into a huge coat pocket, comes up with a fistful of peanuts. Barnum's ruff of white hair flutters in the sea breeze. Stickpin glints, thin bronze lips crack a smile. The kid balances on Barnum's big shoes. Light dims on the round island of clipped park grass where the statue is set on its plinth, firmly, forever. The great showman's shadow cast on the adoring boy, effect of one passing cloud in otherwise blue sky.

Barnum has nothing to do with the murder. First day, James has jogged to the park, finds it all different, all the same, all suggestive. Incognito, he runs in a nerdy checkered hat, wraparound shades; beard shaved, his face half sickly sallow, half California tan. He has taken a room near the university under the name of Felix Young, a sinister professor in one of his mild disasters, talky script devoid of action. Glenda, ever mysterious, named that turkey *hommage* to Harvard Yard. Dr. Felix Young has a bed, desk, rented Ford Escort out front, no phone in a shingle house on Cottage Street. He has

If yearning for the outcome, you may depart this side of the page, read on in the story—the will he? the won't she? whatever will become of? It's your right, the pleasure you take in how they will meet once more—those threads; or meet the first time, your claim to second-guess our actor fumbling toward Mary Rose. Read on, flip back, dip in. I'm here, a shadow in the murder movies, the fink who tails you and you know it—outsmart me. Or here for you like an appendix—vestigal, ruptured, urgent. My problem, really—you, you go on, read the label, the minuscule prescription, dosage and warning, which frees you to follow the story.

Or here, I'm here like a statue set in the corner—some sibyl or caryatid—ornament of the sort you hardly notice, like the musty Harvard Classics, inkwell, pen wiper—outmoded. A statue set atop a glazed bookcase that once laid claim to store-bought culture. I fancy that when you dust me you'll not confuse me with the empty vase, but feel dense veined stone and know a heart that melts if you simply look to the left, buddy, the driver's side.

Women's softball team underwritten by Raybestos Brake Lining. Not possible in this line of march: their first season 1946. A later adolescent fantasy lodged in James' head: those strapping girls, their big knees, broad shoulders, poke of their uniforms over muscular boobs. How he might manage it with the tuffy shortstop. How they, collectively would ball him. World Title: the Brakettes, 1963. *Nota bene*, the ladies more successful than the bush-league Bridgeport Bees.

Catherine tucked a picture of the colonel (Clark Gable mustache, Cary Grant smile) into the mirror of her vanity. Colonel Henry A. Mucci of the 6th Ranger Battalion liberated American and Allied prisoners from a Japanese prison camp on Luzon, Jan. 30, 1945. James' parade is Memorial Day of the following May. In the afterlife, Mucci was chairman of the board of directors of the Lincoln/Mercury Dealers of America; ran unsuccessfully for public office; in the employ of Sunningdale Oil, drilled off the coast of Southeast Asia. May 5, 1975, made a hasty departure from Saigon.

Whereas Phineas Taylor Barnum…

Hey Rube! Pallas Athena, winged woman (unnatural
as Anna Swann, giantess, who settled to farm in Ohio),
goddess of just wars is out of the limelight.
KoKo, the bird girl, takes flight
in the Congress of Human Wonders, cawing,
pecking false feathers while Winged Victory
flies truly from one world to the next,
out of the Palace of Justice into the dime museum.
In their togas which cross all time,
we have lost track of the gods,
how helpful their intervention. Affairs
taken out of our hands, posted by the accountant.

Whereas Phineas Taylor Barnum…mind your attitude toward the great showman. P.T.'s got your number. His Sea-side Park: land donated just after the Civil War though his first notion of a park for Bridgeport

lived in his room one night, half a day to get what he's come for—essence of old Bridgeport.

James as Dr. Young, a curiously dull but penetrating man, perhaps a sociologist, whizzes past Barnum. Hey, he'd forgotten P.T., but Felix notes all public monuments, dainty Pallas Athena about to fly off Soldiers and Sailors, chunky Columbus (Italo-American Society, 1962). Dr. Young runs back through the arch, takes a right turn toward the defunct factories and wharfs of Water Street. If someone should call out "Hi! Felix!" he'd answer. He'd stop and remark upon the city passed by in the late prosperity which swept the entire Eastern Corridor, Baltimore to Boston. Felix has the good taste to note the elegant line of a low factory seemingly cantilevered into the Sound, on its soft red brick, the faint shadow of a name—Locomobile.

Yeah, he is Felix. Decent, fairly smart guy, more likely a waste product engineer come to teach at the university in one of the remaining old mansions where first-generation college kids are registering for summer courses to become life-sci-eco-health-care professionals . . . new immigrants, new dreams. Felix Young sees this more clearly than James Bray, who levitates in his opening shots, all *mise en scène* stuff ending in an indulgent frame—a boy overshadowed by Phineas Taylor Barnum. Nothing to do with the murder.

If he had a phone—not allowed these first days. In a discipline he's set, James sees himself (and Felix) as deep in meditation of place before he gets to plot. Plot a mere sketch on paper, sold to Ziff. Fuck paper. Fuck plot. Establish beloved city, scene after arresting scene. Okay, if he had a phone, Ziff's call to be endured: "What you got for me besides a prostate?"

If he had a phone, he would call Catherine. That tugs, but he will not these first days muddy the waters . . . dredge up that lost world, won't mourn with his sister the stucco house (*ca.* 1910, bulldozed for the Interstate), almost a Prairie house, almost a triumph with its window seats and stained glass; actual tricycles in the cellar, his mother's dress form in the attic, butler's pantry and linen closet

dates back to 1850 when the idea of a shared green and open space within a city was almost unknown in America. Real estate (squatters' shacks and slaughterhouses) for "the central park" was not procured until 1853. Sunday strolls and picnics were taken in the only parklike enclosures. Mount Auburn (Cambridge) and Greenwood (Brooklyn) cemeteries. Much of Barnum's genius was the ability to sniff out the needs and taste of the people before they knew their own minds. Their own desires. Famous by this time, his American Museum, bursting with junk and true treasure, was the great spectacle of New York; P.T.'s cronies the influential journalists, clergymen, civic leaders of the day; so it is not remarkable that Barnum hired the fashionable firm of Frederick Law Olmstead and Calvert Vaux, Landscape Architects, 110 Broadway, just opened for business in 1865, for *his* park in *his* Bridgeport.

Bridgeport seemed about the proper distance from the great metropolis. It is pleasantly situated at the terminus of two railroads, which traverse the fertile valleys of the Naugatuck and Housatonic rivers. The New York and New Haven Railroads run through the city, and there is also daily steamboat communication with New York. The enterprise which characterized the city, seemed to mark it as destined to become the first in the State in size and opulence....
— *P. T. Barnum,* Struggles and Triumphs

Having chosen his city he was loyal, used it fairly well, but then P.T. approved of all his enterprises—the *Autobiography* in its increasingly respectable versions, his temperance lectures, grand tours with his midget Tom Thumb, upgrading his act with Jenny Lind, the Swedish Nightingale. A poor boy with little schooling, Barnum approved of himself as a type to be emulated. Not a type: he broke new territory in self-advertisement and wily

leaks to the press concerning the backstage apparatus of his successful shows. Demonstrating the cute shuffles, shifty deals, he declared himself and the world the better for 'em. Best not to belittle our hero as the quintessential American trickster for he'll disarm you with full disclosure.

Always the balance sheet with Barnum:

exhibitions of Joice Heth and the Feejee Mermaid

American Museum's first-rate ornithological and conchological collections

Circassian slave girl, displayed with eunuch

abolitionist good works

rowdy street band set atop the museum

impossible D above high C of Jenny Lind's bel canto

where ghosts are known. He's after, with Felix's help, the grit and glamour of a wartime—call it an aura of trust and purpose, a giddy, gung-ho innocence—a moment, in the grand American city, of dramatic reversal.

Okay, smaller. Dr. Young may be a psychologist, discourse on memory's trick, the overscale of childhood—immense house, distant downtown adventure, BIG department store. Yet James, running in his disguise of checkered hat and unsullied anonymous sneakers, finds much of his city useful, thrillingly exact—burghers' self-satisfied houses on Brooklawn Avenue, rough New England granite of St. Patrick's Church, Romanesque porch of his father's courthouse, gilt Deco detail pasted up on the City Trust. He tours in the Escort to discover the perfection of General Electric and Bridgeport Brass, these fortifications more massive than he recalls, to hear the lull of side streets with soundtrack of children's play and long moments of the purest hush, then cars braking softly at stop signs, faint scurry of squirrels in branches overhead.

Second day: Felix points out the boarded-up windows of pillaged movie palaces, the brown glass Hilton (an unwelcoming negative on Main Street), the new courthouse, lowbrow cement. On its splayed porch, the silenced bell from the grand tower of the old courthouse, a shamed and clunky artifact. Tripped by dead tree roots and broken pavement, Felix remarks that much of the charm has worn off the gimcrack workers' houses on Cottage Street. Even James, slightly bored on his second run of the second day, finds the park bleak, uncomfortably empty when once more he circles Barnum. Heart thumping, thighs knotted and trembling, he looks to P.T. as though to beg a blessing or at least a cute Yankee word as to the next smart move with his project—call it art.

"Give them what they want," P.T. says.

"What I want," James says.

"You will find what they want is what you want."

James looks up at the massive lump of bronze dealing him a riddle. Tired of playing Felix, he yanks off the shades, the check-

Large in person and in vision large, like Whitman, who perceived the vast and various appetite of America while walking Fulton and Broadway; the poet self-invented, too, his voice strong to be heard above the tramping multitudes.

Just when you're carried away, install Barnum back on the pedestal…funny that you took him all that seriously, that you walked through the revolving door of history to stumble upon the showman's life. You're a loser like Herman Melville, who got in the ring with the impresario to write *The Confidence Man*

(a tale of hypocrisy and sham, mirror of the times, which did not amuse the public), two years after the publication of *The Life of P.T. Barnum Written by Himself* (a book that walked out of the shops into every parlor). If, like Melville, you don't get your jollies from fraud and moral flimflam, you're a chump or, worse, much worse, you're a no-name poet or pitiful playwright— Federal Writers' Project—who discovers eighty years too late that the illustrious city father was a braggart as regards his gift to Sea-side—10 acres of 340. P.T. rocks on his plinth, belly laugh at the inepecunious Depression *artistes* righting the record. Let them water the elephants, shovel camel dung, be gainfully employed.

History is the best bunk: if it is correct that within two years of 1492, Fra Luca Paciolo, a Venetian monk, made known the beautiful concept of double-entry bookkeeping in which the debit and credit must always agree, then we had surely arrived at a New Atlantis, new world as we more simply named it, wherein no inaccuracies or altered circumstances are admitted, wherein no daybook or mere journal will stand the check of the other side of the ledger. All previous systems with their date, expenditure, narrative—that slippery word that descends to the personal account—from that date, postdated. Why, one might as well keep a commonplace book in which the fixtures and furniture speak like facts, for themselves. *What I want*, said Mr. Gradgrind, *is Facts. Facts alone are wanted in life.* —Dickens, *Hard Times*

Not to blame Olmsted and Vaux for this coy arch, barrier to their view of the horizon, look of a Tinkertoy set up so little cars may be run through it: no Arc de Triomphe commanding the radiant expanse of Place de l'Etoile; nor can it seduce like Stanford White's lofty monument that draws us down the bustle of Fifth Avenue to the promise of Village beyond. James' triumphal arc, erected in 1904 by the widow of a Mr. Perry, civic-minded treasurer of Wheeler and Wilson Sewing Machines. The City Beautiful Movement (1900–1910) in full swing: in Cleveland, Cincinnati, Baltimore, Rochester, moguls made their money, made a mess with their factories, warehouses, railroad lines, tenements—a filthy, uncivillized mess. Now to tidy and embellish. In a great wave of bourgeois environmentalism, neoclassic arches, colonnades, pergolas, nymphs, goddesses were loosed upon the land. The widow Perry's dinky arch is the work of Henry

Bacon, who designed our revered Lincoln Memorial. When the grand and grave statue of Lincoln by Daniel Chester French was finally installed (1920) like a mammoth marble puzzle, shinbone fit to kneebone to thighbone, Abe, with satanic

ered hat with its slope-brim reference to Sherlock Holmes. A small-time professor, Barnum, Seaside Park have nothing to do with the murder, the good war; can in no way inform his role, the leading role—Billy Bray, detective.

P.T. says: "It is the last hope of a second-rate actor, that he has merely been miscast."

"Who the hell . . .?"

"Am I?" The bronze chair creaks under P. T. when he CHUCKLES. "A humbug."

If he had a phone. Second day: James calls his wife from the Ocean Sea Grill on Main Street to say like the old days, days unknown to Lilah, the chowder is full of clams and he's . . . so hyper he's hallucinating, then hears a plaintive snort, hoof stomp. Falada restless with a persistent low fever. Lilah on the extension in the stable, waiting for the vet, her voice gutters out with worry. Glenda—he's in O'Connell's pub *sans* credit card, reversing charges—Glenda says: "Statues crank arms, blink eyes, break into song. Mozart, babe, pre-Spielberg. Also your art pix of the fifties."

If he had a phone . . . recurrent thought that evening in the rented room as he sits over a sheet of paper, the *Ur*-blank sheet of artistic anxiety. Latino music, BURSTS of TV laughter, students' rock 'n roll, whiffy low-tide breeze, not California dry lemon scent far above freeway whoosh, surf rumble, if . . . then he might call his ex-wife he's not spoken to in years. She'd remember corrupt stench of America, incense-heavy dreams, angel dust, obligatory jaunts to flowery other worlds. Voices? Mired as she is in the sixties, she'd recall a woozy reality, heightened awareness. You bet, voices. But from her rarefied Mendocino view she'd accuse him: their son has become a banker. Painting her miniature flora and fauna, shrinking the natural world as she had once blown it up for studio mattes, it would be James who lacked all proportion. James lost in filmfolk extravaganza, sure, he might commune with Barnum, the ghosts of Griffith, De Mille, Mike Todd. If he called her, Eamonn's mother, she would make it clear that the burden of his ephemeral fame, his

beard, cavernous nostrils and eye sockets, was terrifying as O'Clancy the Irish Giant in the raree show. It was a matter of spook-house uplights hastily corrected by General Electric so we'd love him in the warm spots gleaming down like God's own sunshine.

Not to blame Olmstead, though Seaside is one of his few failures: he designed the wooded gardens, lagoons, and islands that were the only relief from the grandiosity of the beaux arts hodgepodge for that nervous, assertive look backward, the Columbia Exposition, which opened on May Day, 1893. Intended all for show, the White City in Chicago was constructed of staff, a cheap substance for temporary buildings that dribbled down to many a Mrs. Perry marble arch.

...the damage wrought to this country by the Chicago World's Fair will last half a century from its date, if not longer. It has penetrated deep into the constitution of the American mind, effecting there lesions significant of dementia.
    —Louis Sullivan, Autobiography of an Idea

Statues, a foolish summer game enacted after supper on the lawn. Four or five Parrott Avenue kids: one by one, the leader spins her playmates off as in swing dancing, calls out—"DiMaggio!" "Lone Ranger!" "Betty Boop!" STATUES! In a split second assume your pose—sliding into home base or flirting tippy-toe—and FREEZE! How we thought of statues, the human body immobile, lifeless. If you were judged the best— miming the Slugger at bat, howdying Tonto,

the Indian brave, miming (therein lay the invention)—you were next leader and called out—"Flash Gordon!" "Dopey Dwarf!" "Dracula!" Or, bringing it home, the slouch of the idiot

vegetable boy, Bennie; the hump of the witchlike widow, Sister Brown. STATUES! We had seen statues of our benefactors in the parks of our Park City and at the crossing of Park and Fairfield avenues, a Caucasian mermaid atop a soapdish fountain—amazing creature suckles a fishy babe while holding a light bulb aloft. She is the work of Gutzon Borglum, the sculptor of site-specific Mount Rushmore: his work much improved with scale. I had knelt before realistic colored statues of the Sacred Heart, the Virgin, Saint Theresa of Lisieux, knelt and prayed to their calm contemporary faces, casting my eyes down humbly to their flesh-colored toes, until rote prayer gave way to such intensity it was communion and looking up again felt their response, their blessed favor. Therein faith and my invention. *Greet, one another with an holy kiss. All the saints salute, you.* —Corinthians 13:12

depthless make-believe has made their son acquisitive and dull.

   Looking up from the blank page into the evening dusk, James hears the compelling ting of a bike bell, the crack of a baseball bat, a mother rounding up her kids. With renewed hope, he watches a fat girl bend to the window of a sexy Trans Am, shriek with flirtatious laughter. End of the second day and by Christ if he had a phone he'd call Ziff: "What I've got, buddy? Box office Americana."

Short of breath, P.T. leans on his cane. Years of hard living have taken their toll: an impressive figure nevertheless, broad-bellied stature much admired in the Gilded Age. Up one flight, he raps on the door with the knob of his cane. James has fortuitously poured himself a finger of scotch before he answers to the knock on Cottage Street. Barnum sails into the lamplight as though drawn by a pair of white stallions in circus version of Roman chariot. Leonine head held high, he tours the cramped room to see what he can make of this, even this dead-end boardinghouse arena. The old man's face is ruddy and very large. Unlike the smooth surface of statue, his broad forehead is heavily lined with actual thought or care. Mighty worldly, P.T.'s tight-lipped smile, not benign; the nose bulbous with acne rosea as that of a stage lush; thick chins and full throat have fallen to rubbery decline.

   James, a kinda normal 5' 9". Upon occasion angled up by the camera, never stood on a box like Robert Taylor, Alan Ladd. Under the enormity of Barnum, he feels freaky, not even the little kid who peeled off from the Memorial Day parade, just a tiny toy man.

   "Cottage Street," P.T. PROCLAIMS, "built over the protest of old fogies who could not share my vision. From the time that I turned my attention to the opening and beautifying of new avenues . . ." The powerful voice alternates: cynical, adenoidal W. C. Fields; righteous, plummy, as though from podium or pulpit. James folds himself into a corner, far from this masquerade. He might be in the last cheap row of a magnificent lecture hall, the orator, seeking him out, phony as the clack of wooden nutmegs yet theatrically convincing.

Thomas Ball's seated statue of Barnum (book and pen in hand) was dedicated on July 4, 1893. Kitsch-free, rather wonderful until we turn to Houdon's Voltaire: then the old promoter in his gentlemen's haberdashery seems all studio pose, his comtemplative brow done with academic accuracy "from the life," while the philosopher's smile lives in a barbed thought come to mind. Voltaire's hands grasp the classic *sedia* as though to push away from the restraint of marble that might make him saint or god; or perhaps

three-legged race, or physically joined near the heart like Chang and Eng, who, they say, did not get along, though when they became citizens of this country chose a common name—Bunker. And built separate houses. Fathering twenty-one children but could not go their separate ways. It's regular work, though I find it stuffy this lockstep of annotation. It seems, how shall I say without offense, partial. *An association is almost always commonplace. Disassociation discomposes and uncovers latent affinities.* —Jules Renard, a stay-

to merely stand and welcome "Belle et Bonne," his adopted daughter who gave him much happiness in his last years. His toga, worn easy as a sweatsuit, is less costume than P.T.'s unyielding boots, his cumbersome business suit. *In Aevo Eterno* on the pedestal of Barnum's statue. In the life to come? In the eternal life?

Facts as turned up in the course of investigation. The bookkeeper's all wet. Pay him off. Hard to justify your tricks of the trade over mine, dear reader of stories, bound as we are in a

at-home writer, who lives on, if at all, solely in his *Notebooks.*

Let me point out that life-size (small) statue of Elias Howe which was intended for Central Park and never got there. He stands with hat in hand as though it was no big deal inventing the sewing machine and he'd just as soon look to his toes and scrub grass close to the factory. Hardly his doing, the gasser: "Let me take you to Seaside and show you Howe standing up"; nor can he be held responsible for the production of

The great man boldly PROFESSES *his own chicanery:
"First procured Joice Heth, hundred and sixty-one years old—three*
THOUSAND *dollars—and* EXHIBITED *the black woman, nurse of
George Washington. No small sum, the year, my friend, was 1835."*

As in a set routine, James reads his line: "Bought her?"

*"Poor crone had been improperly displayed. In need of
dazzling gas illumination. I lay Heth costumed as a household nigger
upon a table, the better to demonstrate her gray matted head, hooflike
nails, wizened mouth from which she sang spirituals and babbled
touching stories of her Georgie boy."*

"Sold her?"

*"The old girl died." P.T. leans upon his cane, this object
ebony, gold-tipped, its nob of ivory engraved with royal crest. "Heth
was no half measure, a grand investment, rigid in her coffin as she was
upon the stage."*

*"In God's name!" James dashes at Barnum, a move from
long forgotten melodrama.*

*The windbag, all benevolence, holds him off: "Buried her
grotesque remains in the family plot. If you are in the show business,
my boy, you must simplify these knotty moral questions."*

"Never!" CRIES *James.*

*P.T.'s breath, musty as the tomb, his flesh stone cold as he
pumps James' hand, a repellent touch, what's more they have no deal,
yet the entrepreneurial light in P.T.'s eyes encourages the actor, who
has seen filmfolk scratch and claw, to defend his property, what he now
calls "My Story." Hey, telling the great man the plans for his movie,
which might be for a tree house, penny theater in the garage, James is
that excited, for in his mind "My Story" takes a fantastic new turn, not
the treatment he's foisted on Ziff like a three-dollar bill. Fuck paper.
"More honest," James* DECLARES, *"epic, dark. The murder Billy
Bray solves—okay, no knotty moral questions. Soldier boy exonerated,
seductress condemned. The city stars, wondrous-ethnic-dream-come-
true American city. Strong unions, vigilant police . . ."*

"Ah, the police. Straight from the bog," P.T. CHORTLES,

Dr. Warner's sanitary corset which made the "human form divine." Six thousand a day turned out on Atlantic Street, courtesy of Howe's miraculous machines; nor is he to blame for the garments' rustproof stays of buffalo horn and whalebone; nor for Dr. I. DeVer Warner's disfiguring lectures on the female figure—woman's body turned to stone. The saints are all men of business, someone said. Tom Thumb, I believe, whose head was knocked off the statue on his grave, an image he commissioned before his growth/decline. His wee foot was cast and sold as souvenir.

A translucent ball, Cath lay in bed delirious. The facts of her body gone wrong from the start, information she could not learn and stow away. Square shins and wrists, broad breastbone, thick waist, as though not child but matron in the loose dresses her mother smocked. As though in her plaid school jumper and velvet collared coats of Sunday she pretended little girl. When James, playing Barnum, thrust a rusty rake through her lip, the tetanus shot went screwy. She lay on exhibit, her blown-up body a wonder to many doctors. From the watery depths she swam up to watch them watch her—exotic in this shape, at last desirable. Lightly blaming her brother for the injury she enjoyed.

Freaks: the Museum of Human Mistakes their father would never let them see. Cath strained to peak behind the bally artist at Iron Jaw Wilson, the Bearded Venus, the India Rubber Boy—their extraordinary bodies within the dimly lit tent. "You only look at 'em," James said, "and pay extra." How confident they must be:

it was none of their fault. She wanted to look upon their flesh that went wrong, to feel wonderfully normal, yet it was the freaks who starred, were lucky or endowed. She did not think lucky, the midgets, at least, who toddled on their stubby legs in the Big Top, looked worse than bored, wretched as they scampered from big barking dogs, tumbled in the sawdust after full-sized clowns.

We are as God made us.—Tom Thumb. His dilapidated house, three blocks from the Brays', no commemorative plaque or sign. "A flophouse," Billy said. In the midget's front yard, the Tom Thumb Florist—poinsettias, Easter lilies, tasteful arrangements, when sadly needed, delivered to Redgate's Funeral Home. "A *boardinghouse*," said Nell. No one took an interest: rotted clapboards, pavement sprouting weeds. Bravely Catherine had sidled by the florist truck, walked up on the porch hoping for a tiny door, a dollhouse window. A terrible woman with broken brown teeth, red legs in slipslop slippers, told her to go way.

Charles Stratton was four years old, 2 ft. 1 in. high, 15 lbs., when P.T. found him in Bridgeport (1842). Rechristened, a quick study, natural song-and-dance-man: his body worth many times its

weight in gold. Not a freak, that is the reward in studying the Little General's success. "...nature put a *veto* on his further upward progress, ordered him forever after to remain in *statu quo*."

raises James' whiskey glass. "You do well to keep them happy."

"My story. The murder . . ."

P.T. lowers his grand bulk onto the daybed, which SQUEALS in pain. Listening to James' movie (Kinetoscope or stereopticon slide will not bring the public in), his skin grows porous and gray. Then: "Unless it be the great tragedies, Hamlet or Macbeth, murder is not worthy of the stage. It does not uplift or entertain."

"In my story," James PROTESTS, "the sordid crime seeps into the gentle wife afraid for Billy's life, will forever haunt her children . . ."

"Hmmm, the small domestic piece," P.T.'s voice WINDS DOWN, piping and thin as an old Caruso record. "No money in it, boy. Take the . . . big risks. Astonish and amaze . . . the populace. Mount . . . the great ex . . . hibitions, the . . . tri . . . um . . . phant show."

He's gone. James can't say whether the last of him was flesh or stone, though Phineas Taylor drew himself to monumental height in the dark hallway, rewound, gave one loudmouthed Yankee GUFFAW: "Frame houses! The Lord forgive me the profit I cleared providing for the workingman. East Bridgeport had its problems, but Cottage Street, a veritable coup, so near the Sound with the delightful prospect of the millionaire mansions for the less fortunate to look upon." P.T. tapping at the rotten wainscot. "Firetrap," he says, and did he in fact descend the stairs or did the disembodied voice TRAIL OFF in gaseous recitation? ". . . whatever lay in my power to extend and improve that charming city. I was exceptionally anxious that public parks should be established, especially one where good drive-ways, and an opportunity for the display of many fine equipages for which Bridgeport is celebrated . . ."

James examines the fat fanny impression on his bed, the moldy green smudge on his whiskey glass, believing, before a night of childlike sleep, that he has heard in this pompous, self-adulatory bullshit the last of Barnum's words.

A promoter's dream: "Unlike many other dwarfs, the General is exquisitely proportioned, his head being not large, but of the proper symmetry and his hands and feet the prettiest ever seen.... His canes, of which he has several, are from 10 to 12 inches long and his hats for various costumes are of themselves curiosities."

Cath's roller-coaster history of denial and plenty: the naked want of many men and their rejection: for a bitter blooming season she was slim. That body, normal as Gulliver's, but with curve to its waist, trim hips, high bosom, had seemed always an impersonation; posing, passing herself off for the girlie show. The General, by contrast, sound as a tiny bell and in no way threatening to his audience. His antics suggest we may start over, like bouncing water babies begin again. To be always a child or even small husband to doll wife perfectly evolved, so reassuring in the first shock of Darwin's claims to descent with modification. Let the cartoonists and scientists pursue the ape theory. (P.T. secured and exhibited the Missing Link). Better to cherish Mathew Brady's photo of "The Fairy Wedding," Charles Stratton to Mercy Lavinia Warren Bump—Grace Church, Broadway, Feb. 10, 1863—grim days of a lengthening

war, conspiracy, disaffection, the impeachment of Lincoln plotted. Better to read of the (dis)proportionate wedding gifts:

Miniature silver horse with garnet eyes, chariot embossed with rubies— Tiffany & Co.

Chinese firescreen of gold, silver and pearl
—Mrs. Abraham Lincoln

Tortoiseshell case from which a phoenix with real plumage rose and sang—P.T. Barnum

"Prince Charles Stratton of the Dukedom of Bridgeport in the Kingdom of Connecticut," the little trouper announced to the crowned heads of Europe. Never with the circus, the Thumbs and their small company held levees. Of all the General's acts, Napoleon, Frederick the Great, Highland Fling and Hornpipe, *The Grecian Statuary* was "the most beautiful and wonderful portion of his performances. His 'tableau' of Cupid with his wings and quiver; he looks as if he's just been removed from an Italian magic-board." Triumph: his diminutive Samson, Slave Whetting a Knife, Ajax, Discobulus, Cincinnatus and David (a natural). Spare us *Le Poucet,* Hop 'o My Thumb in nude body stocking. Spare us the filler script, delivered in piping falsetto, of derring-do with sexual innuendos, kisses for the ladies who delighted kissing at last a harmless boiled-down man. Nor is it true that the flamboyant Cora Pearl—cockney courtesan—that Cora, mistress of dull brother of Napoleon III, served up T.T. naked like a roast piglet at her table before

Bray is no patsy. Third day: he sets out at dawn for Seaside Park. Barnum's baggy bronze suit, a chalky cupreous green, is the same with same limp pockets, same big buttons match big buttonholes, same smooth bald dome, neat fluff of hair, but the old guy looks worn, not wise. Overweight, over the hill, P.T. contemplates the landscape of his choice, this flatcake of land, spoonbatter ragged at the edges, view of a dank puddle; in morning mist the chipped rim of Long Island barely visible. Even the renowned Frederick Law Olmsted couldn't do much with this stretch of shore. Winding roads circle each other in an American do-si-do, end up in folksy circles to avoid the rigid geometry of Rimini or Cannes.

In any case, the show is over. No sails, one ferry plies the route to Long Island. No strolling citizens of Bridgeport, only James in the Escort and a squad car wasting time. Mo & Jessie, that mild graffiti scrawled on P.T.'s pedestal across a bas-relief—funereal stuff, must have been stamped out by the score—Greek maidens with lyres and lads with the laurel in dutiful pagan procession. A cross stuck in to cover that base. Piss-poor tribute to the man who invented the circus parade: fleshy women undulating in elephant saddles, clowns cartwheeling down Main Streets, calliope's seductive call. Here, even the high tide sucks the shore in dispirited sighs.

Bray on a park bench, his backside to Barnum. Okay, last night's wigged-out dream a hoax, an old repertory cornball sent to bring him to his senses. Anything can be set up: De Mille destroy Rome, Ford the Sioux Nation, Barnum knock on the door of his rented room surely as James can taste a blood capsule between his teeth, let the slippery no-taste of simulation drip from his mouth. Yeah, he can make his jaw leap with a spasm of pain. Why curse an apparition or a statue? Barnum has nothing to do with the murder.

Solved or unsolved, the murder is his, the city his. Fuck Ziff, the show biz. "My Story" is not up for grabs. Arse from the bog turned to Barnum, (well, from Hollywood where myth begets reality), in any case James Bray watches a small wooden trawler with a couple of long-ago lobster traps putt-putt into the Sound. A mother,

removing the platter to her boudoir. Nor that in the wake of the scandal, P.T. hustled him back to America to produce the little folks' courtship and wedding in America. Tragedy: he grew many inches, gained weight, his scraggly beard and puffy eyes were not adorable. The most famous midget in the world, he'd not have been hired as a Lollipop boy in dippy pasteboard hat, much less Mayor of the Munchkins. T.T. as yachtsman, horsebreeder, real estate magnate suffered in the Depression of the 1870s. A great smoker of diminutive cigars, he was buried (1883) with full honors of a Fourth Degree Mason.

Lavinia went on to marry the Italian dwarf Count Magri, a dreary, punishing fellow; went on as a "Lilliputian Atom" in the most godawful acts. STATUES! "While suspended in the air, the Countess will be placed in different positions and dressed in several different costumes to represent several different characters, concluding with THE GODDESS OF LIBERTY." Said to be the most photographed woman of her time. In the good days, Lavinia's

cartes de visite were set in photo albums beside the pictures of dear ones, midget and Mother sharing the studio backdrop, the gilt-edged page with Sitting Bull, Yosemite, Vatican Views, Ulysses S. Grant. Two big books came to rest on the parlor table. The Photo Album and the Bible seemed not to be at odds. The Album was of our making, more or less. Less, we thought, though never tired of turning its pages and seldom thought...what is it seldom thought? That the photos can be cropped, rent, or rearranged. That we can paste a gold star, ticket stubs, cutout of Monroe—James or Marilyn, depending on our theme, if theme, not catchall of memorabilia with dance card, lock of hair, pressed flower above the wide white smile of Johnny We Hardly Knew Ya. Still, it was our cabinet of curiosities, a book of life. Unaccountable history, displaying good bets and our mistakes. Why did we flip the Album pages as though struck dumb under the glow of gaslamp, pleasant as the indirect light which shines on our TV?

The Album, had we cherished it, allows free association (an oxymoron if ever), permits the aphoristic wit and wisdom of others, yet all rather...hmmm? Sure, all self-revealing, and all, all of our choosing. I enter:

In 1919, the miniature grand piano, gift of Queen Victoria to the newly wed Thumbs, brought $11, a year after the Countess' death.

Alone, afraid, ashamed, in the foulness of the tent, I looked around me in the silence; and beyond, above—the Universe of night and space. All my life but the feeble rustlings of a mouse in straw.
    —Walter de la Mare, Memoirs of a Midget

I write poetry and prose,
Holding my pen between my toes.
    —Anne E. Leak Thompson, armless wonder.

managing inflated beach ball, real pails and shovels, scampers after her kids down broken cement steps to a strip of sand, so fuck Glenda's patronizing tone which makes "My Story" unseaworthy as a toy boat in the studio tank. For that matter, up Felix Young, his classroom commentary. To his right, a pulpy soft woman in a faded housedress, citizen of Bridgeport, walks her mongrel pup on a gold leather leash. To his left, trim retired type, Red Sox cap, begins an ardent wax job on his fine equipage, the family sedan. Shred the proposal which buckles to cramped plot before the restorative power of memory yields to the grand sweep beyond set or location—succumbs to this city, this honorable place. Fuckin' gull's grace the same, sun glitter on the Sound beckons as ever. To James' right, to his left, his faith in "My Story" is restored by prim, immutable begonia beds.

Catherine awaits. She's bypassed the turreted courthouse where their father scribbled the fruits of his investigations on yellow legal pads. James will find no records there, only the offices that process human services, and perhaps encounter prepped-out Vic Benino or Mary Boyle suffering her casework. From the adored movies he grew up on, James will know to come bumbling to the library for his murder, for newspaper clippings of the trial, drawling his dumb requests like Jimmy Stewart. This once outsmart him—coy as a ditsy sleuth in one of her genteel mysteries, Catherine will distract, forestall, and so has made her way back to Broad Street without a false step, taking the old route from the North End bus, quick to miss the soaped and boarded windows, the populace reduced to two drifters and a banker, two bankers and a drifter. The banks still glorious amid the rubble, live as the patch of grass now called McLevy Green that fronts the outmoded city hall, a Greek Revival beauty worthy of her notice, but Catherine scuttles along in stiff pumps, shell earrings, Nell's pearls, unmoved by downtown. It's all as Mary Boyle tells her, postindustrial with the death wish of gentrification in a bit of Belle Époque brass, a smart green awning here

Confined as I am, Ladies and Gents, to the left-hand side of the page, one leg to stand on, tail end of the coin, but if we had invested in the Album, more or less. Less *papier mâché* rocks, potted palms, less Sunday best and christening gown; more honest as to our use of Gog and Magog, of *Tannhäuser*'s worthy dwarf, Tweedle Dum and Dee—the oddities we set beside our photos to exhibit our own tasteful proportions;

more open to the candid shot in which we appear headless, squinting, or, alas, in the jersey bathing suit which clung; less dense as to the revelations of double exposure, that gorgeous gaff with its instant imprint of present on the past—we might have called upon the Album to tell my story, or James' or Cath's.

STATUES: In Rodin's *The Kiss* note that the ardor is hers, not his. One *Kiss* of his many was selected as Art for the Chicago World's Fair; upon its

uncrating X-rated, admission upon personal application only, while Little Egypt, cooch artist, unveiled on the Midway. Would that Barnum had lived to see her pop out of a pie at a gentlemen's dinner in New York, his son-in-law Charles Seeley among the company charged with an offense to public morals.

Oh, the grass is greener where the lean, linear actor moves forward in his love story, away from mere sequence and moral dilemma. Spin, spin me in the backyard of summer once more. Call out: "Aphroditty!" "September Morn!" "Stag at Bay!"—STATUES! The Monumental Bronze Co., 354 Howard St., used zinc to produce their famous white bronze which "will withstand the atmospheric changes of time without deteriorating effects." Actually blue-gray, one-tenth the cost of the real thing, cast as medallions, mural tablets, cigar-store Indians, infinite public drinking fountains (courtesy of the temperance movement). Big business in Civil War monuments, Union or Confederate soldier, $450. $600 with personal head. Without inner armature, the white bronze "crept." In civic triangles and squares across America, soldiers, buckling slowly at the knees, leaned forward at unlikely angles. Who were the unheralded sculptors of Bridgeport? German metalworkers, Italian craftsmen kept busy at the end of that century, for laborers, clerks, housewives favored man-made items in the name of progress; their garden urns and grave markers, mail-order art.

Skulking on the other side of the page as marginalia, diddling with apocrypha, I take extreme—no, views that are privileged as though granted the unbuttoned freedom of speech allowed royal dwarfs or those of the Papal Court of Cardinal Vitelli or Pince Charles Stratton, Dukedom of Bridgeport. As though looking on, looking up at big bellies and breasts, the underside of chins, I'm entitled to the abasement and cruelty dealt out by Charlie McCarthy, the wooden dummy of radio fame,

and there. But in the Georgian lobby of the Public Library with its pasty smell and reverential hush—her knees go quivery and queer.

She took this as her holy place—1944 or '45. At first glance the radiant spread of main reading room diminished the dim incensy aisles of her parish church. Catherine embraced the new rituals: Dewey Decimal System, her carefully written requests granted or denied, the set hours. When the lights dimmed their warning at wartime dusk, she could not bear to abandon the big oak library table, leave an eternity behind. As the oversized door swung behind her and she stepped into the street, she was not with them, the shoppers bustling out of department stores at closing time . . . unlike the grown women with goods from Read's and Howland's. No better, only different—a child, clutching her borrowed books like daily bread, she would dash through the dim unfashionable arcade, not to brave the crowded sidewalks, to feel her difference special as a wound.

At the top of the curved double staircase a bright green cursor dances on a screen. No Rip Van Winkle our Cath, she'd plugged into a miraculous glut of information when she last worked at *Time*. Today the library computer brings to mind the parochial data bank—Bridgeport abuse, Bridgeport disease—which Mary Boyle feeds into, a system which calls up a stunning murder rate. Familiar urban body count of recent years, not, thank God, the small scandal of one poor soldier slain in elegant surroundings. Her spinster calves strong with treadling loom and wheel, but the second flight does take Cath's breath away. She kerplunks on a velvet love seat in the Bishop Room. Glazed bookcases display artless local histories and exhaustive city records which may be read by electrified oil lamps, a likely setup to investigate the past. James will figure to come here for the murder. Miles ahead of him, today his sister's waiting is not the maiden's curse.

"Waiting," she says lightly to the young woman who asks, what files or records? Then, the old fear upon her, her purpose dissolves: it's not her limited arrangement with Mary Boyle or the

who suggested, even to Cath, true believer, that there might be a question: Who manipulates who? So on with the popcorn, elephants, circus! James like most everyone is a sucker for Barnum's last enterprise, the Greatest Show on Earth. Bridgeport as winter quarters for Barnum & Bailey's Circus, peanuts compared to cultural catchall of the American Museum. Stale peanuts to the boy—his father's oft, oft repeated tale of watering the animals for a free ticket to the show; Billy's report of Wild Bill Cody sauntering down Main Street, the fat lady hoisted into the streetcar, raffish keepers and clowns in South End saloons and THEN, if he can trust his father's tale, the great fire (Nov. 20, 1887), wild animal show in flames. A Bengal tiger pacing the Brays' front walk on Division Steet, collapsing, paws over eyes, into a soft household pet while trumpeting elephants stampeded for the Sound.

But Jumbo, best-loved pachyderm, was already taken from us, his great skull crushed by a Canadian freight train in 1885. Barnum bought this magnificent beast from the Royal Zoological Gardens, made hay of all fables surrounding the

African elephant so far above and beyond, that zoologists took Jumbo to be a new type specimen. With fame came Jumbo plates, jugs, jawbreakers, infinite toys, animation—of which more later. Thousands of children rode on his

back. According to his keeper, Matthew Scott, he ate and drank legendary meals, guzzled a quart of whiskey when not feeling fine. At his death he was shipped to Henry Ward's Natural Science Establishment, Rochester, N.Y., where Carl Akeley, the naturalist, launched his career stuffing Jumbo to Barnum's requirement "that the skin be made considerably larger than in nature." Akeley stretched the hide (1,538 lbs.) so that Jumbo might be shipped, bigger than life, on posthumous tour. Hey Rube! STATUES feathered and furry, nearly alive, nearly immortal. In Peale's Museum, which Barnum bought (1843)—lock, stock, Dodo bird and puffin

—stuffed specimens were exhibited according to Linnaean principles—i.e. naturally, behind glass. The Peale boys, Rembrandt and Rubens, saw the value of coupling show biz with science, but their entertainments, like earnest *National Geographic* films, couldn't cut it, whereas Phineas Taylor Barnum. And besides they operated out of Philadelphia. Tuck in, sweet dreams with Teddy and Tigger; declawed, with button eyes, they are our familiars. Not that long ago they were wondrous strange, when Nature was pitiless, not to be pitied.

Bless Barnum, bless him for the poultry show, the fattest baby contest. Damn him for the gelatin made of Jumbo's ground tusks, served up to society ladies in Gotham, as a promo. Harder to imagine a wobble of that primitive concoction on my spoon than it is to envision the mastadon grazing the New York Thruway up near Newburgh where they found him, though the reach is still longer to a nation that read with damp eyes Jumbo's obit.—"The pillar of a people's hope, The centre of a world's desire." Mascot, molting burden,  gift of P.T. to

Poor Old Jumbo's Skeleton.

monotony of her coverlets she hides. James has free access to look upon her defeat, but she'll not have him pry coffin lids. It will be the undoing of them all—the story of their father and that murder.

Felix hat stuffed in his pocket, he arrives as James Bray, a gaggle of teenage girls in attendance. Readers and librarian look up, a crackle of excitement in the air. Bray's sister knows that signal. He goes to her directly, dry kiss on her wet cheek.

"Where else?" he whispers.

"Don't be nuts," says Catherine. "I haven't been here in thirty years."

"Don't cry about that, Cath-rinnn," crooning her name as Nell did in soft exasperation. She blushes, gray and puffed, older at fifty than James at fifty-two. They speak in shushed fragments, years to cover. Not their private parlor, James feels the Bishop Room as a tight set. Mellow lights burn on their reunion. He plays it close, warm—not where his day was heading. For Catherine, the cherished present, spun double-twist like her valued hanks of wool, all unravels. She might be a fierce competitive child cowed by James' magic, or a jilted young woman seeking her brother's protection. Balanced on the edge of the borrowed love seat, she tips toward the punishing past, closes her eyes in a trance. Bridgeport's own Madame Blavatsky, her pronouncement flat and too loud: "You have come to the place where the caskets must never be opened."

But he's signing an autograph for the one fan bold enough to ask, all the while charming the young librarian. "You're the expert," he says. "Barnum? What's around?"

"Books, letters, deeds."

"Real stuff. A coat? Perhaps a cane?"

"Not here." The librarian somewhat put out, key in her hand to open a case of mere histories, memoirs. "That would be the museum."

"Do you remember a black walking stick?"

"The museum's being renovated."

"A frock coat? Big buttons."

Tufts University, the beloved beast went
His bones live on Central Park West, Museum of
Natural History, Dept. of Mammalogy, of African
elephants he remains the biggest and best. I do
presume the infinite heart.

Felix was immensely entertained. He had called it
a comical country, and went about laughing at
everything he saw. You would have said that
American civilization expressed itself to his sense
in a tissue of capital jokes.... Felix might have
passed for an undispirited young exile revisiting the
haunts of his childhood.

—Henry James,
of Felix Young in The Europeans

Glenda refers to the animation of the statue of
the Commendatore in *Don Giovanni*. "The eigh-
teenth century, which was so deeply terrified of
losing the natural power, betrayed its preoccupa-
tion with it in its fascination with the apparently
magical and self-moving activity of automata and
mechanical toys, metaphors under which it
sought to ensure the continuation of its own
threatened potency." —Brigid Brophy, *Mozart,*
the Dramatist. The Glenda sensibility feeds on the
retort, continues the game. The result—trivia of
reference, a flashy amnesia as to what the hell
Mozart intended with the singing statue. Ah,
Glenda with her game-show brilliance, or is it
contract bridge in which she pretends the thin
hand, holds the ace, jack, queen for a slam to find
she has no partner. Solitaire. Plays with herself.
    But what can I say of Glenda that's not
envious, that she's free, not accountable. Or that
all she knows—Mozart and old movies, *Dr. Fau-*
stus and impeccable French is
spoken in a life beyond page
or office. Somewhere—a
post-moderned bungalow
in Santa Monica—Glenda

says: *Let me recite what*
history teaches. History
teaches.—Gertrude Stein.
And like Gertie holds
forth in her monologue
while I backslide to anno-
tation, keep the reluctant log of the actor setting
forth on the choppy Sound, unable to cross over,
warn him off, strapped to his leaky enterprise
while Glenda sails on: "Balanchine, babe, ballet
sequence, *The Goldwyn Follies,* 1940. Statue—
Vera Zorina rises en *point* through plashing fountain. Shimmer of now, sweetheart, reflection."
    While I rummage in the dustbin for dear
life: "The health of the eye seems to demand a
horizon. We are never tired so long as we can
see far enough." —Ralph Waldo Emerson, babe.
Recycle: "When you're not on Broadway, everything is Bridgeport." —Arthur "Bugs" Baer.
There's no justice: the chains go slack, rattle in
their pans. In Cocteau's *Blood of the Poet* (1930,
Glenda's wrong, wrong! Off by twenty years),
the statue/know-it-all speaks from the great
unconscious and furthermore our Glenda fails to
see that Spielberg as Pygmalion is head over
heels in love with his own creations. Hey Rube!
Natural power under the spell of graphics, pix-
art, morphing. Animation—of which more later.

Yes, the infinite heart. It's the insupportable
present goads me to project on the defenseless past, brings me back like James to better
times. He's primed for his movie, his art, which
gives us the sensation of living without direct
experience of life. Please, forgive me that last if I
enter a slight adjustment to the books: *I do not*
talk to any intellect in nature, but am presuming an
infinite heart somewhere into which I play. —
Henry David Thoreau, Dec. 24, 1840. Play—as
an actor? Instrument? On a Christmas Eve play

"I'm from Detroit. I don't know that much. About here."

She's a looker, a dresser. James gives the midshot smile, distant yet tender: "So what's a nice girl like you . . .?"

Catherine swipes her brow in broad relief. *Barnum!* Never much for the library, James doesn't begin to suspect there's a world of yellowing files with flaking *Post* photos of their father disgraced on the courthouse steps, of the acquitted woman in a sober pinstriped suit, triumphant padded shoulders. Her brother has come for Barnum, nothing to do with the murder. She flops back in the love seat, deflated, delighted.

Mary Boyle alone thinks of the city as real. Like the librarian from Detroit, she has been assigned here. Mizz Bee understands how workers in the line of service move about this vast and needy country, how nice girls have their calling. When her degree at Columbia was finished, jobs were posted in Baltimore, Cleveland, Atlanta; far down the list, this city with the bad press, the Park City as Catherine insists on calling it with a wry smile. Sure, Cath is why she came here, but it was the look of the place too, half built and half abandoned. When she got off the train to be interviewed, Bridgeport won her heart first day. The city looked as though a natural disaster had swept its main streets or she had arrived in a developing country where hope, as well as funds, had been ripped off.

Official buildings sat about in the rubble and the nice sections faced away as though discouraging events had never happened. Vic Benino drove her through those better neighborhoods with safe two-family houses. Her guide, her Saint Anthony—done up as a corporate executive on holiday, Vic showcased the nice new condominiums where she might live in safety. Safe and nice came up throughout the day. Mary Boyle felt on the other side of the world where she must observe embassy precautions. Vic's tour of Father Panik Village, the project she would work in, was fast as a drive-by shooting. His lengthy lecture cited confounding statistics, praised his own juggling of federal, state funds, but she got the

into, as to an audience or congregation, surely.
Lord, it's good to come up with the answers, but
abandon all thought that I am second sight, able
to predict from my side that Cath won't on her

life, that James will for the hell of it. STATUES!
There's the free moment for both of us, live footage taken on the summer lawn at dusk, before
the pose, the freeze.

Niobe, the weeper, punished for pride,
has lost her nine children. All. All—
not eight or five. The girl with the lisp,
boy with cast eye. For legend's sake—the clever, the dumb,
the one with milk breath, the one with scraped knee—
rest in short graves. Lord, we are blessed to abandon her story.

I confuse with fireworks, a fair,
that spoiled picnic when the Thermos broke.
Awash in lemonade, we feasted
                        on olives
Blotted ancient history, pale stain on the page.
Remember, now that I remember,
headstones, mossy, pitted with age,
their legends dim as to sister and wife,
when they departed. To this green place
we came for the joy of it, knowing
not one of the dead, husband or son
with names out of fashion as archangels.
Fine names we might use in a script.
Without supper, births and death filled us
as sun set. The bawdy sky carried on
while we grew grave noting garlands, willows, weed—
sorry for our sighs, stock as tablets pressed in bronze,
Pat. pending.

Iconography let us off the hook—
lambs for the little ones. Lilies, a cross
let us claim Grief and Glory,
Innocence, living two days. Remembering—
Now fades the glimmering landscape on the sight.
Ruined still life of bread and cheese, soft stone,
brittle grass transposed to colorless mourning.
Our fingers blind on the folds of crimped garments,
whether angel or saint we could not say,
trunk or tail of the beast. Or of Niobe,
the mother, who names her nine children—
the girl who skipped rope,
the boy with the buckle come loose on his shoe.

message: the Village was Beirut, Calcutta, East St. Louis, chip off the South Bronx. Long before Vic talked sick days and benefits, the few persistent shrubs, littered walkways, and barred windows of the red-brick housing project claimed her. Mary Boyle, figuring the threat of the place is what she came for, figuring to invest herself in the Village, in the lost intention of that word, figuring to reverse its inevitable fate, assumed her mission first day.

"So, what's this?" Benino says to Mary Boyle years later in the safety of his office *cum* boardroom, manicured hand on her sleeve. "You got some new style?"

They laugh, her friendly cohorts, good civil servants who would just as soon puncture Vic's fat tum through his rugby shirt, let the hot air out once and for all. They laugh obediently as Mizz Bee looks down to greenish bleached-out stains that speckle her seersucker suit. The stains must not tell their story of lice-zap shampoo she used that morning on Peaches' head before she drove her, second day, to school. It is a warning that in her pursuit of the child all must seem ordinary. So, she's happy when Vic turns to his daffy demographics, checkered charts, and pillared graphs, when Benino's dose of daily denial is over and her custodian suitor sidles up to her in his van.

"When you gonna make me a happy man?"

"Set the date," Mizz Bee yells up to him. She has never noticed the grinning iridescent Lucifer painted on the back window of his Cherokee. Some hellcat, her lover. She feels the security of their routine, his one tired joke, her lame retort; and stops on her way home in alien territory, enters, bravely, a toy shop, where she buys a rainbow pack of Magic Markers, sticky tape, glue. Dewboy's head had tumbled off his slack body in the night. Floyd, as though actually flying, has somewhere lost a shoe. And thinking to upgrade the child's efforts, thus to deliver her from that horror house of family, Mary Boyle pays out fifty bucks for French watercolors and sable brushes to bring to the bunker. Rewarding herself, perhaps for

The Arcade

We have but one arcade, which runs from Main Street to an alley at the back door of D. M. Read's, our finest department store. Half block of wonders which, as a girl, she did not notice, short cut to the bus that's all, no one to see you though in the eerie light Cath could see herself swimming through handbags and fedoras, wedding china, empty eyeglass frames; herself among the goods. The shop windows displaying, reflecting her with (YALE) locks and plump Topstone cigars.

    Well, you might wonder who sold in the arcade, who bought under the roof of glass, bluewhite as skim milk, lid of haze, insubstantial, yet through all the years…Its great age, older than icehouse or livery stable. Untrue, our arcade was of the nineties, novelty item from Paree where the allure of the *passages* had recently been reinvented. So, its foreignness: *here* yet in another city—arcades of Berlin or Milan never heard of, don't know aura from enigma and wanderin' the modest Holyoke mall or the unending splendors of the Galleria in Houston, I mythologize—that my arcade in Bridgeport was uninhabited, save

for a man with a push broom and a waiter. The sweeper, in striped overall and matching cap, makes a neat pile of ticket stubs, wrappers, receipts, and silt which gathers mysteriously in the sealed arcade. The waiter in black tux waits at the Italian restaurant upstairs. There, on a narrow balcony—teeter tables, chianti bottles in straw corselets.

Veal Parmigiana   *$6.95*
Spaghetti, red clam sauce   *$3.50*
Tortoni or Spumoni   *$1.25*

Heaven in few words. I do not share the arcade. Or share my dreams, speaking them out makes a fuss. You tell, then I tell…forcing tales as to the prosthesis emporium, its ghastly wonders of mechanical knee, flesh-colored foot with full articulation of the toes; Davis & Hawley's disembodied velvet neck with graduated pearls; wrist-

having escaped another day with Peaches, she sings scraps of a song come to mind, ". . . playin' a part an' don't need no rehearsin'." In the convent, long after pop went down and dirty, the naughty ebullience of the Beatles lingered on and on.

"Size of the front-hall rug." Catherine paces that out on her worn linoleum. "The gray platform."

"Gray?" James asks.

"Weathered. Two steps up, fenced in."

"That so?" says James on his second whiskey, not buying any of this—weeds and Ba Ba wool from the rafters, loony loom. Worse than apparitions in the night, to find Catherine alternating between crazed fright of his movie and mad tranquillity. He sits at her chipped kitchen table in his Felix hat, unsettled by her calm insistent story.

"In front of Nell's roses. *You*, playing Barnum." She's changed into hopsack and sneakers. "Look here," Cath pulls down her lower lip, "you waved a rusty child's rake." James puts on mammoth Harold Lloyd glasses to see the slight hillock of tissue in the flesh of his sister's mouth. Her teeth spaced, stained, gums inflamed, he looks away. "A gray platform," she says, "like all the special things we had, puppet theater, the village for electric trains."

"Billy loved that stuff."

"On the gray platform," Catherine says, "playing Barnum."

"I honestly don't recall."

"The game was circus. You made me pay admission."

He is sorry about that and the brutal scenes she ticks off with such pleasure—rusty rake, stitches, tetanus shot that made her swell. Cath, rapt in her drama: "I was a blister, a human blister. Many wise men, doctors, came to see the show. You nearly killed me."

"Curious," James says.

"Nell ripped the guilty platform down at once. Then, only

watch plunging on the quarter minute into a tumbler of murky water when I'm already in the tank.

Then you would agree the arcade is a glass coffin, as they say?

Huh?

Or subaqueous dream palace in which the many shops sell your desires?

All's I said is um...ur...mall.

The Pallisers, George (1848–1903) and Charles (1854–?). Englishmen, their careers blossomed in Bridgeport, where they did, in fact, design the workers' houses on Cottage Street, not for Barnum. It was P.T., however, commissioned them to

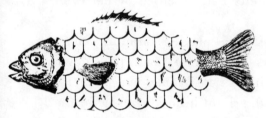

throw up block after block of speculative housing. Then they saw the ingenuity of duplication and published the ever popular *Palliser's American Cottage Homes,* which included drawings and specifications, articles of agreement as well as detailed plans for built-in sideboards, bathtubs and dressers, for fences, gateposts, brickwork, gingerbread scrolls, and their playful use of fish scale and diamond shingles. Tooled pieces promised infinite variety, yet once a Palliser house is registered in the eye you can tell one anywhere in America. Neighborhood Victorian, the ample house in which to presume the perfect family life. Not Charles Addams' manse with sticky cobwebs that cracked us up on *The Munsters*, but studio houses on the exemplary set of *Meet Me in Saint Louis* and the enchanting reproduction of Main Street unveiled at Disneyland, that's your Palliser house of Bridgeport and Albany and Oakland, of Plainfield and Butte. And of the bur-

geoning burbs, the Palliser brothers got hold of that one. You may choose the $4,500 model with its simple gables and veranda or may afford the $13,000 extravaganza with octagonal tower, butler's pantry, double parlors, and fernery. You will be happy there. The linens will be freshly washed, lightly starched. All modern methods of ventilation and sanitary gas registers ensure your comfort. Preserves and relishes, set in their proper dishes, will be spooned with their proper spoons; Czerny exercises played on the piano, and in the sunlight's beam the calico cat stretches luxuriously on floral carpet. Dreaming, you let your novel (*A Lady of Quality* by Mrs. Burnett) fall, sink back in the Morris chair until the thud of the evening paper is heard on the porch. The Palliser house wraps round you with the hearty odors of dumplings and chicken fricassee, rice pudding for dessert. Home: of all the possibilities—saltbox, Cape, Federal—in our Hollywood hearts we yearn for our Palliser home.

In the arcade, which is in ruins, I watch myself on the monitor, newly installed. Actor and viewer: the dream state. I move naturally at first, then, aiming to please, lift my eyes to meet straight on my winsome smile, my confident air. I speak of the silly Surrealists (1921–   ), how they courted the irrational with Ouija board and

mud in front of her washed-out roses." These many years later, Catherine forgives with laughter, but throws a wine cork at her brother.

Now, at the screen door, Mary Boyle. They've not heard her drive up. Catherine, who raged at the head shot of her famous brother, is nowhere to be seen. Some goon in nerdy cardboard hat, owl glasses takes the place of James Bray. She freezes at the door, can't take it—the happy sight, everyday sight of brother and sister. Silly unaffected children: the girl bops a cork: the boy lobs it back. Mary looks down into her sack of hopeful art supplies. Plump fingers of pain constrict her heart: her obsession with Peaches is unnatural and . . . and literally criminal. She knows that as she trips into the scene.

James wants a second take. That night he moves to the Hilton, where specters and out of work character actors will not be allowed upstairs, but he's back at his sister's kitchen table wanting to take it again, the wince when Catherine bopped the cork still registered on his face, then, a shadow against the screen. Next, the slapstick of paper bags collapsing as the door springs open to reveal the sorrowful virgin looking on at life. Cath dashing at the Magic Markers fanned out on the floor. His jumping from the kitchen chair, grabbing at the woman (he had taken it too fast). No—his rising from the kitchen chair in one smooth motion, his hand held out to hers. She steps lightly across the full spectrum of colors, coming to him as though invited to the dance.

Registered as James Bray in the Hilton, where he should have holed up in the first place. Dumb notion, undercover in the gritty city. Cath, in full disclosure, said that after their mother, wielding a crowbar, ripped up the play stage, that patch of yard was cursed. Then he remembered mud, no lawn, and nearly killing Catherine, not playing Barnum, so that when Glenda tracks him to the Hilton—"How's the grisly downhome murder?"—he continues to see Catherine as a festering sideshow blister and cannot answer.

seance; quest for the *real* world. How they elevated the funk of arcades, peopled their *passages* with ostrich-feather whores, patent-leather dandies, the demimundain drawn to great cities.

"…the double game of love and death, *Libido*, which nowadays has enshrined itself in medical books, loiters about here with a little cur named Sigmund Freud at its heels." —Louis Aragon on the *Passage de l'Opéra*. In 1921, Aragon's sometime friend, André Breton, went to visit the little cur in Vienna soliciting—diagnosis, affirmation? Was it not true that the unconscious lent itself to artistic experimentation? Freud said, "Close, but no cigar."

The monitor is second nature to me now. My image, perfect and instantaneous, runs without sound in the arcade where my footsteps echo, where an occasional breeze through a broken pane flutters the cardboard clockface on the oculist's doorknob—"I will return at ⏰." The Italian restaurant folded. In the arcade I am careful to wear an androgynous jacket, shirt, slacks—which tell next to nothing about me. On the monitor, in miniature, I am ordinary. I will not be invited to the Magic City Ball in Luna Park.

Barnum appears to the actor. Consider that they are regulars in the world of illusion. Alone, in a room stripped of toys for the back-wall projection, James is ripe for visual and auditory phenomena. Yet, he must doubt, explain, diminish, while his sister never questioned her comforting/maddening ecstasies. To each child assign the appropriate text:

When as a young man, I lived alone in a strange city, I frequently heard my name suddenly pronounced by an unmistakable, dear voice, and I then made a note of the exact moment of the hallucination in order to inquire carefully of those at home what had occurred at that time. There was nothing to it.

On the other hand, I later worked among my patients calmly and without foreboding while my child almost bled to death. Nor have I ever been able to recognize as unreal phenomena any of the forebodings reported to me by my patients.
—Freud, Psychopathology of Everyday Life

To the medical mind these ecstasies signify nothing but suggested and imitated hypnoid states, on an intellectual basis of superstition, and a corporeal one of degeneration and hysteria. . . . To pass a spiritual judgment upon these states, we must not content ourselves with superficial medical talk, but inquire into their fruits for life.

—William James,
Varieties of Religious Experience

In self-imposed exile, James is close to anon. Exile is home, the place of James' first two-wheeler and first kiss. What had he imagined? More than a treatment, third of the money down. It could make a would-be director inflate the past to atmosphere, light as a helium balloon, such fun till it gets away. The past can make a grown man cry or see double or Barnum. It has been forty years since he entertained the idea of visions on holy cards, in comic books. Why this unwarranted testing? Falling asleep he holds to the apparition—dank smell in his nostrils, tap tap of cane to tap roots and finds the dream. No. Breaks with the dream, starts up in the dark. Like a gumball or shooting mib, just one that is perfectly round and pearly discovered in all the driveway gravel: he had, in fact, been Barnum in frock coat padded with pillows, doffing his grandfather's top hat. After the safe platform of the parish school, junior high—big stage, real lightboard, velvet curtain. Some talent show or pageant he'd directed, done up as fat old Barnum, talcum powder in his hair…Master of Ceremonies waving the knobbed cane Billy brought back from Château Thierry. The tap-dance sisters, the comic in innocent drag, Joey Montera's magic violin zipping through "Flight of the Bumble Bee."

"The series," Glenda says. "I can make a sweet deal."

"Script control?"

"Thanksgiving with the Arabs," and so forth, but he's thinking how comfortably Cath inhabits her big body; her cheerful industry, how Nell would favor her daughter's projects . . .

"Love ya, babe"

. . . and thinking he'd like to get it right, his shopworn actor's smile on the wistful face of Mary Boyle.

Catherine said: "Make your movie."

"It's only a story, Cath."

The thrum of his words telling; no voice coach, hell no, James sounded like that in second grade. Like all his gifts, the arresting vibrato delivered early and complete, makes you believe more's there. In the uncertain registers of adolescence, got him what he wanted. Got him what he was after tonight. Compelled by that voice, she was eight years old running across the backyard where there was not a stuffed elephant or doped-up Bengal tiger or crack of the training whip to suggest a good show . . . only James flourishing Barnum's cane, a rusty wand to transform her to a curiosity. Tonight in the kitchen, James calling to her and she paid her nickel. "Go on, make your movie."

"It's only a story, Cath. Billy Bray dazzle," tilting his checkered hat back with a gesture that belonged to their father, "his cocky virtue. The war that made the city ripe to bursting before the nasty trial."

"The nasty murder," she said.

"Small story. How it breaks him. Sleaze—society woman and soldier boy. Lust."

"Whose lust, James?"

"Oh, the woman's!" The alluring undertow of his voice, telling his fake movie—smoking gun and wanton woman. Clear conviction of the murderess, yet heartbreaking disillusion of the city. Why? And why does it follow—end of Billy Bray's career, end

The audience hollering, stomping for more. They had played for themselves, for each other. In back-stage comradery that only the amateur...even Viola Pistey who exceeded her reach in "Indian Love Call"...they had all kissed and wept in the wings, moved by the honesty of their performance. M.C. That was the talent show.

Which means?

Means, madam! I know not 'means.'

That you approve of James' recall, nub, subtext? Male construct as it were?

Hold the phone! Means you are single if not simple-minded. Means I'm tired of your time that would have Willa sashay out of the closet...

Your time?

My time, dull age that would have Isadora drop twenty pounds, coax Emily down from her room to drive into town for necessities. "She's doing much better," we say.

Then you are a woman?

Yes, I am that.

Ghostwriting: James is jogging past Remington Electric Shaver. In the middle distance— Locomobile, ever so retro-romantic, produced handmade luxury cars, four a day. Didn't hold with Henry Ford's Model T production, an innovation which belongs, in truth, to Bridgeport. Elias Howe, inventor of the sewing machine,

came upon the efficiency of the assembly line when working on his repeating rifle during the Civil War. Andrew Riker, an engineer at Loco-mobile, is responsible for developing the first useful gasoline engine in 1901. A fleet of Special Locomobiles was designed for General Pershing, Commander of the American Expeditionary Forces in World War I. Tufted calfskin rumble seats, handpolished brass radiators, upon occasion Tiffany accessories, electric intercoms, always the infinite coats of lacquer: insistent that quality must never suffer, Locomobile dissolved in 1930.

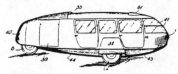

On October 18, 1933, U.S. Patent 2,101,057 was issued to Buckminster Fuller for his Dymaxion car, constructed in the Locomobile plant. "I knew

everyone would call it a car. It was the land-taxiing phase of a wingless, twin-orientable-jet-stilts flying device." In speaking of his car Bucky revved up, more than usual. The car, like his geodesic dome, Dymaxion house, tensegrity sphere, was of our universe, the real, not other-world. His zoomobile a beaut, drivable on high-ways, on Fifth Avenue. Three-wheeled, steered from the rear with a rudder, better than special effects of a Batmobile, sleeker than moderno jet, ideal transport for Bucky's Phantom Captain, that self-balancing boyish adoptive biped—man. "You could hook it around 180 degrees, a turn no motorcycle could make. Like if the cops came after me, I could turn and go in the opposite direction. They could never catch me. It was lots of fun. They just wanted to rubberneck this thing, and take me to the station so they

of his belief in the courthouse, of Daddy's stake in justice? When she understood he had it wrong, pure hokum, she said, "Make your movie."

Find Nell if he can in the work of a competent aging actress, still elegant, creped throat, bruised shadows under her eyes. The boy must be elflike, clever as the wind. The girl solemn as stone. Park what's left of Golden Hill Street with snub-nosed 1940s cars. There will surely be a lunch counter with brass and marble fixtures like the one Billy and Elliot, the hippety-hop reporter, frequented. Establish the homefront—virtue before small violence. She cannot help thinking her brother will lift green lawns and sparkling sidewalks at their corners so his movie will feature predictable maggots in the mud.

Still, Cath ran to the gray platform, paid for the burr in his voice. Make your show, but how will he play Billy though he affix bow tie to double chin, fatten to his girth? She cannot figure how he'll play their father, who gave himself so fully in performance, yet never acted in his life. "Make your movie," she said, signing the release. It was then she threw a wine cork at her brother, just as Mary Boyle fell in at the door, into the family banter. His arm held out to save her, she caught herself. Ex-nun looks on movie star, holds him in her eyes: "I've fallen in love with a child." Meaning to say—how clearly Cath saw it—Mary Rose meaning to say, I will not fall in love with you.

James at his morning pushups on mauve carpet in the Hilton. No more running in this ghost town, God knows who you'll meet— Carol Lombard, Jimmy Dean. Through the brown glass windows the shambles of Victorian railway station, listless harbor, handsome post office appear in sepia soft focus. It's hours before he can get at Ziff, say (no need to mention the co-opting of his sister) that the atmosphere has thickened—disturbing flash of that Isabelle Tully or Toole, sultry social climber among dutiful gray war workers; forgettable pawnlike beauty of the Polack kid; buoyant detective,

could show it off." Three Dymaxion cars were manufactured, exhibited as fantasy. One may be seen at Harrah's Auto Museum, Reno, Nev.

In Sir Francis Bacon's *New Atlantis*, written when he'd fallen from power (1623), it is the inventor, the experimenter, who is entrusted with the prophetic vision for humankind. The science of the useful was to bring about the ideal commonwealth; had brought it about in Bacon's Utopia, for Bensalem is all set up, functioning in the South Seas. There are museums of science and industry with statues: "*. . . we have two very long and fair galleries: in one of these we place patterns and samples of all manner of the more rare and excellent inventions: in the other we place the statuas of all principal inventors. There we have*

he were about to move away from something at which he is now staring. His eyes are wide open, mouth agape, wings spread. The angel of history must look like that. His face is turned toward the past. Where we perceive a chain of events, he sees one single catastrophe which keeps piling wreckage upon wreckage and hurls it in front of his feet. The angel would like to stay, awaken the dead, and make whole what has been smashed. The storm from Paradise drives him irresistibly into the future to which his back is turned, while the pile of debris before him grows toward the sky. That which we call progress is this storm.
      —Walter Benjamin, Theses on History

I-95 soars above Bridgeport: the city is seen as rooftops, domes, spires, much like James' open-

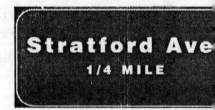

the statua of your Columbus, that discovered the West Indies: also the inventor of ships: your monk that was the inventor of ordnance and of gunpowder: the inventor of music: the inventor of letters: the inventor of printing"…and of silk, wine, corn, bread, sugar. "*These statuas are some of brass; some of marble and touch-stone; some of cedar and other special woods gilt and adorned; some of iron, some of silver, some of gold.*"
      In 1882, the Smithsonian requested a bust of Barnum to be placed with those who distinguished themselves "as promoters of the natural sciences." P.T., who had generously donated "duplicate curiosities," moved quickly, proudly, to have the life mask taken.

There is a picture by Klee called Angelus Novus. An angel is presented in it who looks as if

ing sequence, much like the cartographer's sweeping view from aerial balloon. You keep on going to New York or New Haven. It takes less than a minute to traverse the city from the first exit, Black Rock Turnpike, to Stratford Avenue, the last.

Running, the actor's jog controls the architectural tour, though he need not be in shape to play his roly-poly dad. Perhaps developing the directorial eye; figuring what's left of picturesque banks on McLevy Green, one of the few commons in New England with no house of God; seeing the courthouse, Richardson Romanesque, to be yet and always the perfect fortification for the administration of justice; framing his principles in a long shot, the murderess and the detective turn from each other swiftly—descend the steep pitch of granite steps. Running, running by—

firm finger on the moral pulse of his small city.

Call Ziff, say it: "Hometown—all you can eat, buddy, fuckin' salad bar."

"Fuckin' bacon bits, garbanzo beans." In the inevitable fuckin' over he hears Ziff's excitement.

And Mary Boyle bending his mind worse than Barnum, nothing to do with the movie. Insane reversal of some goddam story conference, in which saint becomes whore, crook written out for good guy, Civil War updates to Vietnam. Mary stumbles toward him, holds him with her lovelorn eyes . . . a swift breaking of the spell. There is no mistake: in her shapeless stained suit, she is the exiled princess.

Shoot it: delicate planes of her head, halo of blue-black curls, okay; though hot beat of her temples, warm breath upon his cheek can't be captured on the screen, nor the primitive power of first touch. Surely it was foretold she would steady herself, hand to his shoulder. Flustered and comic their beginning, he'd flipped his hat, head to toe, a vaudeville maneuver during which split second twenty years transpire. Living with Mary Rose, nice Bridgeport girl, his Mary Rose in a scrapbook of stills—dancing at the Brooklawn Country Club, safe upon the doorstep of their white Colonial, frantic over the mortgage, over the crib of a sick child. They have dismantled a dozen Christmas trees, endured teenage contempt, attended the deaths of impossible parents, vacationed in Maine and Bermuda, argued, voted, paid the bills. He has spent a lifetime with this woman he doesn't know, but knows profoundly, sweetly in prehistory, all beside the point of his pushups and his movie.

Deep focus: black cradle phone, ivory nail buffer, reading glasses, gold pocket watch. Billy wakes to homicide in movie dark. Hear Nell's alarm. Sudden streak of lamplight on polite studio photos of boy and girl. Rising in grumpy fits and starts, the detective's thick body obliterates bedroom paraphernalia. Heard before seen: footsteps firm with courthouse authority. Long shot: Billy's march through the great hall under dizzying arches. Cut to crunch of gravel before the

better exercise, run up those steps, sweat as he reads the scribbled notice:

> KNIVES, STEEL TOE SHOES, DRUGS AND ALCOHOL PROHIBITED. NO GUNS. ALL REGISTERED GUNS AND AMMUNITION CHECK AT THIS DOOR.

But James is running, running by.

I banish from the arcade the work of Sylvester Zefferino Poli, a Sicilian modeler of wax figures for museums, until he discovered in Bridgeport the mother lode of real estate and movies. I do not admit mechanical pianos, melancholy electric globes, gossip sheets, wind-up toys, African masks, broadsides of **SALE!!!**

Exceptional Values!!!, posters with time

and place of bygone shows. Props which the Surrealists needed: a boys' club, really, charming their circle. Elevation of innocent vision. Grim fun of their pranks. Bored, waiting for something to happen, they brought it about— happenings, avant gibberish, begging the catcalls, the rotten tomato. Café morality: claiming anon, while creating public scandal. Poets with pistols contemplating beautiful crimes. The name of the game— Chicken. Only Marcel Duchamp called them on it, walking the waters to New York, where the wordless play of the chessboard would entertain him all his life. One just man, it says somewhere—
A few righteous men. Genesis 18:22.
The Bible, the Daybook. The word is sacred in the arcade. Shakespeare, as Barnum advises, with few adjustments plays to the masses, whereas those Frenchies...
And Krauts?
Them too, readin' our detective stories, our funny papers, watchin' our gangster movies. "Oh, Texaco, Esso, Shell, the great inscriptions of human possibility! Soon we shall make the sign of

the cross before your fonts." —Louis Aragon, *Nightwalker.* You believe that crap?
Then you are an American?
Nobody laughs at me.
Not in your arcade?
That's right. Not in this day and age.
Which age?
This age: The Age of the Envy of Movies.

Nell with her Puritan streak disapproved of the movies. That you'd give up God's day, go into that night. Took the joy out of her kids' Saturdays at the Rialto. Or tried to, for the boy deftly screened out her displeasure. As though she could save them from the dark dreamland, from the flickering harm of the show. She had seen Charlie Chaplin in the old days and gone twice more to the movies. Once, to the Depression comedy *You Can't Take It With You* and laughed herself silly, for years identifying with the wacky bohemian family in the Kaufman and Hart script as though her father's solid house, Billy's paychecks, her nourishing meals, were mere frippery and they lived on the zany brink. Perhaps the artistic life—for she painted flowers and fruit on tole trays, sculpted sweet clay angels—was her deep desire and she rightly feared the common undertow of the movies. A second time she took her children to *Fantasia* at Rockefeller Center, a cultural event: quite overwhelming, "The Dance of the Hours," "Night on Bald Mountain." Small weight on her heart, James swiping her change to sneak off to the movies, take himself downtown to Poli's Palace or Majestic, sucked into the fancy playhouse she could tell by the stunned look of him. Wasn't she glad when he went out for the higher principles of the stage, for Shakespeare at Yale, Chekhov in New York. It was only Billy thought

6—REEL COMEDY—6

detective gets out of his car, looks to expanse of Tudor mansion, pats body holster down to the neat bulk of his gun. His (our) first sight of the killer. Costumed as a girl, she swings the front door open to stand defenseless in cold sunlight.

It runs in his head, you bet, but with repeat of the scene which fits nowhere, the one with the unasked-for woman he's known always, falling toward him in a clatter of kid stuff, scoring off him, saying she's in love. Huffing and puffing in the muted Hilton view of Bridgeport until the sun rises upon the reality of California, James Bray doesn't know Mary Boyle from Minnie Mouse, from some cute extra, day hire on a film. Their intimacy crisscrossing time is the wily trick of an old Hitchcock thriller; or maybe his coming home, call it that, casts him back to lovesick boy, a role he never had much time for. Dream dozing, idly flipping the pages of Conrad Hilton's *Be My Guest*, he presumes this unfamiliar yearning is no more than the buttery breakfast wrenching his middle-aged gut.

Unaccustomed to celebrity, the front desk sends her up. On the pretext of returning his hat, Mary Boyle enters the programmed comforts of the room—chairs match carpet, drapes. Silk lilies in colors off the tranquillity chart. She's pert in pressed jeans, blue Keds, a scarlet blouse printed with tiny repetitive balloons. And savvy—allows how he must travel in disguise. James flings the checkered hat of cheap manufacture across the room. Shivering in the Hilton chill, Mary Boyle looks to the sealed brown glass windows. "Hot, it's hot as hell outside."

"Sorry."

"It's not your fault." With a tremulous smile she watches James hang the *Do Not Disturb* sign on the outer doorknob of the room. Tears dribble, then the unleashed flood, which she stops with angry fists. Her face, salty and raw when he kisses her . . . what follows in this room the director of "My Story" has not imagined.

"Tell," he says.

him a fool. The time came, before her gentle end, when she went to the movies. Catherine would come from the city to take her rather ceremo-niously to a bright new theater set among shops, first mall on the outskirts of Bridgeport, where she would watch James and know it was perfectly ridiculous, both the story he played in and the choke of her pride turned to tears. If ever he was finally taken from her, if ever she possessed him, it was in the movie dark. His sneaking off, she needn't have worried: James was alert in his plush seat at Poli's, watch-

ing the beam of light from the projector, the studied movement of lips and eyes, play of shadows more real to him than the fanciful surround, which was for children, exactly as his mother said.

The twin theaters, Majestic and Palace, were built for Sylvester Zefferino Poli in 1922 by Thomas Lamb, architect of the first luxury movie house in America (1913), a doge's palace named the Regent, which still stands to the north of Central Park. Lamb, a Scotsman, was in his Adam period when he built the Bridgeport theaters.

Nell would not have minded the Wedgwood bas-relief, dainty opera boxes, recessed marble columns or the pretty damask sofas and chairs (not nailed down) which made the mezzanine lobbies into the drawing rooms of Edinburgh; and fortunately would never have known the encrusted excess of Lamb's later barococo and oriental theaters. Twenty years after his blindness to the charm of Poli's, James grooved on the polychrome embellishments of Orpheums and Paramounts, the ecclesiastical vaults of Loew's Orpheum, L.A., and the atmospherics of the Arlington Fox, Santa Barbara, so close to his Spanish Revival home.

Ghost story: Holmes would have no interest in the uncomplicated murder of the Litwak Boy. *"My mind," he said, "rebels at stagnation. Give me problems, give me work, give me the most abstruse cryptogram, or the most intricate analysis, and I am in my own proper atmosphere. I can dispense then with artificial stimulants. But I abhor the dull routine of existence. I crave for mental exaltation. That is why I have chosen my own particular profession, or rather created it, for I am the only one in the world.*
—*Sherlock Holmes in* The Sign of Four

The case of the jaded beauty holds no obscure motives, exotic clues. Did James ever take hold of the doom beneath idle dalliance that led to Litwak's murder? Will he portray death with

"Not now."

No one, certainly not Ziff whoring after the public taste, could predict the POW effect—tragic Little Boyle controlling the scene. "Hold your calls," she says.

James obliges as she unties the drawstring of his sweats, grabs his hard cock, strokes the wet tip. Oh my, checking him out, determined. Her fingers flick at the mother-of-pearl buttons on her blouse, snap at the laces of her Keds. Naked, willing a martyrdom . . . then, then her brave purpose dissolves, her hands cup modestly over erect pink nipples, thin shoulder blades quiver in shame. Wave after wrenching wave of sobs.

"Tell," he says.

"Not now." It occurs to Mary as the refrain in their established litany.

For James, a perfect take. Bride over no threshold, yet the fleeting thought *virgin* thrills as he scoops her above the enormous bed. Arms thrown around his neck, begging to be set in place, though she plays at resistance and he forces his knee between her legs before she arches toward him, opening with small unpracticed hands the swollen lips of her glistening vulva. See! See what she has, here in the tangled pelt, like no other, her rosy flesh, like no woman in the world, losing herself in that hope. His hands press into the tight curve of her waist and he enters her easily (yet another surprise), thrusting up as though never before, as though no end to what he needs from her while her nails rake down his sides urging him further. Pushing him off to prolong, she kisses the love welts she has inflicted, kissing him down, her damp ringlets cool on his body. So their quick claim upon each other in a rented bed is done with violence, with tenderness—a giving up, a giving in.

"Mary Rose," he christens her, choosing, with the silky growl of his voice, that name of an old-fashioned girl, then urgent above her again, come into the need of her body. "Now?" James cries, free of himself, bound to her. What sort of question can that

more accuracy than *noir cliché* in which the body glides by on the screen at its best angle—a pleasing distortion? *There are also a few badly scarred champions of the formal or classic mystery who think that no story is a detective story which does not pose a formal and exact problem and arrange the clues around it with neat labels on them. Such would point out, for example, that in reading* The Maltese Falcon *no one concerns himself with who killed Spade's partner, Abner (which is the only formal problem of the story), because the reader is kept thinking about something else. Yet in* The Glass Key *the reader is constantly reminded that the question is who killed Taylor Henry, and exactly the same effect is obtained—an effect of movement, intrigue, cross-purposes, and the gradual elucidation of character, which is all the detective story has any right to be about anyway. The rest is spillikins in the parlor.*

—Raymond Chandler,
The Simple Art of Murder

Murder provides the occasion for an actor's return to home base, apprehension of small cityscape. Rejecting the sloppy spring thaw of that fated day to fix his parade on Memorial Day (at that time an unmovable feast), he recaptures Main Street on Saturday: shop windows…manikins in halters, culottes, a snood here or there; women—in Bemberg sheers, spectator pumps. Perms and pompadours revolve through revolving doors for Howland's White Sale, bustle into D.M. Read's for high fashion; men—soft hats, Palm Beach suits—appear affable but mighty busy. Aerodynamic La Salles, veed grilles of the old Mercurys, slab-sided Hudsons. "Don't you love the look of it?" The erotic facade.

Broadway As Symbol

It was during the commercial period that the evolution of the Promenade, such as existed in New York at Battery Park, took place. The new promenade was no longer a park but a shop-lined thoroughfare, Broadway. Shopping became for the more domesticated half of the community an exciting, bewildering amusement; and out of a combination of Yankee "notions," Barnumlike advertisement, and magisterial organization arose that omnium gatherum *of commerce, the department store. It is scarcely possible to exaggerate the part that Broadway—I use the term generically—has played in the American town. It is not merely the Agora but the Acropolis. When the factory whistle closes the week, and the factory hands of Camden, or Pittsburgh, or Bridgeport pour out of the buildings and stockades in which they spend the more exhausting half of their lives, it is through Broadway that the greater part of their repressions seek an outlet. Both the name and the institution extend across the continent from New York to Los Angeles. Up and down these second-hand Broadways, from one in the afternoon until past ten at night, drifts a more or less aimless mass of human beings, bent upon extracting such joy as is possible from the sights in the windows, the contacts with other human beings, the occasional or systematic flirtations, and the risks and adventures of purchase.*

—Lewis Mumford, City Development, *1945*

be? Yes, now. Permission granted, now that they are naked, undisguised.

Just folks: lying side by side it's not so bad having made love in full view of a bleary brown sky. Freaks to discover in the Hilton universe, in middle age, in unserious times that there's love to die from. A dozen movies a year (nothing Bray's cast in), nightly tube, continuing run of soapy novels might have instructed these rumpled misfits in true love. It's got shelf life, the poignant pull to sadness which underlies the triumph of unlikely mating: bearded ladies, albino giants, dog-faced boys, and creatures too clever to display our deformities, searching for who'll take us—hairy, unpigmented, hunched—take us as their own. *"My own,"* Billy Bray sang courting Nell, his pure tenor not yet coarsened by three packs a day, sang it at Matt Devlin's Steinway: *Sweeter than the Rose of Erin. Come be my own, come light a flame in my heart.* The sentimental lilt of those lyrics not available to Mary Boyle and James Bray.

"No sequence." He's telling her about the movie business. To be fair, she's asked, "Why'd you come here?"

It's his life, the movie business. How he no longer trusts it, but this time wants it tough, no path of least resistance. So maybe impossible? Ah! she's not buying that. You see, he despises the people who stand in line to see him. In New York on a Sunday, 28°, he leapt out of a cab, shouted at the shivering fools, "Go home. Fuckin' dummies, go home."

"No sequence. No continuity." For at other times he loves them, men and women who wait for his practiced gaze into the face of evil. Millions, they are his millions waiting in the dark for the cold eyes, lantern jaw, bone at the bridge of his nose. He turns to Mary Rose: now his unwaxed hairline, indistinct lashes would ruin the look, distract from the seamless surface of action so smooth you never notice the love story is flimsy, there's no motive for the bloody kill. How dear her tousled head in the crook of his arm as she listens, girl breasts softened to cream with a divvy of jam. Nell's puddings he thinks and thinks how perverse that boy love of vanilla, tapioca,

Would you say that the monitor is a mirror?
It films me. Reflect on that.
In case you shoplift?
In case I mug for the camera. All must be natural in the arcade. No plastic palms, silk flowers ready for your next set of lovers at the Hilton. Consider it a greenhouse, if you will, earth smell, moist and warm to perfection.
As a new-baked bun?
The dream is not known in its final state. In places the arcade unexplored, a wilderness: where once the boot black with his snapping rag and kit of polish, now the precarious gorge with lichen covered rocks; hot mineral springs where Karpilow Locksmiths: Alarms and Safety Doors. Sunrise bleeds off the balcony. All such violent landscapes, not the work of man, inspire awe in the arcade, never to be exploited by Sunday painters. Yet there are areas of cultivation—civic parks, formal gardens, the Okefenokee Swamp.
Utopia?
Go for it. The detailed fantasy: ornamental edibles—tiger tomatoes, ebony corn we will savor; grandifloras—Sweet Surrender, Sheer Bliss, violets big as your fist; Biblical quaffs of mead and honey, the cup that cheers. And here disrobe for each other like curious childen. Silence and music allowed, little speech.
You were nuts about words.
Useless exchange of words. Oh, there will be endless stories and song in the arcade, history as consolation. Notices and proclamations posted in the grove beyond the Fanny Farmer store. Words to live by: *"Bridgeport, why that is the place I had those elegant fried oysters."*
—*Abraham Lincoln*
Why that tone, a toad in your terrarium?
Lighten up. Shadowboxing in the shadow box.

Often words break the frame in the comic strip *Pogo*. Yeow!, Wozzat!? or more simply, too big for the panel. The emotion, that is. Cast of critturs—possum, turtle, owl, skunk, worm chile, etc.—being caught in extraordinary adventures. Plotwise they've much to say: "We gotta figger a way to get POGO to marry mam'selle so's he'll have a first Lady when he's President…. "Thoughtwise, too: "Well, THAT'S Life…a fleeting shadow, Darksome seen as in a rearview mirror." The remark of Howland Owl (named after Bridgeport's second-best department store), but most often POGO, the possum (bewildered/self-possessed), gets the aphoristic line so's to be quoted by Nobel laureates when speaking on TV. "As POGO said: "There may be people up there as intelligent as we are." Human beans, specially on TV, miss the double edge. Or edge that wobbles as in the strip where panel 2 looks back at or seeps into panel 1, for *Pogo* is chock full o' common terry an grab a dream. Hole cloth of funny papers, those that are suitably funny. The only suit worn by a verbose bear, P. T. Bridgeport, unless you count the pirate costume of Simply J. Malarkey, that fat pig. The animals, playing us in inspired strokes, never depart their parlous, homey habitat, a landscape at times so sweeping in its narrative Walt Kelly widelensed it across the page.
Educated guess: Okefenokee Swamp is Beardsley Park, the other park. The swamp is

the mound of mother's sweets while once . . . once in Glasgow, he tells her, the set a big greenhouse of a place in which Commie Cubans blast Interpol. Victorian cast iron and glass, the People's Palace, a museum preserving relics of the industrial past . . . the available light faded early on that northern location. So back to the hotel where, at a movie house nearby, a tribe of Indian men in Gunga Din getups were buying tickets to another of his efforts. They turned from him, angry to see the man they'd come to see. "One more affront in that friggin' dark cold country," James says, "like a hoax."

Mary Rose draws round the sheet: "A hoax is intended."

He speaks to her of Barnum, making it plausible to himself—that the statue in the park suggested the apparition. He'd come back to play his father, the great showman a likely substitute. "An old circus trick—load the cannon with the live dog, the stuffed toy shoots up in the air."

"Would you like to believe it?" she asks.

"That I communed with the dead?"

"That you're a nut job sighting UFOs. No better than hysterical girls who see the Virgin. I believe it. I believe an old man breathed his damp breath on you from the tomb, if I believe this." Flapping her arms to include their wide bed, rose-mauve amenities, flimsy brass-glass glamour, rotogravure glow of the ruined city beyond. Draped in her sheet she marches to the bathroom, looking like one of the classical maids on Barnum's pedestal. Those rigid nymphs don't cry like Mary Rose. He discovers her sobbing into a Hilton bathsheet. Through the black curls, coarse gray hairs he's not seen.

Sad story: "Catherine saw me. She misses nothing at that loom. You left your hat. I thought to drop it at the desk." Smart-mouthed through her sniffles: "I had that crap—stickum, glitter glue, the goddam pot at the end of the rainbow—to give Peaches, more important than your old hat."

"Relatively new," James says. He puts on an antique ki-

bosky and beauteous as Beardsley, built to Olmsted's design (1893) by Miss Elizabeth Bullard, who managed the Irish and Italian workmen just fine, thank you. Walt Kelly, the cartoonist (East Side, Harding High), *genius loci* of Okefenokee, hung our elms with Spanish moss, transplanted cattails and bullrushes of Miss Bullard's rusticated swimming hole to the imagined pastoral of Georgia.

P.T. failed in his attempt to purchase the half-timbered and wattled birthplace of the Bard in Stratford-upon-Avon, install it on Broadway; but the Ladies' Art League unveiled a thatched, mullioned, posied replica of Ann Hathaway's cottage in Beardsley Park (1916), upon which occasion Rachel Petrona, a young girl from the public

school, recited the mad scene from *Hamlet*. The cottage, which Catherine loved, was in decline—all dusty, littered, the second-best bed and furniture untended when she rode her bike one day as far as Beardsley. As she was growing fast, she now saw that the house was half-size, like . . . like the dwarfs' house in *Snow White and the Seven Dwarfs*, which of course, it may have been, since Kelly worked for the other Walt as an animator on movie of same name . . . vine over the small door, country-cute windows, woodwork unfortunately Heidied, but Cath knelt to touch the very knots in the very floorboards which Snow White sweeps. All surmise, since Kelly came to the Disney Studios in 1936, but we are certain of *Fantasia* (1940)—his work on Bacchus, the donkey, the fauns.

Dumbo—he animated on Dumbo, ringmaster, roustabouts, kids. Bpt. story: reverse grandeur and grace of Jumbo, you get the inept, forlorn, the littlest elephant who triumphs in the end. Leaving the sea of studio animators, cartooning alone, Kelly bought the worthless swamp wherein an obscure possum...the rest, as they say, is histree whether or not it's the sugar maple in Elizabethan garden of Ann Hathaway's cottage in Beardsley.

Be Big: *Think Big. Act Big. Dream Big.*
It has been my experience that the way most people court failure is by misjudging their abilities, belittling their worth and value. Did you ever think what can happen to a plain bar of iron, worth about $5.00. The same iron when made into horseshoes is worth $10.50. If made into needles, it is worth $3,250.85, and if turned into balance springs for watches its value jumps to $250,000.—Conrad Hilton, Be My Guest

Ah, you are getting to the love story.
In the arcade we do not intrude. We leave lovers to their fate, which may be glorious, fleeting, enduring, banal. We do not second-guess matters of the heart. If we were to steal cross-page, it would be softly:

> *O, Mary Rose, how came you here*
> *Where child was not awaiting?*
> *How lay you in the way of tears,*
> *A bed not of your making?*
>
> *Your star has traveled from the West*
> *To touch you e'er so lightly,*
> *School and hold you to the test.*
> *Will passion be your playing?*

And so forth, though the ballad is always postscript, consequence, or choice that never was. The tearstained kiss, depth of feeling, their love

mono (courtesy of Ziff, Lilah disapproves). The slither of old silk feels costumy as the stiff sleuth's hat.

"Your dumb hat," says Mary Rose, "but first I wanted to see my child. Mizz Bee on a mission, drivin' down East Main with the care package, cereal and milk, set on giving the head lice a second dose. The master plan had blossomed, how I'd be awarded Peaches. Made for TV movie with the liberal judge and ever after she's with Catherine and me around the real Christmas tree, Peaches opening her presents. I'm this perfect anglo mama, dealing out the goods, that's how wonderful I am. Peaches in a swell school uniform, her little round face first row. She's waving her chub golden hand. Peaches knows all the answers. Fractions, social studies, communication skills. Reads, tucked under Catherine's woolly blankets, Peaches reads—*Little Women, The Secret Garden*—book after classy book. I think Peaches is so smart she reads Dickens, about all those English orphans, and appreciates her happy days with queer old Aunt Catherine, Sister Mary Rose. It's a series: Leave it to Peaches; Peaches goes Hawaiian. Can I have cold coffee? I want a cigarette," says Mary Rose. "I haven't since I left the convent."

"One sin or another." A comeback line as he delivers it, moving back from her confession. Her story for his story. All this while she's perched on the side of the tub, the bathsheet slipping off her thigh, and he wonders if she knows that the milky crystals she scratches are the spill of his sperm. Unworldly child with gray-flecked hair, it's not what you tell your lover, that you've had him on the rebound from a project kid.

"The sin was Peaches," she says. "Virgin birth to phantom child. By the time I pulled into Father Panik Village she was *summa cum laude* in a cap and gown." Mary Rose clutches the towel across her breast, nice Bridgeport girl. Again, he's stirred by the crazy closeness, has long known her retreat after sexual abandon, a wordy, anxious drawing of the veil. His own misery is unexpected. The bathroom, full of mirrors, reflects his pied face, foolish as a callow boy in love.

in a plain word, cannot be fathomed. So we turn in the arcade to our puzzles—Adam's navel, Darwin's ovaries, Virgin birth, whether the Spotted Boy was white on black or black on white. Sad to say, the arcade is in color, but we have the answer to that one: in the 1850s the new cadmium oils became available. The American landscapes of Fitzhugh Lane and Frederick Church transformed our twilights to theatrical, assertive Sublime, so that the purples, reds, oranges filter through these glass panels, stain the terrazzo of the arcade, ricochet off the crumbling walls. Then too, when Technicolor, *Flowers and Trees* (Disney, 1932), first blazed before us on the screen in a second coming—there was no turning back.

And the monitor?

Oh, the monitor is lovely black and white, grainy, unstable. In the arcade we dread the coming of virtual reality, fractional invisibility, all cybernetic punk.

The computer steals your soul, as they say?

"They say, they say, they say. Ah, my child, how long are you going to continue to use those dreadful words? Those two little words have done more harm than all others. Never use them, my dear, never use them."
　　　　　—*Aaron Burr in William Carlos Williams,*
　　　　　　　　　　The Virtue of History

Only you are allowed to speak in your glorified specimen box?

Mind your beeswax.

Only you are seen on the monitor?

Look. We know that we live in a parlor fern case, that we are a decorative curiosity, barely self-sustaining. That children stand on tiptoe and peer in, disappointed that we don't

swim, chase tail, blow bubbles, entertain in any way. We are bugs in a jam jar thrown a leaf to consume, not granted chops and ice cream, our last request before the sentence of suffocation. We know our haughty second person to be forsaken, lone. That'll be the day—when I see, not myself, but another in the monitor—whiskered, young, in a celluloid collar or varsity sweater, my lips shaped to form the consonants of another time. Then, the seasons will come again. I will declare autumn days of meditation, winter days of mourning. A feasibility study will prove me incorrect and on the button, nevertheless able to go on.

To push on: *Words cannot express the joy that the sun brings to all living things.... Yes, Love comes even to the plants. Males and females, even the hermaphrodites, hold their nuptials (which is the subject that I now propose to discuss), showing by their sexual organs which are males, which females, which hermaphrodites.... The actual petals of a flower contribute nothing to generation, serving only as the bridal bed which the great Creator has so gloriously prepared, adorned with such precious bed-curtains, and perfumed with so many sweet scents in order that the bridegroom and bride may therein celebrate their nuptials with great solemnity. When the bed has been made ready, then is the time for the bridegroom to embrace his beloved bride and surrender himself to her.*
　　　　　　　　　　　　　　—*Linnaeus,*
　　　　Praeludia Sponsaliarum Plantarum

Sexy, but discredited.

You were hankerin' after the love story. In the arcade there is no release as in the movies.

Out of the shower she's all business until the second run of overwhelming tears. Well, it's this: She parked in front of the Benner/Benez building. The usual vials, dishes of cocaine scum in the halls scattered after the night's revels, roaches (both kinds), fresh urine, familiar carcass of burnt mattress, dead pints of Ron Rico. Hall light shot out. The unlocked door did not open, open so that Chi Chi and Ty could come back and inhabit their photos, so Flyin' Frank could be grounded, Dewboy fried for good. She pounded hard with her fist, thought Peaches harmed or dead, drew back to batter against the door with her shoulder—the way they do, she says, in movies. The moment to call the cops. She could not. In her head it's still Peaches and Mizz Bee: the tape in which Dorothy hugs trembling Toto, Oliver begs for more, skips to the safe ecstasy of Disneyworld, Mary Boyle and her love child spinning in the Mad Hatter's Teacup. The door would not give. On the dirty wall along with the names of the half living, dead, and departed of Father Panik Village, crude engorged shaft, blown-up balls. She must have passed that cock so many times, never seen its dimension, hopeless crowing two dimensions, its flapping cunt of a companion. Peaches has grown up with these signs, not quite grown up and maybe died here. Mizz Bee can do nothing about it.

At last the door flung wide. Michelle in a frilly apron, bad-ass pants, satin halter laced over swollen tits. She stands firm in silver sandals, giving Mizz Bee the welcome.

"Mizz Bee," she says, "you need somethin'?"

"Peaches?"

"Schooltime, Mizz Bee. María's gone to school."

And the whole place cleared. All wonders gone. She could see behind the brazen body of that ten-dollar skeeze—Lloyd's empty chair, no slack-belly Paco—all gone, those men Peaches had put in their place.

"You want somethin' here? You wanna do my paperwork, Mizz Bee?"

"Gone!" she cried, looking over Michelle's shoulder.

The lights never come down, yet all is not clear.
Surely—
No surely. We search for the chink, the gulp of fresh air.

Joseph Cornell lived on Utopia Parkway in Queens. It is well documented, the modest house and untidy garden, the corny figurines and TV tables of the reclusive/friendly artist's studio/home, the excess of his dossiers, overflowing with scraps, gimcrack, jetsam, baubles, plastic shells, childish cutouts, etc. waiting to be chosen for the timeless set. To be boxed in a Cornell box, sealed under glass in a little showcase of objects—string, twig, words, maybe a Ping-Pong ball or feather, tatter of net placed before the painted backdrop. Assemblages you cannot possess, for the master has arranged the shop—

there's the pipe for your pipe dream, time in a drift of sand—but no matter your desire, he will not take your money. Nothing for sale here—it would seem all is fixed, all given—stars, castle, *the bird one never had a second time in life,* butterfly, carte du jour, dove, dancer, egg, maps,

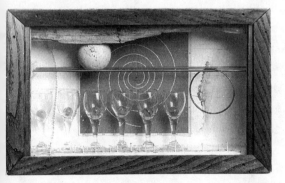

moon. All is set, then Cornell's scenes shake down, travel the mystery route from his memory to ours: his gift to us being our investment, our retrieval. Album of no pages. The glass cover of his boxes not looking glass, not monitor screen, not chalky arcade panes. No ticket, plush seat. No plot, program, scrim of transparent theory. No...no attitude. We simply enter.
Your arcade is not perfect then?
No one knows himself—Novalis, *so long as he remains merely himself*—Novalis, *and not at the same time himself and another*—Novalis.
Your arcade is not perfect?
YES, it is not perfect.

Bridgeport, 19 January 1875

My dear Clemens,

...if you should happen to be in a writing mood and could in your inimitable way hit my traveling hippodrome so that people could get an idea what is coming next spring & summer, it would help me—but I neither ask nor expect nor desire such a thing unless it so happens that in the way of your literary labors you can make the hippodrome the subject of a portion.... If you can't bring it into your regular work, I shall be very glad to pay you the same as you would want from any publisher....

Last August I had an immense tent made, over 800 feet long by 400 broad, and transported it to Boston, where I built seats to accommodate 11,000 persons, & I transported my entire hippodrome to Boston. There were over 1200 men, women, & children engaged by me; 750 horses, including 300 blooded race horses & ponies; camels, elephants, buffaloes, English stag and stag hounds, ostriches, &c. &c. (Don't mention

"I cleaned up that mess."

It was a scarred shoulder, razor sliced by Dewboy. Mizz Bee remembers that paperwork. Long time ago when she was green, the babies still at home, boys so close in age. María Benner or Benez maybe five or six with little-mother ways, so common in these families when the real mother was a wayward child. One case among many. Mama cut up—one incident among too many which had removed Chi Chi and Ty from a dangerous environment. With her spanking-new degree from Columbia, Mary Boyle, in full command of her distancing techniques, had done that paperwork. Now she's crazy with grief looking over the slick scars of Michelle's shoulder to the gummy strips of Scotch tape still stuck on the black screen of the Sony, to the fallout of plastic limbs from the raggedy tree, and she's screaming at her client, "Where the hell were you?"

"Where'd I be?" says Mama Michelle, up early in the morning, shine on her eyelids, rings in her ears. Up early or late, she is treacherously pretty as she touches a long red fingernail to the dainty gold cross at her throat. They wear these crosses, all of them. Them, these women.

"Don't hand me that shit, Michelle. Where'd you be? You'd be roastin'. Butt fuckin'. Blowin' half the pols in town."

From Peaches' room, what Mizz Bee thinks of as Peaches' room, a big guy—pumped up, heavy bull head—stomps toward them. Mama's new steady.

"You snitchin', Miss Boyle?" Michelle's snappy, showing off for the stud. "Didn't do your paperwork!" By Christ, they had her: she had not turned the abandoned child in, left Peaches to drift in make-believe, her make-believe. For half a moment she's terrified of this woman—a tossup, a tramp—so who'd take her word against that of Mary Boyle fully invested with forms and files. Never afraid to come to the Village, she sees this mute guy could finish her errands of mercy with one clout. Smoothing the ridiculous apron, Michelle says, "You don't know how to work the street."

Code words: the street, bum's rush, shit row . . . paper-

menagerie of lions, tigers, & other wild beasts, for I don't take them traveling with hippodrome.)

I can easily lose half a million of dollars next summer unless I can in advance so awaken and electrify the country. . . . I carry blacksmiths & blacksmith tents to do all my horse-shoeing, repairing of chariots, wagons, &c. I also carry harness makers. I carry carpenters and builders who precede the show ten days to build the seats. I carry wardrobe men and women to repair and care for the wardrobe, which has cost me over $70,000 and which I use in processions and all the various plays, scenes, and the great street procession which occurs every morning. I take two immense bands of music, first-class.

My hippodrome exhibitions include the Roman chariot races and many other acts that were shown in the Roman Colosseum 1600 years ago, and on a scale that has not been witnessed in this world during the last thousand years. My Roman chariots are driven by Amazons instead of men.

But I show besides scores of thrillingly interesting scenes which Rome never saw. I give a scene called Indian Life on the Plains wherein scores of Indians of various tribes appear with their squaws, pappooses, ponies and wigwams. . . . They encamp, erect their wigwams, engage in buffalo hunts with real buffaloes, give their Indian war dances, the Indian pony races, snowshoe races, foot races against horses, lasso horses and other animals, and both Indians and squaws give the most amazing specimens of riding at full speed. The Indian camp is surprised by the Mexicans, and then

ensues such a scene of savage strife and warfare as is never seen except upon our wild western borders.

The great English stag hunt wherein 150 ladies and gentlemen appear on horseback all dressed in appropriate hunting costumes, with the English stags and a large pack of real English stag hounds, depicts a scene worth going over a hundred miles to see.

Then of course we have hurdle races by ladies; Roman standing races (the riders standing on bareback horses); flat races by English, American, and French jockeys, with the best blooded race horses to be found in Europe; races by camels ridden by Arabs; elephant races, liberty races by 40 wild horses turned loose; ostrich races, monkey races, and the most remarka[ble] performances by elephants and other animals. Taken altogether, this is a colossal traveling exhibition never before equalled and what no other man in this generation will ever dare to wish. . . .

Truly yours,

P T Barnum

P. T. Barnum

work. She was their coupon cutter, paper lady. There were no free samples in the Village. You pay for what you get. Bunk. Caviar. The price of dope sets the value on sex. Need for disease, vice versa. Reversion to barter. Dollars might be the saffron-and-rose-petal currency of a board game. Anyone can play and sometimes you win. One working girl—this in her file: "What you want, Mizz Bee? I cleared six thousand last week. You want me to work McDonald's?" What's she to say to such logic? Nothing left of last week's six thousand but your audiovisual, leather jackets, gold chains recycled with wonderful efficiency.

The silent guy moves in, his huge body paved with black jeans, black silk shirt. Peaches would stuff him with comic accuracy down to his sucked-in gut and beefy balls. He stands behind Michelle, no words, gleaming high beams puncture his empty pie-tin face. Over one pierced ear, a crescent shaved on his head, which Mary Boyle makes no more sense of than the cross on Mama's neck. Michelle is a Christian: she takes that no further.

Collecting herself, "I brought breakfast," Mizz Bee says.

"We ate breakfast."

Half hidden in the kitchen door, the topknot of ringlets, one bright amber eye—María. Discovered, she steps out bedecked in splotchy bright new clothes, gaudy flowers all up and down her plump body. Sassy, she tosses her head, shifts to one hip. Mama's girl. Does Mary Boyle imagine a flip of the child's hand to be a subversive farewell? Bye-bye, Mizz Bee. Or, that Peaches glances down at her new lemon-drop sneakers not proudly, but with regret. Probably. That is what Mizz Bee wants to believe as she heads blindly across the crumbling tarmac, away from the solidity of that family group. Wants to believe that Peaches might tell a wicked tale of Big Jo-Jo, no tongue in his gravel head, that she'd capture its mean shaved streak—not with Brillo, with coarse play yard grit.

Mizz Bee's face stings as though Big Jo-Jo had smote her. Stroke of the Lord's anger burns on her cheeks, sweeps to her groin searing the love out of her as she barrel-asses out of the Village. She

Mark Twain, the one man in Barnum's generation who dared to wish more of a traveling show: he was writing *Tom Sawyer* at the time and only ran into a bit of trouble when attempting the sequel, *Huckleberry Finn.*

(Tom Sawyer's Comrade)

The adventures of Huck and Jim did not yield to Twain's rambling prolific ways and were not published until ten years after his refusal to write in the "show line," though he might well have been inspired by Barnum to outdo the exhibits of hippodrome. The circus in *Huck* is the bulliest ever seen, the ringmaster the slickest. Surely Twain thought of Barnum's letter when he wrote of the bareback riders "a gang of real sure-enough queens, and dressed in clothes that cost millions of dollars, and just littered with diamonds." As well as the Duke of Bilgewater who could "sling a lecture" when need be, and of the Cameleopard, a giraffe or perpetrated freak straight out of the American Museum and of the brass band, first-class, that unravels a cruel Barnumesque hoax, leads Nigger Jim back to town as a hero. P.T.'s immodest solicitation is all over *Huck Finn,* but not over Huck, harmless liar, the boy who knows when play goes wrong.

THE LIVING HAPPY FAMILY

The Clemens connection: friendship of sorts, the families visiting back and forth, Bridgeport to Hartford. A sense in Twain's letters of his self-reflective *interest* in Barnum, in the entrepreneurial spirit they shared, their mutual popularity. Twain, fascinated by the trickster in himself, wondered how they might make use of each other. He'd done just that, made fun of P.T. when he ran for the Connecticut legislature in 1857, calling upon his happily managed menagerie to become a template for human affairs. Barnum considered it good press. Twain lost his fortune investing in a newfangled typesetter: Barnum was humbugged by the innovative brass works of the Jerome clock. Both men recouped by exhausting lecture tours. Ah! to take your seat in the village opera house for Twain's artfully natural performance piece in which he played himself, the American Author. P.T.'s orations—"The Art of Money Getting," "Success in Life"—would seem pure camp. Nice that Twain had sailed to Europe with the commission to write *Innocents Abroad* on the same boat as two of Barnum's procurers of curiosities and wilde beestes for the American Museum—looters all. He devoured Barnum's autobiography, *Struggles and Triumphs,* that vainglorious,

ASTOUNDING!

carefully edited second edition—not a moment's self-doubt—quick trip through the struggles, a spate of tragic relief from the triumphs. When Twain came to write his own autobiography it was so dark, such an excoriation of his fame, which he loved, such a mistrust of the fruits of democracy, such a naked and still boyish cry from the troubled heart, he would not allow it to be published until after his death.

P.T. among the famous: Thackeray looked him up at the museum. They got on. Barnum wrote to Oliver Wendell Holmes, beloved poet, honored doctor, who accepted complimentary tickets to good shows and happily endorsed P.T.'s Aquarial Garden, his genuine tattooed Greek, Capt. Djordji Costentenus, and a (stuffed?) Dodo bird. Like Holmes, Barnum was an irrepressible optimist: P.T.'s Universalist beliefs so free of dumpy old Calvinist gloom that the afterlife admits all comers with a quarter, children half price.

The Greatest

**THE LIVING
MONSTER SNAKE**

The Aquarial Garden,

had believed a small person made the world. The sharp grip at her heart: "Well," she says to James Bray "that mess is cleared up."

As they quit the room, the phone rings.

"I'll get back to you," Bray says to whoever in California. Mary Boyle assumes California from his tone—conspiratorial, edgy. "You're on fuckin' hold." She sees they could have drawn the drapes with their repeat of exotic lavender birds and blowsy peonies in maybe Chinese vases and that the day through the brown windows has changed, a series of thick-bottomed clouds pressing in, filthy through the tinted glass.

"I've got someone here, buddy boy." He sounds right— curt, clever—then turns to her with his dear old smile, the one she's known for a couple of hours. "The grand tour," he suggests in a husky whisper, and that sounds wrong.

She had not called it that, only listened to his historic renovation of the city and said, "Let me take you round." She had thought to be gentle, then he would at least come back to her with his script complete, with his crew, and park the streets with movie vans. The way he feels for his glasses in a pocket, checks his watch, gives her a sense of time allotted. So, she'll make a quick job of it. A good house husband, he switches off the light. In the dark of the windows their bed reflects stone gray, a rumpled catafalque.

When Mary Boyle fled 4C in fury and pain, she'd thrown Mizz Bee's tote in the car. Now she clears the passenger seat of her files. It is almost noon, going to rain. They will not come out the better end of this day. Oh, she will—that thought a tight knot in her chest—survive Michelle and her pimp, why not James Bray. The pale suede of his jacket smells animal clean. It will be ruined in the rain. He can well buy another.

In the threatening gloom, she drives east, then north. Meaningless directions. South End, West End collapse into an uncharted city that might be any of a hundred across the country run out of steam; any of a thousand cities placed this way or that, toward

Fires which leveled two museums, his oriental mansion Iranistan ("truly celestal"), and the inferno at the winter quarters in no way defeated him; P.T. dusted the ashes off like a gentleman victorious in a street brawl. *Build me more stately mansions, O my soul:* in Holmes' poem "soul" is lowercase, practical.

Horace Greeley, Commodore Vanderbilt, Queen Victoria, Abraham Lincoln, Hans Christian Andersen—the illustrious quite natural in the course of Barnum's business, until you come upon the visit to Bridgeport of Matthew Arnold. Arnold, listed by Walt Whitman as a literary dude, delivered himself of the lecture "Numbers: or the Majority and the Remnant," divvying up the world into the cultural haves and have-nots. Barnum said the lecture was grand and found no presumption in placing himself among the chosen. He'd invited Arnold to stay with him at Waldemere, his third mansion: "You and I, Mr. Arnold, ought to be acquainted. You are a celebrity, I am a notoriety." If P.T.'s visitor looked down his long nose at the flashy decor, the "library" of Waldemere, our great impresario didn't give a damn. Somehow it is unnatural, uncomfortable, and even uninteresting, this meeting of the purveyor of the best that has been thought and said with the Papa of Pop. Encased in their own versions of Victorian morality, they would have nothing to say to each other. No tension here, no game: the two lecturers would greet each other, despite Barnum's mock humility, in the airless rented hall of their fame.

East Bridgeport (1851) was Barnum's sensible Utopia, imagined to the last dime. Big Daddy rules of sobriety and Christian conduct. Call it speculation if you will; delete modification of Utopia, though the scheme of P.T. and his partner William Noble was reasonably unreal. *The new city was laid out with an eye to beauty and convenience as well as profit; trees were planted, and an eight-acre grove was set aside as a park. Then Barnum and his partner began to sell at cost, reserving for themselves enough property to guarantee a large profit when the new city should begin to flourish and property to be in demand. The purchasers of lots were constrained to build after a style of architecture approved. . . . they planned a city which for neatness would be an example to other communities and which would harbor enough manufactories to keep its happy population out of mischief. —M. R. Werner,* Barnum
The gratification of the model city was immediate, but even P.T., bilked by his tenant, Jerome Clock, even his failure paid off in the end, doubling, tripling the holdings of the self-made man.

$$\$ \ \$ \ \$$

Catherine, archivist from age twelve, hooked early on queer secrets of the past, knows the Bishop Room. Collecting dates, names, inventions, acts of God or man—truth of it all, not like the tarnished souvenir spoons, centennial plates in the Devlin china cabinet. The alluring truth: that James' "Wheeler mansion" was built for a Mr. Harral, saddlemaker, to the design of Alexander Jackson Davis, whose mentor, Alexander Jackson *Downing,* wrote the first book of American landscape gardening (1841), in which he proposes the public park "to soften and humanize the rude, educate and enlighten the ignorant and give continued enjoyment to the educated." It's Cath knows the worst of Barnum,

the sea or railroad or river that caused it to be writ on the map, now turned in on its desolate center, inhabited by what in truth should still be called the underclasses and the banks, their indestructible vaults with great steel doors swing open on ingenious gears at nine, close at the end of each banking day on bricks of gold and stacks of greenbacks, on diamonds cut in the old style, on yellowing deeds to excellent corner lots and fine commercial tracts sinking into the sea, on unclaimed bonds for the constant improvement and many envelopes with silken baby curls, unfaded ribbon in tissue, diplomas and marriage certificates with shattered wax seals, silver spoons and tea sets. All that had its spoken value such as patents, contracts, mortgages and wills safely stowed away, unseen like veins, nerves, tendons under the last layer of fatty tissue in the body of a city eaten away, still breathing.

Black men huddle in the doorway of once Woolworth's as the heavens open. Screeching girls run for the Do-nut shop: a trading post—"Give you nickel bag for cocktail," says Mary Rose, "Quaalude for half a Valium, good as gold. At the foot of Golden Hill Street, you have to love it." Driving blind in the storm as she heads up to Billy Bray's courthouse. It's hers now, peopled with Vic Benino and her faithful suitor in his green custodian's uniform, with parole officers, guards, the methadone gang, and raging families stunned into respectful silence as they approach the mediation center. And files, years of her files with reshuffled plots. One classic: cute girls with scars and crosses, menacing thugs, resourceful children born to the roller-coaster ride of indulgence and inattention. The turret, porches, pillars of the courthouse are hers, and farther uphill a large stripped lot.

"The Wheeler mansion," James says, but this vacant site is hers, too, where a client on the run burrowed in a crevice for a winter week, before passing from her files to a pauper's grave. And why the hell should Mary Boyle know what James Bray knows of the razed Gothic mansion where every Bridgeport boy placed his beloved Boris Karloff; or possess the memory of copper beeches,

who blacked and wigged a genuine Negro for the minstrel to pass him for acceptable make-believe: and the best, that in his decline he earned his good notice in the reward books, which praise him as "the children's friend." Cath, who checked the dates and quotes, the facts of the world, double-checked for *Life* and *Time* until the quag-

mire, until with a swift kick she closed the files, threw away the key. Mum's the word, while James is undone by historicity, snakelike hiss of the word. Our director has no idea what to ask for in the Bishop Room—top hat or cane? Was it Ava Gardner played the statue in *One Touch of Venus?* Why does bronze turn green? Is sequence the dull child of continuity? Gosh, that's a lifetime in the library! 1945—Memorial Day, was it fine or did it rain?

Henry A. Bishop gave us the parlor with the many files and records, courtesy of his railroad fortune—New York, New Haven & Hartford. Our arcade, the Post Office Arcade, so called after a useful branch office, was built by Henry A. in 1889 and owned jointly with his brother, William D. It is 130 × 25 ft., 40 ft. at its apex, where large sheets of glass fit to iron struts in a plain geometric pattern; a straight passage in the Queen Anne style with no crossway connecting grand boulevards, or sad to say, no labyrinthine turns. The arcade is the work of Longstaff & Hurd, a firm with a trunkful of trendy references (the usual fin-de-siècle uncertainty of who we are.) Longstaff & Hurd, who designed the Islamic-Romanesque Barnum Institute of Science and History (1893), which we now call our Museum.

BRIDGEPORT, a city, a port of entry, and one of the county-seats of Fairfield county, Connecticut, U.S.A., coextensive with the town of Bridgeport, in the S.W. part of the state, on the Long Island Sound, at the mouth of the Pequonnock river;

about 18 m. S.W. of New Haven. Pop. (1880) 27,643; (1890) 48,866; (1900) 70,996, of whom 22,281 were foreign-born, including 5974 from Ireland, 3172 from Hungary, 2854 from Germany, 2755 from England, and 1436 from Italy; (1910) 102,054. The harbour, formed by the estuary of the river and Yellow Mill Pond, an inlet, is excellent. Between the estuary and the pond is a peninsula, East Bridgeport, in which are some of the largest manufacturing establishments, and west of the harbour and the river is the main portion of the city, the wholesale section extending along the bank, the retail section farther back, and numerous factories along the line of the railway far to the westward. There are two large parks, Beardsley, in the extreme north part of the city, and Seaside, west of the harbour entrance and along the Sound; in the latter are statues of Elias Howe, who built a large sewing-machine factory here in 1863, and of P.T. Barnum, the showman, who lived in Bridgeport after 1846 and did much for the city, especially for East Bridgeport. In Seaside Park there is also a soldiers' and sailors' monument, and in the vicinity are many fine residences.

In 1905 Bridgeport was the principal manufacturing center in Connecticut, the capital invested in manufacturing being $49,381,348, and the products being valued at $44,586,519. The largest industries were the manufacture of corsets—the product of Bridgeport was 19.9% of the total for the United States in 1905, Bridgeport being the leading city in this industry—sewing machines (Singer Manufacturing Co. is here), steam-fitting and heating apparatus, cartridges (the Union Metallic Cartridge Co.), automobiles, brass goods, phonographs and gramophones and typewriters.

their leathery leaves spread wide, an umbrella of dark blood branches over downtown, beautiful not scary. Life's blood as he walked home from high school. Yes, he had thought to become a reclusive rich man behind the massive carved doors of the Wheeler house, a baron of industry surveying from on high the well-oiled hum of work and pleasure . . . until Billy said a retired cop, Joe Flaherty, sat guard all night long with a gun outside Arch Wheeler's bedroom door. Rain streams down the windshield rendering the granite hulk of St. Augustine's insubstantial; the minarets and oriental tracery on the legendary curve of Barnumesque apartments shimmy. Trembling white letters on the big green Interstate sign announce New Haven, New York, his old escape routes.

A long take in which he watches Mary Boyle's face narrow with the purpose of her disastrous show-and-tell. "Which bridge?" she asks.

"Stratford Avenue." Amazed as he speaks that name, that the bridge is still there with his recall of oystermen, oil tankers and ferries in the wreckage, even then, of silver-gray pilings and splintered wharves. At a stoplight he asks, "How long were you in?"

She gives no answer.

The rogue and the lady, remake that one. You wouldn't have to stop short of mild skin flick in the Hilton. Clean up Michelle—no scars, no pop tracks on her frail brown arms. A heart tug reclaiming her child. Opportunity of apron and cross. Who do I have to fuck to get off this picture? Letting his mind play dirty, not to like himself as he sees the nice Bridgeport girl veer off from him, from what might-have-been, that one-faced coin of promise and regret.

"There!" James calls out. Where the charred sign for mufflers and auto parts flaps in the storm. "There! The dowdy dress shop, best in town." Where Nell took Catherine to outfit her for college. He speaks of his sister in those days, the high pitch of her hard work, insufficient offering of good grades. How she had studied without

Ghost story: the third Walt—Benjamin (1892–1940), man of letters, collector of books, quotations, photos, and toys. His unfinished work *The Arcades Project*... his great unfinished work is a collection of aphorisms, quotes, contemplations accruing to the industrial culture. The indoor-outdoor of the Parisian *passages*, urban marketplaces of the transitory—their tawdry left-

over goods, malingering mores yielding stories like fossil shells and ferns—made them places of wonder to Benjamin. All that we have of *The Arcades Project,* twenty-three years in the mak-

ing, is 900 pages of fragments which at times crystallize into essays, as though the writer must have *done with it,* meet the unnamed commitment, or, having lost track of his calling, like a fledgling academic, bought the scare tactic of publish or perish. There are hints in Benjamin's letters of the *Project*'s design which sound like misleading clues or forced attempts at net profit, what we call bottom line. At times he imagines a vast scenario: "to set free the huge powers of history that are asleep within the 'once upon a time' of classical historical notation." At others, a strict

agenda: "the fetish character of commodities stands at the center."

Scholars, disappointed or elated, assemble and reassemble the bones of the beast, but Benjamin's great project remains an exhibit with P.T.'s label "What Is It?" Not *The Key to All Mythologies,* not the *History of the Modern World,* that grab bag of detritus carried as a prop by the grimy Harvard eccentric Joe Gould, a character both Catherine and James remember panhandling in the Village. Walter Benjamin's 900 pages are substantial, not failed, grandiose or mad: ongoing and maybe, just maybe, exactly as intended: *Every passion borders on the chaotic, but the collector's passion borders on the chaos of memories. More than that: the chance, the fate, that suffuse the past before my eyes are conspicuously present in the accustomed confusion of these books.*

Writers are really people who write books not because they are poor, but because they are dissatisfied with the books which they could buy but do not like. You, ladies and gentlemen, may regard this as a whimsical definition of a writer. But everything said from the angle of a real collector is whimsical.

—*Walter Benjamin,* Unpacking My Library

In his *Arcades Project,* a consuming, continuing work, Benjamin expected no less than to alter our relation to the page, to let us *shop,* that's the whimsy, through his chosen topics and cultural totems; to rifle the bins of "Dream City," "Museum." To touch—doll, fashion, whore—feel the goods. Read the price tags on Marx, photography, newness. To fear the preconceived package which does not let us discover our own correspondences, will not let us destroy what we must in the old city.

Yet Benjamin warns us against baby out with bathwater; snip and

benefit the pageboy, the chignon, princess dresses; had blocked out the samba, paced it unrhythmically, and once, Billy, to prepare her for a dance, had spun her round the living room in a two-step, clutching his daughter to him, cheek to cheek in the jittery fox-trot of one-reel silents.

"Catherine," she says. "How could we?"

"How could we *what?*"

Mary Boyle wanting to shred the day: "Catherine is family, if you can understand that."

"Let's just stop," he says.

Childish, literal, she slams on the brakes: smallness of her chest hunched over the steering wheel, her little heart-shaped face strained but in no way defeated. The storm ends abruptly. She draws into a flat lot big enough for your mini-mall, one lonely car in what Bray, scraping the stubble on the million-dollar chin, experiences as unreliable East Coast sun. Explaining, she demolishes his city: in the improbable aerodrome they face, Basques play jai alai. "Gambling. The fix, the take." She's prissy. "You know about those things, increase the tax base . . . a bunch of dog-track losers were supposed to bail the city out."

Explaining—oh, my, Mary Boyle can't stop herself explaining, and as she does Bridgeport becomes aftermath, the Sound rising to swell the Pequonnock river, only the rim of safe suburban hills above the floodplain. People's Bank, City Trust bobbing like tub toys; solid triple-deckers, flimsy new condos floating toward better prospects in Stamford, West Haven. Flotsam and jetsam of corsets and guns, of sewing machines, typewriters, and fine equipage, the city's manufactured items swept out to sea. Bridges out, he is stranded with his guide on a dry strip of East Main where low ramshackle shops compete for small trade in yams, cigarettes, lottery tickets, spongy bread. Where candy stores sell more than candy.

"They drink quarts," she says. Indeed, they do. Dark men on a stoop with exhausted eyes pass round the big Bud.

paste, imagine our order, but first to make the redemptive choice as though we have inherited the dossiers and cartons of trinkets tumbling off the shelves on Utopia Parkway, where Joseph

Cornell often popped the glass lid on one of his boxes to alter his fantasy in some small way. To rearrange: never cut, splice, print the release, ship it out in the can.

Walter Benjamin killed himself at the Spanish border fleeing from the Gestapo, trying to get to America by way of Lisbon. The flip side of *Casablanca,* minus the music and love story.

Zentralpark, the title which Benjamin gave to the last work he sent out for publication (rejected), is fragments on the city poet Baudelaire. It has as much to do with Central Park, a place he would never see, as the poet's *Le Voyage* has to tell of a trip not taken. The protection of the *Arcades* had been removed like a glass bell: Benjamin was released from theory into events. Out in the open like the angel of history, he looked back to the Paris of Baudelaire, Second Empire city of broad new boulevards, lofty cast iron and glass, of the *passages* in their glory. City of pleasure about to wear thin, of spiritual bankruptcy and of the eccentric poet's vented spleen, his warning. Benjamin looking back, his body not driven irresistibly toward the future in America, toward the comfortable life projected if he got from there to here.

Central Park, the essay, is darting, buoyant, at times frantic. We search for the scrap that might have saved him: "Fashion is the eternal recurrence of the new. Are there nevertheless motifs of redemption in fashion?" Or "Redemption looks to the small fissure in the ongoing catastrophe." But gravity pulls: no angel, Benjamin chose to cross the finish line of despair rather than run the race of the intellectual life, which in our American cities had become marathon, an exhausting careerist affair. There is, too, his fear of seeing what he had imagined—the statues of unknown heroes, park benches of exile. Walter Benjamin would have admired the accounting system set up by the young storekeeper Phineas Taylor Barnum, in which even the future Prince of Humbug could not escape a stark Yankee reckoning and entered:

Balance......... to running away.
Balance......... to death.

We musn't worry it, though it's a great shame Benjamin did not live to collect us, to squirrel away *Pogo* strips, remark upon our park's Wollman Rink and Shakespeare Garden, for he had already begun to figure us, even the other Walt, Disney, whose work he found to be "without the slightest seed of mortification."

And did not live to see the arcades of Paris become (re)current fashion—Galerie Vivienne, Coller Reynard, the Palais Royale with spanking new bistros reinventing peasant fare, with chic international goods to be found in Tokyo, Miami, Rome, displayed under gussied-up lamps, all mystery gone. In the guidebooks noted: motifs of redemption—the cast-iron tracery, terrazzo restored.

About your arcade. You do see the pathos and pretension of the great Parisian arcades popping up in Bridgeport—your little glassed-over alley! Sorry if I demolish, but you're impossible. Really imperious, sniping in all directions.

Howzzat? People in glass houses shuddn't throw stones?

Bear with me. I never would have swung the wrecking ball, now I see you scuffling about

Or the Sacher torte. That a half mile of urban blight should call up
Vienna. Hey, that was the grand tour. Twenty years back on a pic-
ture—third-rate Third Man *that would make him a middling star, an*
old cameraman had taken him around in one of those futuristic Citro-
ëns suspended on air. A Viennese Jew who fled to Hollywood with
Lang, sharing—forcing his Sacher torte on the young actor. "Ach, you
must attempt it," a wonder of his imperial city. On the one hand,
waltzes and whipped cream, Lippizaner horses prancing in Hapsburg
sawdust, bright misty-eyed kitsch from the old pro honored for the
brooding shadows of his lush expressionistic lighting: on the other
hand, the little gentleman's haut bourgeois heaven—elegant rationale
of the Ringstrasse, willed temples to politics and trade. The museums
of art and natural history faced off on a monstrous plaza that shrank
the cameraman to a worshipful child, reduced the actor, James Bray,
recently discovered, so full of himself, to anxious and insecure.

Each time they stopped—Opera, Rathaus, Burgtheater—
the Citroën wheezed down on the indestructible paving blocks in a
genteel fart. James' sentiments exactly. From the first day's shooting
Vienna seemed to him a museum before museums got friendly, supe-
rior and chill. That picture: counter-espionage ornamented with inge-
nious surveillance; treacherous young widow (unreconstructed Nazi)
played by a European stage actress. As it turned out, she worked well
with the American actor, who had learned to pull back, move hardly at
all for the camera. His small gestures confident: steady eyes, steady
smile. The woman's fussy acting betrayed her, gave away secrets, set
up Bray's toneless, impersonal pursuit.

He had not thought of that picture in years or of touring
with the gnomish cameraman, who wore thick glasses, thick leather
sandals, and a smock, who tucked a beret over the beeswax polish of his
bald head. Once an artist, now a hack, the man had showed him a
dream city, Vienna without the Anschluss, without the Jewish ques-
tion, Vienna of the nursery and operetta. Ach, you must attempt it—
Fräulein had dressed him in a fresh sailor suit that he might run to
meet Papa, home from his bank. Mama reading Herzl by the gas fire

on the cracked pavement, white with plaster dust as a marble muse of tragedy, dodging huge icebergs of shards, picking through notices of The Drunkard, Othello, Captain's Courageous, Beach Blanket Bingo, finding the sweeper's striped hat, the Chianti bottle unbroken in its life jacket of straw.

Sake's alive! No more than a BB gun you used on them panes. Kids do it all the time. At night, when we have night, the little holes appear as planets and in that glow our monitor, our guardian angel, waits with us here in the railway station, which admits God's sun when we have day. It is true, what you guessed, that we yearn to leave, cross over no matter how painful the story of James and Mary Rose, who, for their running time, for some part of that time, love truly, transcend all envy of the silver screen. Perhaps if they had stopped to eat one simple meal together...still, we are thankful to Henry A. Bishop for the oil lamp, love seat, city records, photos, and files, and settle to our work: Is it not shocking that a fellow, name of Clap Spooner, sold his family farm for the Brooklawn Country Club? Splendid that Kiddo Davis made it to the majors. We are not for a moment surprised that Barnum had a child by that strumpet Mlle. Ernestine, no better than Isabelle Poole, such are the matings, the passions for all we know, and cannot help but think of the grand tour. If the nice Bridgeport girl had stolen with our star through the shattered door of the arcade where, safe from inclement weather, from the hush worse than din of dead street....We look up from our labors in the Bishop Room to the first broadside (1881) of P.T.'s final memorial to himself. Far, far beyond Hippodrome, folks! The immortal three-ring circus!!!

In the triple ring the single actor with his tiny skill was lost; everything must be bold, whirling, changing; no brilliancy of lights can quite illuminate the monstrous top: flying color, the inevitable magenta and sky blue and silver stars, the grin of clowns and the swift turn of the acts, revolve and pass, projected against a void. Here at last was wonder, though Barnum never spoke of it—beauty amid that showy aggregation, an exquisite precision which seemed aerial, and informed the whole long march, and even the faint high fretwork overhead.
—*Constance Rourke,* Trumpets of Jubilee

Grand—but I stand single under the iron strut of the Post Office Arcade. Too tiny to be mounted alone in the specimen box. I'd like Peaches to cross over, the Peaches Benner or

Benez that was. That would be company. Together, we wander the arcade buying pie tins, masking tape, Brillo, and buttons. And I explain, like Miss Bee who can't help her explaining, that in the art of Joseph Cornell...that many of his boxes work—kinetic games, manual toys. Watch! Watch as Peaches taps a lever, observes ball roll into cup, feather flap, thimble spin. Knowing child, innocent of nostalgia. Cornell programmed scene after scene with his stories. A beginning: a middle. Early cinema toys. Childlike man, nostalgic for innocence, knowing. Yes, knowing dream-thoughts' translation, peep-shows and Freud. But watch, please watch with the monitor. Peaches tilts, turns the boxes—sand shifts, springs turn, words slide. Too bad they are stuck in museums, the child knows...magic boxes should live in the Arcade. Each story, each ending —different each time.

and so on. It was a view made up solely of longing. They stopped at an apartment house fit for financiers and university professors. There, under the heavy Renaissance cornice, a window where once the Friday-night candles had burned throughout an opulent meal. An extra serving of schlag for the boy who brought home honors from the Polytechnik. The cameraman selected for James Bray the shimmer of casement window, the sensuous scroll of balcony, the tasteful art nouveau sign over the tobacconist's shop at the corner. His lively eyes, made miniature by the lens of the almost blind, framed scene after scene. In a cameo performance, Freud might pop around the corner, frail in his weighty double-breasted overcoat, the platonic Homburg; street girls cavort to the Messianic strains of Mahler. "You cannot imagine!" the old fellow said to Bray, who had lost track of which quarter they were in, Ring or Reichstrasse, which café the artists, which intellectuals.

He'd been chosen for that tour in the Citroën; the troll in that arty smock, famous among filmfolk, figuring him a blank slate, as yet unknown; he hadn't bought the schmaltz, and touring the shattered East Side can still remember his aversion to both cute and grandiose Vienna, how lighthearted he'd been packing for the next location, a garish hotel in Nice. It was a picture that gobbled up cities.

The cameraman had requisitioned one young actor. Driving through the ruins with this love of a graying girl, Old Vienna flips to Jolly Wartime Bridgeport, his own distorted dream. BOFFO box office. Cinema I, II, III—let them stand round the block for his nostalgic view of Bridgeport. Okay, he is within seconds of bagging his art, the hopelessly romantic picture, entire city cut back to McLevy Green with the courthouse blocked in, his father's courthouse. Kick the druggies out for the duration. Hose down Cottage Street, give it definition. Spiff up the gingerbread house where he'd rented that eerie room. On his set no ghosts need apply.

But the city is Mary Boyle's, a shanty back-lot arrangement. Hers the rotted porch railings and crumbling stoops of blind-eyed, gap-

The Dictionary of the Mix

A a

In the beginning was the picture. It was the initial A, peak and crossbar simpler than drawing of horse upon the wall of cave. Simpler, though much later; beginning of the Mix which we shall examine only in its U.S. of A. manifestation, provincial to be sure, discarding all marks we do not understand—hump of Hebrew Aleph, Islamic wisps and squiggles, accomplished Chinese brushstroke, to name but a few worldwide. In our pursuit of A we acknowledge, truly we seek limitations that foreshorten to our day, deny the pleasure of the capital conceived as scribal ornament, whether standing apart from the text or drawn into its body, always on display in gilt upon vellum; precious in abbey, in library, in museum under glass at 65°, writ by whose humble hand or hands we do not know, the A affording slope and angle, arch as well in which interlaced beasts, processions of birds, angels, and saints, all personae of the legend raise the curtain on the story. And A we must forgo of block print and etching, bold black on rich rag paper of AD—the Anno Domini to signify an historic beginning in the book, that tool of history. Also the big letters of single page which make of A ant or apple pie aping the sound for children with harmless inaccuracy and the A of good grades on our homework, on sacks of potatoes, often doubled, tripled on bonds as well as AA and lest we forget the A Train or Scarlet Letter, a misnomer, being gold embroidery upon red cloth. All capitals rejected, even the astronauts' high sign from the heavens—A-OK.

You may well ask what's left us. The lowercase, the actual and ancient problem (we're not a-historical) of making our words known to another as they were to the gentle audience when *the bawdy hand of the Dyall was now vpon the pricke of noone.* Or making ourselves known, however shamefully, with stock gesticulation—Jew's shrug, Paddy's wink, flailing arms of all Sicilians. We got by with showy smiles, with shudders (cold or fear), with no, no, no we did not mean to say, my dear. Hey, never!—James dismisses the capital from art much as we swallow the final vowel in nostalgia, gulping for a time when, upon entering the Village we were not struck dumb.

The Tale of Yellow Mill Village

On a creek between Newfield and Stratford, a mill—gristmill, no manufacture. Frame buildings, clapboards we detect from the "yellow" and surmise the mill a landmark that obliterated the creek's native name. So it was called when the Lottery Bridge (1701) crossed the Pequonnock and so called until the expansionist era of P.T. The Yellow Mill Creek lying within East Bridgeport, incorporated into his grand design of factories within walking distance of those large houses prescribed for the managerial class on Noble and Barnum avenues: tenements for the workers by the swampy mill not included in promotional material, rickety outdoor staircases climbing to the fourth and fifth level on which we picture gaiety of laundry flapping, immigrant imps at play,

mouthed tenements; hers to exhibit, the scourge, the char, the stomped-out roofs where an unfriendly giant has trod at random through a neighborhood, punched his monstrous foot through landlord's cheap tar paper and middle-class cedar shakes. Even the brittle slate on the mansard slant of a few grand old houses has not been spared. Naked foundations stand, shaming all odds. Yet, around a corner, the white picket fence: lilac in bloom over a plot of neat mown grass and by the garage early tomatoes staked. Love apples in backyard Edens, the garden again, turned away from boarded-up factories, cave dark camps without water or light where survivors, throwing off filthy blankets, welcome the sour sheets of summer. Hers to show him, the marauding bands of children; the listless, the vigilant; the corroded mermaid above her fountain, dry at the tap.

A hundred years ago with his first wife . . . a movie with subtitles. Foreign film emporium in Brentwood? Santa Monica? The artist wife who, after faking it in the studio all day, developed a passion for documentaries and this film of real people with their real bundles in hand, pushcarts laden with household goods; a baby carriage stuffed with pots, pans, a lace tablecloth, a fiddle. Their energy. Which people? Armenians or Polish Jews leaving a small city. The lucky few in autos and beside the highway (a paved country lane) only the gray stubble of winter fields, a lone farmhouse: the city which they flee burning in the distance, left to its fate. Mournful music, sympathetic voice-over, the urgency of that exodus.

Explaining: the beat of her words, like a teacher's tap of the pointer at each site. "IV needles, cookers, blood rags in the cemetery." St. Michael's where Nell and Billy lay side by side. "At night you hear the gunfire." In Beardsley Park, the other park, where James and Cath fed monkeys in the zoo, spotted rackety-raccoon in the wild, a thrill for city kids. "The death rate of premature infants takes the prize." St. Vincent's where his tonsils were badly cropped, bequeathing him the actor's voice. "I go in there. They might kill you." Stock

newsy exchange house to stacked house. Natural History was the craze in the recessions of the 1870s and '80s, High Age of the Envy of Science: when the economy is off look to animals, the earth, the recently proven perfectibility of all living things. It was then the workers' tenements were appropriately named beehives. Labor cheap: the factories hung on until the plenitude

THE MCLSON ARMS AND AMMUNITION COMPANY, BRIDGEPORT, CONN.

of World War I when Bridgeport was christened Arsenal of Democracy.  The Garden City (yet another) Movement brought war workers' developments—Gateway Village, Old Mill Green, etc.—two-story brick, inner courtyards, which acknowledged the danger of the old tenements but did not bring them down.

Until the next cycle, the Great Depression, when Stephen Panik would not tolerate the infested firetraps within his parish of SS. Cyril and Methodius. A young priest come to succeed his cousin Gaspar in a parish that spoke Slovak, Father Panik was born in the Carpathian mountains, the nephew (or grandnephew, it is given both ways) of Marlic Hatola, professor at the University of Praha, philosopher and linguist who composed the first Slovakian grammar attempting to unite his people. Stephen did him proud: out of the East Side there came Slovak newspapers and magazines, but for the dream of decent housing Father Panik learned the language of the banks and politicians, fought with the skinflint Socialist mayor and advised the Housing Authority in elegant English: "...of faces marked by misery, faces alienated by despair and indeed, faces on which the crushing malevolence of the slums has already made its mark." A short fellow, chubby, one imagines well fed by a housekeeper from the Valley of the Vah where noodles and dumplings, steaming cabbage and pork...his round face never smiling in the photos whether it be with the school band or with officials from the Department of the Interior, as though, a man of God, he finds these public roles a strain. But we make up that Stephen Panik.

It is a grave injustice that Yellow Mill Village was renamed after Father Panik's death, that it is legend in the *New York Times,* on the evening news—Village of drug and welfare culture. A rotten shame that Mary Boyle took the Village as her beat. She cannot speak the language, has memorized the phrase book: "I am on holiday. Do you have cinema? I wish no butter on my bread." But Mary Boyle's no slumsister; a profes-

footage, the Village with 4C, squat two-story project, thousands across the country. James laughs to himself, cutting her out.

"What's funny?"

Well, it's this: though he will never say it—Catherine wins. In need of no further instruction, he understands as Mary Boyle heads back to Long Island Sound that the Great Flood would profit Father Panik Village, that "My Story" is her location. Deploring the more-in-sorrow set of her mouth, the fun balloons on her red kiddie blouse, and the unbloodied sheet at the Hilton, "Nice Bridgeport girl," he says, low and mean.

"I'm from Pittsburgh."

"You slumming, or what?" He turns her innocent face to look at him and the car jumps the esplanade newly paved with vintage brick, comes to a screeching halt inches from a Victorian lamp post.

"No." Mizz Bee is cool as a stuntman, for hasn't she thrived in this town on risky business? "No," she says, "I'm a tourist, like you."

They end up under Barnum's tuberous nose. The impresario looks far beyond a skeletal young woman on the stroll who pouts, cuts her deal before she hops into a car.

"Where we necked." James, barely audible: "I went all the way."

Lovers no more, they amble the seawall. Cold now: the zinc waves still tousled by the storm. She wears his grand suede jacket. In less than a day they've run through their story. Mary Boyle and James Bray watch the gulls swoop at a damp paper bag split with decaying riches. How to end? They feel that.

"Burnout," she SIGHS. "I've lasted longer than most."

He sees that selfishly as his line. Weighted with disappointment in themselves, they walk toward the reef where the old lighthouse is no more. Clouds play with the chill Eastern sun. Not

a

sional, heroic as many workers in the field; her days virtuous, though until the golden child she's taken small joy in her duty. Pity ourselves if we cannot pity her, unable to speak: the argot remains in her files—*pink ass, geekin', beam me up;* buzzwords she can fit into a sentence—*shitkick, cooker, stooge*—often confusing verb with noun and has not noticed that modifiers are missing. No degree to *rollers, chill pill.* A language so in flux, today's hip lip excludes her tomorrow. ă is for assed out.

No translation in the Mix, no second meaning, third, but many variants to show how remorselessly clever. Professor Hatola, studying the patois of the Village to spare his nephew's name, could not design a grammar for this language of destruction, anger, abandonment, and loss.

SS. Cyril and Methodius. 9th C. Missionaries like Mary Boyle. Brothers from fine family in Thessalonika, thus the double moniker of Stephen Panik's parish. Apostles to the Slavs—Cyril the brains, but their time was of great learning overall. Methodius, the older—activist and politician, which tends toward the binary story, though as always, we prefer to separate out, to sketch faint character of each saint, lend our substance to his holy. So Cyril figured the Slavonic language into 38 letters to make clear the word of God, to speak the Christian rituals. The Slavonic tribes listened, were converted, for the words—communion,

salvation, mercy—were their own. Flak from all sides who held with Latin. Methodius won the case for the vernacular in Rome, knowing the truth of it for his people. His smart young brother died, so he traveled alone back to the Slavs: but language is power and in his absence the Germans, the Magyars had whittled away at Cyril's alphabet. Methodius died Anno Domini 886, the Latin mass encroaching. We see the brothers in flat Byzantine, their robes fall in stiff repetitive patterns, but their warm eyes so alike—wide ovals, dark rings of sorrow, the long family nose.

Particularizing: sin if we do: sin if we don't. Mary Boyle's loss of professionalism ill serves her social purpose in Father Panik Village. She felt the springy roots of the child's hair, the sting of medicinal soap on the pads of her fingers; heard the child's sudsy complaint, the easy laugh that passed between them. In that lived moment Peaches became irreplaceable. Long ā as in ache.

Short as in ă-muse: I. (a. O.Fr. amuser, to cause to muse, to put in a stupid stare).
It's not until—

4. To divert the attention of any one from the facts at issue; to beguile, delude, cheat, deceive…

that we begin to catch up to—

7.a. To direct the attention of [one] from serious business by anything trifling, ludicrous, or entertaining;

passing to—

b. To divert, please with anything light or cheerful.

And we're home free at last.

To divert:
If you had a noise, you might as well have a funny noise, not that you'll have to hold your sides when you behold "plink," but I think it's about 3 times funnier than crash.
—*Walt Kelly, KA-PLATZ, 1942*

his climate. He would welcome Felix Young nattering on about the migratory subculture of the city's Puerto Ricans, on the unassuming statue of Elias Howe, but more than anything he wants to talk to Ziff, shitface talk over a fifty-dollar bottle of California wine, bad-mouth the world.

"Fill my father's shoes," he ANNOUNCES to no one in particular. "What's the point in that?"

"Some kind of hero?"

"Yes, ma'am. Cops and robbers." Pulling an old-time radio voice, "Billy wore the sheriff's star."

"What's that?" she asks. "The put-down?"

"Just . . . I do Billy, always could. His needling and the follow up of charm. Tell me, now tell me, sweetheart. *And with pro-pri-e-ty they say Ma-ree.* Sing his songs. What's the point in that, darlin'?" He feels drawn to the edge of the seawall after that performance, urged to jump into the shallow pocked waves, pushed by the rough bully of the city behind him. It is the city has cancelled his project, third of the money down. Or Mary Boyle with her bleak documentary. Or the bright boy on his bike who suspected forty years ago there would be no astonishing story to bring him back to this burg, yet who believed there was no plot beyond his invention. Or the actor, unaware of any audience, who can at last amaze the populace, turn down a phony script. James recalls there was an actor's exercise—the Private Moment. Heartbreak, you bet, this moment in which he finally gets it: "My story" is partial, bitter-sweet, its neat incident of murder triggers a small domestic piece. There is a vast plot in the rubble, real stuff with proper names and dates, a long terrifying plot—dull, uncinematic—the erosion of time and place, the ruin of days. There will be no feature film. The scene before him is aqueous, Long Island Sound surreal as the rushes he once watched at the end of a day, assessing his work in a probable hit, watching himself, snorkelless in clear Caribbean water, evade scuba evil. Tropical fish kept the tone light, all that crazy phosphorescence while he was trapped in the embrace of an

a

To please with anything light:

In 1945 George Balanchine went to Sarasota, Fla., to choreograph "The Elephants' Polka" to the music of Igor Stravinsky for Barnum & Bailey's Circus. Mr. B had a ball. Vera Zorina, his then wife, rode atop Medoc, and in the finale both ballerina and elephant bowed, touching their foreheads to the sawdust. The work was canceled after the season for it was said the elephants did not like Stravinsky's score.

E *e*

Mule of the alphabet, everyday e: with t's to form, from the French, feminine or diminutive in the misguided past. E looks forward on the page. Our forward is from left to right. How we proceed. Not up and down on frail ratchet holes with the story.

But E, you say, is for Envy of Movies, the age we have been assigned to. Watch the dailies. We are often edited out.

Track up like a clown on toy ladder, flip over, climb down, climb up, climb down! Never to turn the page? Jack in the box, mechanical bank—up down, up down?

Come now, your verso text—you want it both ways. The split screen passé, if not fuckin' pretentious. Work the Disney side of the street, buddy boy—VAX with the JPL simulation.

Never forget, sweetheart, it's imitation. Left to right, how we proceed with the word. "Money talks. Bullshit walks."
　　　　　　—Morty Ziff, hardly original.

E for Edison: *I had some glowing dreams about what cinema would be made to do in teaching the world things it needed to know . . . when the industry began to specialize as a kind of amusement proposition, I quit the game. . . .*
　　　　　　—Diaries and Sunday Observations

And for Miss Dickinson, who in line after line of her poems made of grammar such invention, took bold strokes with the dash—

It were infinite enacted
In the Human Heart—
Only Theatre recorded
Owner cannot shut—　　　　　　[741]

When—suddenly—my Riches shrank—
A Goblin—drank my Dew—
My Palaces—dropped tenantless—
Myself—was beggared—too—

I clutched at sounds—
I groped at shapes—
I touched the tops of Films—
I felt the Wilderness roll back—
Along my Golden lines—

The Sackcloth—hangs upon the nail—
The Frock I used to wear—
But where my moment of Brocade—
My—drop—of India?　　　　　　[430]

Fantasy over, curtain rung, the India shawl disappears, or becomes ink upon the page where her poetry draws us, back to the dense black and white footage of Kansas or Amherst or Bridgeport. Dashes—drawing us out of the Mix so that we must look up from the page, read out from the page to hear her fragmented narrative of loss for gain. To listen, though we are not blessed to listen as discriminately as our Emily

animated octopus, holding his breath as he holds it now beyond endurance, waiting to be rescued by a gimmick.

Lucky boy, were he to take the leap, it's an easy swim through the oily clam suck of low tide to sand bar as, Hey!—temporary refuge. A stranger to these parts, the perilous gull cry and the dead rumble of the city's response, its clotted diphthongs, globular vowels make no sense to him at all—an Esperanto of general decay, livable despair. This is the end of it. James Bray, who has never played without the daily pages, without searching out a script, wants the end of it. The rogue gleaning manners, morals from the lady: the lady . . . he had never intended, not this time, hanging that sign on the Hilton door. He has been looking at her for a while through the Harold Lloyd glasses; she is feeling the soft suede of his jacket, which she wears as a thing apart, apart as the soggy salt air to him, the Eastern damp after a storm. He has been looking at her in parts; wayward curls, pursed lips, gray—gray eyes like his wife's, but grainy, unreflecting—narrow impatient feet. Dismembering Mary Boyle, until lovely limb from limb she is . . . the love interest. Then what does that make him? Senseless, you bet, not savoring the loss of her, knowing the end's in sight with perhaps one last scene, Long Island Sound parting as in *The Ten Commandments,* two rigid walls of sea-green sea and De Mille's sandy highway to salvation, color of yellow brick.

Shoot the reverse—isolate her; his veering off to this tactic while looking at her for a while on the seawall and she with her mind intent, wrapped in her explaining. Her many names spilling from her, each drained of whatever faint color like drops of blood in water, Mary Boyle, Mary Rose turning to him as though to his publicity photo in the *Post,* or to his face filling the screen, figuring him blown up *there,* if there for her at all. Then what does that make her? Our Lady of Long Island Sound, Sister Mary Roommate, assumed to heaven in a starched seersucker suit. Where else to go? She's used it up, the city behind her, the language she could never

e

upon all occasions. When young she traveled the seven miles from her father's house to Northampton— *. . . how we walked in silence to the old Edwards Church and took our seats in the same, how Jennie came out like a child and sang and sang again, how bouquets fell in showers, and the roof was rent with applause—how it thundered outside, and inside with the thunder of God and men—judge ye which was the loudest—how we all loved Jennie Lind, but not accustomed oft to her manner of singing didn't fancy that so well as we did her—no doubt it was very fine—but take some notes from her "Echo"—the Bird sounds from "Bird Song" and some of her curious trills, and I'd rather have a Yankee.*

—Emily to Austin Dickinson,
July 6, 1851

And let E memorialize the giant electric light bulb that turned on and off, on and off with the pull of a Hubbel Link Chain; a fantastic illumination facing the railroad tracks, welcoming the traveler to Bridgeport and when they were first thrust out in the world, lighting Catherine and James safe home.

I i

No authority. I—persona non grata.

Inside info: the Mix refers to the drug culture. Strictly speaking—Northeast, Mid-Atlantic. Verbal voyeurism, it's a kick to know that lingo, as it was once delicious to speak a word of necromancy, incantation of Black Mass, or let slip the secret code as in the wartime movies. Transgression without risk. How it enlarges us, the inside info—to speak like punks in an alley, like Rosicrucians, charismatics—I, I, I know.

O o

The surprise, the alarm—O! Perfection of shape, pleasing. Om, om, **omm, ommm, ommmm, ommmmm.** Ozone of primordial soup we live in, which would kill us in pure form, but which P.T. recommended as beneficial in Seaside. Naught, yet in the beginning: Once upon a time, contract between teller and all children, by which I mean us kids, lead-in to magic remodeling of reality. And the inviting o of ordinary, dark as a rabbit hole in which the world is experienced as quite extra-ordinary though we strive to make it daily, to fit us, to fit in.

As in: Once upon a time, Jasper McLevy was born in a tenement in the South End, his father a Scot slater and roofer. As a boy he worked the buckle factory, $2.60 a week and of

the poor, remembered the poor when improving himself through the International Correspondence School at night. It is said he became a Socialist reading Edward Bellamy's *Looking Backward: 2000–1887,* a best-seller that cheats, for while the millennial novel exposes the greed and indifference of the rich, the abject lives of the Boston poor, Bellamy's model for the utopian

rightly speak—cocktail, shit row, high beams—useful phrases in the guidebook. Now that will be María Benez's language—skeezer, date. Where to go? Not with them, those women who would have no part of her, into Village paperwork. Where else? Not home to Catherine. She's spoiled all nests and perched on the rocks recalls her swift flight after long disaffection with the convent, how fast the end came. After a troubled night of prayer for faith she had reasoned clear away, how she wandered at dawn toward the shared bathroom and a door was open, the door to the cell-like room where a simple woman, an old kitchen nun, slept. The woman was kneeling naked. Her white head jerked up with the pain of each stroke as she flailed herself with a stiff knotted rope. The nun's soft old flesh speckled with scabs and fresh wounds. In that instant the convent was over and she packed her few things to leave as she knows she will pack up quickly and turn from the experience—no, from her adventures in Bridgeport, from this man she can't leave fast enough. He has been watching her for a while, the way she now stands, alert as a small bird with a twig in its mouth.

   The patrol car, rounding one of the loop-de-loops which is all Seaside Park has to offer by way of invention, notes them as domestic dispute. The woman trots off in a mincing girl's run; man in a penitent jog at her side. The limp air cannot absorb their misery. Swallowing attempts at small talk, out of breath with their belittling, it's better for them, buckled up, driving off. No further incident for these two, just one peculiar bit: the actor, who as actor reveals so little of himself, rolls down the window, YELLS, "Money grubber," at Phineas Taylor Barnum. "Fuckin' green giant," and addresses a Bronx cheer to dumb, dazed Christopher Columbus, "You, too, you son of a bitch." He's got her laughing. Would that he had the funny hat. "What's the point, darlin'? I can't work his magic." The golden thrum back in his voice, James says, "Besides, Billy was short and fat."

PULL THE THIRD LEVER!

state which will come about swiftly on "the great stage of history" is highly militaristic. Besides, the great populist plays Hollywood tricks with time, the future is now and so forth. His hero wakes from the wretched dream of reality, is restored to bourgeois dining table where the company does not welcome his passionate cry, "I have seen Humanity hanging on a cross!" Chastened, deprogrammed—in a garden on Commonwealth Ave., he is awarded Edith, the wealthy girl, "consummate flower of the century."

Young Jasper McLevy woke in a flash, was lost in the socialist dream. For twenty years he spoke on street corners, on soapboxes, by factory gates. Never a figure of fun—only look at the early photos, the Celt face, dour and lean (so like the young Beckett), taut with his fiery message of the forty-hour week, the fair wage, of crippling corruption. Cracked uppers, down at heel, oily band of his battered felt hat; threadbare pants hung from frayed suspenders. The workers began to take note of this cycle of patronage and graft, and of McLevy. In 1929, with the scandal of Yellow Mill Bridge rebuilt for a fortune, Jasper was in. For 23 years the people of

the city would speak with pride as though *they* were extraordinary, having elected a Socialist mayor, a roofer and slater by trade.

A druid's circle drawn round him, charmless man, slurping his coffee from the saucer, eloquent on the podium, crude in the bars, where he drank not a drop. No one called him to account for embracing Eugene Debs, for being embraced by Earl Browder at a Communist rally. Joe McCarthy didn't bother to get a lead on him, but that's toward the end of the story. With nary an image consultant in city hall, McLevy, understanding the successful politician's coupling of distance with familiarity, made himself a character, always called Jasper. O as in ouch concerning our leader, who attempted a Socialist agenda for a few months, but his cronies never got the hang of it. Jasper was blessed with Roosevelt's largesse in

TO PROTECT YOUR OWN WELFARE

FOR AN ORDERLY SOLUTIO

the Depression, which saved the city before the saving grace of the next World War. Oh, he built sewers and silly esplanades—narrow cement patches down the middle of the streets; it put men to work and our mayor invested his faith and his frugality in the Civil Service—but Jasper's socialism was saving pennies in the porridge pot. An embarrassment to the real party, they threw him out: he sued to get back in and won his case. The banks, who knew their man, contributed to his campaigns: fearful of federal money as he was now of national unions and (Bellamy's) state control, he fought Father Panik, then took credit for the projects, Yellow Mill and Success Village.

Oh, here is the love story. Jasper married both his sweethearts—Mary Flynn, who loved him secretly for many years 'cause she was Catholic,

Double entry, designed to place equivalencies . . . when something is missing . . . when something is lost, you simply set down a number on the other side of the page to compensate, reconcile . . . as if to balance, naturally . . . as if to insist that the beautiful system must hold.

nurtured his young man's ideals, taught him grammar, and died in childbirth; and Vida Stearns, Socialist born and bred, secretary of the local party, who spent her days painting flowers. With Nell, side by side at the Ladies' Art League, where they spoke of color values and warm pallets, of gold leaf and distemper, trompe l'oeil and japanning. Nell, whose father made the tidy fortune on handsome contracts awarded him by the Irish mayors, and Vida of the Workman's Circle borrowing back and forth mat varnish, burnt umber, mineral spirits of an afternoon as they captured a vase of homegrown pansies, depicting the flower faces so artfully, accurately copied you could not tell Nell's from Vida's, Vida's from Nell's, on tin boxes and trays, mostly trays, and they ended with surplus on which to serve their husbands, both men of power in the small ellipse of the city, the world that so surely enclosed them.

"Regards to Jasper."
"Best to Bill!"

We can say with certainty that Jasper read a modicum of Marx at night in the rotting South End beehive, that in those early days his faith in the unions was in place, that he stood firm on the Socialist platform, but never heard, as the busy years in city hall went by, of Gramsci's *City of the Future* or of Horkheimer, Adorno—any of those heavies in the Frankfurt School—theory he had no need of before or after his election, and often, we blush to confess it, used the charged word "dialectic" as a joke in after dinner speeches to the businessmen of Bridgeport. They knew their Jasper, who kept his distance from the Spanish Civil War. He was not slippery or self-serving, just your New England pragmatist who took the consensus on Main Street before he made a move. Our mayor was conservative, parochial— honest, he campaigned for Claire Booth LUCE!

But we believed…what did we believe? That we were exceptional in Bridgeport, just ordinary folk, and Jasper our righteous reflection. Until the character role wore thin as the seat of his pants and the textbooks he bought for the schools twenty years back hung in such shreds children could no longer read them and the Interstate was planned to pass us by and Jasper was out and the absurd proposal of a Fronton called JaiAlai or JaiAlai called Fronton, some crossword-puzzle word was to be built in the shadow of Father Panik Village, though you would never have to see that disaster to play or bet the quenella, just swing off the highway into the parking lot where under the concrete Jimmy Hoffa's body was dumped, so they say. For twenty-three years we were decent, if shabby and deluded, delighted not to be swindled. So we love Jasper, defend him, compare his rangy form, his boyish smile, to Will Rogers, the American humorist, once miscast as Barnum in the movies, and, as you know, P.T. was for a term our honorable, unremarkable mayor, which leads to the nagging thought: our Socialist mayor was a consummate showman—yep, Jasper was Barnumesque.

Oh, my! Mary Boyle can't park her vestigial amazement, though she can identify a stick knife by its glint across the Village parking lot and smell the stuff she can't name cooking through the phlegm and blood, jism and bile that rise like ooze in scary science fiction (or Dante's *Inferno*), seeping through the broken pavements into the halls and barricaded rooms of the Village as though from the old Yellow Mill Pond.

But oh, how strange the streets of the City of Pain really are. In the seeming silence of noise against

noise, violent, like something cast from the mold of the Void, the glittering confusion, the collapsing monument swaggers.

—*Rilke,* Tenth Duino Elegy

Michael Harrington (1928–1989) spoke frankly of his party, the Socialist Party, how it lost force in "hair-splitting theological arguments," and since they had no power there was nothing to fight over. He spoke of the "intact poor" unto the third and fourth generation as in the Village and spoke, in his last television interview, as he always did of hope for new models to rise from the ruins as they must "for the benefit of all contending classes."

Gosh! We should have said. My side of the page, no obligation. When it is unamusing, just go on, go on with the story. Catherine has won this round by default. James will not make his movie. For the view of East Bridgeport, the prescription is rose-colored glasses:

The first person I noticed in the street was a glazier whose piercing and discordant cry floated up to me through the heavy, filthy Paris air. It would be impossible for me to say why I was suddenly seized by an arbitrary loathing for this poor man.

"Hey! Hey?" I shouted, motioning him to come up. And the thought that my room was up six flights of stairs, and that the man must be having a terrible time getting up them with his fragile wares, added not a little to my hilarity.

Finally he appeared. After looking curiously over his panes of glass one by one, I exclaimed: "What! You have no colored glass, no pink, no red, no blue! No magic panes, no panes of Paradise? Scoundrel, what do you mean by going into poor neighborhoods without a single glass to make life beautiful!" And I pushed him, stumbling and grumbling, toward the stairs.

—*Baudelaire,* Paris Spleen

U u

Poor U, confused with V, interchangeable consonant and vowel right up through Dr. Johnson until good old American Webster, and it is only the 21st letter of our perfected modern alphabet which concerns us, though U may count its blessing, since it does not appear in *The Human Alphabet* of Jo. Theodor and Jo. Israel De Bry (Frankfort O.M., 1596), wherein naked bodies of men and women are contorted into letters, I and T being the only decent approximations, the V particularly obscene, legs in the air, bottom and balls exposed as in sinuous maneuver of Indian erotica, we suppose, and much prefer *The Animal Alphabet* of Joseph Balthazar Silvestre (Paris, 1843) in which the curve of U is a spaniel taking a pratfall on what must be an icy pond while a haughty heron forms the standard among upright reeds, quite in his element, you see, while that dumb dog…

U the lucky horseshoe, the devil's prong. It is unlucky that Mary Rose and James, touring the venue of Father Panik Village, where a U bolt would not save a runner's bike, come within a few blocks, but do not see the birthplace of Robert Mitchum, 476 Logan Street. The house (1893) would be for bookkeeper or foreman in Barnum's scheme, but has been fitted out with picture window, vestibule, split-rail fence and looks as though it has slipped down into the small city lot from Cath's exurban tract. But "Mitchum Estate" it says on a plaque put up by Don and Debra Pettway in 1980 when officially deemed famous. It would have done James a world of

476 Logan Street
Location:
Built: 1893
Style: Victorian
Historic value: Bridgeport's famous ho
EastEnd Historical So
named: MITCHUM ESTA
Purchased by:
one family/full cel
members will be persons
membership will
U.S.A
CLUB:

good to look in at the gate as if the ghost of an East Side kid would pop out the screen door, run down the walk to the privileged boy from the North End, and tell him how it's done, for James

is right—Mitchum is a great movie actor and Sir Lawrence Olivier was wrong; "I suppose this anemic little medium can't take great acting." But what would James say to his home-town idol whose mother worked as a typesetter at the *Post* and had great plans for her son, who, by his own admission, was a hobo, bouncer, bartender, sailor and adagio dancer, stevedore and powder man before he became a star and who studied tap dance with Dan Quilty in the Ritz Ballroom while James was chauffeured to the cotillion in Fair-field, which was false as Nell's ambition for her boy, who could, of course, as a man, phone Mit-chum up and ask why he will never speak the lan-guage of filmfolk like a native and how you cross over as an actor, discard the script—the other fella's lines.

Delight of a U-turn, but no exit for James, who says, not unkindly, to Mary Rose, "Hey! It's like the movies. Stuff happens." She does not *get* his flip, shamefaced line—whether "stuff" refers to Peaches or the Hilton. As she watches a hooker work the seawall in Seaside, the body language of the working girl's dry smile and twitch of revulsion remain unseen by Mary Boyle, like the book of her own life with many uncut pages.

Unspeakable:

Dearest, if you want to know just how much Reit-man has hurt me from the first day I met him, just go out on the streets awhile, as I foolishly did when I was about twenty-one, and go with strange men for money. For a woman of your knowledge you are strangely innocent. I ask no forgiveness of the language I used toward him but I do ask for-giveness for my anger. He has received from me just

what he has given me—no more—no less. He tackled the wrong woman when he tackled me. I have had a deep horror of him ever since he met me at the N.Y. station. I understood him thoroughly as soon as he grabbed my arm as we walked along the street. I used the same kind of language he did. Please ask him that, for the sake of the Cause, if he ever goes to meet another sin-laden woman who is beginning to see a glimmer of light—please ask him, for humanity's sake, for his own sake, and the woman's sake—not to begin "fuck" talk. Please ask him to remember that he stands by your side as representing anarchism.

. . . Perhaps Ben is the way he is thru suffering—just like myself. It warps one.

—Alameda Sperry to Emma Goldman,
July 27, 1912

And unworthy:

Unworthy of these sore heads, James Bray and Samuel Clemens, their commentary on Columbus: *"Oct. 12. It was wonderful to find America but it would have been more wonderful to miss it."*   —The Diaries of Mark Twain

At every turn reverse, undo—the impotent desire *re* our histories. Undo, lift the gauzy layer, the softening gel or film of dust and scum, stretch the image tight—no stroke of our brush visible—until it is hyper-real, the past illusory as in the movies. For all their unbalanced equations of dream with waking, their dismembering of time, the surrealists never came upon this sane American definition: PAST, n. *That part of Eter-nity with some small fraction of which we have a slight and regrettable acquaintance. A moving line called the Present parts it from an imaginary period known as the Future. These two grand divisions of Eternity, of which one is continually effacing the other, are entirely unlike. The one is dark with sor-*

*row and disappointment, the other bright with
prosperity and joy. The Past is the region of sobs,
the Future is the realm of song. In one crouches
Memory, clad in sackcloth and ashes, mumbling
penitential prayer; in the sunshine of the other
Hope flies with a free wing, beckoning to temples
of success and bowers of ease. Yet the Past is the
Future of yesterday, the Future is the Past of tomorrow. They are one—the knowledge and the dream.*
— Ambrose Bierce, The Devil's Dictionary

Uplift is what we've come for in the end, grand
finale of Hippodrome, the crowded stage, for we

are multitude who once were few. Delivered from Babel we will speak *every
man in his own tongue wherein we were
born, hear them speak in our own tongue*
if not of the wonderful works of God,
as they say, at least each to the other,
post-Pentecostal, and shall deliberate
with clarity upon the shade of meaning
between Ultima Thule, the farthest
point on the map, cold but known,
attainable—and utopias with their
pleasing arrangements we can only
imagine, as in—*I obferved, that all who
went took the right hand, and all who came the left
(a). This fimple method of avoiding obftruction
has been lately difcovered; fo true it is, that all
ufeful inventions are produced by time (b). By this
regulation all obftructions are avoided, and every
paffage is left free. From the public feftivals,
where the greateft concourfe of people refort, to
enjoy an entertainment of which they are naturally
fond, and of which it would be unjuft to deprive
them, each one returns to his home without detri-
ment or danger.*

> *(b) This method, I am informed, has long
been ufed in the imperial city of Vienna.*

— Sebastian Mercier, Memoirs of the Year
Two Thoufand Five Hundred,
*translated from the French
by W. Hooper, M.D., 1772*

And sometimes

Y γ

As in the awkward human alphabet. Arms of the
referee flung to the sky, in celebration of first
down. Arms raised to heaven in supplication at
Gesthemene. Arms held high in surrender—for I
have long given up the steering wheel for the
yoke, admit we are a harnessed team. Beasts of
equal burden,  never free of each

other. The right hand knows well what the left
is doing—my side, your side—the balancing act.
I am in your debt: I trust you are in mine, but to
that I cannot answer.

   With the nuns and the girls, Catherine
sang off-key at Marymount:
> *Te-ell me why-γ-y the stars do shine?
> Te-ell me why-γ-y the ivy climb?
> Te-ell me why-γ-y the sky so blue?*

Love, the incomprehensible answer. Cath
knew the red stars' brilliance is synthesizing car-
bon, that ivy is heliotropic, but love the true
answer, simple as close rhyme. And why, you may
ask, is this dictionary only of vowels? Because
they are the given, the origin of all our lamenta-
tions and of our song. When Billy was dying in St.
Vincent's, James came from New York. Then, as
now, each patient's name was posted on the
door: William Aloysius Bray—the full name got
off some document—and in the next room Sadie
Klotz. Unable, James stood in the corridor, not as
an actor prepares, but unable to go in to his
father, and listened to Sadie's continual cry of *Oi,
Oi, Oi, Oi* to her Maker whose name she dare not
speak, and to Billy's gasping *Arraugh, Arraugh*
from the Irish bog, far beyond the pale of
Bridgeport.

The Music Man

A dandy walking down Main Street: no one to note his wing tips, double-breasted blazer, knife crease of the lemony pants, not on these blocks as he makes his way past the remnant of circular drive, striped canopy of the Stratfield Hotel, its many windows now sealed into the rest home which one day may claim him. He marches smartly by the men who loiter at this end of town, colored men, as he calls them, joined in the slow commerce of this day's survival. Now and again a man touches the beak of his cap, "Sir," with a sly smile, or "Cap'n," for he cuts a fine figure, a Sunday-morning man.

He is Jerry De Martino, pleased when they greet him: come on down from his condo, though he can't recall what was there before the trim maze of walks and shrubs, the toy-town roofs and balconies that make up the mini-village where he has lived a dozen years—whether it was the Sunoco Body Shop or the fluorescent sprawl of Kay's, a dusty department store. Under the dead marquees of twin movie theaters—Poli's Palace and Majestic—Mr. De Martino makes his way rather grandly. Not so much of a main street that he can't take it in stride, past the new courthouse and down to

299

the Barnum Museum. A few blocks on, coming out of a bank, an office or parking lot, one of the kids will call to him. "Jerry!" they call to the old bandmaster, a note of hope—that he'll signal the next inspiring tune. Jerry's brown as a farmer though his time in the field no more than parade drill on a football grid and, of late, his daily walk in all weather. "Jerry!" He listens for the call, overshooting discount drugs in his single-rank strut, pivots at Fairfield Avenue. Jerry, not Mr. De Martino, if a kid played in his band. His sharp outfits, military carriage, takes them back: a neat memory jog for the kids (the youngest well up in their thirties) calling this spiffy old guy by his first name. And he is fond of their familiarity, so few left in a town lively people abandon. If not today, then tomorrow a bandsman will call to him in the city which is heaven on earth to Mr. De Martino.

Born Geraldo, in or about Palermo, to a courageous commendatore and hopeful lyric soprano, he pleased his parents by inventing tunes on a penny whistle, that tooting all Mama needed to project a grand career. In his mother's version, they fled moments before the commendatore was taken by the fascisti; she, in dramatic widow's weeds, with one steamer trunk and her boy, to a cousin who made it to streets of gold in Bridgeport. In the trunk, the family laces and linens, her gowns of cut velvet and spangled georgette worn to the opera houses of Catania and Bari; at Teatro Bellini, her one audition for the chorus. Tucked among her corset covers and petticoats, the precious instruments—Geraldo's oboes, recorders, an ebony clarinet. The cousin, an enterprising tailor who parlayed his craft into a coat factory, thought them an unpromising pair, the Signora with her outmoded trousseau; Geraldo, carrying mama's artistic shawls. A sallow obedient boy, eighteen going on forty, flattened as though he'd been packed under the linens and operatic finery, under the libretti and sheaves of music for classical clarinet. *Da vero*—how were they to live?

Geraldo remembered his father not as Mama's patriot with Garibaldi mustache but as a sickly postal clerk. Never mind, there was the misfortune of his death, the trunk and the prosperous tailor in Bridgeport who procured a contract for G.I. overcoats hours after an unprepared America entered the Second World War. Never mind, Mama advertised Geraldo as professor of woodwinds, took in a few pupils herself. A conspiracy of two in this outpost of workers and bosses, radio shows and movie houses; how they adored reviling provincial piano recitals, the inept State Symphony; how Signora lived for their pilgrimages to New York, where, with opera glasses in a beaded bag, she swept into the glittering lobbies of Carnegie Hall and the old Met. What sights from the dress circle—Melchior's chest swelling, the fluttering throat of tiny Lily Pons, broad back of Bruno Walter, but *O Dio, Dio*—Toscanini among the mortals. Their return trip euphoric, until at Stamford or Norwalk the pathos of their destination came to mind, the front parlor on Thorn Street where they received unmannerly children who could neither sing nor play, the soulless sons and daughters of merchants, managers, policemen.

O Dio, it was their sustaining joy, knocking flat, discordant Bridgeport, the smug swank of the place with a couple of parks, oil tankers chugging gaily into the shallow harbor as though it was the fabled Bay of Naples, greasy "Apizz" parlors, the colorless promenade on Main Street; the very street that Jerry looks forward to each day, seldom thinking of Signora De Martino and her attentive boy, how with cherished ticket stubs they returned from the great concert halls to exile. The old master, brown and brittle, can't recall a young man, pale and limp among soldiers and sailors with their duffel bags who rode the trains, who slept like babies on benches in the Bridgeport station when Signora, long past midnight, commandeered the one and only cab. His mother dead these many years, it has faded: Jerry has let such scenes turn milky as aged Kodachrome—their flat on Thorn Street paid for by the cousin, sun kept

off Lucia (the fat piano) by tattered window shades; display of sec-
ondhand instruments, coins dropped into his palm at the end of a
lesson, the indignity of dimes and quarters making up three bucks.
From the kitchen, *Ger-al-do*, the shrill claim of her contralto (Mama
lost the upper range). Admonishing, wheedling, flirting—*Ger-
AL-do*.

Weeks after the Signora's final callback for that grand opera
(bouffe) in the sky, her son stood under a basketball hoop, faced off
with a high school band. Dressed for the grand tier, he introduced
himself—Geraldo De Martino. A blubbery sousaphone (Bud Shea)
scooped a stray volley ball, smacked it at the skinny teacher, "Hey,
Jerry!"

"Think fast," Geraldo cried, miraculously returning the
ball. He could hear his own frightened words, his precise immigrant
voice, spin off the high ceiling of the gymnasium. Scared, they must
never know, these big American children, that he'd lost his whole-
some lunch in anticipation of this enormous room smelling of wax
and disinfectant and the sweat of all their games. Must never know
the rehearsal of his pep talk, a hundred times the feeble jokes run
through, and his stern unflinching order: "Practice at three. Instrument in hand."

Little notion where to go from there, but he had survived
a flabby sousaphone calling his number. His first days in the uptight
fifties, the worst of it, more painful than the desecration, many years
later, of his flag formation during Vietnam, more humiliating than
the flotilla of condom balloons released at a homecoming game by
an insufferable tuba. So he had to thank that fathead Bud, who
married (unfair, unfair) a penny-bright piccolo, along with the
Board of Education which took a chance on his conservatory credentials, inauthentic as "the works" on pizza pie; and thank his first
principal, indifferent Miss . . . Miss? . . . Monahan, a tone-deaf
woman who referred to De Martino as the music slot.

Discipline, routine, no marching band without it; all psychology as well as parade maneuvers gathered out of a handbook from Schirmer's music store, first trip to New York without Mama. He could hear the full scale of her outrage: *"O Dio-o-o-o.* A brass band?" Buffoons who passed the hat in public squares, led funerals through back streets of Palermo. Yes, Geraldo answered, all of that—a band. He'd never talked back to Mama; now the words came quickly as he passed the stations at Stamford and Westport, looking up from the unmusical English words in his bandmaster's instruction book. *Da vero,* the rousing marches somewhat ridiculous on the page, but his students' faces had been eager, not like the sullen children who suffered instruction in the chill front parlor. Yes, a *marching* band, he corrected Mama, because he could not pin a hero's mustache on Papa, could not stroke her gowns believing she had reached in those legendary auditions the mad ecstasy, *O Dio, O Dio, O Dio,* of Lucia's romantic excess. *Really,* how was he to live? A burden at the cousin's dinner table? Forever looking through the wrong end of the opera glasses at a minuscule "studio" where, even in the cold, the dark, his instruments mysteriously split in the central heat? It was a good job, the cousin said, who had quickly arranged it, impatient with the black band on Geraldo's sleeve, uncomfortable with old-world mourning that smacked of Sicilian fate. A job, after the war, when jobs in the city were running scarce; the cousin never guessing that Geraldo dreaded a menial role at the coat factory and that upon grand occasions in the concert halls of New York, he'd looked long upon young music students with their gossip, their laughter—and hoped they did not see him with his mama.

Instruments in hand, the kids showed promptly at three; in a magic few weeks could Break to Block One in style, Cross Field March, come to the Flourished Halt playing "Our Boys Will Shine." Grueling rehearsals, drill in the sleet, in the rain when athletes left them the field. In the early years, Jerry asked himself why, why their performance for a mighty mouse maestro, famously strict. He'd dismiss his lead trumpet for a cigarette stub (later roach) in a uniform pocket, yet not mark a windy fife absent when he knew the girl to be six months with child. Why, mainstream or misfit, did they show? Give up weekends and holidays for a chinless stick figure blowing his toy whistle with wet lips? A drummer might think to be Stan Kenton; a cymbal date a halfback. That was no answer. Why Jerry? Their mascot, he supposed, in the green and white uniform with parade of brass buttons, signaling to the right flank—Mark Time, Flash Kick; to the left—Side Step and Pivot; their little general with bristling cockade, gold soutache on his shako. Simple music, open and free—"Hi-Dee-Hi," "Stars and Stripes." The way he knew to please with "Muskrat Ramble." Jerry abreast of the times, "Jingle Bell Rock." Holding back the new sheet music till the end of practice: then, he would walk ceremoniously among his bandsmen to distribute—Go, Jerry!—"Blue Suede Shoes." "The Star Trek Theme."

Why Jerry? Maybe his kids knew the simple heart of a man who lived through them and for them, not quite an adult; but did not guess that in cities, particularly a workers' city, folks value the few loons, the wounded eccentrics that make them whole and fit.

In this entry on Geraldo De Martino, deletions—happy humdrum summer trips with teacher friends to Williamsburg, Quebec, Howe Caverns; noted—one move downhill from Thorn Street, then another in which the grand piano did not make it up the narrow stair to rooms over Gold's N.Y. Deli, each flat closer to the high school; noted—the luminous spring of '58, his passion for Mimi Marr, a sultry saxophone, that racked him like a devastating virus. Mimi, heavy golden hair fell to her epaulets which once she'd asked him to untangle; pouted and teased when Geraldo's hands shook with love. He had placed her in the first rank to see the wind whip her short skirt, caress her thigh, though Mimi could not play the clarion trills, and to cure his desire took up with Jane Crim, teacher of Home Ec, timid and graceless, whom he squired about till she went nuts in the late sixties with jug wine and weed, took off with a leathery woman to bake grainy breads. The maestro's record at once ordinary and amazing, a story of survival/transformation which Geraldo/Jerry, released into his life, no longer questioned, though on a winter night in '62 . . . One blustery night held for Geraldo the answer: still in the North End, he stole from his bachelor pad over the deli through back streets, pulled his coat collar up, slipped into the back row of the neighborhood Rialto.

The show: Robert Preston in *The Music Man.* The very title made Geraldo wince, a professional anticipating the amateur performance. Knowing something of the story, he'd come to scoff, for a moment missing Mama. The movie is skillful, slight—a carnival man suckers an entire sugar-water town in gullible mid-America into buying tubas, vibraphones, etc., all the razzmatazz of a vulgarly imagined marching band. Unlike the facile Jerry, this con man can't play a note, yet dupes widows and children, sips strawberry phosphate. He is played by Preston, too old for the part. By a rustic bridge in moonlight, the Music Man pockets his cash even as he makes love to the beautiful librarian, holding out hope of song and life. Now Jerry leans forward in his seat. He has pulled this cheery scam. He, too, is an amusing American type, the flimflam man, show-off for crowds who love to be taken.

Each night of *The Music Man*'s run at the Rialto, Jerry is stirred by the cocksure Preston without conservatory credentials, by his harmless, heartwarming fraud. And watching, tracks the quick reversal of his own fortune, which might be taken from the bizarre turns of plot in his mother's beloved Donizetti or Bellini, only her boy is not destined for tragic derangement or death. His life is a Hollywood musical—foolish, wonderful, improbable—without the pretty girl. His spindle limbs blow up to screen size: the Music Man leads his kids through the once dull city of Bridgeport, which blossoms under a Technicolor sky; the patched pavements in his order of march, State Street to Park Avenue, are a shimmering sweep of Warner Brothers' dance floor. Clutching the broken arms of his seat (the Rialto is folding fast), Jerry waits—yes, for the famous finale when the movie children, unable to blow or toot, when, suckered by pure need, pure flash, their seventy-six trombones, hundred and ten cornets play the air. But waits for the moment when the kids' ill-fitting mail-order uniforms switch to splendid red coats and creamy pants, those colors reversed on the bandmaster so that as Robert Preston marches toward him on the Rialto screen, gold braid on glimmering white jacket, his trousers, even his shoes turn truest scarlet as Jerry high-steps into the real dream.

Never mind whether it's this humid summer day or yet another when Earl Fabray, his first colored horn, comes swinging through the glass door of City Trust: "Jerry! You stay fine?"

"Just fine," Jerry says. Earl hitches his shoulders back, ashamed of his comfortable belly. Earl with the perfect ear, a soft man in a business suit embracing middle age, can't jump strut, never mind connect with his trombone. He'd come into the gym after practice, a knot of contempt on his black baby face, asked Jerry if he knew the Bird. The bandmaster handed the kid a slide trombone and struck "Dark Town Strutters" from the repertoire. A delicate matter the repertoire, though the Hispanics had pressed for their cha-chas and mambos. At the arcade, he turns full circle, pain in his hands remembering aspirin. Except for the gnarled joints of his fingers, just fine, though he forgets in his charge down Main Street the agony of lacing wing tips, knotting the slippery rep tie. Can't signal Cease March, tap his slender baton. For a few years there had been orchestra. He kept those children clear of Mozart, fed them florid arrangements of Offenbach, let them maul Strauss and Tchaikovsky. Never mind, it soon dwindled, one cello and two whining violins. But the band, it was all spoken grandly at his retirement dinner, reported in the *Post*—the band played on to win medals and trophies. Plaques for his novelty numbers: the peace sign contracting, swelling into a dove; Apollo II blastoff—timpani, cymbals. He had traveled with his bandsmen to Pittsfield and Cleveland, to Orlando, and once marched down Fifth Avenue, saluted the Cardinal on St. Patrick's Day; though it was payment in full, having polished his white shoes, to proceed toward Seaside Park, his ranks maneuvering smartly around the esplanade into double file under the triumphal arch.

He marches through the magic doors of discount drugs, the girl at the checkout counter a perfect twirler—strong back, chin up, quick fingers with the change. There was that, too, the old bachelor (not that old at the start), how he had longed, only longed for that one girl in tasseled boots and short white skirt, Mimi, and with restraint others, their hard thighs and firm butts. His supple fingers guiding their awkward play in private lessons, a harrowing contact sport. Pure bandgirls, he was not much for the twirlers.

Jerry shakes the aspirin bottle: "The chill," he says, "I feel it in the joints."

The girl tilts her head at him, looks out to the hot downtown street, steaming after the first summer storm. She has all the attributes—squared-off shoulders of a majorette, pert breasts, and there's her naughty snicker as she slams the register. His kids, much he did not want to know. Often, on a bus trip or as they came out of the locker room they'd see him and go silent. Jerry, the believer in ump-pah and upbeat, designer of fluttering flag formation. He knew they sheltered him from their nefarious teenage lives, and now, having turned from the mocking beauty, so knowing at her register, the maestro is marking time on Main Street when it comes at him, this day's greeting a strangely authoritative shout, "Mr. De Martino!" He pivots by the left flank.

"Mr. De Martino!" The man calls from the shine of the Hilton Hotel. All Jerry can see, the eyes not what they were when he'd catch a drummer in the last rank miss his cue, all he can see is the blaze of glass and marches toward it to find James Bray lounging, careless as ever, twirling a soft leather satchel.

"James?" He would not have known him, a splotched face, unshaven, were it not for his fame. Every bandsman well aware that Jerry coached a star; and half resented the gifted boy who haunted their sour notes. Yet who's to say it wasn't Jerry with his picky rules and regulations, his slow burn when you didn't clean your instrument, that bought Bray's ticket out of Bridgeport. Now the movie star was saying in a husky voice, one-on-one sincere, that he remembered the studio, Mama, remembered vibrato, embouchure, the fingering. He had not forgotten—was it the Mozart Double or the Haydn they had played together?

"Still teaching?" James asks by way of being nice.

"No, no," says Mr. De Martino. "We are all so proud . . ." he begins and falters. "And you? What will it be next?"

"Television," says James, twirling his bag, and Geraldo De Martino remembers the redheaded boy, fidgeting with his clarinet case, fetching his mouthpiece out of thin air. In that dark room with the cracked shades drawn, his oboes, recorders, and such displayed as though in a museum. He remembers James taking a glass of wine from his mother and that he was the only pupil who drew her into the studio. She said, *"Non e della città."* He doesn't belong here. James telling Mr. De Martino, telling himself he will sign for a series.

"Then, you are on a visit?" his teacher asks and asks after the kind mother and with a hesitation step, a flush on his weathered face, "And Billy, Billy Bray?"

"They're all gone. Long gone." He reckons how very old Mr. De Martino must be. The strips of glossy hair, yellow pants, natty jacket put him off. Now he sees the neck shrunk within the collar, the knobbed fingers.

Geraldo stands at attention, about to say—when a limousine drives up and Bray with a fond actorish farewell gets in and is driven away. The old man sees a blur of himself in the dark windows of the hotel, the light pants, double-breasted with dull brass buttons, phantom face, faded print of an old comedy short in which he turns unsteadily, toddles down the empty street, not on his usual course today toward Barnum's museum by way of the library to read for free in the paper that the mayor is squabbling with his men, that the Christian Democrats have held their seats in Rome and local clams are once again unsafe while a new mall will open in Danbury or Stamford. He looks up to discover the route back to his condo where the many paths and doors create such confusion, a daily jumble of sameness.

James, in an eye mask, crosses the country. A turbulent dreamlike state possesses him; deeper than sleep his rocky journey through the past few days; the speed which flies him away bringing him closer to home. Which home? Mary Rose takes on the look of how many girls—young actresses, P.A.s, a zealous student of film at USC—their look of blank adoration. If he can keep her that way, but the gray, no-color eyes blink on, switch to clear assessment as she reasons their time together away until it has no life, is not even a romantic story. Her eyes are slate with faint chalk dust—erased, yet younger than the many girls, darkly passionate. Yet older, old as Nell but so unlike his dreamy mother. He does not believe his mother was passionate. Once, just back from his father's funeral, she let out a primordial cry, like the yelp of an animal. One cry. He had run to where she stood under the stained glass windows in the dining room. Drowning in the greenish underwater light, she turned to him with an apologetic smile: "Never mind. Never mind."

Not to forget Mary Rose, though he's forgotten the others. Road meat, Ziff calls them, as though they were slow creatures who couldn't keep out of his way. "Was she an otter or a skunk?" Not to number her among them. "A chipmunk? A toad?" He can't rid himself of the ugly system, though he wouldn't let Ziff in the same room as Mary Rose. A ground dove who could not fly. There was blood on the fender this time. Slim evidence he could have lived with a woman in that deflated ball bladder of a city, gone each day to a job like his father. There would be no more, no more . . . in his voluntary blind man's bluff, James can't tag what will be no more, gone as in a card trick. No more acting. That must be it, if he were to wake each morning to the gray curls, the seeing, unseeing gray eyes.

Such conceits invade him as he crosses northern Pennsylvania heading to Ohio; demons, too, absenting himself by the sleep mask from the crockery and cork popping of first class—Isabelle Poole, Barnum, Mr. De Martino, Billy Bray, all costumed, cast as themselves, are out of sorts with James, who can't please them. They loom on the black mask announcing their recriminations, that he will not make her story, his story of murder and mayhem which seems to be one story. Tilted up, slowly breathing, arms crossed as in sleep or death, James flies over the Midwest, can't resist flipping off the mask to see what movie—last season's buddy bomber. Silent figures romp on the screen, crossbreeds from television, pie-in-the-eye guys, fumbles and tumbles.

One by one the curious flight attendants come to view James Bray. He is older, shorter, beak nose jutting from the black mask, shine of his scalp through almost a bald spot; not handsome, but you can't tell without the eyes. Pretending sleep over the Great Plains: on the black stage Catherine appears in her weaver's smock, the awful garment she'd put on as soon as they entered her house. Fat Cath in her sack. They'd laughed like kids, entirely happy. Her house with dead flowers, the wake long over. Proudly, her hands held out to him; stains under the nails, the gray-blue cuticles that would not come clean; the dyer in that poor house more alive than he'd ever seen her. Why then had he said they were all gone? Catherine from her post at the loom still tracks the scene of all their crimes. "Long gone," to Mr. De Martino, risen from the dead in dapper duds. James counting up the years, figures the man can't be alive unless . . . unless Geraldo was *young* when he was a boy. Or an apparition—Barnum come to life and then the music teacher. Such ghostly thoughts pursue him as the pilot announces the Rockies jutting through cloud cover. . . . unless preserved in the airless dark room with the exhibition of precious instruments, Geraldo has lived on, untroubled by life beyond the racket of pupils coming up onto the porch, the nuisance of their no talent or talent thrown away.

The steward, tucking away blankets and pillows, can't

keep his eyes off James Bray: a fair bod, worked on, the nose a disaster with the Zorro mask, hair and neck on the way out. No hot shot, maybe coked up—the celebrity fingers tapping like crazy on the armrest, the lips moist, sucking air. On the black stage, James appears, shakes the spit out of his mouthpiece, replaces a split reed. Instrument up, such a clever boy maybe he can fake it: a wise apple, unable to recall the fingering of the Handel overture, unable to cross the break, but then the music comes, the Brahms in F minor. "The most exquisite," Geraldo says, snatching away the music, too good for the boy, too good for Bridgeport. From memory, James plays on right through the grand arpeggios. As the final notes fade, the ungrateful boy is offered a glass of pulpy homemade wine by Signora in her ashen shawl.

Mr. De Martino's tale skips, bars played off sheets of music that flip in the wind; from fussy immigrant pretender to lovable American fraud to . . . there the notes scatter and the score is held down with an arthritic hand. The old eyes squint, see double, see one movie actor—Preston, then another. The Music Man glad-handing round the secret of his selfish, selfless purpose like invigorating tonic; not unlike James Bray on Main Street conjuring the past, not wanting to display his own transformation worn so very thin. In a reprise Geraldo falls behind these tricky, fast-stepping men who duck like a couple of mobsters into the Stratfield, the hotel Dutch Schultz used in the thirties, a safe and proper distance from the great metropolis; the celebrated hood playing cards with Park City lawyers and bankers. With Billy. That's history, before the Black Shirts cuffed Papa, before Mama packed the steamer trunk, before the prick of "Studio" on Thorn Street.

Jerry's drill began in the Central High gym, a trembling note, his pomaded head under a basket ball hoop. Halo or noose?—never mind, for in his modest condo there are many trophies. The occasional visitor—a discreet, lonely neighbor—comments on the rewards of a successful life. "No," Jerry says, "up at the school, there's your trophies!" The school no longer up on Golden Hill, moved out from dead center. "It was the band, all my kids." And there are the photos: St. Patrick's Day (1965); Orlando with Pluto and Minnie; the competition at Ohio State. They were invited round. In black and white (Corbit Studio), the big B formation. His signature, as it were, before each flourishing finale, B for the city, and on the last day, his very last drill, the kids would not obey his command, Quit the Field. The B, snaking to no tune of his arrangement, froze in magnificent J.

No one to show the old programs—coated or cream stock, a crisis each year. His teacher friends he believes to be living on, baking bread in Ithaca or Arizona. In fact, he is a lone survivor, and were it not for the trophies, the group photos in green and white, the walk to the library where today he's met Lulu Montour, the names always clear in his head. Montour, a frail child who staggered under her bassoon, was with a surly fellow who grumbled, popped gum. And someone else, one of the kids. Hanging his yellowed creamers in a dresser drawer, folding his soiled shirt . . . but the man had not called to him, "Jerry!" He pivots: the room presses in with aging faces and cheap golden statuettes which he knows you buy at Blinn's trophy store and give out freely for drills and deportment, for consolation to second and third best. He is alone and has been since the day his mother died. Never mind, on the floor his instruments lie in their cases, dusty as her garlicky black shawls. It's been a while since they conspired, since she sang out *Ger-al-do*, always in part a command. *Geraldo*, straining for the high note. With whom had she sung the exultant duet—*O Dio, O Dio*—certainly not with his mild weak-chested father. He thinks if he can show her the tickets from the beaded purse she will not see him in his musical-comedy hat with the bristling cockade, the betrayal of his slick smile as he Salutes the Visitors. "*Really*, Mama, how was I to live?"

"But this place, this place!" Does she revile this city or the cluttered condo without the baby grand? Her scolding soprano reaches down to him from the celestial heights of a perfect E-flat: *"Che posta là, Ger-AAAl-do!"*

The tickets are to the Haydn, the Vivaldi, to the Poulenc clarinet concerto she preferred to all others. There was never a Mozart Double, a false step. Geraldo remembers his order when the line of march strayed or faltered: "As You Were!" A merciful command, but wing tips and blazer buttons have taken their toll, news of polluted oysters and those gypsies who call him "Cap'n." He can't snap his pajamas or open the jar of decaf espresso without considerable pain, then he remembers the high-breasted majorette, aspirin from the discount drugs, remembers to place the tablets on his tongue and swallow, leaving his clawed fingers upon pursed lips as though to instruct a blind uncaring boy. See! See, it is like a kiss upon the mouthpiece. Laying himself out straight as a bandsman, instrument up. Only play your piece, Geraldo. She will bring you bitter wine.

Circling in the shit over L.A., James replaces the mask to search for the granite of his grandfather's curbstone, hoping to find a few feet of it left under the steel supports of the Interstate. To replay and set forever the sequence of his driving up home with Cath to see where the highway erased Matt Devlin's house, the rough gray-green of concrete pilings mimicking the spectral stucco. To watch as they get out of the car: it's dangerous the embankment, a steep ramp at this point where our yard with gray platform . . . though all the neighborhood yards, far as we can see to the hospital, are now perfectly flat, but there is this wild swoop of blacktop through the back porch, cars sideswipe our mother's stove, an enormous Allied Van careens through the pantry door into the revered dining room table. No *corpus delicti,* but we come up the front walk anyway and peer in through the beveled-glass door. Nothing to mourn, that's the shock, and if we were to smash back at the Interstate with a bulldozer we'd find not one white suspender button off Billy's pants, no gap-toothed comb of Nell's, nor tin tray with her hand-painted posies, no stacked deck nor headless Our Lady, not one chip of Catherine's lovesick 78s. Amazed, brother and sister laugh nervously at the untrustworthy world as though with luck it might be a game of peek-a-boo, all gone.

We drive away in careful silence. I gun the sluggish rented car up through the marble-top dresser next to our parents' bed, a desecration but my heart leaps up, for across the oncoming traffic, we see the dread cemetery of childhood looking New England quaint. And on our side of the highway a fresh grove of weeping birch, geese on a shapely body of water glistening in the sun . . . some landscape gardener's dream of oriental boulders and fashionable grasses. "My God!" we cry to each other. "Seeley's Pond!"

Screenplays

MIRACLE, n. An act or event out of the order of
nature and unaccountable, as beating a normal
hand of four kings and an ace with four aces and
a king.   —Ambrose Bierce, *The Devil's Dictionary*

1

*The window of a plane with rounded corners. Indistinct whiteness of
exposed film or watermarked paper moving by. In fact, thick sunlit
clouds which thin to wisps in blue sky. Tilt to scene below.*

I had taken off the mask. The mountains were now the
Sierras; pockets of snow; above the timberline red clay and shale
that often crumbles to the touch; Western vegetation—among the
defiant California pines and cypress, cleared or burnt-out patches.
Beyond, yellow-brown smog smeared across a big VistaVision sky.
The plane banked and turned, turned again waiting for a runway.
At times it seemed we'd got our tail wind and might take off across
the Pacific, then we'd bank and head straight back to the mountain,
come low enough I could discern a trail, a possible cabin, a stream.
Toying with that mountain from above.

*James' voice, its pleasantly rough texture—public, accept-
able as the fabric of the window shade he now pulls, a pattern of
repeated blue logo and gray unflappable wings.*

If I knock on the mountain it will open as in the children's
story: that other mountain in *My Book House* Nell read to us. The

hero, a curious son, ventures out into the world, comes to the mountain. There is no path or way, but something like a door. He knocks, calls a spell of words, calls out a magic thrice. The mountainside—trees, rocks, babbling brook and all—swings open, sings on its hinges. At first the story proceeds within the boy's known landscape: mine would be the outcroppings of ironstone with mica in Beardsley Park, a trickling branch of the Pequonnock, neighborhood oaks and elms, no doubt the cutleaf maple my father, a man not tuned to nature, planted soon after I was born. The boy's journey is long, hard, heavy with riddles. He grows to be shrunken, hoary, old; yet boyishly he breathes underwater, flies safely, not as I am flying to Los Angeles, where the control tower may fail us, the landing gear stick in the belly of the plane. The boy is fearless through all his trials in an unstable alchemist's world, never more self-assured than early on when that mountain opens. It was full of rooms with false doors leading to many clever, deceptive halls. My sister loved that story, for it involved a very pretty girl with similar adventures.

Quiet of anticipation on a transcontinental flight when the last fuss is over. The seat in first class next to James is empty. Above his head the reading lamp on him like a spotlight. He plays to the captive audience in a trapped voice-over, never heard by the passengers as they perform their restless, rumpled mimes.

I direct this one. It will have to do. It will do nicely, play the art circuit. P.T. would scorn the small houses, invent some hoopla—public scandal, work over our insatiable appetite for freaks—run it in the Big Top, send the audience away glad they've been cheated. Hey, I'm a mere actor trained like the natty midget to the hornpipe, like Jumbo to the ballroom dance, but I call the shots on this one. No affected hand-held camera. Professional work, fantastic color, spacial imaging, and by golly clean, dusted-up sound—every footstep of my choosing, each intrusion of motor, plunge of the blade, off-camera shuffle and cry. There will be silence, yeah, a little coercive, so's to make you see. . . . Corny cuts—what teachers of high school English, trying to lead us through a bit of Shakespeare or Hardy, once referred to as leaps of the imagination.

Okay, overdirected, that's your dollar for my hole in the doughnut. Where's control, you don't set the hurdle up?

2

The window of the plane like a television screen framing gawky palm trees, cusp of sand along blue shore—lead-in to a travelogue. Then Bray in the hooded tunnel which connects plane to terminal. His voice echoes, lending conviction to his delivery though he walks without progress on a stationary track.

I came down in L.A. feeling I'd been on a binge, fairly mean—cursing the flight attendant, cutting an innocent fan. Flat sunshine. I was inside the mountain and I hadn't knocked or called, the route clearly marked, next lap of the journey, fly me up the coast—home, though I'd been home. Nowhere to nowhere. Ziff, straining at the gate to meet me, could find me upstairs in a whorehouse. No mystery by this time: On the phone Ziff locates Big Foot, Judge Crater, I presume. Bury him with the goddam switchboard on his desk, he'll ring me up from hell, money on the line.

"Yo, James! Sir James, E.C.T."

"No, you don't."

"Eastern calcified turd. You know what you look like?"

"Tough shit."

"Smart, too. A college boy."

An assault of white papers in my face: "Velcum. Velcum ho-ome." Ghoulish Peter Lorre voice: "All iss pre-paredt," flapping, I'll never know, the contract for the resale of my soul. Poke, jab—wasn't that Ziff and me? Buddies, always a flick to the left, a couple of pals in the ring, that was the model, the glamour of violence barely concealed. Shit, I lashed out, unlike the old Hollywood clinch, feints in the movies, whammed the guy. His papers scattered at first swipe. He flops on the floor to retrieve them.

When he got up he had this big fuckareeno smile comes when he's about to kill a half-created script. "Big balls," he said with the big smile, not yet sure if I was kidding. I was not.

"You gotta da big boccie balls in Bilgeport," Ziff said, thick tongue, trickle of blood.

I fought dirty, bucked with my head. It seemed natural, absolutely natural to punch out the bad guy. A small crowd gathered as though we were on a set, then someone spoke my name. "Sorry," I cried as I took off for my connection, running for my life.

Ziff's in better shape: caught me, wrenched me around to see his killer smile, "Sorry butters no herring." Until that moment I never got why Ziff, not an actor, went to the million-dollar dentist for the caps. The filthy grin wiped me more than words, more than his fist with the topaz ring that cut across my nose. "Fuckin' homeboy. You know what's small potatoes, Father Jim?" *Boys' Town*, Mickey Rooney sob in the throat: "It's you, holy kamoly, bangin' the belle of St. Mary's."

He'd been on the hotline. Like one of those wily wizards in *My Book House*, never surprised when the kid turns up in his drippy grotto, Ziff knows why I'm running, nowhere to nowhere. For half a second I think I'll sign what's in his hand, only now it's tucked in his slubbed silk jacket and the band of spectators forming again . . . I'll sign then know who I am. But I socked him, this time light and easy as in the movies.

He reeled against the flimsy airline rope: "A town full of girls can't keep their pants on, you travel for the novelty item."

Then we both look ashamed, even my buddy who knows no shame, thinking of the bad press—fisticuffs in the airport.

"Look, I put it together." Straight, no impersonation from the classics: "Your fuckin' blarney, fuckin' foot-of-the-cross Irish-cop picture."

"It wasn't worth the plane fare. You knew that." They were holding my flight to Santa Barbara. He looked like a kid who lost by the flip of a card, sad but with a nasty edge. In a whining gravel voice Ziff said: "Is this the end of . . . ?" It didn't play.

3

Bray in a taxi, through the window behind him sunshine of postcard California works as backlighting. His features blacked out, head and shoulder in silhouette. Latino music on the radio fades.

  The way I come home: at the small airport scooped out of an orange grove, I take a cab. Thrill of the sea, the mountains. A resort with healing powers. I am a visitor among the palms and citrus, though my wife has taught me fan palm from date, portulaca along the freeway, bougainvillea, oleander as we wind uphill in Montecito. It was spring of a sort, both lush and arid, burnt-out lawns, the town reverting to desert. Morning, with morning fog that will lift. They have a scrim of white fog and say, "Not one of our better days." Demanding everything in paradise, ex-presidents and bums on lower State Street are of one mind about the weather.

  "You have to come out West," I'd said to my sister.

  James pays the driver, stands in the shade of a giant More-ton Bay fig looking at the arrangement of spiked agaves and lesser succulents that define the driveway up to the patio, stands there with his shoulder bag before moving in close to the camera, at first flinching in the sun. His face in this exposure, an almost memorable actor's face when free of flesh-colored paste, rouged shadows, has come to life with exhaustion and a raw scrape across the nose. His voice natural, un-projected:

  "You'll have to come out West," I said to my sister.

  "I'm months behind!"

  With the damn bedspreads? Woolgathering in the work-shop, hell of a lot sounder for Cath than my home on the range. So, being driven up to the ranch with Mex music I could of heard in

Bridgeport where you can get caught in a spring shower seeking the afterimage of Wheeler mansion where once an ancient copper beech. We should have been struck by lightning, me and Mary Rose. Anyway, Cath would feel a stranger to my dusty pasture and dry pool, unplashing fountain in the drought, to snorts on an intercom babysitting horseflesh of no more use to me than ornamental swans. There were cars, too many cars, yet no one home. The house serene, as my wife makes it, cool. On reentry, that's when I look close at our museum pieces—Indian baskets and pots, the Hopi blankets. Early, too early, yet beds unslept in, even my daughter's black barge to the underworld. No sign of breakfast. Then a whisper: "Sweet girl. My sweet girl." Grief and love in the empty kitchen.

I ran out, up through the sharp home smell of eucalyptus in the morning air. Still in Eastern harness, I had not unhitched my shoulder bag, keeping my arrival tentative. Jen, at the stable, turned to shush me with a kid's worry and wonder. Together we looked down through the feed window at Falada, my wife, the vet, the vet's assistant. Lilah, crouched on the rubber stall mat, cradled the mare's large head, embracing Falada's pain as though she could take it from her. The mare fixed one eye glazed with terror on her mistress. It had gone on too long, a bad birth they call it. The foal was halfway out in its dense white sack, a bag of luminous bones that would not take on form, assemble. And the mare working, working at the matter, her front legs stretched as though at a hurdle she could take, but her belly exhausted with heaving, then working again, and Lilah's gentle urging, "My girl, my girl."

The vet with fine capable hands in plastic gloves. "Now," he said, his voice muffled by a mask.

"No," Lilah said, whispering her secret to Falada's ear. She'd done that always in the show ring, said their favored words. The equipment laid out was surgical. I hadn't understood until the assistant—a wizened jockey or groom—handed the oversized scalpel to the Doc. I remember the comic look of big scissors, a needle with a giant eye, vaudevillian pincers. My daughter didn't look away. Lilah, I'm sure, did not know we were there. Then I noticed the new wood, that in my few days' absence the stall had been enlarged for this birthing so that Falada could lie comfortably on her side. Now it perfectly accommodated those in attendance at her death.

So much blood and the breathing of the mare lasted too long, overlapped with the colt's first whimper, the mumbled orders of the vet. But my wife did not cry out until her mare was injected and well dead. Imagine, back in the empty kitchen—a scream from a scary radio show, thick whispers, clotted sighs. But you'd have to see my wife shudder as Falada gave up the ghost; the Arabian's quivering nostrils tense, her head pulled back as though to refuse an unfamiliar gait or barrel. You'd have to see the little groom's swift management of the caul to get the glory here. You'd have to smell the antiseptic and manure crossed with the black red of animal blood, not in the least theatrical, and take note of the loss on the woman's face, blinding so that she doesn't know us looking on at her tragedy. Her wandering husband, her kid. And the orphan foal raised to his feet, a star on his head, higher on the nose than his mother's, a royal decoration. Hungering life, the faltering step.

James shuffles in the driveway pebbles, his face drained of that moment's existence, breaths deep, smiles apologetically as he turns to move on to the patio, walks by the lemon trees and into the sheltering cool of the house.

4

Like a bandit, the masked man in first class. Close-up of the gray stubble on his chin, the etched line across his brow, red hair going to white where the elastic band of the mask cuts across his temples. The mouth moves as with fully formed words.

A hip guy—pierced ear, tinted gold-rimmed glasses—perhaps a student, looks down at the masked man through his camera, changes lenses, gets the actor in his sight, gets him with jaw tense and a quick jerk of the head backward as though he is running, short of breath. CLICK. *A still of this shot, another of the man unmasked—headshot with wry, inward smile.* CLICK, *a camera's click as though in a studio, shot after shot of the actor, James Bray—dour, crafty, seductive, semitough. Poses that suggest range. Serious glasses, various hats; bearded, mustached, bleached, dyed—no acknowledgment of age, the eyes always playing to the camera, catch-me-if-you-can eyes, as though he's been tricked into this enterprise. Finally, an exasperated snort, as Bray, made up for the camera, moves toward it, wipes out the lens with the palm of his hand. A blackness gives way to the black mask, its elliptical shape on the screen now framing—the mother on a deep brown couch, her boy on one side, girl on the other. She is reading.*

The mother old-style, hair knotted up softly, wash dress and flowered apron of the thirties. Fine bone at the bridge of her nose, fair eyebrows melding into fair skin make her long oval face vague, translucent. Cultured voice, tender but spirited, a mite solemn—what was meant by a lady. She takes pleasure sitting on her couch, reading out loud to her children in an awed story voice: "Meantime it had grown quite dark in the wood. The rainbow alone was visible by its own light. But the moment the moon rose the rainbow vanished, nor could any change of place restore the vision to the boy's eyes. So he threw himself down on the mossy bank. . . ."

The boy fidgets with a loose button on his heathery sweater, working to get it free. The mother's child, fair and freckled, with distant, amused blue eyes. Attentive, then partially gone, twirling his tortoiseshell button while the girl, dark and sturdy, is absolutely rapt. There is nothing for her outside of the story, no brown couch or pleasant living room. She leans toward the book, eager for every line, while her brother lolls back against the pillows.

"When he awoke the morning sun was looking straight into his eyes. He turned away from it, and the same moment saw a brilliant little thing lying on the moss within a foot of his face. It was the golden key. The handle was curiously wrought and set with sapphires. In a terror of delight he put out his hand and took it, and had it."

The button has come off the boy's sweater. He flips it like a coin. It's hard to catch and on the second flip the button disappears between the cushions.

"Then he jumped to his feet, remembering the pretty thing was of no use to him yet. Where was the lock to which the key belonged? —for how could anybody be so silly as to make a key for which there was no lock?""

The mother's hand upon the page, then her face projected on the black mask, looking directly out from the screen, her voice uncertain, barely audible: "To bind them to me . . . with pie and fairy tales so the world could not feed them its thin story, so they would . . . never outgrow East of the Moon . . . The Golden Key. Keep them with cake, turning pages . . . keep them from the ordinary pictures up at the Rialto."

The girl moves the mother's hand from the page to see the illustration, warm blues and golds against a deep green forest. The storybook boy, pictured in buckskin and tights, his auburn hair clipped at the shoulder, is turned away feeding a dappled fawn, while the girl with her apron held out, full of nuts and berries, is central. Her bright beauty fairly jumps off the page. A kind girl, too, the woodland creatures surely know it, for they dance at her pretty bare feet. Her long flaxen hair is banded with white ribbon, the white yoke of her dress pure against sky blue laces of her bodice. The mother turns the page:

"What is your name? asked the lady.

The servants always called me Tangle.

Ah, that was because your hair was so untidy. How old are you?

Ten, answered Tangle. How old are you?

Thousands of years old, answered the lady.

Ah, but, said Tangle, when people live long they grow old.

I am too busy for that, said the lady. It is very idle to grow old. But I cannot have my little girl so untidy. Do you know I can't find a clean spot on your face to kiss."

The boy digs down in the cushions, retrieves his button, which has a metal loop on the bottom. He finds he can twirl it like a top on the palm of his hand.

"Then Tangle saw a deep tank. It was filled with beautiful clear water in which swam a multitude of such fishes. The fishes came crowding about her. Two or three of them got under her head and kept it up. The rest of them rubbed themselves all over her, and with their wet feathers washed her quite clean."

The actor, James Bray in Lone Ranger mask, reaches out blindly, raises the shade on the white sun, white clouds. The screen blank. His breathing, airplane thrum, indistinct voices. The student with the camera looks down, memorizing the actor's jeans, classy loafers, gold buckle on snakeskin belt. James reaches for the blanket beside him, tucks in pretending sleep.

The button spins, forming itself into a dome, a big mushroom now, but slick and hard above the mother and children who sit under this speckled umbrella washed in a pool of tawny light, their living room at the edge of the storybook forest, brown couch on their island of oak floor with oriental rug, fringed lamp, end tables, the big button twirling above them. The camera moving up and back on its crane, the mother and children growing small on their small stage, cultured voice fading:

". . . carried her back to the fire, the lady having dried her well . . . the finest garments smelling of grass and lavender . . . and over all a green dress, shining like hers and soft like hers. . . ."

5

Middle shot: the actor in a studio—modern, clinical. A man in a lab coat, grown to his late years intact, polished bald head, prominent glasses, look of the inventor in old futuristic movie, trace of Viennese accent. Bray's hand spreading Victorian illustrations that have been cut from a book. Close in: the pictures marked with arrows and numbers where they are to be enlarged or cropped. He chooses the picture of the boy feeding the fawn.

Old Man: The one without movement? (*He instructs the actor gently, quickly choosing out three or four action shots.*) Why the one without movement?

Bray: The peaceable kingdom.

Old Man: And the boy three-quarters turned away?

Bray: You can fix that.

Old Man: We can do anything. Switch figures, get the girl's snarl, you say? Rat nest, her hair.

Bray: *No.* No way.

Old Man: You will come then? (*The camera tracks back to disclose a large studio, sketches and storyboards. One matte painting dominates: an iridescent blue pasture or sea, not of this planet. The old guy switches on a projector.*) Here is the lineup. (*On screen, the Victorian illustrations blown up: the boy and girl crouched in a dank, sweating crevice, their horrified faces turned toward a radiant fearsome light. Rays move up the page, no—move up the small screen until they burst.*) Ach, you cannot imagine! Or here— (*Manipulating a joystick so that the illustrations, dusted with color, are smoothly animated: a mottled yellow snake slithers toward the children; a dark lady in royal blue swings toward them through the clouds.*) So why do you favor dead Disney? Tell me?

Bray: You are remarkably like—

Old Man: Ach, they say that, young filmfolk. (*Pushing his glasses up on his slick bald head.*)

Bray: They can't all have had my father. (*The old man lights a cigarette and hacks.*) You're right. You got the look of it. It's gotta move—Wonderland, Scared to Death. Good, bad—easily forgiven. The whole fuckin' myth. Timelessness. Misremembered color.

Old Man: I take it you are sentimental.

Bray: Anything but. (*Ruffling the pages of the destroyed children's book.*) Look, you're the expert.

Old Man: Yes, James, I am.

Clatter of hammers and saws. The camera pans the studio. Carpenters on a scaffold knock together intergalactic space ship aimed toward an icy star. A young woman in overalls gilds the dome of a bisected temple, backdrop for mystical effects—molten marble of baroque plinths, drooping sci-fi candelabras. Bray and the old master technician come upon a polished bronze maquette of P. T. Barnum seated in a chair staring at a small-scale model of the old Bridgeport courthouse, which has been relocated to McLevy Green. James touches the little trees and park benches.

Old man: From our point of view it was a nice project.

Bray: Sorry about that. No script. You can't shoot the deal.

Old man: (*Shrugs.*) The trial and error, ach, you cannot imagine. (*A happy elf, he pads to the door of his studio in thick Birkenstock sandals.*) Come, you must see. (*Bray follows the special-effects maven down a tiled hall with Romanesque arches, paneled oak doors with ancient transoms—Circuit, Superior Court, Judge's Chambers. The strains of the Strauss brothers' "Pizzicato Polka" ushers them into a dim room where the old guy works at a light board until the sun comes up on a burnished mountain complete with rushing streams and snow-capped pinnacles above the tree line. It is a three-sided mountain, laurel and wild flowers, the nuts and berries of* My Book House *botanically correct; a sheep meadow at its base, woodland creatures in a clearing. The old man plays the lights, the mountain goes blue to purple in moonlight. The whole edifice midsize man, tall as James Bray.*)

Bray: Jesus, it's the mountain.

Old Man: Beautiful, yes? (*He stoops with James to examine the meadow flowers, a tiny ladybug on a blade of grass, but coughs painfully, straightens with a stricken face.*) It had better be your mountain.

328

Bray: Hundred and ten percent! (*The old man takes James'*
hand, guides it from a granite terrace to an upright stone flecked with
mica. James knocks and the mountain swings open: cheap scaffolding,
amorphous clumps of gray fiberglass, tangled wires, a system of pipes
and plain string.)

6

James Bray stands at the door of his dead screening room, steals in
and lightly touches each piece of equipment, goes to the window. Now
his face caged behind the Spanish scrollwork.

ZIFF IN TIFF. BRAY GETS NOSE JOB. It's in the trades. Hey,
I've pleased the network gang, launched their series. In truth,
launched fabricated press releases before series. Glenda grooves. I'm
waiting for my lines, the corporate decision on location, further
definition of my character. For Glenda I keep up the patter: "High
definition, low concept. An actor prepares." Tough luck, giving up
my story, fake as it was—City of Brass, Billy Bray with no answers,
yet this notion I still deserve to direct home movies—Lilah nursing
the foal; me shoveling shit, mixing the dip, not a natural, prisoner of
these routines.

He turns, starts for the Cube chair, thinks better of it, stands
back at the window to be free of this place.

Then one afternoon Lilah's gone too long to market. In
fact it's suspicious. We live on Jurgensen deliveries up at the ranch.
Jen sleeping the day away in the black pit. I phone round to the
horsey friends. At dusk I hear the jeep grinding uphill. Prize horsewoman, my wife can't shift gears.

She has a baby goat, ducks, and these speckled Christmas
card birds. The lot of them are installed up near the stable. She leads
the foal out. "He needs his kind," she says.

"A goat? Birds?"

"Yes. His kind. He doesn't want us." Not in boots and

jeans, wherever she'd gone. In a floppy goosegirl frock: incredibly young, hair loose, feet in canvas shoes; cut off from me with her animal lore. I take her by the wrist which, with the slightest pressure, turns a trot to canter. I pull my wife behind me—stable boy with milkmaid. In the barn on clean hay, I have her. Pulling her hair back, settling her roughly in coarse straw. Her gold on that base yellow. My hand up under her dress on bare breasts that fall from their perfect center evading my harsh caress. I cup them together, big pears that I suck at, my mouth splotching the summer dress. She cries out. Not resistant, her legs swing up around me, pull me down. I want to know my wife, that's in mind, but my cock has taken over; to know her though I mean to break her. Unbuckled, I wait. I feel her thighs, stroke her wetness until she arches herself up with a moan. I ride hard and come quick. After, we don't touch. Lilah with an inward smile—not contentment, but, hey! not mockery of a jump in the hay or my lust. Something she needn't speak. Lost her canvas shoes in the fray and walks barefoot out of the stable in her soiled, suckled dress. I start to the eucalyptus path, turn to watch her squatting on her haunches with a handful of creep grass. The spotted birds come to her, the goat, the foal. I could reach back and touch the chicken wire that contains them, worlds away.

7

Long take as I enter.

A black wall: white objects—phone, TV, white desk, black and white movie stills: Ingrid Bergman stumbling downstairs to freedom, Gloria Grahame smoking gun in hand, Ida Lupino mopping the prison floor. Bad girls of my boyhood dreams, misunderstood girls who need no one. Otherwise a white fan, white Venetian carnival mask with hook nose, bleached skull of a coyote. A mirror in which I see myself, an intruder, sitting on my daughter's black bed. The camera's view of the one white wall—cuckoo clock with birdie, mellow pine shelf on which peasant doll, souvenir mugs (Rome, Athens, Epcot Center), faded yellow ribbons of junior riding events. The camera pulls back. I'm standing in the center of the room I've begot, and like a thief move toward the white desk on which black CD and computer, black paper clips and, trying my patience, a rubbery knot of licorice ropes. My guilty fingers tapping, then flipping open the cover of a speckled black and white notebook.

My daughter's accentless California voice, calm, reading from the notebook—revealing next to nothing of her smarts or her rage:

So, it's this place, a village, high up—Sherpa land or the rain forest of Brazil where wires rot—there is no reception. The signals are there, but no screens or radio tubes exist to gather the noise, the image. Every day the indigenous, that's to say natives, go about their sleeping and cooking in huts, dark abodes which barely resist inclement weather, unaware that the infinitesimal signals hover. One day some malcontent will reach up and draw the particles of electricity to her in a swarm. Grown big as bees, they will form their patterns and their sounds, which will be mysterious, meaningless for a while until the people construe, interpret, understand. Their village will no longer be sought after by white hunters and snoopy professors except in movies. They will only live in movies. Under their grass hats and padded jackets they will wear T shirts with dopey slogans when they enter the big world.

My father was born on Krypton. He is the twin not heard of after the destruction. If you stick him in a phone booth, my father will be arrested for disrobing.

Eamonn wished that his father would act in a horror movie. He whispered how he loved creatures with slightly misshapen heads, almost normal, who invade. That was when he was little. How little? And when did he tell me this secret? He said he would not be frightened to watch the features dissolve, the face of his dad, into a slick humanoid mask. He must have been my age or older to have spoken of genre, to say he wasn't frightened. I hate horror movies. I hate scream-ing to prove I'm alive.

Black and white. Not more authentic to me. I'm color. I'm a kid. Technicolor's gone out of the color business now someone's got it per-fect. I believe what I see—color film. The black and white's a response in the dumbo dialectic. Am I a creature of fashion, i.e., marginal or eccentric exception?

There is this one movie of my mother as Lilah Lee. She's up on a horse, NATURELLEMENT. *Actually, it's TV. She is heigh-ho-silver at the Tournament of Roses. Hey! Beautiful, okay, you bet, but Lilah Lee can't act—her reprieve, antonym for saving grace.*

I turn through the blue-lined pages filled with my daugh-ter's contemplations written in her cramped obedient script, open a desk drawer to find a stack of speckled notebooks. Quite on its own my hand trembles as I pull one, then another out until the mottled black and white covers blanket the desk like the pelt of a jungle animal, a trophy from the last unexplored world, a territory I can only circle with bearers, guns, medical supplies. As I look through her journal, Jesus, the careful aim of the kid's declarations; how dependent her findings upon this family as though we are a race. (*The cuckoo clock chimes, its pendulum wagging as an animated blue bird flaps wooden wings.*)

Notebook: *Remember useful words: animate, inert, dispatch, indo-lence. Memorize to forget: indefatigation, pandiculation, circumstanti-ate, countervail. I buy my ticket from a girl in a booth who doesn't have to be there. It's a nice touch, like popcorn. I go into the theater, which is already dark, and find a seat. Half empty, half full. Cozy not crowded. My film comes on my terminal. Words in funky black and white. Only perfectly chosen words. I select an appropriate typeface. I'm a conventional kid—neat Helvetica for "My father's name being*

Pirrip, and my Christian name being Philip, my infant tongue could make of both names nothing longer than Pip." Futura light: "1801—I have just returned from a visit to my landlord—the solitary neighbor I shall be troubled with." Clear Caslon on 13 point body: "You don't know about me, without you have read a book by the name of The Adventures of Tom Sawyer, but that ain't no matter." Times Roman: "This is America—a town of a few thousand, in a region of wheat and corn and dairies and little groves." AND THIS IS THE CLASSIC THEATER, it says that out front in Deco neon, tip of the hat to the past. Whole stories are displayed here, not a word left out. The machines are fixed, replay but no fast forward. No pictures. It's ideal, even the laughter that comes from the guy beside you when your words are too sad, or the heavy breathing and uncontrollable sobs down front when your words form a happy conclusion. The words are perfectly assembled, memorable and require no test.

Only sixteen lip positions are needed to simulate English. When arranged in proper order, displayed thirty times per second, they talk.

Suppose Christ never came, like billions of people suppose. Suppose Edison never got it moving, the light bulb behind the celluloid, behind the lens, suppose that.

Eamonn took me to the movies. A picture I was not supposed to see as if I had not seen everything. This movie starred James Bray. Eamonn was sore about something, perhaps his loot that summer was not overwhelming. I doubt that. We drove out to this Taco Bell ghetto where college kids live. We went to Multiplex or Cinemart. My father's rag about the Arlington Fox, the old Majestic. Well, we went into 2 downstairs from 1, next to 3. Autres magiques, autres temps. My father was a cowboy. Is that why I was not to see this movie? He did not wear the business suit of the minor diplomat or secret agent, but modified cowboy gear of some present year. It was violent. Animals are killed as well as the usual humans. Perhaps why the picture was forbidden,

certainly not the way the cowboy nails the girl, that was the worst,
slow motion haze, unsexy like a friendship card. The plot is kind of
Monarch Notes for The Virginian. *Eamonn slouched, feet up in the*
air. It was the afternoon, the theater empty and I could tell he liked the
show, liked the story of modern rustlers flying over bewildered cattle.
And I began to like it, too, my father getting in and out of a red truck
that was his horse, which made him powerful but plain. I forgot he was
my father and cared when he almost lost, almost won. The girl, the
ranch, the grateful cows couldn't hold him. Doomed to ride alone, he
drives the red truck into the distance. If I wrote to Eamonn. If I wrote
to 4 Clabon Mews, London, S.W. 1, Eng., I would ask if he remem-
bered the title of the picture, if it was mainstream or a send-up? The
forbidden movie at Cinemart? Multiplex 2?

No reflection in the mirror, my daughter's mirror. My face big on
the screen, streaked with makeup, mustache of nervous sweat, nasty
scrape on the nose scabbed over. Close in: sharp chin, pores, network
of black and white bristle. Camera up: white of the eyes mapped
with red veins; atop, below—vegetation of lash; the black pupils
grow in light until the rings of blue iris are swallowed. Pink mounds
of tear ducts glistening, enlarged. Track back: I'm just sitting at my
daughter's desk, looking up from the page where the proper school-
girl script reveals her anger, her fear, tamed to blue lines.

8

Shoot the page:
  James closes the last of Jen's notebooks. The cover dissolves
into speckles which sort themselves out into blurred pixels, then denser,
clearer images. Morty Ziff—surfing shorts, oiled chest, unbelted ka-
rate jacket—on the phone by his lap pool. He lies in the contrived
shadow of a steel and Plexiglas arbor. A girl in a tank suit and white
rubber cap swims a long-stroked Australian crawl. Thick corrugated

cement walls containing Ziff, pool, pool equipment, a couple of lounges, no flowers. Not a domestic situation. Below, two men can be seen getting out of an ordinary black coupe. They size up the hi-tech iron steps which lead up to the pool. The layout of Barbara Stanwyck's suburban villa in Double Indemnity. Posh subdivision up Cal. hill: nifty street with nifty houses overlooking Ziff's stylish concrete wall where the pasture and stable would be, for—hill, house, driveway, stairs duplicate the layout of Bray's ranch squeezed into a narrow lot. Chic aluminum and poured-concrete bunker for the long low sweep of Spanish Revival ranch.

The men climb to the pool, the stocky one puffing, sweating heavily under his gray felt hat. He wears a three-piece suit of another place, an earlier time. Even as he struggles to catch his breath, he scratches a wooden match to light up a Lucky. His sidekick is thin with fluttering Hugh Herbert fingers, a courtly bearing, many pockets, buttons, pointy white shoes. Serious as Laurel and Hardy on a mission, deadly serious as they face Morty Ziff.

The girl has started a lap of splashing butterfly strokes. Ziff, shaking water off his karate sleeve: "Save some of that, sweetheart." The men, Chub and Beano, move out of range.

Chub: Cash for the gear?

Ziff: Upon completion, gentlemen.

Chub: That's not how we do, that's not polite.

Ziff: A third up front?

Chub: (*Shoves back his hat, pleased with the deal.*)

In a lineup with Ziff's Porsche and a modest blue sedan with Connecticut plates, Chub's black coupe. Beano springs open the trunk: a small arsenal of repeating rifles, wires, detonators, flares. As they move the ammo around, both the fat and thin guy are seen to be toting semiautomatics in shoulder rigs.

Ziff: You know what the hell you're doin'?

Chub: It's classic. Relax.

In the house, L.A. retro: fifties amoebic coffee table, lava *lamps, orange freeform couch. Picture window on pool. The girl's long smooth sidestrokes. Ziff counting out greenbacks. Dead sound. The three men watch the swimmer: Chub with a knowing smile. Beano bobbing in time with the bob of the swimmer's white cap. Ziff with coarse proprietary leer. The money handed over to the Chub, who flips his burning butt into a giant ashtray.*

Chub: I'm outta here.

Sound—a blast of Woody Herman's "Body and Soul."

Ziff: (*Shouting to be heard.*) HIGHWAY ROBBERY.

Chub: Retirement pay.

Beano, hands flapping to the music. Ziff cups his balls in an obscene gesture. Music down.

Ziff: (*Still shouting.*) A FUCKIN' WAR ZONE, TO-TALLED!

Chub: You got it.

By the pool. Ziff rips off the jacket, the big topaz ring. Close-up of girl's mouth sucking in air, breathing out into the water, breathing, spewing bubbles, breathing. Ziff dives, comes up under her, grabbing her ankles, feeling her up—legs, mound of Venus through the silky tank suit, her small belly, her breasts, pulling her head up into the light, his hands on her pale throat. The swimmer is Mary Boyle. She snaps off the white rubber cap to reveal a severe boy's haircut that makes her an urchin, defenseless and hard. She slithers free of the producer's embrace into a slow backstroke, her gray eyes, untroubled by the sun, absorb the gray concrete and stylized arbor, leaving Morty Ziff treading water at the epicenter of yet another unsalvageable project.

9

Shoot the page:

Bedroom of the ranch. Moonlight on Lilah's pillow. She sleeps deeply, her mouth slightly open, golden hair fanned. Beside her,

James, awake, watching the wavering shadows on the ceiling bend against the Spanish brackets and beams. A rustle, disturbance under the window; he turns to the clock, actually a gold watch, his father's, which hangs under a glass bell. Delicate hands, thin Roman numerals. It is three o'clock.

He gets up—floppy pajamas; naked from the drawstring up, thick at the waist, stringy arms—shuffles into old moccasins. Each footstep heard, his own throat cleared, a lazy cough, he moves through the dark hall past closed doors, toward the great room, the living room with its baskets and pots, bold patterns of Indian rugs. Moonlight through the arches and on into the kitchen, where he grabs but decides against the Eveready with the headlight beam, wanders into the bright night. On the eucalyptus path, the podlike leaves of low branches strike his face. He's still swiping their sting away when he comes to the gate of what is now a narrow barnyard set against the stable. Metallic click, stir of animals. James in Falada's stall, feeding the foal. The fine cut of the Arabian's chestnut throat, white star on his head, downy topknot of mane.

Zing of bullets strikes the stable wall, a second volley strafes the red tile roof. James pulling the foal down into the bedded stall, terrified. His stifled breath under the squawking and braying. A round of shots in a crossfire between house and stable. Lights on in the great room, the kitchen. Beano drawing himself behind a patio pillar, hands tapping nervously at his buttons and pockets. Floods go on along the eucalyptus path and up in the pasture. James running for cover to a water trough, a pitchfork his weapon. Crouching, dancing low into the underbrush. Above, a scatter of shots. Silence.

Lights off in the house. Lilah punching the buttons on the dead phone in the kitchen. Jen in her arms. Shatter of glass, music. A frantic mickeymousing soundtrack follows every action. James crawling downhill on his belly toward the kitchen door, flap of ducks, speckled birds flying. Chub, behind a potted lemon tree, sights James as he runs for the patio, takes aim along the slim barrel of his automatic weapon. Brightness of Spanish tiles, the fountain plashing.

James turns in full moonlight, raises the pitchfork at his unseen assail-
ant. The Magnum's aim. The thud of a shot strikes center chest. He
falls with a clank. Music down. Red seepage through the fingers of
James' clutching hand. One slipper flies as he scrambles down the
drive, falls, screaming, "You fucking clowns," as the black coupe, a
comic book taped over its license plate, squeals away.

> *Night silence as James dusts himself off—torn pajamas,*
damage of blood pellet, his sweat-smudged face as he limps toward his
wife and child.

> *Jen breaks from Lilah. Her father holds her mop of*
squirrely yellow hair against his chest, then turns her tearstained face
up, leads her to a terra cotta drainpipe, and begins to rip the planted
wires off the house.

> *"Timers. Short circuits," he says. "The whole place set up."*
> *"When?" the girl asks.*
> *"This morning? Must be when we drove into town. You*
were sleeping." Even now, a tone of parental impatience implies that
she is sleeping the summer away. "Come on now, darlin'," he says and
they march in their nightclothes up to the stable. The brown birds
puffed with sleep. Colt at his basin.

> *"You see," Lilah says to her daughter, voice shaking, "he*
knew it wasn't real, Falada's boy."

ZIFF HOAX: Hey, I'm an actor, but that sequence should be cut by
five minutes, not cut altogether.

Through a new wave of cries, Jen asked: "Don't you want
to kill him?" I wondered what she might write in the speckled
notebook where we impersonate ourselves, where the world is reduced to movies, my business. Movies both problem and answer. A
moody actor scared shitless, I could not hate Ziff, his sleaze and foul
mouth part of my routine. Imitation being the insincerest form of
flattery. Yeah, I'd like to kill the bastard. He'd rise up without a
scratch. Wardrobe has a duplicate silk jacket should there be a stain.

My wife and daughter drinking milky mugs of tea. Lilah

in a white robe I bought years ago in Siam, her hair pulled back as she wore it to ride in shows. That was how she seemed now, as though she was to go off early with Falada to Santa Rosa or Monterey, shoulder-in and half-pass—intent on her dressage. In possession of our separate terms. Her concentration, her solemnity a reaction shot to her child's anger.

"The publicity," Jen said contemptuously, ripping at the carefully ripped shirt she wears to bed. "You want the headlines?"

"It's over," I said. "Joined at the hip is over."

"You think he had a permit, Dad?"

"Enough," Lilah said. She got it, Ziff's elaborate prank, that I was to retaliate, stay in the game. "Enough," she said to both of us. Her look at that moment comprehends the crude male pride I've taken in sex, paltry Bridgeport adventures, and my failed prospects. She simply *sees* it, unlike Ziff with his magic phone.

Gunfire again, ill-timed. We went out to find the upper pasture in flames, a fine sight in the white haze before dawn: set up on a fireproof mat, dress rehearsal for the burning of Rome or Atlanta. This time the animals took little note. The colt would strut there on his show lead in an hour.

Ziff, that fucker'll never know how completely he won the day. I had not given full value. You bet, in a story conference I would have pushed for the rewrite in which I do my own stunts, levitate over our nicely planted drive, pitchfork held high, hurl it at Chub, who twists round to face me at the moment of kill, impaled, sputtering his last, falls by the getaway car to die. A grisly scene: not enough, never enough to please. I move toward the body. Felt hat has tumbled off Chub. His bald head shines, double chin slack under a jaunty bow tie. His dead eyes upon me. Horror, my horror. The hired thug is Billy Bray. My bloody hands fumble at the familiar watch chain on his vest, then slowly I rip off the rubber mask with its cleft chin, snub Irish nose, off the dead-white face of a kid who worked on Ziff's last production.

The cops arrive—a chief called Carlson, thick neck with

gold cross. His boys—trained to housebreaks, taking nose candy from rich children—scramble up the eucalyptus path after Beano. Poor Beano's white shoes light the way as he makes for the noisy barnyard. In the stable they stalk him. I cry out when Carlson, failed dairy farmer out of Minnesota . . . I cry out when he plugs a bale of hay. Falada's son goes crazy, hooves in the milk pan, frantic stomping, circling in the stall. The big cop scared as the colt breaks through his gate, runs wild out of the barn. Figuring the little horse won't draw their fire, Beano scuttling along, stick arms and legs flail as he makes for the pasture. Simultaneous shots, whinnies, cries. Beano, his arm raised in an unlucky command. Shame on my freckled face, intolerable shame as I peel back the weak smile of Geraldo De Martino. Here, too, just a kid—an extra, a flunkie. We pivot from him, move in; move in slow rank toward Falada's son. First Carlson with his big blank stare, then the boys in blue—wide-eyed, unbelieving. My turn in the processional, limping slightly in my torn pajamas, play blood on my delicate paunch. We men look down at the colt's heaving ribs, trembling withers, the small clean wound above the shattered shank, long curve of the neck held back with dignity, royal jibbah on his head that will never be crossed by a bridle.

Jen has run to the house. She stands pinned to the patio— wiry yellow hair roughed by the warm Santa Ana. Web cast by an electrified Spanish lantern over her small blanched face. From here she can't see, only hear us. In her white robe, Lilah moves toward the men, toward the sun as it rises over our mountain. Blurred, yet mysteriously bright, she floats, a perfectly animated spirit, as the tumbleweed moves in the desert she moves effortlessly toward us over the dry excuse for a pasture. Girl of the Golden West, she takes Carlson's pistol. The sun has come up. We are seen from above, all of us in a small circle: there's the sprawling white ranch, red tile roof, empty blue pool, dry fountain, the shine of our lemon trees hung with yellow fruit. Jen, motionless on the patio; stiff gray agave, the great dignified crown of the Moreton Bay fig, excess of wild geranium and bougainvillea spilling down hills and far below the toy town with its Mission; fogged-in beach ringed with palms and white spume, first glisten of morning light on the Pacific. Paradise here on our mountain. Lilah with Carlson's pistol. The colt moves its forelegs daintily, practicing an untutored gait.

Jen against the whitewashed adobe in her pauper's shirt. She holds a speckled notebook to her chest, looks dead ahead, then up at the half ball of blinding sun. The shot rings out. Silence as the black and white splotches of the notebook fill the screen. Its white square with COMPOSITION, Name_____, Date_____, Subject _____, on which the credits role.

10

Shoot the page:

Watch. I can make this button disappear right into my shoe. They're shoes I order from Italy. Pretty damn nice. So's my hundred dollar work shirt, but I am particularly fond of this old cardigan, hand-knit—green, in some lights gray. They don't make 'em like this anymore with the real tortoise buttons. I vow I'll be good and not play with the button here on the worn brown velvet couch, vow to myself for I'm half listening as my mother reads. My sister on the other side of Nell. We did that verboten thing, speaking to each other, called the parents Billy, Nell. Well, she's reading to us, our mother, in that mellow voice women no longer use, full of promise, even rapture.

He examined the face of the rock. It was smooth as glass. But as his eyes kept roving hopelessly over it, something glittered, and he caught sight of a row of small sapphires. They bordered a little hole in the rock.

"The keyhole!" he cried.

He tried the key. It fitted. It turned.

Catherine, as I say, is on the other side of Nell. She has pushed her bluntly cut hair behind her ears to better hear the story. Her sack dress is crisp, freshly starched for this occasion. She looks as though she's in a school pageant wearing a brown paper bag to play the baked potato. Every now and then her hand reaches up to touch her string of pearls, not hers, but Nell's. It's odd she is allowed to wear them.

"How beautiful you are, Tangle," he said, in delight and astonishment.

The brown couch rocks, comes unhinged from the floor. No, it is the hardwood floor itself that no longer holds the ground, for it's no more than a small stage set in a green wood or glen. Trees for the living room walls—all manner of willows and maples, California palm and citrus. Ever so smoothly we ascend with the fringed lamp and end tables. Set loose from our moorings at last. At last.

"You are like the oldest man of all. What did you do after I lost you?"

Our mother weaving her spell, tells it off by heart to her overgrown children.

They told each other their adventures, and were as happy as man and woman could be. For they were younger and better, and stronger and wiser, than they had ever been before.

We are in the treetops. I rip off a maple pod, stick it on my nose. Cath grabs a lemon. She will make good use of it. Our music is Aeolian, not harps or trumpets—a perfect mating of clarinet and glockenspiel. Track back. Wide lens. Brown couch central. On my right, Mary Rose Boyle in the driver's seat of her baby blue sedan, the roof transparent so we can see her pinning back the vestigial veil, buckling Peaches in for safety. That is Peaches with her hair braided, navy blue knee socks, plaid skirt of a good parochial school. And to my left, his shako scrambled with gold soutache, stuck with scarlet plumes, white gloves immaculate—Geraldo does the Field

Flash for Mama, who is thrilled to death, as much by his performance as her new Spanish shawl.

With magic devices not seen since the big musicals of the thirties, the living room floor sprouts platforms and there, in a silver spray, Lilah and Jen perch on the rim of our fountain. My wife, in the velvet hard hat, frock coat, and britches she wears for International Dressage, beats her crop in rhythm with our sound track, smiling into the middle distance while Jen studies a humongous book, so big she must use both hands and with effort turns the page. In the story Eamonn drives her. He is a worthy skilled carpenter or lively academic. They enter an old movie house with gold sconces, red velvet seats. Angels bless them from the ceiling of Poli's Majestic as they watch a bona fide classic in colors never seen. She is head to toe in her favorite black, save the angelic Harpo Marx curls, and stops to look across at us—her father, her Aunt Catherine, figures the lady to be her grandmother, Nell. Nell with *her* book, which is just a prop, for the end of the story is coming which she knows so well.

The light came from the moon, but it did not look like moonlight, for it gleamed through the seven pillars ... and one pillar was of the same new color that he had seen in the rainbow ... and he saw a sparkle of blue. It was the sapphires round the keyhole.

And, a step below us, Lala and Anna in a golf cart. Cleated and labeled (Izod, Lauren), they exchange presents: for Anna a Prince racket, diamond in its sweet spot: for Lala a useless sterling silver tee. While, in the limpid twilight of Seaside Park, Michelle in sneakers and old jeans sits by the baseball field cheering on two little boys who run the bases. Home free.

Glenda's office, a cozy cabin in the sky, tidied of contracts and the trades, swings like a funicular traveling up, up to the heights where she devours *The Magic Mountain* and late Henry James: in a clear Brooklyn accent quotes Tacitus and Shaw. Free of deals, her pop eyes popped in, her fright wig neatly bobbed, she gathers from her *Radcliffe Bulletin* that she has been awarded, *honoris causae*, humane letters.

The brown velvet couch, light as its goose feathers; oak floor come to rest on a sun-lit cloud, floats up and over the depleted sandbars of Long Island Sound and the famed surfing waves of the Pacific, over the pretty piddle of Seeley's Pond, over the exhaust of L.A., over old blue Manhattan with only the choice skyscrapers—Chrysler, Woolworth, Empire State—over Liberty Enlightening the World and over Boon Hulburt brought to Christ by Hetsie among the matchbox tract houses metastasized over the reclaimed desert which features the show-off spread of Rancho Grande, over the improbable integrity of McLevy Green and the scar of Father Panik Village, the lofty date palms along Cabrillo Boulevard and the silver dome of Barnum's last provincial Institute of Science and Industry on the ruins of Main Street. So it was before the aeroplane that itinerant artists imagined, beyond their view, our geography from aerial balloons.

He took his key. It turned.

But above Nell, above us—the snorting, chirping, honking, all the animals grazing, the floor thickly strewn with peanuts, pellets, hay. Falada and Falada's son, despite their lineage, are not affronted being in the ring with Howland Owl, a flirtatious skunk, the pompous self-promoting P. T. Bridgeport—the whole Okefenokee gang. Indeed, the foal breaks from his mother to follow the wisest most befuddled possum in the world. Bootsie included, roused from his stupor by a milk bone . . . guinea hens and goat, a circus Appaloosa and over all Jumbo, his magnificent trunk swooping, swaying to the music. Raising his great body, he waltzes on hind legs in thin air.

Quite alone, Sister Brown, fry pan hat and fearsome reticule, shrunk in her library chair, checking through her spectacles—Catherine, that big girl, and Jen, her new discovery. "Are you a foundling?" she calls to my daughter in imperious Yankee.

Now Nell seems to rest, her hand on the sleeve of my sweater taps the seconds off. Her eyes close. The lashes thin, glints of red still in her faded hair. Her long cheeks powder white, her lips violet—age, for she never tampered with what she was given.

"Mother of God, you *were* Barnum!" Cath cries in theatrical dismay.

"Wrong. You happen to be wrong."

"Darn you, James."

Our mother's eyes open. She's cross with our banter. It's then Nell sees us—the stout, plain woman beside her, dulled by her craft and resignation; the smiling insubstantial boy in his dandy play clothes. It's worse than any wound, her disappointment. She closes her book, reaches down into my shoe, and retrieves the hidden button just as his hack, his catarrh scrapes through the heavenly music. It's Billy Bray, of course, nails clawing the parlor floor. That's all we see, his nicotine fingers tearing at the precipice. Disembodied, they travel the edge like a breathtaking scene in a Buster Keaton movie. I get off my duff at last, leave the brown couch. Only an actor, yet I'm the only one who can save him. Amazingly easy, I grip his wrists as though schooled by the flying Wallendas. Why the hell not? Come aboard, Billy. He huffs and puffs and cuffs back the felt hat, swaggers toward us, come home with courthouse convictions. We, his little family, can do no wrong. Nell blushes. We children are transported as though he has just sung to us, the invincible tenor, one of the lost Irish songs.

"*He took his key,*" my father says.

"*It turned in the lock.*" We all know our lines.

"*A door opened on slow hinges.*" Nell, smoothing her housedress, moves downstage to Bill.

Cath lumbers toward me, takes my hand for the North Avenue crossing.

"*The key vanished from his fingers.*"

"*The door closed behind them.*"

Together now: "*They climbed out of the earth; and still climbing rose above it. Far abroad over ocean and land, they could see the fragile walls of the earth whirling beneath their feet.*"

Okay. Heads up! Hooves, paws, hands—Salute to the Visitors! Mark time smiling—ears, tusks, whiskers up. Eyes bright, march forward into the light, the applause. March! March toward the Flourished Halt.

The Spinster's Tale

... the priest, whose forerunner imagined Saint
Patrick driving his chariot-wheels over his own
erring sister, has to acknowledge, or to see others
acknowledge, that there is no evil that men and
women may not be driven into by their virtues all
but as readily as by their vices ...
　　　　　　—William Butler Yeats, *Explorations*

Once in a pleasant land. Don't expect the baggage of kingdoms—milkmaids, cobblers, wise old women with legendary goats or hens. Once, 1945, in a pleasant land, a favored city, the people worked and though they made little of it, played. Work was their glory, a gratification that went beyond the weekly pay envelopes, their hours punched into a time clock so their labor could be reckoned to the nickel, the dime. Cash—a man or woman could feel the fold of bills, feel the coins fallen to the bottom of the brown envelope, check the week's earnings against the possibility of human error, though mostly in the large plants—Remington Arms, Sikorsky Aircraft—in the small shops—gunsights and kinkless pull chains—there was great good feeling, trust. Particular good feeling, for tough times had done the city in.

　　　　You were but a twinkle in your father's eye at the start of the Great Depression, which ran its course and now was over. No spells, no potions; actual events of foreign wars brought the place to life. A stranger getting off the train, finding his way through heavenly streaks of sun cast from high windows of the station, passing the earthbound lunch counter and homey newsstand, that stranger breathing the almost country air would be quickened, feel life's hustle, walking the two blocks to Main Street. If he came on business, which is most likely, he'd be driven off to the pulsebeat of factory running day and night; an official figure from out of town with his government contracts or patents, all the works above and around him as though he stood inside a big body with miraculous energy or a cathedral busy with birds, music, masses, vendors, stonecutters and carvers at dizzying heights and the outsider, quartermaster or army engineer, would sense at once the spiritual story here as well as the commercial.

Castles, there are none. Row upon row of houses, double deckers—dark green, gray and brown—set close, families stacked beside, atop one another on solid wood floors. Thick plaster, modern cross ventilation. Parlors face the street; kitchens the backyard. Clothes dry in the sun. Orderly, but ever interesting, the way the plantings vary: the rambler rose so different from clipped privet, privet from hydrangea, hydrangea from althea, and so on. Yet curtains, white or ecru, much the same; voile, net, muslin veil the view. Porches, porches rubber-stamped. Churches—steeple, steeple, gilt dome, green dome, steeple, steeple, though grand variety of one family dwellings on ample lots. Here and there a neighborhood so blest in which Conquistador, Colonial, Queens Anne and Bess, Mission, and Monticello happily combine on wide tree lined streets. Maples, chestnuts, elms.

One such house stands alone, determined not to be overgrand, pillared porch to view of bus stop and Sourian's fruit stand. A gray-green structure, color of wet cement, its back windows facing stacked workers' houses just behind. It's in this house you clean the kitchen. What a treat, for it is not your job, the scouring of a pot until it shines, sour milk done away with, curds worked down the drain; cups and saucers set straight as to color and design. You place a white pitcher here, then there, *there;* an ivory bowl with blue band upon a narrow ledge where it shows off, round and pleasing, in lamplight; lay a cloth you've chosen, a cream and sky-blue plaid which you drape in points like a hankie that might dangle over a surprise to be unveiled. Though it is only the kitchen table laid for breakfast, you fetch from the cold porch a sprig of some waxy plant.

Your mother is ailing. You are a child and this is not your job, but you fancy with the bowl and oddity of cloth's arrangement, with the pot shine and now a cut glass . . . yes, you have gone into the china cabinet with the key . . . a cut glass dish which you fill with coarse golden brown sugar . . . you do fancy you do it all better. Your father is partial to brown sugar on hot cereal. She never, never thinks aforehand, must always go and root out the Jack Frost box, put the box, torn as it is, on bare table.

She is seldom sick, so this is your big day. Or night. That is how you see it: your kitchen, your fine arrangements. As you hang up the damp dishtowel, wipe your hands across the wet stomach patch of your apron, her apron which hangs well below your knees, you are so very pleased. It has not been done before, the table laid at night. Next, the nicety of silver napkin rings you've found abandoned in a drawer. You have made it as it should be for your father, who is not at home. He has gone out with his gun on a late case. The danger. He has gone to solve a murder. Brave, going out like that in the night, deserving of all your housewifery. Above, all is still. She is down with a complaint that doesn't have a name, so your brother must not toodle his clarinet, the nightly entertainment.

You have drawn the black shade, though the war in Europe is over and the city has turned on its streetlights, but you do not want to be the girl who lures the Jap bombers to the North End, the very center of the world. Turning from your handiwork, you mount the back stairs. Halfway up, you see she is there, there in the dim hall, the brown bathrobe that has always been old clutched around her, her hair in mild disarray, all the white of it gone in shadow, the worry from her brow gone, so that she looks more the girl. Your sturdy form stopped on the stairs: the solid mass of you blocking all view of your sweet artistry in her kitchen.

"Come up," your mother calls through her sickness, "come up to bed now, Catherine." Your name tumbles toward you like a pair of rolled socks she has lovingly darned, like the gnawed rubber ball of the departed bulldog, Bootsie, which she keeps in a cupboard drawer. No small thing to be her treasure. She smiles down. "Catherine," she says with effort, "turn out the light."

"Yes," you say and run to do her bidding. At the switch you fail. The bowl with blue band, plaid cloth and glint of napkin ring to welcome your father, you can't leave it in the dark. You cannot leave the moment. You in the dark, your own hair gray, dry as scoured fleece. Woolly gray, you do not have to see to know, that is your game, foot treadling, wheel spinning, wetting your fingers when necessary in the dark, your yarn stopped at that moment when you disobeyed those years ago, left the light burning for your father, who had gone out into the city with a gun. Those years ago. That flame.

They made so little of it when they played. You are a solemn eleven, have left all play behind, yet you are curious when your mother and father go out to play cards. You note her good gloves and Sunday hat, his rehearsal of joviality at early supper. So envious of their once or twice a month auction bridge with a highball of rye and ginger. They come home with little favors—Chinese fan, ceramic ashtray, pastel mints. A chocolate eclair in fluted paper: so curious, so envious, you eat it before you go to school. "But that was stale," Nell says. "I only took it to please Marie McCall."

"Did you win?"

"Win?"

You can't grasp why they go to play their cards, in no way comprehend these modest round-robin parties that take them out at night.

Telling yourself, the thread breaks. With the lights on you see the wad of carelessly carded wool. You see that, indeed, light must be shed on the matter and that, strictly speaking, you should not have the loom. Daughters who do not marry are the spinners. The married women the weavers, makers of webs. You have drawn out of yourself the old story, telling again what you wish to hear, from memory made the city grand, betrayed your sick mother, made a hero of your dad. Now you must press on with the shades up. No cat, no kin; you are alone in your one-story house and it's pride that makes you want the world to see you pictured in the picture window working well into the night, spinning the unwashed fleece, oily and rough. You have been good to yourself, only in the tale. Good to them, too.

First what's easy: in the morning as she pours top of the milk into your jug, your mother though somewhat listless, pale, is much as always, buttering the toast, poaching eggs, testing the porridge, calling upstairs for your lay-abed brother. It is your father who looks ill through the rosy shine of his close shave, nicked on the chin, wobbling his head this way and that as though he has water in his ears. And he seems not to hear as she commends your Fanny Farmer kitchen with cottage cloth.

"When it is sliced," she says, "the bread goes dry, even in the bread box." You see she has discarded your slices of last night, is buttering her own. You see that her face is stiff, dead as stone.

"What's all this?" he says. "What have we here?" You remember that his hand shakes, that the cigarette, always between his fingers, trembles as he taps the cut glass dish of brown sugar. Ash on the breakfast cloth. "Well now isn't this lovely," he says with a cough or a laugh.

She turns to him in cold reproof, turns on him her wounded frenzy. "It is *Catherine* you have to thank, not me!"

"Now then," he says. It's not easy to recall how he rose to watch her lift the shivering eggs out of their steam bath, the man who all his years never heeded a stir or boil in the Edwardian-Irish villa built for the ages. "Now then, Nell—" You hear the plea in his voice.

You see the life come back to her as she gives in: "And it was your daughter put my mixing bowl out on a shelf."

"Say, isn't that lovely," he says. You are glad that they laugh at you. You recall.

Spilling the same old beans, how you willed her gone with your efforts in her kitchen that you might be his beloved daughter in a child's tale. Then the uneasy telling to yourself when you stumbled upon the evidence. Telling in wide-eyed fury no one, that underneath the earnest workaday city, arsenal of democracy, behind the gentle card party with the Connors, Fords, McCalls, the Sunday morning pieties at St. Pat's, there lay that other world he frequented. Oh, if there was ever an inspired underworld, Little Miss, patched out of comic strips and radio shows, you made it, fleshed it out with items from the *Post* so that you could picture him on duty, draw him—unmistakable in soft hat, badge, and bow tie—into the lurid panel. Billy Bray with the Polish girls in their thin embroidered blouses, ribbons in their yellow hair, whirling with him to the czardas and the polka, a fifth of whiskey on each tavern table. Hunk Town in the distant South End, overrich with cabbage soup and pastry, with thick sweet wine, Billy staking out its revelries. You placed him in mortal danger down in the Hollow where the anchovy and onion, pepper and sausage of the Apizz parlors covered for the Mafia touts and zips. Golly, blue-lit bars and smoky cafés down to the state line of New York, that city acknowledged hell, but here close to home . . . it would be years before you'd know why you invented the underworld of Bridgeport, let it fester like a low-life scene in Brecht, a pit of writhing bodies in a Bosch. Tell yourself that once at a performance of Genet in Greenwich Village, upon first opening the filth of Celine or maybe just watching a Warhol movie where the girl's head lollygags for hours in the toilet bowl

. . . Prick your fat thumb on the spindle: the arty reference won't pull you through. Blood drips, drips, drips, into the barnyard stench of your virgin wool.

A rich tart killed a soldier. She was blond, dainty, Goldilocks in a fantasy bordello. She shot a boy who most likely did not love her and then seduced your father. This took place when you were eleven years old. She was Isabelle Poole. Billy had the goods on her. Mrs. Poole with a handsome Air Force major for a husband. This was wartime, movietime. You were the detective's daughter. On your Bakelite radio next to porcelain Mother Mary in your room, *Gangbusters* opened each true installment with urgent nasal announcements: a vicious crime committed every forty seconds, every three hours a murder. The woman was fiendishly cunning. She was Isabelle Poole: her Camels with the lipstick print intertwined with his Luckies in the state car. That was the car you seldom entered. No free rides: Billy Bray was honest as those days were long. Later you would often dream of the unmarked black car and wake in terror: a fine spring afternoon, coming home from school with a leather bound copy of *Silas Marner,* one of your prizes. Your mother's big Packard gone, but there was the unmarked Ford coupe, Billy's car with a sheet of yellow paper flapping out the door, the legal paper he wrote on in a surprisingly slender script, wrote out the evidence he would present in court. If you had not loved your father more than Christ Almighty, but you had to tidy for him, Little Miss. Her cigarettes and his spilling out of the ashtray. Only think how nosy, squeezing into the cramped backseat to discover a silk stocking with a runner, the peacock blue belt of a dress. There had been some altercation during an apprehension, you knew that from the radio. The yellow paper, as it turned out, a false lead.

How did you know that day to keep your mouth shut, to steal into the living room and watch him snore, funny-paper Daddy on the couch, his perky bow tie bouncing as he swallowed air? How did you know to listen to the slur of her Southern or Texan when she called? And never answer, just quietly hang up. Tell, how as a meddlesome eleven year old who disdained the neighborhood girls swapping Nancy Drews, those stupid, unconfounding mysteries, you now investigated your father's pockets. The suit jacket that hung limp on the dining room chair revealing matches, tobacco crumbs, and at last a button cut with many facets like a jewel. Once, in his topcoat, a bobby pin bright as her hair. So little to go on, yet you knew the world of crime to be bad as *Gangbusters,* worse to accommodate his fall from grace. Your father's sin which you cover the rest of your natural life.

Once after supper: "It's a date." Listening in on the extension, his reply to the drawling request of Mrs. Isabelle Poole. And thereafter how you ran for the phone to hear her sultry voice before you cleverly hung up. It was always after supper and once he caught you silently replacing the receiver and looked as though he might kill you, his only daughter, plump as a busy brown hen. "You stay well out of this," he said. The calls stopped then.

Tell, how often you pulled out that silk stocking with the runner, exhibited the glass button for one doctor or another to prove . . . prove what? You cannot reckon the many times, like the niddy-noddy with its kiddie name that winds your wool without counting, how many times it came to your defense—the silk stocking, the button or variation on brass bobby pin and peacock belt.

Or so you believe.

Out of your breastless eleven year old hysteria, you declared it to be true. Clear as the deep stain you identified, the Revlon "Raven Red" of her mouth on the butts. Clear as the injury: *You stay well out of this.* Settling yourself in the next doctor's chair when the next man had done with you. Letter perfect girl, tell how you passed yourself around to the inaccessible men—married, near queers, your hard work with a soft member, coaxing a bit of love. Their thrust into your open body, a dead-end street, selling yourself like a working girl, like Isabelle Poole. You got as far as that once or twice in the doctors' offices or in the hospital, too late. Waving the silk stocking like a flag, like *Silas Marner* brought home from school. Honor student, you did not deceive yourself.

Or so you believe.

Now wet your fingers. Detect nubs in the consistency of your yarn. Unlike Isabelle Poole, you were weak, always arranging the ivory bowl with the blue band, putting out brown sugar, a history of such investment. Tell how Billy Bray mounted insufficient evidence and his boss, the dour Henry Stringer, this once slack jawed, bemused, acceded to the defense attorney's motion to dismiss. The woman had killed a soldier boy fighting for his country, the least of her crimes. *You stay well out of this.* You remember that he came at you as you hung up the receiver, pulled you to him in what seemed like an embrace. Strong smell of his smoker's breath, your round body held close then thrust away, thrown from him as in a smooth jitterbug twirl, a swing step to one of your brother's clarinet numbers. The frank horror on your father's face, that he'd laid hands on you, gone too far. Tell how you summed up your case and every time won it, *Gangbusters'* style. You wanted Isabelle Poole dead or alive. Recall how you brought her to justice, the cruelest killer on the East Coast, with a glass button and a bobby pin, how you assigned her to the death chamber.

And tell how Billy twirled you into the lives of those men whose names, each name you can recall, flipped you into punishing installments as seedy as those in his—in *your* provincial underworld. How you let it spin, the faceted button from that woman's blouse or dress, flickering its light over what was hard and maybe real in your story until like moondust in a movie, magic twinkling on the screen, you were Cath, grown up, with your visions. Your voices. *Catherine* they called to you, men and women from the past. Button? Button? Who's got the button? You, always a girl again, a child being tested. Old women of the neighborhood, men of the peaceful wartime city, even Benny of the vegetable cart, a simpleton asking if you wanted beets or beans. An impossible choice. If you said beans, the beets were nice that day. Silent or answering wrong, a blameless child, a sinful woman.

All at once?

Yes, at once. Silent/answering, blameless/sinful, grown/ not grown. Get up from the wooden wheel you've made more live than your body. Stand accused/absolved. The widow of all widows, Sister Brown, black, shriveled, pert pepper eyes: "Catherine! The density of water? Weight of air?" Ancient nuns you pleased in class, soft wooden mumble of their beads, chalk fingers whisking back their veils: "Did Augustine value charity over hope, Catherine? Hope over love?" One by one, they came to you. Alone. Librarians and old maid teachers. Miss Mealy in her nurse's white: "Have you moved your bowels, Catherine? Combed that hair?" Their lone figures calling to you, the mama's boy at City Trust and your brother's prim music teacher, Mr. De Martino, calling to you, *Catherine*, the lone people.

All at once?

Separately, that is to say, alone. Telling yourself in confidence it was like a button that was not a button, the clue as in so many of your gentle British mysteries forced to prove out. Now stand at your window so that anyone driving by must see you pictured, the spinster telling herself of voices, that it was like nowhere more than that point on the dial of the Bakelite radio where two stations come in at once, the Green Hornet and FDR, Benny Goodman and the Symphonette. Out of your control—their arrivals, their questions. And then no more, for you saw that alone you must cross to their world.

At once?

No. Case to be closed: Isabelle Poole and your father. She'll sing. Give her the business. Caught red-handed. Take him downtown, he'll talk. Not at once, slowly, but as though the loners called to you to come over, to accept the transformation. Tell of your conversion to sanity and loom. Tedious, possessed of that newfound religion, tell. Blest be the spinster you were meant to be, the wallflower growing out of the dry crack. Blest be the drafty numbers in your head for Gentleman's Fancy, King's Ransom. Blest be blue's eight to white's five all down the row, shuttle flying. Blest be your songs of hut-sut and doesy. Till your weeds. Suffer the moody Caloric. Ply the narrow craft. Show yourself in prison garb. You serve the sentence, not Isabelle Poole. No time off for good behavior. No voices other than your own, until you confess under the merciless third degree light.

How you went to your brother—ah, like snags in the weft—the brother, the mother so little in your story, when in fact they are necessary to your design. You went on a bus into town, Mary Boyle having gone early to her helpful, hopeless work. You took the bus into town. Two trips in two days into the city you could never leave, the city you had forsworn. You waited for him in the hilarious lobby of the new hotel, its ersatz sophistication reminiscent of one or two of the funny farms you rested in, rested from your trials. There, too, the deceptive love seats, sleek cocktail tables for the clients sworn off booze. Here, a splashing fountain with, inevitably, a few pennies, and, indeed, you wished yourself to be in the Eternal City, to be anywhere but waiting for your brother in downtown Bridgeport, waiting in a setup of funhouse mirrors that block out any small sighting of human life on Main Street. You station yourself among ficus and anthurium as though you are merely waiting out a blustery storm projected beyond the brown glass windows, sealed with hotel foliage in update of atrium, calling to mind old Latin grammars with illustrations of the most civilized family home, the classical life with the *puella* and her *pater*. That is what you have to offer James, a laughably basic text from this mock-elegant pit. Here, on the industrial broadloom, you'll throw Billy to the lions, put yourself to the wheel, Saint Catherine, telling him, handing it over, the one true, the only story.

How James came undisguised, a reporter in tow whom he sluffs off without offense, much as he rid himself of admirers in high school. You could not sit with such a brother in plain view, so up to his room where a young Asian woman dismantles the scene of their sex. Not so removed from the world that you did not pick up on that one. "Mary Boyle," you said.

"She returned my hat."

"How could you, James?" Now you must tell: it was like all the times you came home to the solid house with a small triumph from the world and wouldn't ya know, your brother received the prize—blue ribbons, gold stars up his sleeves—and the thick stucco walls, chestnut paneling, Matt Devlin's baronial fireplace turned to rubble at your feet. It had become his story with Mary Rose—that good woman, half sister, half daughter. Startling, as though you had turned to the last page of one of your mysteries and for once not guessed the improbable/predictable answer. Infamous, their coming together whatever their need, their use of each other while you, you with your great secret, your heirloom flaking to yellow ash like old clippings from the *Post.* Yet sounding like Nell, with a touch of her indulgence: "How could you, James?"

The chambermaid discreetly offstage.

"I could, Catherine. I can."

"She's only . . ." You were about to say a girl. A woman past forty, her days spent with addicts, pimps, whores—the underworld.

"She's fine," he said. "Better off than we are."

You will long remember that.

And tell how you watched him pack his ritzy belongings, discarding the cheap raincoat, but tucking in that bogus hat. His pale eyes spent, wandered the room to check if he'd forgot. . . . Recall that he turned to you, moving in for the close-up, the grizzled thrust of his unshaven jaw: "Cath, we must not let this happen. Let the years go by."

Then, you are moved to tears. *Puellae lacrimae.* By rote, you remember the quick flip of emotion in that scene. Test yourself on this moonless night when the black window mirrors you at fifty, gray girl. Speak to her in your spinster sack. Watch for the glisten of your tears as you hear again James' voice swing low with the offer of a bright kid in California who hardly knows she has an aunt, of his thoroughbreds and horsey wife, lemon trees and eucalyptus, a hillside of wild geranium. He offers you his view of the Pacific.

You say: "But you'll be back with your people, your crew?"

"Not here. If ever."

Confess. Use that word, not to God. Use that word that has so little to do with memory, with actual recall—*confiteor.* Not to God, but to yourself, dropping the veil, intricate screen of first person, how I was made glad there would be no moving picture. The city was gone. The look of that war. "No longer," my brother said, to please me, "no longer men like Billy Bray. It's not *now.* Too straight, the fancy woman and the soldier."

"Too cruel?"

"Or not cruel enough, Cath. I don't know—it would be like some fancy documentary. Cinema stuff. I work in movies." He was steering me out of the room, leaving that segment behind. In the rose light of the hallway we ran to the elevator, pursued, pursuing.

Get it over. Fess up. I said it was just a murder when we were impressionable children. I said, "Insufficient evidence, no plot." The words out of my mouth revealing at last, at long last that was all I ever had—a weak case, a button, a belt, Southern drawl in a city full of women come up for the war work, many raven-lipped women. A circumstantial stocking that would not stand the test of the nightly mystery. I had pinned it on Isabelle Poole, yet I still treasured the smoking gun that would have made my brother's movie, for it was after all my story, the story of a foolish life. And, total recall, my soul, or something like it, fluttered within as we

descended to the Hilton atrium and I ran for the bus with my
shabby secret of Billy and my suspect, some first degree floozie or
who knows? Who will ever know—Isabelle Poole? In any case, my
prize, the golden spindle, won at last.

Waiting for my father in a churchy place, I'm Cath. I guess it's
unavoidable, the tower, moat, and magic potion. Here is a window, a
narrow recessed window with stone tracery as in a castle, not a
prison. View over rooftops—tar paper, asbestos shingle, not thatch
or soft red tile of a princess' lookout in a foreign land. I can only
guess this haunting view far beneath me to be North Avenue without St. Patrick's steeple. But in the distance, a smooth green expanse
and cheerful spill of water. Round puffball trees line the road which
curves lazily up Golden Hill and leads far beyond. It is my father's
kingdon. I am happy here. Wonderfilled as a child with a pop-up
book in which the page plays at three dimensions—real stool, dainty
cupboard with doors that open revealing sweetmeats, warm mound
of family pet, Bootsie we loved but did not care for. Then it goes flat
and all the absorbing details—broom, doggy bone, comfy stove—
collapse as though that sunny slide's been pulled. Dark, without
moonlight, and I must feel around, knocking against a table, upset-
ting a dish that splashes cold-wet upon the floor. My eyes adjust and
I see my mother in a queenly gown, her playing card headdress all
in grays, for like a cat I see no color.

     "Catherine, you have spilt the milk."

     "I didn't cry."

     "Don't say the obvious."

     "You were never like this," I say. "You were never tart.
Each night you fed us cake or pie."

     "Brown Betty. Sally Lunn. A rich vanilla pudding, my
girl."

     "Sorry."

     "Well you might be." She speaks in this stilted stagy way

like the actors who come to town every year with the same old *Rumpelstiltskin:* "Cake or pie, indeed!"

"Nell! Nell!" I cry, but she doesn't hear her name.

"We never called them Billy, Nell," James says, though he's not in the room.

"Always. You had the fresh mouth. I simply followed. We said it together. BILLY. NELL."

"Peach cobbler, pineapple upside down. You will prick your soft white finger." She goes on, my mother, now hunched on the three-legged stool, old crone in tatters. I can see the toe of her royal slipper, the silver girdle under her ragged shawl. That was one thing I never did like when the Trump Tree Majors came to Bridgeport, that they doubled, tripled up as frogs and ogres and good people of the town. I never did buy that. "The king's a billy goat! The prince a snail!"

"Hush, Catherine," my mother whispered, but this one, this Nell cackles: "And on that day your blood will run."

James says: "Try it with a flicker of light, candle stub. This is eerie black and white. Don't fuck up the scene with laughter." He is sitting with Billy by the stove. Our father in his shirt sleeves, wears a heavy leather strap across his chest to tote his little gun. He springs toward me, bucks, paws the ground, raises the tufted white head to interrogate: "Cake or pie, my fine girl?"

Tell how you may now choose, after the few days that seem years later, to turn from your image in the dark window or to wait for the reprieve till dawn when your flat face fades, as the moon fades with the coming of the light, to nothing. A conjurer's trick—all gone.

James. Mary Boyle gone on her way. Alone—tell that you may turn to your wheel or to your loom, spinster, weaver of stories you told yourself and of tales left untold. Take your place on the hard bench, further the design. The blue indigo of your wool with its sweet odor of waste forms the tip of a star in King's Ransom. Now that should make you laugh, but does not, so blind . . . beat, beat your threads close and in order. So blind I cannot tell my tears from chamber lye.

Natural History: II

All the facts of natural history taken by themselves, have no value, but are barren like a single sex. But marry it to human history, and it is full of life.   —Emerson, *Nature*

Legs akimbo, Lilah sits in the great room on green carpet close cropped as a suburban lawn. Her skirt forms a hammock between her knees which fills with blocks, a plush rabbit, plastic monsters until she leaps up to spill these treasures. The baby collapses in ecstasy at this simple undoing. Next his mother must sit, back straight as in the saddle. Then rabbit by block by Godzilla by creepy crawler he loads her lap again. His game, today's game. Across the room the television plays a summer rerun of James' show. That's her game: it's failed. She had thought how William would love to see his father, who's taping in L.A., and detected a moment's interest before he grew fretful and, cleverkins that he is, invented the gathering game.

The boy's a towhead, true Hulburt, so like her brothers who ran wild through Hetsie's patch of tomatoes and squash, California kids with no dreams beyond surfboards and dirt bikes. And so unlike, with a tough armature she can see under his sweet flesh as he heads with industry into the next amazing task. Lilah's the one wanted the picture of James, counts the hours till he'll come uphill in the limo. He's there for her on the screen—tawny, thick in the neck and shoulders. He consoles a frantic woman with matted white hair, lowering the famed voice of his famed series. Lilah knows it is the husky reassuring voice of Billy Bray.

The game has escalated: her lap now piled with cushions, a leaning tower of chintz. She has to peek round gorgeous pink roses and twining ivy to see her son, a small tyrant; to see her husband, America's darlin', who stills the hand of the old woman anxiously plucking at her cardigan. Lilah shares James with thirty million people, men and women who take him to be father, lover, maybe their boy—whatever proves satisfying these past two years. It will not last forever. She shares William with no one, feels a pang of jealousy watching his father carry him up the path to visit Mufti, Falada's son. A sin perhaps; she's a California girl with an under-developed sense of sin, her mother having come to Christ after the hardscrabble days were over.

The tower falls. Will, buried under frilled cushions, gasps in fat full-blown roses, the funniest event in the world, rerun and rerun. The same roses hang at the windows, where they can be drawn against the spectacular view. Then in the evenings the great room closes around them, Lilah and James and this late child they don't deserve; the television right there with expensive bric-a-brac, cheery no-account vases with fresh hothouse flowers. There's nothing here she cares for except the writhing package she pokes at under the cushions and her husband's voice saying something firm and wise. She could reconstruct the great room as it was when James so named it, where the Karok basket hung, on what shelf the Pueblo pots; simple as naming the man she married for the wrong reasons—to cure his cynical talk of filmfolk, leach it out of his mouth with a native remedy while he would peel back her shell of composure. She will never forget the day the great room was stripped. Her belly tight and high with the baby, she tired as the morning wore on, while the anxious curator directed his helper in the packing and crating. It became semisocial with sandwiches and Native American chat she'd never intended, the fussy young scholar constantly thrilled, stroking silky woven grasses, polished black glaze. Greed lit his pinched acquisitive eyes, though he spoke in an undertaker's hush of her bereavement, her diminshed life without these old and beautiful things. It was coming on to nine months since her mare had died.

In her giving, she wished to be anonymous as the women who wove and coiled these useful objects. The Pomo basket was lowered into a crate. She could see its black eagle feathers were safe and that a Navajo rug, with a geometric riff that specially pleased her, was rolled, unnecessarily, in an acid-free tube for its ride down the mountain. Fingers laced over her belly, she had watched them disappear, these artifacts overinvested with meaning, meaning of herself. The helper, a Latino, worked deftly, precisely, carried out the last of the crates. There came a moment of silence in the naked white room, which even the prattling curator respected. He must know he is fawning, unbearable, that she was giving these precious things back—in no way to him. She had trotted off then, insofar as she could trot William kicking inside her, to the screening room, where she grabbed the mended Mayan figure to present to the learned young man. That was a precious moment—squinting, contemptuous, he was unable to say to his patroness that her gift was a worthless fake.

Tumbling on the carpet, William's golden hair spins like a crazy cap. A few seconds before tears, his mother scoops him up. James, wearing his shield, turns on a brash lieutenant. Deep focus reveals his jaw working as he considers his every word. They stand under black trees. Cicadas call forth the threat of summer night. He speaks to the young officer gruffly: "More in sorrow than in anger." It is getting to the end of the script where the white haired woman, a supporting actress of the sixties, must acknowledge her arrogant son has committed the crime. Lilah switches the set off, Will squirming in her arms as she turns toward the kitchen. The soft flip flop, flip flop of María making tortillas can be heard. Her life is full of Marías and Rosas, Juan up at the stable. There is so much money: one reason to live with great care. Flip flop, flip flop—this María convinced that James, the police chief, is sustained by her tortillas, must have them in abundance when he returns.

"Who's that?" Lilah asks, holding Will up to a gilt mirror that came in with the chintz and grassy carpet. The child says his name, but can't witness along with the mirror that his mother's face is now predominantly Okie, brown and stark. Her beauty gone. The baby has finally taken it from her, and good riddance. They make their way out to the patio, where Will runs to the stale water in the fountain. It is forbidden. He stops short, turns to his mother, who snatches him from the scum of algae. She would like the fountain, which recycles a trickle of water, shut off, but then she'd like to move from this place altogether, down to L.A. to be with her husband.

Jen's trunk sits in the drive. It will follow her East to college. She has already flown away—to Yale, where she intends to consolidate her honors, work to complete what her father so easily sluffed off. Her last month here has been happy, each day filled with the tremendous relief that comes at the end of a long awkward visit. They have all been generous, laughing at each other, creating too late a system of family jokes and teasing retorts. James home, when not taping, to see the little boy. Jen straining to leave her parents to this next family, to carry her scars into the world where they may be disguised to seem no worse than her roommates', girls from normal families in Ohio and Tennessee. Despite herself, she's come to care for the baby, though he is no Eamonn. She remembers stalking her older brother on the yearly visit, sleeping outside his room, the guest room, like a lone groupie. William is a tough little customer, Lord of the house and barnyard and pasture. Eamonn knew what she knows, that they are peripheral, assigned to minor roles in the Life and Times of James Bray. On the other hand, William will do fine, coming on the scene at the very moment of his father's second chance.

Air Express arrives for Jen's trunk. Brass-bound, leather-strapped, untraveled; it's Italian, top of the line: there is so much money. Lilah runs down to sign the papers and as the trunk is heaved into the van she notices it is a glossy dark green, not actually black, the choice of a daughter too subtle for her own good. She should have gone East with Jen to pick out posters and curtains for a dormitory room; was not wanted. The van slams shut on the trunk. Her daughter's belongings are driven away. It's only these last two years Lilah's felt hurt, sore-assed as city folk on a dude ranch, knowing that Jen finds her insufficient with good reason.

Fistful by fistful, William is transferring the pebbles of the drive to adorn a dusty open drain. He is a perfect little animal, squatting, running, scooping—pebble by pebble now. That will take a while. She sits under the Moreton Bay fig, which she waters illegally, the great tree planted here when the house was built in the twenties, only sixty, seventy years ago, when the fashion of Spanish Revival swept Southern California. The glamorous past. She would like to leave this place—try L.A., or maybe a sodden green oasis in the reclaimed desert. The pebbles are forming a pattern, roundish. Will does not take time to admire his work or see that his mother is restless. Lilah walks up to the patio. The lemons are huge this year on the potted trees, real to her as they were in the backyard in Riverside. To James they will always look false.

It's clear in the scorching light that when she calls New Haven tonight she must not ask Jen after the roommates, after her courses and curtains in their difficult attempt at ordinary talk, but say it. Say—I miss you shut up in your room, your black magic calling us to account, but I'm glad you've gone East with the *crème de la crème*. We were all that smart once. Lilah Lee, your father, your aunt. Lately, I have been thinking about rodeo. I suppose because your Daddy is a star, I've been thinking how I roped a calf in seven seconds, how I was the only girl let ride the rough stock. I have been remembering that what comes natural may not be good for you.

William is king of the mound squatting on his drainpipe and pebbles, a mess which only his mother sees as a wheel, his own brilliant and first-time invention. Lilah sits on the rim of the fountain, the slightest breeze spraying her with the fetid water. The flip flop, flip flop of tortillas, patient as a heartbeat: she thinks she'll never leave this place now and that she may not speak to her daughter about anything more than the curtains. It's like being out there in the dust and dung of the arena riding the barrels—too easy, you lose track; too hard, you lose your nerve.

Mary Boyle is poking through a tangle of pins and thread in her mother's sewing basket, looking for a button that will do. She pricks her finger, licks a single drop of blood, finds a flat gray button. The eye of the needle moves in, sideswipes black thread, moves in, bats it down. Right way round, she discovers, is thread into needle. Pleased with herself, she ties a lumpy knot. The gray button is held to her father's tweed coat where she stabs it unmercifully until it is clamped to the cloth. The button is small, ill-positioned. She can't cook or clean with out disaster: fat fires, electric shocks pursue her as though she's a setup in the cartoons the youngest of her nieces and nephews watch, a cat or rat in human gloves and shoes who's flattened, blown up, popped back from annihilation.

Her parents are getting on. It was not revealed to Mary on her visits when the Boyles made it ever plausible, the ongoing vigor of family life; convincing skits for their daughter, too saintly for the upscale Catholic school, working among the poor. So they played it, until Mary arrived unannounced on a summer day to find her mother and father unrehearsed, faltering without the defense of barbecue, Pirates, Steelers, no holiday view of the Alleghenies or mighty Monongahela. The Boyles are in need of attention: Mom unsteady, dwindling; Pop's heart on the fritz. Mary's brothers and sisters delight in her return, see it as a natural progression, a woman with no ties. They consider, all except Deirdre, that she's come home to safety, to rest. Dee Dee is not convinced, believes Mary, as most of mankind, resides in a state of unbalance, that her sister's polarities—dutiful girl and daring adventuress—can be harmoniously united by the application of the male Boji stone. The Boyle tribe laughs, but Mary will not discredit Dee Dee's chip of tourist rock from the time of Atlantis. The world *is* out of whack: the smooth black stone is a relic any believer might touch as a saint's bone or fragment of shroud—a cheap ticket to the supernatural.

"Okay, Pop!" Mary Boyle kicks the hard base of the recliner. Time for their walk. Now the tragedy of the small button is revealed. She could weep as the wind flaps her father's coat open. Her mother, a woman with guts as Mary now sees her, has made her torturous way on aluminum canes to the front window and cheers them off. When first home Mary Boyle trailed her father through these streets as one accused, past the brick houses of German and Irish neighbors who knew her, the girl chosen by God. They could see she was no longer special, walking Pop Boyle out, and she imagined a visible thought balloon above her head with repossessed words—shame, penance; the gory stigmata of her discarded vocations on view, until she understood those people had gone, only the Boyles and a few old neighbors left. These streets were now prime, houses with a little age on them offering eclectic charms she can't name—Tudor trussing, Queen Anne gables—to lawyers, bankers, executives at Alcoa, USX, young people drawn, in this cycle of fashion, to the urban life style.

For two winters she's urged Pop on his walk. Living with her parents, working part time for the city—paperwork for federal grants. She might be Vic Benino, keeps that distant from the needy of Pittsburgh. Her father knows the names of the children being strapped into Volvos and Mercedes. Their parents know Pop Boyle and love him—a retired union official with snowy hair, old tweeds. Once the enemy, Mary thinks, now part of their scene, an old Irishman with a middle-aged daughter to air him.

"Daffodils," Pop says. Sure enough, in every landscaped front yard, spikes of green are breaking through. "I did love my King Alfreds all down the walk."

"You did?"

"And the beds full of them; the apricots, paper whites, April Tears." Her father steps out smartly in front of her, clutching his coat. "Your head was buried in the prayer book."

This day's walk is now full of the wounding green shafts of daffodils. For the first time she sees that her parents, Pop at least, have some grievance against her and that she is part of some other design: the crabbed daughter with affable old father an endearing sight, why it's worth buying into this neighborhood, to watch the Boyles walk out for their grocery sack. Today she'll fulfill the new-comers' fantasy: it's going to be meat loaf and mashed potatoes: paring knives and scalding milk, a menu of dangerous encounters. If she had entered the convent ten years earlier she could have threaded the finest needle, sewn the narrowest hem on a shift to be bride of Christ. If Catherine had not cooked and cleaned . . . No *if* she conceives lets her off the hook today. If the world had not turned into Village. The truth, she has more than a faint idea, is that she's neither a worldly nor domestic creature. It's downright uncomfortable being at home and she wonders if, from the very begining, her whole life was not set by her discontent in the Boyle house, the gentle wrangling and affection of family life which never seemed enough, yet made her insufficient.

As the months go by she is stranded, the cartons she brought to Pittsburgh half unpacked in her room, twine rolled in her top drawer. Misery—in Central America, in Asian refugee camps—calls to her. The disabled earth beckons. Her room, once shared with Dee Dee, holds a small library of human and ecological abuse that will show her some useful direction. She's okay without meat loaf and a man, without the protection of Catherine or Pop. Each night ticks off. When the house is quiet, she reads, her door open to hear her father's jazzy snore, her mother's efforts in the night. Mary falls asleep over documentation of torture and heroic resistance, never unpacks or packs. Home is her detention.

The meat loaf and mashed potatoes are a triumph. The string beans stringy and coarse. Thursday, the night of James' show. Her mother and father are devoted to James Bray, think, in retrospect, much better of Catherine for this celebrated connection. Mary sits on the couch where she can't be seen by Pop in the recliner, by Mom in the straight chair holding the rubber grips of her aluminum canes. Mary's gray eyes open wide in the dark to devour the man on the screen until they are alone—no Boyles, no Pittsburgh. His hair has receded, forming a rusty widow's peak. Close, overreal, his face large with pebbly, tarnished skin. She is in the stained seersucker suit and yearns to speak, to have her say, as if he's with her in the television dimness. The story, however, must be laid out with its stock characters and each episode's complications. The sensation of his breath upon her, of her words unspoken, lasts a split second, then Mary Boyle, like the millions she keeps track of in James' ratings, is drawn into the small town, into this compelling story that will make her want the next.

The town is noplace, midsize, mid-America: a Main Street with easy parking, friendly storefronts. Corruption, felony, fraud, plain old marital predicaments with their resulting disorder are undone in fifty minutes by the man who was once her lover. Each week Mary Boyle sits with this secret on the couch, figuring what it must mean, her communion with the actor on her parents' set, something beyond that need of the flesh that betrayed them. It must mean . . . and then a disreputable young woman is shot, an impaired child lost or stolen, a good man falsely accused. James has the fleeting look, she'd seen it in Seaside Park, of exquisite self-doubt that renders him completely human. She wonders if, like the gravel-washed voice and the swagger, it came by way of Billy Bray.

This night of the disheartening daffodils, the first clue that her father has a hard line on her, a view that goes back to her head stuck in a prayer book, Mary settles on the couch. James does not at once appear: a quirky plot with first the murder, a chase; then he comes ambling through the wooden courthouse which is cracker barrel cute. She leans forward about to say and knows she can only imagine they lie together. No, stand together in the deep welcoming light of the Hilton, ready to head out, the grand tour. She says that she has blundered, never chosen, that she leaves when there is pain.

"Tell me," he says. "Tell me, darlin'."

"I pack up, move on. My boxes going out your sister's kitchen door held no more than the footlocker I took to the convent. My baggage, Cath knows, is of another sort. I had discarded faith, then Peaches. Of you, we never spoke. My few cardboard boxes wound with twine were worldly. The world, you see, more immediate when traveling light. Cath insisted on the coverlet. Bad scene: I wouldn't, couldn't possibly, and the next moment clasped it to my chest, would treasure it for life. So we laid it out on the backseat of the car to be stolen at the Joyce Kilmer rest stop on the Jersey Turnpike. Then didn't I cry for my lost coverlet and Catherine? For you, looking at the empty seat, the unlocked door. I'd never mourned any of it properly—the losses. My short-term passion for a man, for a child, were reasonable, fit the profile of the good girl needing to be bad or reckless. That's the burden I take with me, your sister knows, the figuring, the figuring who I am and why. Why is no answer.

"Now the coverlet was swiped by a venal woman—it had to be a woman couldn't resist the beauty of Catherine's work. I was at fault, willful—leaving the car unlocked, wanting to trust the families on their first trips of the summer, stretching their legs after the ride, the kids running ahead to stake out their treats. Of course, I'd dangle the coverlet before them, just as I drove into Father Panik Village testing them, that the poor should prove themselves to a zealous woman in blue jeans who assigned them the sins of the world. Peaches, the grand tour—why can't I let things ripen? Why had I not shown you the plain people of the Village—their grinding survival, not boss? Not hip enough for your movie. The tears gone by the time I hit Pennsylvania, traveling back home to this family I hardly know, but suspect may know their daughter, their sister Mary Rose.

"You will never tell about the coverlet?"

She closes her eyes, not needing the image of James on the screen: "Never tell Cath—the day I went back to the Village, a few days after our outing at the Hilton. I'd quit. Easy, using the catchphrase 'burnt out.' Only my custodian sweetheart trailed me to the parking lot: 'What'sa matter? I didn't buy the ring?' I laughed one last time, bit my tongue not to say, 'Sweetheart, go home to the wife and kids.'

"So I was out of business, had no business going back to the battered door of Peaches' place, hating the cocks and, oh my, the cunts I'd finally noticed on the crumbling walls. Driven by my own unfinished business to say I was sorry to the mother. Some thankless Christian act. It was the last day of school, late morning. Michelle alone, the gold coast dealer, big stone face, had started his wake-up rounds. I'd figured it, the apartment with only Michelle, a knockout in heels, white silk pajamas trimmed up with gold. So the money was coming in and Mama, suspicious but middling polite, mutes the salsa.

"Mizz Bee had nothing to say. Maybe seeing I had no paperwork, she was nervous, hopped around the room straightening the doilies that had appeared on tables and the pictures reframed of her two dark-eyed boys. A hot Mama, you'd love her. You would."

James' chin is thrust forward—solemn, weighty it looks, his blue eyes darkly troubled, not buying the bad rap pasted on a poor frightened thug. Mom and Pop turn from this drama to watch Mary leave the room. Hearing her footsteps on the stairs they call out. When she turns her father looks up at her, not puzzled. She thinks that he might say, "You took your head out of the prayer book, didn't you?" Her mother has come on swollen legs, made her way to the newel post. "Pop," she whispers, "leave her." How long has her mother known and protected her? Known what? Her father says no more than good night. Mary goes to her room, takes the twine from her top drawer where it is buried under winter gloves and scarves.

"You'd love her." She continues her part. "Michelle's a number, the crucifix stuck on the smooth cocoa skin of her neck, black hair braided with a fat curl at the end. Strutting down the hall to show me her butt slung in white silk. A spicy smell in Mama's kitchen and on the refrigerator the tight meticulous drawings. Colored within the lines, a proper dinosaur, respectful Statue of Liberty. María's signature obedient and tamed. Michelle smiling a lot. Maybe she's on, just a little something peppy. Forget it, she's glowing and cradles her belly that will soon pop the pajamas.

" 'Teach me,' I said. Then Michelle understood it was more than Mizz Bee not knowing shit about life in the Village. I wanted to ask her about bodies, her body and mine. Why, if we both mistreated. . . . No, that was dishonest. Wanted to ask if the trust you put in your body is unlike the pain? There in the clean kitchen with cereal and milk, 'Teach me,' I said. And Peaches' Mama, sorry for my predicament, offered me a cup of tea."

Mary opens the dresser, begins to pack up, T-shirts and jeans, a perfect replica of the seersucker suit, and reaching for the twine uncovers a dog-eared pamphlet—*The Scivias of Hildegard,* the saint's swirling heavens and earth look zany, beautiful to Mary Boyle, inspired as Peaches' world before her end. She cannot imagine back to her choice of Hildegard, knowing that she has never had a mystic moment, but considers that the Abbess of Bingen would have ordered Father Panik Village to her liking, learning in a moment the necessary language, would have told off city hall: so *Scivias* is packed with useful socks and underwear. The cartons are quickly sealed and tied. The Boyles have gone to bed. Pop will lie awake till Mary's light goes off. She is reading about the malnourished, the unvaccinated in a hill town of Peru. Not martyrdom. Please God, she wishes to perform one virtuous act with ease. She is reading about the application of papaya to the dead flesh of a pressure sore, about a crutch made of a strong branch and inner tube, when, looking up from the page, she sees the slick black Boji stone on her night table, holds it in her palm. She is figuring that if James, not James of the Hilton, but the kind policeman she watches, the friend or lover she foolishly speaks to, if James has found his incarnation . . . "Please God," Mary Rose holds the ancient stone to the pulse in her throat, "why not me? Why not me?"

"Catherine Bray Raises the Roof." This caption under a picture of the fiber person, puffed with pride. The color photo cannot convey the soft violets and teal greens, the rosy roses of her half-woven coverlet. The roof of the ranch house literally raised to accommodate the overhead hooks, heddles, punch cards of the jacquard loom that make her fancy patterns. This photo, in a crafts magazine, is propped on Jen's trunk. In New Haven on dangerous Dixwell, she lives in a cool, off-campus house with cool, off-campus kids who favor futons on the floor, Japanese beer, bossa nova of the sixties, and a nuked microwave cuisine. Her aunt's picture is actually above her as she sleeps. Each morning she looks up to Catherine, sees her gratification in the frontal pose, her grace in the swift gesture of work like a dancer's whirl or magician's sleight of hand. Groping for her wire-rim glasses, Jen squints at the smile on Catherine's face she can't quite construe, though she could hold forth on the cultural contradictions in "Catherine Bray Raises the Roof."

For instance: the ceiling above Cath's head might be called Sheetrock cathedral, the ultimate elevation of schlock domestic architecture, except, Jen would point out, this is obviously a work space. In the old mills the looms were so low small children ran under the warp and beat the fabric into line. With the import of the jacquard loom—high ceilings, high windows, and, inevitably, in the factories, yards and yards of common stuff became run of the mill. There is a skylight above her aunt with a square of blue and out the picture window a slice of modest suburban house, a red stop sign.

This is not country. Through a doorway, new Colonial cabinets of a remodeled kitchen. Jen would have to admit to ample comfort: not care to disclose the source from which all that money came. On one wall, pushed to the side, a rack with indigo and white coverlets in their limited geometry; in full view, the fancy covers with many colors and devices, each one displaying a signature block: Made by Catherine Bray, Conn. 198——. She reads further from the hanks of colored wool, shuttles and spindles, the big loom itself, handsome and businesslike, that the place is a shop.

Though the photograph is professionally lit, you'd have to see blown-up details to name Cath's designs, so free and various: wild turkeys and pheasants, strawberry medallions, eagle borders, remarkably sinuous branches of oak, beech, maple. Re-creations and often . . . Jen would say too often . . . in the work of Catherine Bray the sadly paternalistic buck with magnificent antlers, a doe kneeling beside him in grateful submission to her mighty mate. Disturbing, too, the spiked wheel and Celtic cross of Catholic iconography. She doesn't believe in Cath's belief. Her tenderness toward her aunt will not allow that the head which programs—which *imagines* intricate designs can contain the Old Phantom of a primary narrative myth.

Then there is the magazine—elitist, special interest—for potters, weavers, silversmiths, for fine woodworkers who at the end of the twentieth century are fashioning delicate Windsor chairs, severe Shaker tables. There are feature stories on celebrities like Catherine. The woman at the loom, lending herself to this professional exposure, speaks the technical language of her craft, out of Jen's range. It's left up to the interviewer to comment on Catherine Bray's art, how closely she works within the old forms, but with what invention. The craft person herself is aggressively middle-class. Plump and motherly, she wears opera length pearls, the classic sweater set of a woman who has never lived on the edge. Her hair, tinted an even brown, is smoothed back under an Alice band which gives her a girlish air, not of wonder. Here Jen is left with no system to decode the picture of her aunt. The face of the persistent weaver owns to its age, yet that history gives way to the smile of an amazed child: yep, the very best there is, she's at last won the game.

Not nearly so smart in the hermeneutics of her own room, Jen scans the rattling window sash, the three-legged dresser, the pinpricks of light through the trashed window shade, turns from the overflow of books everywhere to the body of the sleeping boy beside her who, until last night, was a friend. A cold wind slaps at the window. The iron radiator clanks. She adores waking to the rotten weather in New Haven, even the nostril-cracking heat, gropes for her glasses, sees "Catherine Bray Raises the Roof," hardly notes her particular coverlet draped over the trunk with its roses and ivy, palm trees and a repeat of the plashing fountain at Rancho Grande, with the shield of her university, its truth and light, and the perplexing peacocks, no pea*hens*—two of them feeding a nest with baby bird. Why two? For symmetry only? That may be the liberty Catherine takes in her art.

The boy stirs, gropes for his glasses. They turn to each other, solemn wire-rim to wire-rim, no longer friends. They are serious young people and must contemplate the enormity of the previous night. The boy has black hair, black eyes, a wide nose, but she finds something of Eamonn's directness in the clamp of his mouth as he studies her, something of her father's awful charm when he finally smiles. He has revealed to her the horrors of West-chester with its country club culture and competitive greed, of his parents shallowing out, their unendurable cheer. That harrowing story has prompted her to show this boy Eamonn's snapshot of James Bray when he was just their father, a sandy man on the brink of middle-aged despair; and the one of her mother, too beautiful, choked in a formal hunting stock, the shine glancing off her top hat as though costumed for Brit TV; and the one of William-come-lately, who in her bitterest moments she calls the press-release baby. So they have come to each other naked, Jen and Scott, the boy with the striving, assimilated name. They have speculated on the syndication of the cop series, the moral dislocation for the Koreans and Finns who have bought her father's show, the pat Judeo-Christian closure at the end of each segment, the degrading dependence upon genre. They know the worst, having gone together to the Morty Ziff production, purported True Crime, in which, for starters, a psychotic rich bitch kills a soldier to launch a slasher movie. They have spoken gravely to each other, fearing they are born into this bleak time of holding patterns nourished on exhausted forms.

Now they move quickly, lightly, to get up, dress, flip through notebooks, talk of assignments before they seal their uncertainty with a kiss. Jen looks at the corny cuckoo clock from home that she's silenced. It is noon and, fuck all, it's Sunday. She snaps the shade up and there's Cath waiting patiently in her van.

"My aunt," she says to the boy, who knows of Catherine Bray's solitary triumph over the constriction of gender, who admires the weaver's strict adherence to the labor theory of value. Jen demures, for the first time using artifice on her friend—how she would adore to stay. She shrugs—duty, the horn of the van, now calls. *It will do him good to be without me.* Her eyes flutter with a touch of mystery. Unwashed, unbrushed, she throws on her thrift shop coat. Making her destination infinitely attractive, Jen whispers to her lover: "I'm off." To Zembla? The Emerald City?

The density of the afternoon, thickened with memory from the start, got up with sacred scraps and noisy intrusions. I'd only imagined it like one of our good times, taking in a movie, a mall, wandering with Jen into shops where we go through our paces—oh, that she would buy one pretty item; God, that I would leave her to her Cinderella tatters. I had secretly longed for this excursion to Barnum's refurbished museum, to see what they'd made of the one mummy and a molting baby elephant I dreaded as a child. Spooked palace with clown costumes, not funny in themselves, and a dry "don't touch" old lady guarding our heritage as her very own junk.

I'd roasted the chicken, made Jen her pie. What she likes—to come home, forage in the refrigerator, set the table, wash up pots and pans. Play house. Not every Sunday, and I thought as she hopped into the van I'd mistaken the day, her distraction audible as it is during exams, a rush of words filling empty space, a tick of anxious repeats until she comes down, sees it's only Cath, family—foreign to her as apple pie, the kitchen cleanup. This threatening winter afternoon, her manic chatter broken with dazed silence. "Would you rather not?" I asked. The hum of the Interstate answered. "The Museum?"

"For sure!"

"For sure yes or no?" Her eyes worn, cheeks flushed, lips moving in private recitation.

The Barnum Museum is lately embraced by a chill postmodern bank, the effect surreal as an imperial plaza haunted by the toy statuette of an equestrian hero. The warm red stone of the Museum, its fanciful oriental dome, cheery bas-relief of provincial history, reduces the "statement" of the bullying bank to an empty threat. At the big brass pulls of the door, the scare and craving of old. It was my mother, improving us, who dragged us to this bizarre building beyond the department stores and offices where downtown suddenly went dead. Jen lightens up momentarily—a fun place right off: Tom Thumb's teeny boots and brown velvet court suit: Barnum's enormous greatcoat, his oversize ebony cane. Circus music.

With a groan of self-pity, she says: "They took me to a circus. It was Nice or Cannes."

An instructive timeline makes Barnum's life an irrepressible pageant, Jefferson to Teddy Roosevelt. Dickens, Daguerre, Darwin, Twain, Edison—Jen points out dough-faced Victoria, Florence Nightingale, both Mrs. Barnums (accessories), the only women there. As we mount the stairs, I'm instructed: "Museums," she says, "ideal self as possessor. The lesser self as viewer." I am told that *appropriate* and *property* share a Latin root. We are separated, thank

heaven, by a boisterous family. Jen grazes the galleries which hold
no enchantment for her, now and again plaintively calling to me
round a corner, "Cath?"

I look long upon the library of Barnum's ill-fated Iranistan, its wallpaper of noble savages among Adam pavilions, the relics
stolen from Egyptian tombs, bright puff clouds on the oriental ceiling, American tiger-eye maple fashioned into minarets.

"Cath? Where's the elephant?"

Her aunt is lost to her in the Barnum Museum. She wants to speak
of Scott, how he is reviled by his name. His father a Russian Jew
from Brooklyn, his mother corn-belt Reform. He is named after no
one, not a romantic novelist, B movie star, or astronaut. She is Jen
out of Lilah and James, out of Billy and Nell, Hetsie and Boon: her
bland name that of the brat in an otherwise perfect television family
of the early sixties. Trailing Catherine, she relives the boy's first
fumbling touch, his hand placed over hers. They were studying
together and, as was their habit, read their neat discoveries out loud:
Marx wanted to dedicate his great book to Darwin; William James
called pure experience "stuff." Scott's hand is broad with long blunt
fingers, hers fluttered under his like a frail wing as though to escape,
then settled, came to rest. They were underground in their Cross
Campus carrels and he'd reached over a pile of books, an incredible
maneuver, to place his large hand over hers.

Within the Museum, the room from the Wheeler mansion, coldly
opulent. Transfixed, I touch my pearls, smooth my hair, make sure
I'm fit to look upon the gaudy orange stencils, the yards of ice blue
satin, the horsehair chairs—frenchy, tufted, hard. It's worth waiting
fifty years. How long could you sit? Whatever could you say? To the
Wheelers, of their art, the fruits of their sewing-machine fortune
. . . compliment the soapy white marbles; the queerness of the life
size nude coyly draping her privates while the Florentine bust upon
a pedestal presents her sexless cupcake tits . . . admire the green

pallor of the Wheeler boys in long blond curls and white muslin dresses, poor things, poor things. Standing on Golden Hill, I'd yearned for their commanding view of the city through long Gothic windows, a view I now see to be obscured, clotted with machine made lace and plastic ferns.

"So, where's the mummy, Cath?"

In the exhibit of industry, I took my time with each display, loving all. To Jen's delight a couple of pug-faced boys repeatedly entered the room to activate a tape. She laughed each time the ghostly voice proclaimed two-thirds of the small arms and ammunition used in World War I was manufactured in this city, that the city had risen again as a great financial center. Along with the distraught mother of those naughty boys, I wanted to scold her, say it's not that easy, my apple-pie love with your old lady glasses, golden credit cards and rags.

What she couldn't bear—Catherine falling for it. Pop come-on of the place, slick graphics, audiovisual kitsch. Then what?—dented pie plates, boots, manual typewriters, guns, many guns. The perversion of foundation garments. One lousy picture of immigrant workers. You got to think of the tribe that got it together, the city as well as the exhibit; the repeating rifle and the sweatshop girls sewing the big seller—Dr. Warner's Health Corset. Cath seemed not to think, not to consider, walked into the costume drama of those period rooms. No—stood at the door like the Irish maid, until she was not Jen's perfect aunt of the loom, but acquisitive, even—she would say it to Scott—even sort of vulgar like those women in Nieman-Marcus taking it all back home. What she liked: the photos of Barnum's freaks—the bearded lady, Chang and Eng, Albino Family simply displaying themselves in full possession of their strangeness. In the glass case that contains them, her own pale face, pale hair, glint of her lens is too self-reflective. Much as she *likes* the sweet smile of the humped camel girl, you got to turn from that view—she would say it, not to her aunt. You got to get out of this place. Funky fun, she's not unaware. And what she loved: the little traps and carriages made for Charles and Lavinia Stratton, their small-scale sofas and chairs, the wee carved rosewood marriage bed. Life worked out in miniature. She wanted to go back to New Haven. "Cath?"

"Mmmm?"

"How do you legally change a name?"

"What's wrong with your name?"

"Not mine. A friend's."

"It's that bad?"

The friend was waiting for her in the snow. Then she was happy and kissed me. A healthy big-boned fellow skulking in the doorway on dangerous Dixwell Avenue, Jen's boy with fogged glasses, coughing romantically, soaked through. That old plot: why she had dawdled with her chicken, not touched my apple pie, though the soft beginning of the snow as we drove back on the highway was a gift to the California kid, beyond her hopes for this disappointing day.

Snug in my house, though lonely, no comfort in my loom. It sits like a mastodon to be praised for mere skeletal survival. I've not had the heart to read a mystery, in the long run unmysterious, since Mary Boyle went away and have stopped my discordant chant, nonsense songs for children. It was our father had perfect pitch. What's more confounding, I pray. Not on my knees, but in some form, a jabber in which I ask that my brother may be always in his series, that Mary Rose be deprived of her reason, that Jen . . . at this point I'm soppy and ask for the world. Tonight I resort to the tape. It's the tape of James, the episode in which—there's no war—a lacquered woman with pouting scarlet lips wounds, but does not kill, a soldier. That's the story line of this one. I don't close my eyes to listen to the voice of Billy Bray. I watch. I've heard an ignorant commentator suggest some actor's jargon, that James has done much inner work. That's dumb, clearly nuts. The amber beads of sweat on my brother's high forehead are real; his blue eyes sunk deep, ravaged with lust as he confronts the woman. That desire held, given to us. Held and denied as he brings her to justice. James is wasted on the millions. I am the only soul who knows that he acts naturally, that he practiced for hours with the cards and the coins to give, in his perfect performance, this illusion of control.

Story over, I lie in bed. The snow a white landscape on my window; hills mount, shift, collapse; rivers cut their way through creation. I enter the Barnum Museum alone. There is the tiny calling card of the midget, the huge dress shirt of the showman, a case with the books I will always believe he wrote: *Wild Beasts, Birds and Reptiles of the World, The Story of Their Capture; The Art of Money Making; Thirty Years of Hustling;* the unrevised *Life* of 1855. There's the historic progression: the Feejee Mermaid preceding the birth of Lenin and the publication of Huck Finn—all neat as a selvage edge. What had I wanted to show my girl? There's industry: the brittle black Columbia Records of Benny Goodman and Gene Krupa, Frisbie Pie Plates, GE toasters and fans, Dictaphones, cartridges, cordage, odorless rubber, cold-rolled steel, curry combs, and the miracle of 1912—the A, B, C sizing system of the bra. It is all set in order, tagged neatly, as perfectly displayed as the many rooms roped off from me, rooms I once meant to enter with men and children.

And in the last room. She's there—Pa-Ib: I never knew she had a name, Pa-Ib, 2,500 years old, with even white teeth stronger than mine, hair that never turns gray. I give her the fright. My mummy is there for no rhyme or reason, just possession, nine-tenths of the law, and the fact that this last place is an attic. No, it exhibits items from the once American Museum, that palace of profit, edification and pleasure: sharks' teeth, whale tusk, a faded photo of little men at the foot of the Boole tree, 109 ft. in diameter, shells and seaweed, a fiddle and Roman oil lamp. What had I so desperately wanted to show my bright girl? A fragment of neckerchief worn by Lincoln the night of his assassination. Etched Arabian brass, Macedonian cannonball, giant's ring, chunks of Westminster Abbey, a stuffed parrot, and the whistling swan who inspired Tchaikovsky. What had I wanted to show her like a blind woman feeling an elephant—the one moment in which you comprehend it all. Dr. Roderick's astounding vacuum pump, snowshoes, Ming necklace. The two-headed calf with two tails. Zuni pot, Dervish sword, the lantern from the old North Church hung out to save America. The tools of Ulysses.

All that stuff. A leather notebook which lies open, bold handwritten inscription: *I believe this world is in a great measure what we make it. . . .* And so forth, Barnum's bright Universalist view of a hundred years ago that make us still his happy audience. His clever eye takes in at a single glance the insatiable demand of the race for diversion, amusement—all that stuff under glass as well as the living phenomena: wild Indians and educated dogs, sword swallowers and tattooed lady, the Renowned Happy Family; and in the chaste lecture room, a refined moral drama of great interest. I possess the Museum no more, no less, than a woman come from a tenement, poor woman in a shawl walking down Lower Broadway with a precious quarter to spend. It is all curious and entertaining. Enriched with the stuff of the world, I head downstairs, clutch the railing, duped by one of his jokes—TO THE EGRESS.

To the Egress. Not before I see Jen enchanted by the human "attractions," those pranks of nature sitting for studio photos in their Sunday best. She turns to me with her crazy corkscrew curls: "Cath?"

"You want to be special."

The bloom is on her, quite pretty in the plain fashion of the day; this is the child, I thank God, happy to say it, to say that in the afterlife I've been granted, she will break my heart.

"Cath?"

Over the rousing um-pah of the band, I can't hear what she asks, but answer, "You want to be ordinary."

Through the frantic windshield wipers of the van we see

her friend waiting. "Thanks," she says—sweet, dishonest. "I loved your Museum."

I lie tight in my bed under the fancy cover of my making with its old designs in violet and madder rose, the snow pressing as though it will fall on this bed within my room. "Cath?" she asks, looking to the boy with the unspeakable name. "Tell me?"

"No. That will be your story. I have nothing to tell." Snow blanks the window like a shade drawn . . . or the light run off at the end of my brother's films.

And still she calls, "*Catherine,* where's the elephant?"

Now that I can answer fairly. The old elephant is gone.

The earliest known map of the town, not a city, was drawn from the heavens, in or about 1688. You can do no better than the cartographer whom we know to be Braddock Mead, an Irishman, though we cannot know why he used the alias John Greer—what manner of pirate, artist, fraud—but can determine where he stood on Golden Hill to make his astronomical observations establishing Ash Creek, Fayer Weather, Black Rock, the river unbridged, though much of his stargazing is lost to us, lost as the quill pen with which he wrote the legend Devil's Belt across a hazardous shore. His lobe of our Pleasure Beach is lumpy, indeterminate. Yet you can do no better than the Irishman's cartouche, beautifully drawn, in which corn is offered in trade to us by an allegorical Indian, for it was one hell of a bargain, this rich and generous place.

Permissions

opp. 223   Photo: Historical Collections, Bridgeport Public Library.

opp. 225   Baseball/heart symbol © 1992, Courtesy *Fan Magazine*, design by Tony Palladino. Photo: Michelle Novak.

opp. 227   Photo: The Barnum Museum, Bridgeport, Conn.; illustrations, Feejee Mermaid and Jenny Lind: Historical Collections, Bridgeport Public Library.

opp. 231   Photo: Lee Deigaard.

opp. 233   Barnum photo: J. J. Misencik; Chang and Eng: New York Historical Society.

opp. 235   Tom Thumb illustration: Historical Collections, Bridgeport Public Library.

opp. 237   Wedding photo: New York Historical Society; cards: Historical Collections, Bridgeport Public Library.

opp. 239   Photo, Tom Thumb: The Barnum Museum; photos, Lavinia Thumb: Historical Collections, Bridgeport Public Library.

opp. 241   Children's photo: Maureen Howard.

opp. 243   Illustrations: Historical Collections, Bridgeport Public Library.

opp. 245   Photo: Film Department, Museum of Modern Art, New York.

opp. 249   Photo: Historical Collections, Bridgeport Public Library.

opp. 255   Illustrations: Historical Collections, Bridgeport Public Library.

opp. 261   Photo: Historical Collections, Bridgeport Public Library.

opp. 265   Drawing: copyright Walt Kelly, 1952.

opp. 267   Photo: Historical Collections, Bridgeport Public Library; Illustration, (Dumbo): copyright © The Walt Disney Company.

opp. 269   Illustration, Spotted Man: New York Historical Society.

opp. 271   Joseph Cornell, *Untitled* 1956–59, box construction, 10 1/2 × 14 1/2 × 3 1/4, © The Joseph and Robert Cornell Memorial Foundation, Photograph by James Dee, Courtesy of the Pace Gallery.

opp. 277   Illustration: The Barnum Museum, Bridgeport, Conn.; photo: Historical Collections, Bridgeport Public Library.

opp. 279   Photo: Film Department, Museum of Modern Art, New York.

opp. 283   Photo: Terry Schutte; streetlamp illustration: Lee Deigaard.

opp. 289   Photo: Historical Collections, Bridgeport Public Library; group photo, Brignolo Studios, Historical Collections, Bridgeport Public Library.

opp. 291   Illustration: courtesy SS. Cyril and Methodius Church, Bridgeport Conn.

opp. 295   Hubbel light bulb and McLevy sign illustrations: Historical Collections, Bridgeport Public Library.

opp. 297   Photo and McLevy button: Historical Collections, Bridgeport Public Library.

opp. 301   Typescript: Historical Collections, Bridgeport Public Library.

opp. 303   Photo: Film Department, Museum of Modern Art, New York.

Text credits

Letter by P. T. Barnum to Samuel Clemens: courtesy Mark Twain Papers, the Bancroft Library, University of California, Berkeley.

Lines from "K-K-K-Katy": copyright © circa 1918. Renewed 1946 by Leo Feist Inc. All rights assigned to EMI Catalogue Partnership. All rights controlled and administered by EMI Feist /catalog Inc. All rights reserved. International copyright reserved. Reprinted by permission of CPP/Belwin, Inc.